INNOCENT HEART

Suddenly she had no control over the unfamiliar feelings that rose within her. Help me, she cried silently, for I cannot do what I should. Someone else is inside me, someone who knows well enough that my defenses are gone.

Help me—

He reached for her and brought her swiftly to him. Putting a finger under her chin, he tilted her face up to his. Without volition her arms reached up to encircle his neck, and she pressed her body against him. It was too late to pull away, even if she wanted to.

"We can't stay here," he whispered. "Will you come with me?"

Other Avon Books by
Jocelyn Carew

CROWN OF PASSION
FOLLOW THE SHADOWS
GOLDEN SOVEREIGNS

Pavilion of Passion

Jocelyn Carew

AVON
PUBLISHERS OF BARD, CAMELOT, DISCUS AND FLARE BOOKS

PAVILION OF PASSION is an original publication of Avon Books. This work has never before appeared in book form.

AVON BOOKS
A division of
The Hearst Corporation
959 Eighth Avenue
New York, New York 10019

Published by arrangement with the author
Library of Congress Catalog Card Number: 83-90755
ISBN: 0-380-84681-0

First Avon Printing, August, 1983

Printed in the U. S. A.

WFH 10 9 8 7 6 5 4 3 2 1

Chapter One

SPRING, 1870

Sunday, April 2.

The winter had been long and hard, a season to stunt the mind and bring the lonely to the brink of self-destruction. Londoners had coughed through months of choking yellow fog, sharp-toothed cold, and a bitter rawness in the wind that clawed its way through layers of wool garments and insinuated itself even in the snug drawing rooms of the rich.

Only now had the forgiving touch of April come. The air held sweet-scented promises, and the fresh breezes of spring beguiled the Londoners who emerged from their storm-bound captivity like the first men from their caves, amazed anew by the miracle of rebirth.

The winter now in retreat had been exceptionally bitter for Valetta Finch. Her world had been turned upside down when, in a moment on a cold January evening, her father unexpectedly drew his last breath. Her mother had died long before, and now, without a single surviving Finch, she was suddenly and completely alone, and all but penniless.

She could no longer remain in the Dower House on the Quarles estate. Her father had, since the summer, been employed as tutor in classical languages to the young sons of the Quarles family, and lodging had been part of his remuneration. He had left his daughter nothing but a few gold sovereigns in a wash-leather bag, a handful of books in Greek and Latin, and a small trunk, containing her clothing, an ivory-backed comb and brush, her prayer book, and a hand-painted miniature of her great-grandmother.

There was nothing for Valetta to do but to ignore her breeding, her good education, and set out to find employment. Her father's books she sold to the vicar for a modest sum. She packed her trunk and took the stage to London.

After a desperate February, endlessly walking the snowy streets of London with diminishing hope, she had finally come to Mr. Markham's draper's shop on Mortimer Street, well out of the way of fashionable trade. Mr. Markham had given her a position as ribbon clerk. The month of March had confined her to the shop and Mrs. Grissom's attic bedroom, just off Cleveland Street. Deadening as the routine had been, she still had time to grieve for her father, and finally put such sorrow behind her.

This first Sunday of April, then, with its gentle breeze of hope, had come like a long-delayed benison. Valetta Finch, along with several thousands of true Londoners, put the shop drudgery out of her mind and became, in her own fancy, once again Miss Finch, late of the Dower House, Quarles Manor, South Mimms, Middlesex. She could just as easily have called herself Miss Finch of a number of other places, since her father had never stayed more than two years in any situation. She had not had time to make friends, or even to develop a sense of belonging anywhere.

She strolled slowly now, feeling the sun warm her cheeks. The leaves were starting, but the trees were still only bare limbs against a sky the color of a robin's egg. She turned her back on the genteel, but shabby neighborhood where she lived and worked. Toward the east, she remembered, the blocks of tumbledown houses became increasingly dingy. She had seen enough of them while she was looking for work. Even now she shuddered when she remembered the occasion when, near the bottom of her slender store of funds, she had gone too far. Beyond Fleet Street, she had entered a land as foreign as France. She would never be rid of the memory of those female creatures slumped in doorways, their haunting eyes, mercifully glazed over with gin—those women who had no money and no hope.

She had fled ignominiously and never went back.

But the remembered dread came, sometimes, to lay icy claws on her—only money and her job lay between her and a similar end.

This morning she had put on her best dress, of Bismarck brown, made with a double skirt and trimmed with ruching of the same material. She had made this dress herself in December, adding sufficient tassels and rosettes of the same unfashionable color to make it suitable for the Christmas ball at the Manor House. The next time she had worn it had been for Papa's funeral.

She walked down Cleveland Street and crossed Oxford. At once the neighborhood changed from cramped narrow shops and lodging houses to large residences set amid pleasant grounds on wide avenues.

She did not hurry. She felt almost at home among such wealth and finery. She amused herself with fancy—suppose the Finches, once a family of wealth and breeding, had flourished instead of dying out. Perhaps she would now be living in one of these mansions, choosing a gown to wear to church, or even planning for a day in the country. For a moment she closed her eyes. Dreams did no good, she believed, but a moment's indulgence could scarcely harm.

The breeze from the river lifted the ribbons on her tiny hat, made in a style called a cap coiffure. It was no more than a lacy brown band threaded with matching ribbons that tied at the nape of her neck, revealing her great glory, her magnificent mass of copper-colored hair, brushed until it shone in the sun like a sheet of bronze.

She reached the Embankment. Realizing she was tired, she found a bench facing the river and sat.

Standing all day in the shop was difficult enough, but walking for an hour on the hard London pavements was torture. She was content now to let the sun pour over her like a warm tide, stirring only enough to be grateful she was not Danae, and that the flood of golden light now wrapping her bore no resemblance to the aggressively virile Jove.

With the recollection of the Greek myth, her father's face came vividly before her closed eyes. The Finch quarrel, going back two generations, had left its mark on Papa, disinherited for a reason she never knew. The only memento left to her was the miniature of her great-grandmother. If she had ever doubted her Finch inheritance, that hand-painted portrait would have convinced her. Valetta bore such a strong resemblance to it that she could have sat for it herself.

Great-grandmother wore fine jewels at her throat and at her earlobes, her gown was clearly of costly velvet, and she looked out at her world with arrogance and an indefinable recklessness in her sapphire eyes.

And her descendant, on her day off like any servant, now sat, feet burning, on a public bench overlooking the Thames.

A little way off, playing on the grass, was a pair of little girls, dressed of course like miniatures of their mother. The older one wore a polonaise of striped foulard, trimmed with matching narrow braid of a sort called galloon. Her sister, perhaps nine years old, was dressed in a light blue mozambique with two rows of flounces around the hem of the skirt. The smaller girl was no doubt bound for a scolding, for already the bottom flounce was torn and hanging in a soiled scallop.

Val caught herself. Six days a week in Mr. Markham's shop had warped her mind! All she could see, even on her free day, was fashion and fabric and trim.

Like Miss Wilson, the senior shop attendant, her world had already shrunk to the dimensions of the small shop with its dress lengths of utilitarian foulards and confection-frothy gauzes.

Casually she turned her gaze away from the little girls to the bridge crossing the river, and there she stopped. A man stood on the river bank near Westminster Bridge, his level gaze unmistakably on her. He was taller than average, his shoulders wide and powerful beneath a brown sack coat. His bowler hat shadowed his eyes so that she could not see their color, but somehow she knew his hair was dark and his eyes light.

In an unconscious gesture of vanity, she smoothed the curl that dangled charmingly against her cheek as though it just now had escaped from her tiny hat. Their eyes locked for a long moment, almost as if they knew each other. Or, the strange fancy echoed in her mind, as though they were destined to know each other. Nonsense, she told herself, irritated. A man like that would never find his way to the obscure shop on Mortimer Street.

She rose from the bench and turned toward St. James's Park. She could not keep from looking again at the man. He was still watching her. Seeing her interest in him, he smiled broadly and touched the brim of his hard, round hat. She could not snub him. She gave him the briefest, iciest nod possible and walked briskly away from the Embankment.

She could think of nothing but the man on the riverbank. His features were not classic, as far as she could tell, nor could she admire his insinuating glance. But in some mysterious way, as though there had been a mutual acknowledgment, he had taken possession of her thoughts. She hastened on, putting distance between them.

She crossed the park and joined the small crowd peering excitedly through the gates of Marlborough House, the residence of the Prince and Princess of Wales. A uniformed guard, looking like a toy grenadier, stood outside his sentry box, tucked beside one of the square pillared gatehouses that flanked the ironwork gates.

Inside the gates stretched a vast expanse of lawn. At the far end was a barrier of shrubbery, faintly green with new leaves, screening Marlborough House itself.

She quivered with excitement. Even the air in this neighborhood felt heavy with wealth and luxury. The parterres were not yet planted, but the ground had been newly turned, making a dark rich stripe across the lawn. A whiff of fresh moist earth wrenched at her heart, a poignant reminder of rural days with Papa forever lost.

Suddenly there was stirring inside the estate. The gates were quickly dragged open. The sentry snapped to attention. Clearly the personages were coming.

An open landau came smartly down the drive. The crowds pressed Val forward. The magnificent grays, held by tight rein, snorted arrogantly as the carriage slowed at the gates. Val could have reached out and touched the prince.

As though he sensed her trembling presence, His Royal Highness turned and caught her eye. He smiled slightly and, bowing, touched his hat to her. As though—she thought with a gasp—he knew her!

Flustered, she dropped an automatic curtsy and watched the landau disappear down the Mall. She shivered belatedly. He seemed to know her! But that was impossible. It was more than likely that he was shortsighted and had mistaken her for someone else. She was certainly unable to believe that the womanizing Prince of Wales had been struck all of a heap, as Mrs. Grissom would say, by a naïve girl fresh from the country.

The days of Cinderella were past. Besides, she didn't fancy herself riding in a pumpkin. Smiling to herself over the absurdity of her lively fancy, she stepped, without looking, into the street.

She was dimly aware of a confusion of shouts down the street. Glancing in that direction, she could see the crowd pressing back on itself and then she saw the pair of horses, snorting and plunging in their traces, thundering down on her. Her feet refused to move. The runaway pair galloped out of control, themselves too frightened to see her in their path.

Paralyzed, as in a dream, she stared at their wide flaring nostrils, their tossing heads—

A hand closed on her upper arm and jerked her backward, out of the way. Her heel caught on something, and she felt herself falling through space, her fingers clutching at empty air.

She sat down on the pavement, hard.

Around her, but as if through a fog, she could hear cries of dismay, even of horror. "The poor wench, scared out of her wits! Idiot jarvey, he was, didn't ought to be let loose with a horse, let alone a pair! The prince's friend, that's who she is. I saw him bow to her! Jarvey's good as in Newgate now, serves him right!"

Val closed her eyes against the terrifying image that burned inside her brain—those wild, snorting horses with rolling eyes and obscene yellow teeth. She was stunned, scarcely aware of the sounds of barking dogs as they followed the runaway hack receding into the distance.

A voice spoke in her ear. "Are you hurt? Can't you speak, for God's sake?" The voice, deep and resonant, was persistent. She waved it away as though it were a buzzing wasp.

"Can you stand?"

"Oh, don't bother me!" she cried. "Get those bees away!"

Her interrogator burst into laughter. "Bees? All in your head!" Tentatively, she opened her eyes. He was kneeling beside her, peering anxiously into her face. She flashed an indignant glare at him. Much too late, he added, "Ma'am."

The man who had rescued her from the certain injury under the giant hooves was the same man who had smiled so insolently at her at the river. His eyes, she realized, were gray, the deep gray of the North Sea in winter.

His strong arm slipped behind her shoulders, holding

her. The world seemed to tilt dizzily and she closed her eyes against it. He pulled her gently to lean against him. Dreamily, she could feel the muscular strength of his chest supporting her and his heart beating fast close to her ear. She was right—he was powerful and commanding and—

Suddenly she came to her senses. What a spectacle she must be making—sprawled on the curb, her limbs awry, her gown likely rucked up and torn! She uttered a quick exclamation and tried to sit up. He took her hand and pulled her to her feet. His grasp was hard, solid, almost comforting.

She must have fallen harder than she thought, for her wits scampered about as unbridled as the runaway team. Why had he called her ma'am, rather than miss? Had he followed her here from the bridge? And for what purpose? She was utterly incapable of answering these questions. Indeed, she could hardly form them in her mind, for she was intensely aware of him standing next to her, his deep-set eyes full of concern, his hand tight on her arm, holding her close lest she faint.

His lithe body, obviously powerful even in his loose-fitting sack coat, was at such odds with the softness of the few men she had known—Papa, Mr. Markham, even Mr. Quarles, and of course the elderly vicar—that he seemed sprung from another world, a world where exciting things happened, where life could be a full beaker of delights—

How ridiculous! The fall had addled her wits. She pulled herself, not without effort, into a more seemly state of mind.

"Surely the accident has not paralyzed your tongue?" he demanded in a much too familiar manner. Now she could detect a slight burr in his speech. A Scotsman—no wonder he seemed from an alien world.

How strange she felt! She noted with embarrassment that her bonnet was awry and her hair was escaping from the net that bound it.

Her rescuer eyed her with disfavor. "You could have been killed!"

Anger came to her. "No doubt I could have been," she said, her low voice quivering. "If I had known that a mad jarvey would lose control of his team at that precise instant, I likely would have taken forethought on the incident."

Like many another man when baffled, he took refuge in wrath. "It was stupid not to look where you were going."

Valetta lifted her chin and gave him a long, level stare. "Nobody, sir, asked you to supervise me."

"Someone should!"

Her fingers automatically smoothed her skirt. They touched a rent in the fabric, and she exclaimed in dismay, "Oh, my dress!"

Her rescuer released his grasp on her arm as though her flesh were burning his fingers. He glared at her. "All you care about is your gown?"

She fingered the edges of the three-cornered tear across the front of the skirt. "Such a great tear—!" It was truly a disaster. Her best gown, even though unfashionable in color, was now ruined beyond mending. She groaned slightly, biting back a sob that threatened to rise to her lips.

The crowd was sympathetic. "Of course, the poor child is worried. She's all of a muddle from her fall." Their combined glances, sent the gentleman's way, were unfriendly.

"Now then, you, mister—what's your game?" This demand came from the jarvey, hurrying up to them. He had regained control of his team and quieted them. Now he meant to deal with the consequences. Clearly he believed bluster would save the day. "She ain't hurt, mister. You trying to make something of it?" The Scot turned to stare icily at him. "Oh, sorry, sir. Didn't see you was a real gent. But she ain't hurt."

She protested plaintively. "My gown is torn."

Her rescuer turned angrily. "A tear in your gown!" He did not try to hide his disgust. "You stand there, your bonnet awry, your hair—quite glorious hair as it happens!—coming unpinned! You could have been killed! And all you concern yourself with is a rip in your skirt."

"It's a disaster!" she exclaimed. "You wouldn't understand."

"Of course not," he said, reverting to sarcasm. "I suppose it would be too much to expect you to be grateful that you are still sound of wind and limb?"

She caught her breath. "Oh," she cried, feeling a flush creeping up her throat, "I am sorry! I thank you, sir, for saving my very life! I thought I had already done so, but I must surely be mistaken, for you apparently keep ledgers on such things."

She knew instantly she had gone too far. He turned suddenly white with anger, his eyes hard as a rocky cliff rising out of the sea, and she thought he would strike her. She did not flinch.

"Twisting a man's words to suit your purpose," he gritted at last. "How like a woman!"

She took a deep breath to steady herself against the anger that shook her. "Why not?" she inquired with dangerous sweetness. "I *am* a woman."

An odd expression crept into his eyes. "I noticed." In a different tone he said, "May I escort you to your destination? I suspect that you are still somewhat shaken from your fall."

She could not think quickly enough of an excuse to put him off. His anger had vanished, giving way to a different emotion that she could not decipher. But her knees still trembled, and in truth she was glad of his offer. He took gentle hold of her elbow, nodded civilly to the thinning crowds, and led her away into St. James's Street.

Leaning on the welcomed support of his arm, she followed where he led. He chose ways that avoided the larger Sunday crowds—Piccadilly, Conduit Street, leading northeast into Regent Street. She was more aware of him than she had ever been of another person.

She had loved her father, but she had never come close to him, nor had he ever sought to know her thoughts and dreams, to understand her. Sometimes she had fancied her heart enclosed inside a hard outer shell, like a Norman keep within the curtain wall, believing that everyone kept their true self protected from invasion, as she did.

But now the oddest thing—she felt as though a small breach had penetrated in her protective shield, opening a channel that could admit all manner of intruders, all sorts of new, delicious, and frightening shapes. The man walking beside her—his hand frequently touching her elbow as they crossed the streets, his lavender-scented soap strong and clean in her nostrils—had in a way she could not understand jarred her old self, causing a disquieting tremor to pass through her.

The silence stretched between them, not companionable but fraught for him with speculation and, on her part, an intense absorption with her own tumultuous feelings.

He said finally, "You will not remember me, I am sure, but we have met before today."

"No," she murmured. "We could not have."

"In Paris," he continued, overriding her protest. "Last summer."

"I have never been in Paris."

"A reception at the embassy," he insisted.

She stopped short. They were standing at the curb on Oxford Street. Behind them lay the fashionable houses of the elegantly dressed aristocrats, the milieu of the upper classes of England. To cross Oxford Street was to enter streets and neighborhoods of gradually declining fortunes. As one moved away from the great artery, a barrier even more unbreachable than Hadrian's Wall, into the farther reaches of the city, one moved even lower on the ladder of prosperity, until in the extreme east lay the slums that Hogarth had delineated.

"You must," she insisted, "have mistaken me for someone else."

His expression altered, deep in his sea-gray eyes. "You must forgive me. I did not mean to intrude upon your ladyship's privacy."

"Truly—" she began and then stopped. "You do not believe me."

"On the contrary," he said stiffly. "If you wish never to have been in Paris, this is your choice. Believe me, I shall not mention it again." He gestured across Oxford Street. "I have taken you greatly out of your way. Will you accept my escort back to your hotel?"

"Hotel!"

He looked down at her, his mocking eyes darkening. Suddenly she was uneasy. There was great strength in this man. He clearly did not believe that she had never been in Paris. He must mistake her for someone else—but whom? She longed to question him, but she feared to learn too much. Perhaps he had made love to that other woman? It was not beyond belief, for his attitude bordered on the intimate.

It was not envy she felt at this moment—not at all!

She refused to meet his eyes. He said only, "*À bientôt?*" Then he was gone.

Impertinent! she thought. She would take great care to avoid this man. If he were now to follow her, to find out where she lived, she would quite simply call a policeman.

She crossed Oxford Street and plunged into one of the side streets. Once she looked back, but he was not in sight. She walked on, feeling very much alone. Strangely, the sunlight had gone out of her day.

But the sun was still shining on Mrs. Grissom's patch of yard at the back of her house. Valetta opened the gate and slipped inside.

Mrs. Grissom clung fiercely to the notion that she must have a garden in the midst of teeming London. She cared lovingly for the scrap of grass and pampered the small bushes that stood along the side fences. From shrewd bargaining at the back of certain flower stalls lining the pavements at Covent Garden, she had obtained damaged bulbs and flowers past their prime and had patiently coaxed them into sturdy life.

Already in early April pink hyacinths bloomed along the edge of the grass, and yellow crocuses made a carpet under the one stunted tree, near which Mrs. Grissom now sat with her cousin.

"Taking the air, we are," called the landlady when she caught sight of Valetta. "Come along and sit."

Her cousin, Mrs. Yonge, had sharper eyes than Mrs. Grissom. "My land, the child's been in an accident. Torn your pretty dress, my dear? What happened?"

Mrs. Grissom exclaimed, "Was it a man? Did he—try—to compromise you..."

Suddenly, knowing she was safe, Val's knees gave way and she stumbled. Maternal arms eased her into a chair, and the universal cure was pressed into her hands within moments. Cradling the cup of hot tea, letting its warmth creep into her fingers, she managed a grateful smile.

"Now then, you're going to tell us what happened, aren't you," prodded Mrs. Grissom. "Some man, like Maggie said. Seeing a young thing like you all alone. Did he make evil advances?"

"Esther," reprimanded her cousin. "Can't you see the girl's had a bad time? Not that I hold with the notion that there's naught but evil men out there lying in wait for a pretty bit of a morsel like Valetta. But my Thomas is nothing like that. Land, I don't know that he'd even know what to do with a lass if he did catch her! I don't worry a bit!"

The bickering exchange between the older women went its comfortable way. Full of wisdom garnered over years, they gave Val a chance to drink her tea and grow calm. Now that she was safe, buttressed against danger by the ample bodies of her companions, she realized tardily that she had indeed been within an inch of being trampled underfoot by a pair of crazed horses.

"Now, dearie, tell us all about it."

Valetta obliged. "It wasn't my fault, truly." She told the story of her day, dwelling on the crucial point of her presence outside the gate at Marlborough House, watching the emergence of royalty into the outer world.

"And the oddest thing—the prince looked right at

me and bowed! I think that was what made me so absentminded when I stepped off the walk."

"I wonder why he did that?" remarked Mrs. Grissom.

Her cousin snorted. "It's plain, Esther. She's a pretty girl."

"But a bit beneath his touch, I'd say. Not that you're not a lady, to be sure, and a head full of learning, too. But they's no question about it, you're not the aristocracy. And just as well, too."

"Beneath or above his touch, either way you're lucky. Goes for stage actresses, the prince does."

"Truly he made a mistake," insisted Val. "But he did seem to know me, and I know I never saw him before. He simply thought I was someone else." As did the handsome Scotsman.

She related the incident of the runaway team.

"No wonder," said Mrs. Yonge, "that you came home all a-shake. Coachman like that ain't safe out loose."

"Well, child," said Mrs. Grissom some time later, "you get your frock mended, and I'll wash it out for you tomorrow. All the dirt on the streets, like as not your dress is full of it."

Val hurried up to her room. Rummaging in her trunk, she found what she was looking for, a length of ruffling that had been her mother's, years before. Originally white, it had yellowed with age until it was a rich cream. Laid diagonally against the brown of the dress, it covered the ugly tear.

While she sewed, her thoughts roamed over the events of the day—the friendly smile of the prince, the frightening accident. But the face that lingered in her mind was the Scotsman's—grave, disturbingly intimate, real and solid. He had not believed her protests. He was convinced he was acquainted with her, expecting her to respond with sophistication to his overtures. She was both ashamed and regretful that she had never learned the moves in the exciting man-woman game that he was playing.

But she would never see him again, so his state of mind mattered not in the least!

Chapter Two

In an obscure rooming house, only a few blocks away from Mrs. Grissom's, Lady Thorne was scarcely aware of the balmy air of the first Sunday in April. She was not one to enjoy the simple pleasures of nature, even filtered, as the spring sunshine was, through the haze that lay over London at the best of times.

She had had enough of rural life to last her the rest of her days. Now she was back in her proper setting—a cosmopolitan city, offering the enormous variety of luxuries that were her due by birth.

Unfortunately, she could not at this time make an entrance, nodding arrogantly at obsequious servants, in the lobby of the luxurious Westminster Palace Hotel. She dared not even take rooms at the new Langham's Hotel, at the south end of Portland Place, lest she be recognized.

Instead, she looked down into a mean little lane on the wrong side of Oxford Street, searching the faces of the passersby. She saw no one she knew, and at last, wearying of her vigil, she sighed and turned back into the tiny, cluttered, rooming-house parlor. Apparently her departure from Thorne Hall had not been noticed. Or perhaps her absence was marked, but no one cared enough to follow her to town. At least she was still undiscovered.

It was possible, then, that no one had missed the blue case on the bed, containing the Thorne jewels. Magnificent emeralds formed the bulk of the pieces carefully wrapped in jewelers' cloth and stowed inside the case. The stones were splendid, and they set off her coppery hair to perfection. Unfortunately, they were not hers. A stupid idea, she thought not for the first time, entailing the jewels so that any Lady Thorne had only the use of them. She smiled now, her greenish eyes twinkling with mischief. Now that she had the jewels in hand, they were hers to do with as she chose, an argument that could well lead her into the unforgiving grip of the law.

But the jewels were her passport to freedom. She would take them to Paris, where no one would question her about their ownership. Perhaps Raoul could help her dispose of them—

With the thought of Raoul, she slid into erotic daydreams. She had met him last summer in Paris. The attraction between them kindled into a blaze that threatened to destroy them both, until her husband and Raoul's wife joined forces to stamp out the fire. But stodgy mates—as Raoul had written just last week—were made to deceive, and she was on her way to join her great love.

Next week at this time she would be in Raoul's arms. She did not look beyond that delectable moment.

She had packed in a hurry. If Colby, the housekeeper, suspected her plans, it made no difference, for Colby, staunchly Sir William's partisan against her, would be glad enough to see her gone.

But she had not had time to set her garments in order. A ribbon missing here, new buttons needed on the bottle-green foulard, perhaps even a new fichu, trimmed in lace—

She must venture out on Monday to make some small purchases. She dared not go to any shop she knew. Hunter, her husband's nephew, might well have spies watching the shops she ordinarily patronized. Love between her and Hunter had long since died, whether William knew it or not. But Hunter Dyson, on whom the jewels were entailed, was a formidable foe.

She began to make a list of the items she would need. That evening she remembered passing a little shop in Mortimer Street, dingy and unpretentious. It might have ribbons and buttons that would serve well enough. Even if their notions were not of the first fashion, at least no one would expect to meet Lady Thorne there.

She would go veiled—and she would cover up her magnificent copper hair so that not a tendril escaped. Even the Prince of Wales had told her once that no one else in the world had such splendidly colored hair—even though she wished it were less coppery, and perhaps a shade more bronze.

Monday she would shop—and on Thursday she would take the train to Dover to board the ferry to France. And then—Raoul!

Valetta's dreams that Sunday night had been vivid but disjointed. The straining wild horses, the prince, the mended skirt, the gray eyes of the Scot reflecting anger, concern, and at times bewilderment.

But what was most puzzling to her upon waking Monday morning was the apparent recognition of her by such diverse men as the prince and the tall Scotsman. The prince could be excused, for rumor claimed he knew every woman in London, in varying degrees of intimacy, and doubtless he had mistaken her for someone else. Surely such a rascal could not call to mind every woman he had taken a fancy to! But the Scotsman...

She had little time for wondering, though.

Looking as crisp and unruffled this morning as though her accident had never happened, she opened the door to Mr. Markham's drapery shop on Mortimer Street and stepped inside.

She blinked in the unaccustomed dim light. Miss Wilson, a spare, angular woman who, judging from her usual demeanor, breakfasted on vinegar, was not in sight. But she might be closeted with Mr. Markham in the small room he called an office, just off the narrow hall at the back of the shop.

Miss Wilson—Valetta had never heard her first name—had been the shop assistant for twenty years. She was more than half in love with her employer, as anyone with a shrewd eye could discern. Since Mr. Markham had recently become a widower, Valetta would not be surprised to learn that Miss Wilson's suspected ambition was about to be fulfilled.

She listened for a moment, expecting to hear the murmur of voices from the secluded office. There was nothing but silence. Perhaps they were in Mr. Markham's apartment upstairs, she thought, pleased to speculate that affairs were marching so swiftly.

Whatever the activities of her superiors, her own tasks were clear enough. First the dust covers over the display tables had to be lifted off carefully. The counters were to be dusted. Mr. Markham took the shutters down every morning, but today he had not yet done so. The few rays of sun that could filter through the narrow ways between buildings were allowed to come discreetly through the front windows. The sun was never allowed direct access to the bolts of fabric, lest it fade them.

Mr. Markham was an indulgent employer, not like some she had heard of whose rules robbed even the lowliest shopgirl of her self-respect.

"The clerical staff will not disport themselves in raiment of bright colors," was a universal rule. Some shopgirls were not allowed even to talk to their fellow workers, and in many shops eating was allowed only between eleven-thirty and noon—but work was to continue while they ate.

Of course, there were only the two clerks in Mr.

Markham's, and there was therefore no need for harsh rules. Miss Wilson was as dry as the goods she sold, and Valetta was desperately dependent upon her wages in order to eat at all.

Valetta loved the look of the bolts of silk, spread across the tables like so many rainbows, distilled into bits of muted, shimmering color in the darkened shop. Now, with the dust cloths removed, folded, and ready to be placed in the cupboard along the far wall, she paused to enjoy her surroundings. The new fabrics for summer had arrived, particularly silks for town wear in various hues of brown and green. Taffetas would rustle when Miss Wilson turned the bolts to display lengths of fabrics for customers.

Valetta was not yet allowed to sell from the bolts. Miss Wilson was jealous of her prerogatives. Indeed, whatever love the older woman had to give was lavished on the foulards, the grosgrains, the poplins, silks, crepe de chines, poult-de-soies, the gauzes light as fairy-dress.

Valetta had the management of cloth roses and leaves for hair wreaths, gaiters laced in front, rosettes, pearl buttons, narrow velvet bands in colors to match the Scotch poplins, embroidery silks, silk fringes, silk cords, tassels, and small buckles.

Now she moved without haste among the tables, passing in and out of the slanting sunrays alive with swirling dust motes. She bent to search in a cabinet for the feather duster and torn rags to wipe down the glass counters so that the rainbow colors of the ribbons might catch the eyes of the day's customers.

Suddenly she knew she was not alone. The prickling of the hair on the back of her neck told her that someone was watching her. She had not heard the door open, but neither had she heard Miss Wilson's steps. Slowly she straightened, feeling strangely uneasy, and looked behind her.

"Oh," she exclaimed, half laughing. "Mr. Markham! You startled me."

Her employer was a short man, concocted of a series of various-sized circles—his rounded cheeks, his curving potbelly, his bald skull crisscrossed with wisps of graying hair. Even his walk was rolling, his bowlegs giving him a peculiar gait.

"Right on time, Miss Finch," he said, pointing out the obvious. "This pleases me. In fact, everything you do pleases me mightily."

"Th-thank you, sir."

"Yes, indeed," he continued, teetering slightly on the balls of his feet, "a lucky day for me when you came. I must say you were a godsend, for my poor wife required my attention, and I needed another hand in the shop."

Was he going to tell her that now he did not need that extra hand? A cold fist squeezed her stomach. She needed this job!

She stood a short distance away from him, her feather duster raised as though she were holding a torch.

He said briskly, "Miss Finch, I should like you to come upstairs. There is something I would like you to do for me."

"But—"

He stepped aside to give her room to precede him. She did not know quite what to expect. A man living alone might well make a muddle of his housekeeping. Perhaps he wanted her to straighten the rooms, even tend to the household washing. She had not bargained on becoming a domestic servant. But she had had no choice. She had walked for miles in the February slush, looking for employment. Everywhere she had been turned away, sometimes kindly, more often with a brusque, uncaring dismissal, and a few times with the offer of a "position" quite unlike the one she applied for. It was only her hearty reserve of courage which had kept her from a disastrous, final rendezvous with the Thames.

She passed him now, aware of his pungent unwashed odor, and moved into the small hall at the back of the shop. Inwardly she shivered. A door on the right led to the cluttered office, and ahead rose a narrow winding stairway to Mr. Markham's rooms above the shop. She lifted her skirt with one hand and went up the steps, her mind ticking furiously. What could be in Mr. Markham's rooms that she must see?

The landing at the top of the stairs was hardly more than a broad step. She waited in the obscure light for him to lead the way. As he passed her to open the door he touched her arm. She hoped he did not notice that she shrank away from him.

He threw open the door to his apartment and motioned her inside. The building shared common walls with the buildings on either side. The minimal light came only from the windows overlooking the street.

The rooms held the distilled odor of recent mortal illness, of dust accumulated and forgotten in the urgencies of sickness, of stale food, stale linen, and the stale body of her employer.

He watched her from a few steps away, a satisfied little smile on his full lips. Bewildered, she turned to him.

"A pretty set of rooms, eh?" he remarked. "A bit better than that attic room of yours at Mrs. Grissom's, I don't doubt. Now then, Miss Finch—I should like to know what you think of them?"

She tried to find words that, while satisfying him, had no chance of offending. "Very nice."

"Is that all you can say?" he demanded. The self-congratulatory shine in his bulging pale eyes was not dimmed by her response. "Oh, I see now. You're set all of a-flutter by it all. I like that. Maybe I should have warned you, so to speak. Give you time to take it all in. Likely it's all too much, but I know you'll get used to it."

The man was crazed, she thought, mouthing words that made no sense. Get used to what? To doing dishes, dusting furniture? She had long since become accustomed to chores like those. But was she to get down on her knees in gratitude?

"I doubt I shall," she said, keeping her voice neutral.

"Well, giving thanks comes hard to some," he said indulgently.

"It might help," she said carefully, "if I were informed precisely what I should give thanks for, Mr. Markham."

"Mr. Markham!" he echoed, grinning. "I'll change that! But time enough to call me Alf. Time enough."

Time enough, she decided, to get back downstairs. He was clearly moving along a road she would not follow. He was the victim of hallucination, to put it kindly.

"I really should—"

"I know it might look funny," he interrupted, "but who cares? You've got no people, and I been alone too long. Molly wasn't what you'd call a wife to me for better'n a year."

"Mr. Markham!" said Valetta, determined to put an end to this lunatic interview. "Had you not been my employer, I should never have agreed to come alone to your rooms. You have put me in an embarrassing position. I shall be obliged if you will explain exactly what you mean."

"Mean? Why, I mean to marry you, Miss Finch. Valetta, that is." He gestured grandly around the mean little room. "I'm offering you all this, *and* a proper marriage."

It was worse than she thought. A domestic servant could at least give up her job if the necessity arose, but a wife—never!

She did not know she had spoken aloud until he repeated, totally disbelieving, "Never?"

"I am sorry, Mr. Markham." She had been too abrupt. She had never before seen such an expression on his bulbous features. His eyes were about to pop out of their sockets, his cheeks were red as a turkeycock's, and—to her horror—she noticed a thin stream of saliva oozing from one corner of his mouth.

"Sorry! *Sorry,* you say! Better say *crazy* to turn all this down. You'll never get another offer this good. Nor any offer at all. Look at that dried-up Wilson woman. Who'd want her? You'll be like that yourself if you don't get a man to give you what you need. Better take my offer, miss, or you'll wish you had!"

By now she was thoroughly alarmed. He had planted

himself between her and the door. She was sure he would not allow her to leave, at least until he had argued his case longer. She had best put an end to this hysteria at once. But her wits were wandering and she chose her words unfortunately. "You must be fevered, sir. I shall go down and tell Miss Wilson that you are not well and have gone to bed."

He seized upon the last word. "Bed, is it? Maybe you want to try me out before you say the word. Is that it?"

She was appalled. He took a step toward her. His voice suddenly altered, taking on a note of urgency, even of hidden violence. A cold finger of fear touched her. This man was one she had never seen before, an unknown quantity wearing the appearance of her fatherly employer. She had to escape at once.

She shot a furtive glance around her. Now she could see that the rooms in which Mr. Markham spent his nights were badly furnished and unclean. They were in a small square parlor, jammed with ugly, squatty furniture ranged like sentinels around the walls. A door to the right stood ajar, and beyond it she saw an unmade bed, the sheets slewn off the mattress, as though its recent occupant had writhed, sleepless, through the long night. A door on the far side of the room without doubt led to the kitchen.

All this whipped through her mind in an instant, pointing out the obvious conclusion. There was no escape except through the door to the stairs by which they had entered.

"Mr. Markham, I must go downstairs and—and see to the customers."

"Customers be damned!" roared Mr. Markham. "Now confess it, my dear, isn't this fine apartment much more to your taste than that attic room? It's all yours, just say the word."

"The word," said Valetta with more calmness than she felt, "is *no.*"

He was momentarily taken aback. "I do like a shrewd woman. Making a bargain, eh? Ah, we'll get along famously. Want to see how I perform first? Well, you won't have nothing to fear along that line."

To her utter shock, he loosened his collar and undid the first two buttons on his shirt, allowing her to glimpse the wispy gray hair on his thin chest. He reached out for her. She raised her hands to ward him off. She was mildly surprised to find she was still holding the feather duster. Its ragged fronds brushed across his face, and he waved them away like a pesky fly.

She backed away, trying to reach the door. To divert his attention she poured out a torrent of words. "Mr. Markham, you are mistaken if you think I have any interest at all in your living quarters. My attic room suits me fine. In truth I am used to a confined space, for you must know I have always lived in less than spacious surroundings. I am sure *you* are quite comfortable here, but I assure you I should not be—"

He circled with her, keeping between her and the door. "You're not thinking right," he told her. "Your father would tell you my offer is the best you'll get."

Indignant, she burst out, "Don't mention my father! You're not fit to mention his name."

He stopped short and thrust his head toward her like a belligerent tortoise. "Hoity-toity! I'm offering you honorable wedlock, and even your father would approve of that. If I were you, I'd not sneer about an honest offer. You've got no money and no family. If I say the word around town, you'll never get another job—unless you go to the streets! Maybe that's where you belong!"

"Mr. Markham, you're insulting!"

"Am I?" He pulled out his shirttail, letting it hang loose over his trousers. "You stand high on your pride and you'll fall off into the gutter."

She lost her caution then, abandoning her slow sidling in the direction of escape. Instead, she picked up her skirts and made a rush toward the door. Her fears rang in her mind—the man was mad! She could not stay in his shop a moment longer! She would beg on the streets if need be—

He moved faster than she had calculated. He grabbed

her arm and hauled her around to face him. She struggled, his face so close to hers that his foul breath made her reel.

His grip on her arm tightened and his free hand reached out to her shoulder. She flung herself away from him. "You're out of your senses!"

He caught her again before she had taken three steps. Quick as thought, she called out, hoping her voice would reach Miss Wilson in the shop below. Surely she must have arrived by now.

He laughed. "She won't be in till noon, so don't waste your breath!"

Desperately, she tried to divert him. "But the shop—who'll wait on the customers?"

"Ah, that's my girl!" he crowed approvingly. "I knew you were just playing the shy miss. You've got an eye to the shop. That's good. It's our living, yours and mine."

"Not ever mine!" she retorted hotly, squirming in his embrace.

"You prefer the workhouse? Or the streets? For that's what it will be, my girl." His breath came short with the struggle. "Settle down now!"

She fought down panic. She was living in a nightmare, and in a moment she would wake up with a shudder and find herself safely in her attic room—

But she was not dreaming. She must get away from this monster. She needed all her wits to escape.

He grabbed at her, pinioning her wrists within sweaty palms. He tightened his grip until she cried out with pain. She pulled back from him, her only thought to ease the hurt. He followed her in a kind of crazy dance step, still holding her wrists, until she felt the wall at her back.

In a quick movement he thrust her arms behind her and pushed her hard against the wall. She felt his loathsome flabby body pressing upon the entire length of her. She twisted, lowering her shoulder, shoving it into his chest. She heard him grunt as the blow took his wind. Her victory, though, was small. He wrenched her arms apart, throwing her hard against the wall again, and a pain shot up from her elbow to her shoulder.

"I'll give you a taste of the gutter!" he murmured, his words slurring. His ugly face touched her cheek and she shuddered with revulsion. Wet with saliva, his loose lips moved along her jawline, searching for her mouth. He writhed against her, the hardening lump of his manhood rubbing up against her thigh.

The trembling emotion that engulfed her now, turning her knees to jelly, was unlike anything she had ever felt before—this was true fear. The man's eyes were no longer hot and wild. They were cold, calculating, cruel.

He found her mouth and took possession of it. His tongue forced her lips apart, and she gagged against the thick invader. She turned her head away, a scream hovering in her throat.

She could not escape his slobbering kiss. He followed her, his mouth enveloping her lips, his tongue on hers, on her teeth, moving constantly. She heard an elemental, animal sound, and knew that it rose involuntarily from the outraged core of her.

Still pinning her arms behind her against the wall, he let go of her wrists. His hands moved on her throat, slipping beneath the cloth of her frock to glide over her bared shoulders. His hands slipped down over her satin skin to her breasts, pinching the nipples until, against his stifling tongue, she cried out in pain.

She fought him with all her strength—for an eternity, it seemed. But as dastardly as his deception had been, taking advantage of his right to order her services in the shop, the ultimate betrayal was her own body.

Surprised by the unprecedented assault on its virginal senses, her body turned traitor. Involuntarily her breasts began to tremble under the cruel fingers, her thighs surrendering to the pleasurable sensation of the other's limbs moving against them. Now, in defiance of everything her heart held dear, her body began to respond with a life of its own.

With each caress, she felt him moving closer to victory. Surprisingly his pudgy body was stronger than she had ever imagined. Her knees quivered, and she sensed they would in moments give way. His mouth left hers, making a wet trail from her lips over her slender throat, and came to rest on her breast, his tongue teasing the sore nipple.

He had sensed the yielding in her, then relaxed his imprisoning hold on her in the belief that her surrender was only a matter of moments—he fancied, heaven help him, perhaps at last she found him irresistible.

She took him by surprise. Jerking her knee up violently, she heard him howl with anguish. Taking advantage of his unexpected helplessness, she flung a fist at him, the blow by good fortune landing in the middle of his face.

She did not pause to watch him bent almost double and hopping in pain, holding his streaming nose. She flew to the door and down the stairs, her feet scarcely touching the steps.

Her rush took her into the middle of the shop before she stopped. There was no sign of Miss Wilson, and Val was grateful for the respite to mend her disheveled appearance.

Now safely away from her employer turned ravisher, she paused to think. There was much to consider, all of it unpalatable. She leaned against the ribbon counter, giving the pounding of the blood in her temples time to relax. Three deep breaths, held as long as she could, served to calm her.

She looked around the shop as though she had never seen it before. The wide display tables burdened with fabrics in light rainbow pastels for the summer season, the shiny glass-topped showcase against which she was leaning, the folded dust covers ready to be put away for the day—she must have begun the day's work only half an hour before. Now it seemed as though she had been there at least a fortnight.

She could not stay here a moment longer. She pushed away from the counter, testing her knees, finding them still unreliable. Now that she could hear her own thoughts over the frightened tumult in her head, she could remember snatches of what were, after all, threats. Mr. Markham had spoken simple truth—if he chose, she would find no door of employment open to her in London.

She wished futilely that she had never revealed the true state of her funds to Mr. Markham, but he had seemed so paternal, so interested in her. When she first came to the shop she had already searched for employment for three frightening weeks without success. She had been grateful for the thoughtfulness she thought she saw in him and responded openly to all he asked.

She had learned this morning more than she wished. She felt her cheeks flaming as she recalled her body's betrayal of her. Then an errant thought came—would she have fought so hard against violation if the man had been less repellent? If, supposing, it had been the tall Scot who had rescued her yesterday, could she have yielded herself willingly into his hands? She would never know.

Valetta was accustomed to facing her problems squarely, logically. She had learned to deal with most things by herself.

So it was now. Her senses knew a curiosity that she herself had never admitted. There was a basic mystery between man and woman and she longed to penetrate it to its core. Some day she might. But never with Mr. Markham!

She picked up her small purse. She seemed to be moving as though under water, slowly, in a dreamy, unreal world. She dared not stay, even though, having escaped once, she was not afraid of him. Her immediate future might be safe from bodily harm, but she had no illusions that he would not use every mental torture he could devise.

She had reached the street door when she heard a sound from the flat above. Had she injured him more seriously than she thought? She could not really leave him unconscious on the floor. She halted, hand on the latch, listening.

Faint sounds came to her—a kind of scraping noise, as though a chair were being moved over bare floor, and then at last the sounds of slow, dragging footsteps. She held her breath, tracing her employer's movements by the sounds. He crossed to the bedroom, pulled out a drawer, went into the kitchen—

He would very soon come downstairs. By the time he appeared, she must know what she should do—to try to hold onto her job for a bit longer until she could find another, or simply disappear into the milling throngs of London without lodging, without employment, and without friends. She had no more illusions about the "fatherly" Mr. Markham. If she did not accept his proposal, he would ruin her. He had said so, and from the remembered tone of his voice, she knew he would. She was entirely, so he thought, at his mercy. Neither could she leave the shop and still live in Mrs. Grissom's attic room. It would be the work of half an hour for Mr. Markham to winkle her out.

She had concentrated too long on possibilities. She had not heard him come downstairs. Startled, she realized that he stood just inside the shop, at the doorway of the small dark hall. His eyes were fixed on her.

He had changed his clothes, and now appeared as she was accustomed to seeing him. His white shirt was neatly tucked into black trousers, his black vest buttoned decently, black sleeve-holders fastened above the elbows. She could almost believe that she had dreamed the dreadful scene upstairs, except for the redness of his nose where she had struck him.

He called to her. "Miss Finch?" When she did not answer at once, he added, "I am half blinded by the light. Miss Finch, is it you at the door?"

She answered. She was safe enough, her hand on the latch, the width of the room between them.

"Miss Finch, I fear that you and I will have to deal with our customers this morning. Miss Wilson will not be in till noon."

He spoke in a thin, drawn-out voice, like an invalid whose fever had at last broken. She gaped at him. He seemed to think that the episode upstairs had never happened.

Then she understood. It was an olive branch—if she said nothing about his outrageous behavior, he would not discharge her out of hand and hound her out of her attic room and indeed out of London itself.

A truce then. The workhouse faded in her mind. He understood her feelings. There would be no more trouble.

A truce it should be.

"I imagine we will have a quiet day, Mr. Markham," she said, pleased to hear that her voice bore no trembling trace of the humiliation she had been through.

Her choice of words could have been interpreted by a sensitive man as a subtly suggestive warning. He did not seem to notice. He turned back to his office, leaving the shop to her.

Little by little she relaxed. She had held the latch so tightly that the imprint was still red on her palm. She resolved to go about her work during the truce alert and ready to flee. She could not endure a repetition of the morning's assault.

This time she would be on her guard every moment.

Chapter Three

The morning, like any other day, wore on toward noon. One part of her mind was grateful for the steady stream of difficult customers, for they kept her from thinking about the ugliness just past.

She bit her lip more than once to keep from offending some pretentious woman whose taste had been hardly well developed. Imagine putting cerise ribbons next to a set of scarlet buttons on a brown-and-white-checked bodice!

Even so, that customer was not as unreasonable as an earlier one, who insisted on matching a certain pink ribbon, faded from its original color. The match was impossible to make, but since the purpose of the ribbon was to be drawn through the yoke of a nightgown, Val was hard put to avoid saying, "What difference will it make?" After all, the woman was at least fifty years old, and any man who was not initially put off by her sour expression would not at all mind an odd ribbon or two!

Val took advantage of a momentary lull to kneel on

the floor behind the counter and busy herself in rearranging the buttons, disturbed by the cerise-obsessed customer who had insisted on handling all the goods herself.

Val winced when she put her weight on her knees, souvenir of her narrow escape from the runaway team. By tomorrow, her arms and back would remind her of Mr. Markham's brutal assault. But at least those aches would also remind her that she had not been more seriously—damaged.

Miss Wilson arrived just before noon. Val's worries, at least for today, seemed over. By tomorrow she must decide upon some course of action that would leave Mr. Markham and his outrageous demands behind. Today, she was so distressed that she could not gather her wits together.

The senior clerk removed her hat and cloak and went to hang them in the small hallway that led to Mr. Markham's small office and to the stairs to the apartment upstairs. Valetta was suddenly seized by a powerful flash of insight. Now that Mr. Markham was a widower, Miss Wilson had altered. Informed by the episode of the morning, Valetta believed she understood. Miss Wilson had developed what could only be termed a proprietary air. The shop seemed in some indefinable way to become hers. Valetta suspected that Miss Wilson also considered Mr. Markham himself to be hers, if not yet, then upon the lapse of what she could call "a decent interval."

Valetta's heart sank. The truce, such as it was, that was proffered to her by Mr. Markham was a weak thing. It could not survive long, and Miss Wilson's dream of empire would soon be shattered as though it had never been.

Whatever was to happen between Mr. Markham and Miss Wilson, Valetta must not be there to witness it. Her path of action was clear now, and the essence of it was speed. She must at once find a new position, locate other lodgings, and then inform Mr. Markham that she was leaving—before he had a chance to blacken her name to a new employer. Perhaps she could accomplish her goal by mid-week. She could endure this ugliness, with its distressing and complicated overtones, only that long.

The choice that Valetta thought was hers vanished in a moment.

Miss Wilson remained in Mr. Markham's office for what seemed a long time. Once Valetta glanced in that direction while she was answering a customer's question and noticed that the door was closed. Usually, the office door stood open, since Mr. Markham liked to keep an eye on the shop. Val wondered now what might be transpiring beyond the door. Her fancy suggested that Miss Wilson was being offered the matrimonial position that Val had turned down. But surely it should not take this long to resolve, for Miss Wilson must be more than willing!

At length, when the last customer in this small spurt of business had left, Val heard the office door open. She held a few coins in her hand, the proceeds of the sale she had just made, and went to the large cash box hidden under the measuring table. She had only the previous week been allowed to make change from the cash box, and she was still nervously careful not to make a mistake. She counted the money in her hand again, concentrating so hard that she did not hear Miss Wilson and Mr. Markham approaching.

She glanced up, startled. "I—I didn't hear—"

"Obviously," said Miss Wilson, coldly.

Valetta straightened slowly. At the edge of her mind stirred a cold intimation of fear to come. The woman's voice held accusation, but of what? Surely Mr. Markham had not confided to her his actions upstairs?

"What do you mean, Miss Wilson? I was merely surprised to see you standing there."

"With your hand in the cash box?" Miss Wilson's lips twisted with irony. "I should imagine you were."

Val flushed slowly. The warmth crept up her throat to her cheeks.

"I see you understand me," the woman continued. "A hand in the cash box can mean only one thing. How much have you stolen?"

"Stolen! You cannot be serious! I have taken nothing. I was putting money in! Surely you saw that?" Val stretched her hand out toward the senior clerk, palm up, the coins shining. "That customer who just left—she bought five buttons and a buckle—this is what she paid!"

Val looked at Mr. Markham, her eyes full of appeal. His expression did not change, but his little eyes were alive with satisfaction. She had scorned him, had dared to fight him, brought him, nose bleeding, to his knees, and she would pay for it. She saw she could not hope for any help from him.

Valetta turned back to her accuser. "You know very well that I have stolen no money. You may look in my purse to see if you can find the money you say is missing. I had ten shillings of my own, and that is all you will find there."

"Ten shillings! I'll wager there is five times that in it." Miss Wilson seized the small bag and rummaged through it. Clearly unsatisfied, she turned the bag upside down and emptied it on the measuring table. Valetta felt her face muscles turn rigid.

"You see?" she said, watching Miss Wilson scoop up the small items and return them to the bag. "Only my ten shillings."

"Where did you put the money?"

"Nowhere! Can't you understand that? I—I—didn't—take the money!" She spat out the last words as though hammering them into Miss Wilson's head. "I have no pockets in this frock. Where do you think I could hide anything? Search me if you wish!"

Mr. Markham spoke for the first time. "No, young lady," he jeered, "nothing as nice as that. The constable can search you. Likely he won't be as gentle as . . ." *I was,* was his clear meaning, but he finished, "as you would like."

"Constable?" she gasped, suddenly sick. She could

almost feel the brutal hands on her body, backed by the law's majesty, searching her nakedness with, most likely—according to Mrs. Grissom's gruesome tales—more than hands on her. "You wouldn't! You know there's no truth to this mad accusation! You know why—"

He interrupted her quickly. "I know nothing."

His senior clerk, not usually sensitive, was nonetheless aware that there was something in the atmosphere that she did not understand. But the unacknowledged jealousy that had gripped her since she first saw Valetta's fresh complexion, her magnificent bronze hair, her slanted sapphire eyes, drove her on now. "There, miss! I'll not rest easy until this saucy thief is behind bars, in Newgate Prison where she belongs. I'll send at once for the bailiffs!"

There was no escape. Val slumped on a stool behind the counter while Mr. Markham stood over her, as though daring her to make a dash for the door. Val spoke weakly. "Sir, you know the truth of this. Help me." But it was too late. Miss Wilson, awkward in her righteous anger, had already gone into the street in search of the law.

If Mr. Markham had hoped to escape his senior clerk's design on his future, he had failed. He had been wounded, both in his aching body and in his private dreams, and he glared maliciously at the instrument of his disappointment. He shook his head slightly, and Val knew she had made an unforgiving enemy.

When she returned, Miss Wilson said in triumph, "The constable will be here in a moment. Then we'll be rid of this baggage."

Val's gleaming eyes turned smoky in futile rage. She had no hope of escape. Her two accusers stood before her like wardens, and she had heard enough about bailiffs not to expect mercy from them. And even if she did escape—

"Even if you got away," said Miss Wilson, echoing Val's thoughts, "we would see that you never got another job. No one wants a wanton who seduces her innocent employer."

So that was Mr. Markham's version of what had happened upstairs! She should have expected it. "I never dreamed of such a thing!"

Mr. Markham cleared his throat. "Whether you did or not, that's the word that goes out from here. It's gaol or the workhouse for you, miss." His eyes glittered in satisfaction. She read his thoughts clearly. *I told you this is how it would be!*

Val gathered her wits and her rage together. She stood up with dignity and started toward the door. "You cannot hold me against my will. I have committed no crime." She was pleased to hear that her voice was steady, if only a little higher than usual. "Mr. Markham, you know the truth, even if you're too proud to admit it."

"Mr. Markham!" Miss Wilson shrilled. "Don't let her out!"

He was slow to move. Val glared at him, daring him to come closer. "Let me go!" she warned, "Or you'll be sorry!" This time she was ready—ready to pummel and kick and scratch—and her intentions were plain in her defiant eyes.

She had reached the door when it opened behind her. "The police at last," cried the clerk. "You're slow enough. She almost got away."

"Now, now," rumbled the constable. "What's all this?"

"I'll tell you—" began Miss Wilson at the same time that Val clutched his arm and cried, "They're both lying!"

"Grab her!" shrieked Miss Wilson.

The policeman, rotund and not shrewd, knew one principle. Let no one get away, take the prisoner to the magistrate, and let them all sort it out.

He grabbed Val's wrist. She writhed against him, pulling away, gasping against the pain as he tightened his fingers. She cried out, a wordless scream of protest and hurt. She was aware of Miss Wilson's harsh voice and the officer's sharp words of command.

Her situation was desperate. She closed her eyes while

she struggled, trying to blot out the vision of the open doors of Newgate Prison—or, if she escaped gaol, the workhouse or even the streets of The Rookery, and the gin-drenched creatures. It was no use. She could not return the money, for she had taken none. And Miss Wilson's appetite for punishment of the younger, lovely woman would not be easily appeased.

Nor would Mr. Markham's revenge fade away.

None of the participants in this incident knew when the street door opened.

The veiled woman who entered the shop caught her breath in an audible gasp. She felt suddenly dizzy and reached out to the counter for support. It was as though she had already lived through this very scene. *Déjà vu,* the French would call it—an experience come again.

The policeman, the copper-haired girl struggling in his arresting arms, the accusers—

"What is this?" She had found her voice. "What are you doing to her?"

"Now then," said the officer, responding to the obvious gentility of the newcomer, "it's all right, ma'am, just a thief we're taking away."

"Thief? What has she stolen?" she demanded. Pray, she said to herself, that it is not emeralds, that that idiot Hunter Dyson has not found this girl and made a deadly mistake. If they say *jewels,* I shall quite simply leave the girl to it, even though the resemblance is uncanny—

"A few coins, ma'am," explained Miss Wilson in a tone intended to be soothing, "but dishonest in little, dishonest in much."

Not jewels then. Lady Thorne, always one for drama, stepped closer and, with a flamboyant gesture, threw back her veil. Mr. Markham's eyes bulged. Miss Wilson gasped and stepped back. The constable looked from his prisoner to Lady Thorne, bewildered. Without thought he relinquished his grasp on Val's wrist.

"Good Lord," breathed Val. "*You* are *me!*"

"Not quite," said Lady Thorne in her amused, throaty voice, "but near enough."

A peal of laughter rang out, prettily, like a chime of bells. "Oh, my goodness!" she exclaimed. "I quite see what a shock I must be giving you!"

She was larger than life, thought Valetta. And the uncanny likeness—the same abundant bronze hair, not quite as burnished as Val's. The same slanting eyes, more green than blue, above high cheekbones—the pertly tilted nose.

The two, Valetta the shopgirl and the elegantly dressed customer, stared at each other, Val in stupefaction, the newcomer with a certain distaste resulting from the realization that her double was no more than a clerk in a shop.

With a shiver Val remembered a German legend she had once heard—the *doppelgänger,* one's own image which came to face one just before tragedy struck. How ridiculous! This was a real person, coming into the shop, and very timely too, to purchase real cloth, or buttons, or ribbons. Surely a ghost image would need none of those!

Lady Thorne made a small gesture full of authority. "Now then, officer, you may go back to your duties. I shall be surety for—my cousin."

"Cousin!" The cry came from Miss Wilson and her employer at the same time.

"Cousin of course," said Lady Thorne. "Can you doubt it?" In a brisker tone, she added, "I need a few ribbons. I see no reason why I should not buy them here. At the moment." She eyed Mr. Markham and his clerk. "I do feel, though, that the presence of a constable sadly hinders my desire to purchase..."

In a flurry the officer was dismissed and Miss Wilson, refusing to meet Val's accusing eyes, said, "Madam, if I may serve you?"

"Not at all," said Lady Thorne. "I wish my cousin to see to my needs."

Cousin! thought Val, her head spinning. But I have no cousins! Father always said we were the only ones of the family left. But this woman could be me—the same hair, almost, the eyes, except hers are emerald and mine are only blue—

"Who are you?"

"Did you ever see a likeness of your great-grandmother Finch?"

"Of course!" breathed Val. "You are very like her."

"And so are you. Except that I should judge five years lies between us." Ten years, Lady Thorne decided, was too much to admit to. "You are certainly a Finch. I am Maura Finch, now Lady Thorne."

Her voice held a question which Val answered. "Valetta Finch. But my father said—"

"We'll just forget old family affairs for the moment. Now my dear, let us choose some ribbons and some buttons—those peculiar blue ones take my fancy—and then we will leave."

"Leave?"

"Dear Valetta, pray do not echo every word I say. You cannot think I will allow you to stay here at the mercy of these harpies, do you?"

Harpies were part female, part bird, thought Val, and Mr. Markham was decidedly all male. She flushed, remembering the strong evidence of his sex against her thigh, only a couple of hours ago. She had never felt less motivated to correct a mistake than she did at that moment.

"I can never tell you how grateful I am," she said, her eyes shining. "How can I repay you?"

"Well, we'll see," said Maura. "Now about these buttons."

"Yes, Lady Thorne."

Her new-found cousin adopted an expression of mock severity. "Now, I shall not allow this! You must call me Maura. I do believe you and I are the last of the family. Not that such a poverty of Finches will stun the world when they hear of it!"

Val could find no words to express what she felt—relief at such a crucial intervention in a quarrel Maura could not have known about, and amazement at the advent of a cousin she had never heard of, but whose appearance was her sanction. She was charmed, too, by the sophisticated elegance she saw before her, the careless gestures of a lady of birth and breeding and wealth. It was as though a fairy godmother had waved a wand to display to Val what she herself could be, given elegant clothes and certain experiences. She felt a rush of affection for Maura.

Maura's green eyes swept over her cousin. Val saw an expression in her cousin's features that, later, she would come to recognize and distrust. Now she felt only that she was being weighed by some unknown measures, and she sent up a wordless prayer that she might not be found wanting.

Lady Maura Thorne *swept* through the shop. Ribbons and buttons were bought. Val was carried off by her cousin, leaving behind her accusers stunned by the swift change in their victim's fortunes.

Not until they were settled in Maura's dingy rooms did Val recover sufficiently to make small excursions into further acquaintance.

"You live in London, Lady—I mean, Maura?"

"Certainly not. I come from a small village where nothing ever happens and nobody ever has an interesting thought and there is nobody of any wit to talk to." Val was suddenly sure that her cousin meant—no man to flirt with. "The fashions are at least four years behind Paris. So I come up to London once in a while."

"That explains it," said Val slowly.

"Explains what?"

"That man. He seemed to recognize me."

Maura stiffened perceptibly. "Recognize you? How could he?" In an altered voice she demanded, "Who was he?"

"I don't know. I met him in the park yesterday. He called me *ma'am,* instead of miss, that was all."

"Did he follow you?"

Valetta was startled. "Follow me? Why should he?"

"Did he?"

"No," said Val slowly. She remembered the Scot who had rescued her, scolded her, and taken the trouble to escort her nearly home to ensure her from further harm. "No," she repeated briskly.

Now Val understood. He had thought she was Maura. Furthermore, he seemed to have expected that Maura would be—well, *friendly*. She could not stifle a feeling of regret that the attraction in his eyes was not for her, but intended for her cousin. She hesitated, then added shyly, "Are we truly that much alike?"

Maura considered her for a long time. Ten years of living lay between them, altering the original resemblance. She was quite sure that nobody who knew either one well would mistake her for the other unless, of course, he did not know the other existed. She gazed for a moment upon vistas opening in her mind. Her discovery of this look-alike and naïve cousin could be a godsend. She hoped the girl's heritage from their adventurous and broad-minded great-grandmama would prove fertile. Upon reflection, she was reassured. No shopgirl, especially one so recently in the grip of an officer of the law, could afford any scruples.

But nonetheless—Maura decided—she must make sure.

"Now, my pet," she said sweetly, "why don't you move in with me? Get your things from whatever dreary attic you live in, and be back in time for supper. I suppose you have a trunk. Let's hope it is small. But of course, these rooms are only temporary. Do you have money for a hackney?"

"You'll never believe what happened today," said Val, hurrying into Mrs. Grissom's house. She had made little protest against Maura's scheme. The specter of Mr. Markham, seeking her out for revenge, provided reason enough to accept Maura's offer.

"I've washed your brown dress, dearie, and it's hanging upstairs in your room. I was about to put it off, for my cousin wanted me to go with her down to see the flowers on the stalls, but I said no, something just tells me that the child will want that dress." She stopped short as Val's excitement penetrated to her. "What happened at the shop that I won't believe?"

Val told her about Maura's arrival, carefully omitting Mr. Markham as well as the constable. As she finished she said, "I am not quite sure what the quarrel was about, between our grandparents"—how pleasant it was to say *our*, after believing herself to be alone for so long—"but it must have been a deadly rift. My father told me that he and I were the last of the Finches."

"Did your mother know?"

"She died when I was small." She smiled, suddenly mischievous. "Papa wouldn't like it at all if he knew my cousin and I had found each other."

Mrs. Grissom labored upstairs in Val's wake. "It's all very odd," she said. "I don't know that I like it. I don't know what to think. London isn't safe, even on the streets where you could call for help. But in lodgings, with a woman you don't know!"

"I do know her," said Valetta stubbornly. "She's my cousin. My only relative in the world. If you could have seen us together, you couldn't doubt it."

"You'll want to wear the brown," the landlady said, gathering it up. Val removed her shop clothes and allowed Mrs. Grissom to slip the mended brown dress over her head, smoothing the fabric over her slim hips. "I got to admit you did fine with that ruffle. It doesn't show that tear at all."

The landlady's experience of intrigue might be limited, but she trusted her instincts. Instinct rang a warning bell. "Just the same, I'd like it better if you knew what the quarrel was about. Maybe there's some fortune at stake and you'd lose out on it."

Valetta responded shrewdly, "If there'd been a fortune, my father would not have let it go so easily. There was no money when my mother fell ill before she died. He wouldn't have let any quarrel stand in the way if he could have saved her." She grew sober for a moment. "No," she said at last, "it was nothing but a silly quarrel, and that was between our grandparents. Maura and I haven't quarreled."

Not yet, said Mrs. Grissom to herself.

* * *

Two days later, Val felt as though she had slipped into a world she had only previously dreamed about, a world of romance and elegance and sophistication.

If Maura had decided to give her naïve cousin a course of instruction in the customs of sophisticated society, she could not have done a better job. She talked a great deal, seasoning her conversation with wit and what Val considered a daring recklessness.

Maura opened up to her a world in which women—that is, Maura—were capricious and passionate, following their whims without forethought of consequences. Romantic flirtation awaited them at every corner, and one had only to pick from a lavish buffet set with delights beggaring description.

"And my dear husband was red as a turkey carpet when the duke and I returned from the conservatory. Not that we had done anything wrong, you know. William simply thought his dignity had been compromised." Maura gave a brittle laugh. "Not my honor, you notice. Just his dignity."

Val thought that Sir William Thorne had some justification for his reaction. Not every man looked on complaisantly while his wife flirted with a member of the royal family.

"So of course we were never invited to Oakwoods again. I shall never forgive William for that. I felt such a fool."

"Perhaps," ventured Val, "he did too."

"Nonsense!" said Maura sharply. "I was never unfaithful to William—never. Not, that is, that he would know the difference."

Suddenly Val was convinced that Maura was lying. "But if you love William—"

Her cousin's eyes narrowed. "Love? That stick? Love has nothing to do with it. Men, you know, have always had their little bits of fluff on the side, but they have an apoplexy the minute a woman admits to enjoying herself as they do. You know what William said to me once? He took so long, you know, to get himself ready to perform—that was when we were first married—

and I couldn't stand it. So I reached out to help him. And he said—*ladies* do not move! I was so mortified I could have died."

Val had moved in with Maura on Monday night. Her cousin, far from treating her like the unsophisticated child she knew she was, talked to her like an equal. It was an odd sensation for Val to watch the woman she so closely resembled gesturing, laughing, chatting with animation. Val could almost imagine herself dressed in those elegant clothes, looking at life with that same good humor, daringly sampling all the pleasures presented to her. It was an exhilarating experience. Val was so caught up in Maura's magnetic charm that her feet, so to speak, scarcely touched the ground.

On Wednesday Maura came to sit beside Val on the horsehair sofa that took pride of place in the rented sitting room. Her air of suppressed excitement roused Val's curiosity.

"Now, my pet," Maura began, "I wonder—are you ready for a great lark?"

Ready? Val thought, I'm almost ready to die for her. The dreadful abyss of prison or worse that had been her inevitable future on Monday was gone, dissolved by a wave of Maura's hand. Besides, she had never had such fun in her life.

"Of course," she agreed.

"We're so much alike. Let's—just for fun, you know—change places for an afternoon."

"You're going back to Markham's?" cried Val, alarmed.

"I don't feel *that* larky," Maura commented drily. "No, the plot is this—"

Their two heads—one copper, one bronze—moved closer together.

In midafternoon, Val was dressed in a promenade toilette of ecru crepe de chine, fashioned with an overskirt edged with a broad box-pleated trimming of blue silk. Maura helped her don a lace sacque, looped with blue rosettes. The final touch was a matching straw diadem hat and an ecru pongee parasol.

"How fine you look!" exclaimed Maura, stepping back and admiring her handiwork. "See how you blossom? Throw that dowdy gown of yours away!"

"I feel like someone else," Val confessed.

"You feel like *me,*" Maura corrected. "Now let's see if you can act like me. Walk a few steps. No, no—move as though you owned the earth, just *daring* a gentleman to notice and admire you! Watch me." Maura demonstrated a few steps in the tiny sitting room. "Try it. That's better! Tilt your head a little. Now you have it."

After a few more turns around the room, instructed by Maura, Val's excitement quickened and she grew eager to see whether she could carry off the impersonation.

"A bit of practice," Maura assured her, "and you could even fool dear William."

Maura's voice always took on an edge of contempt when she spoke of her "dear husband." It was one of Maura's habits that Val liked least.

At length Maura considered her ready to set the scheme in motion. But Val still protested. "What if I'm engaged in conversation by—some gentleman?" she asked, the Scotsman's strong features in her thoughts.

"That's the point, my pet. Flirt with him."

I *can't!* Val thought, but she dreaded Maura's disapproval, so she descended to the street. She would not admit to a secret wish to see again her rescuer of Sunday. This time—safe inside her cousin's identity—she might deal with him more gracefully!

She had never seen a structure as elegant as the Westminster Palace Hotel. Built only ten years before, it was furnished in the luxury that dreams are forged. Maura usually stayed here, and for that reason—she had told Val—she had chosen it for their first escapade. Val faltered for only a moment in front of the doors which opened into the lobby. The doorman touched his cap, murmuring "My lady" as he opened the door. So far, so good!

Maura's instructions had been clear. Val hastened toward the far side of the lobby. "The only hotel in London with a lift originally installed," Maura had said. The lift was a remarkable device, a cage of iron bars, a wonderful folding grille serving as a door, and ominous metallic clankings from some mysterious nether region.

Val held her breath, marveling as the entire cage began to rise, and the lobby disappeared from sight beneath her.

Her cousin's scheme called for Val to act as though she were a hotel guest for an hour. By the time she had reached the second floor, she felt almost at home in this alien world, and she stepped out into the carpeted corridor with a delightful tingle of triumph. She was going to make it!

Downstairs again, she glanced around the opulent lobby. Her time more than half gone, she decided to spend the remaining minutes in the lobby in clear view. The Westminster Palace Hotel belonged to the rash of new hotels to appear in London, catering to the increasing throngs of prosperous families coming more frequently to town but not fortunate enough to own or even rent town houses. Indeed, for a few weeks it was hardly worthwhile to take a house, bringing up one's servants and linens, carriages and horses, and all the other luxuries that made life in the capital such a pleasure.

The decor of the lobby was not quite to her taste—red velvet draperies, red velvet settees, marble-topped tables with ornately carved legs, a patterned Brussels carpet—all seemed to stifle her. She chose a seat at the edge of the room, near the registration desk.

She had not been there long when she heard a voice nearby, startling her. Although she had heard it only once before, it seemed as familiar as an old friend. An old enemy more likely, she thought.

She turned in the direction of the voice. There he

was, the tall Scotsman with the cold gray eyes. Her blood pounded in her ears. He would turn eventually, their eyes would meet—and he would come to her. Now she could not claim innocence. Not only did she now understand the mistake he had made—but she was trapped in the identity she had once denied.

She longed for him to catch sight of her—and dreaded the ordeal of making false excuses. He was turned away from her now, talking across the registration desk to a clerk. She listened openly. Apparently, he had been staying here in this hotel and was leaving—tomorrow. The clerk's reedy voice carried. "A nice leave, Captain Drummond? You'll be glad to see the lights of Paris again, I should think."

Paris! And he had said he met her there last summer!

She watched him. In just a moment he would turn...

Recognition stirred slowly in his eyes, and he paused momentarily. She waited, lips parted, some words of explanation hovering on the tip of her tongue. They were not needed.

He flicked a cold glance over her and moved past her into the hallway toward the lift. All her dread of what he might say, of how he would receive her fumbling response, had been for nought. He passed her by as though he had not seen her. A snub royal! She *knew* he had recognized her. That small start when he saw her, that momentarily raised eyebrow—he knew her, all right. But of course—he knew Maura, really, and not Val at all.

Indignation rose in her throat and she swallowed hard. She glanced at the clock over the desk. The scheduled hour was over. She hoped she would never see him again. But when she did—*if,* she meant—she would take care he did not snub her again. Great care!

She had been so intent on him that she did not notice the veiled woman, in the chair half-hidden by a spreading palm tree. Maura was taking no chances on the success of her scheme. If Hunter Dyson suspected that she had left William forever, taking the entailed Thorne emeralds with her, he would already be on her trail. The child across the lobby, like a decoy on a pond, would attract Hunter like lightning to a tree. When more than an hour had passed, and Val was approached neither by Hunter or the police, Maura breathed more easily and slipped out of the lobby. In the next street she took a hackney and went back to her rooms. Best not to let Val know she had watched her. This small prank was only the forerunner of the greater scheme in Maura's mind. On the way home, her thoughts busied themselves with the details of the next great step.

Chapter Four

"How did it go?" cried Maura when Val climbed the stairs to their lodging. "I can see you made it all right. Your face is such an open one, I can read everything you think. Did anyone recognize you?"

"Several," reported Val. "The doorman, of course. One or two gentlemen passing through the lobby bowed and spoke. They really thought I was you, Maura."

"What great fun! We'll have to celebrate. I've already ordered a meal for us. At least for once we won't have to eat that underdone mutton and that cold soup!"

Val changed back into her brown dress, ignoring Maura's *moue* of distaste at the sight of it. The food was good, even though not as hot as she would have liked. But there was an abundance of wine. Val was on her second glass, noting that she was only slightly dizzy. Whether it was the excitement of dressing up in Maura's clothes and pretending to be her cousin, or the shame she felt under the mocking eyes of the Scotsman, she could not tell. But suddenly she felt very, very tired.

She stood up. The room tilted around her in a very

odd manner. She had had only two glasses of wine—she could not be drunk!

"What's the matter?" demanded Maura, pouring her fourth glass. "Sit down again. I want to talk to you."

"You've been talking to me," said Val, carefully forming her words.

"I want you to do something for me."

Val felt suddenly sober. Here it comes, just what Mrs. Grissom warned me about. With surprise, Val realized that she had not believed in Maura's basic kindness or generosity. Nonetheless, she owed her much—at the very least, her freedom, and—knowing the filth and disease of Newgate—probably her life. She sat down on the edge of the chair. "What is it?"

Maura leaned back, sipping her wine, and regarding Val steadily. "I want you to go to Paris."

Val knew, from the amusement in Maura's eyes, that her own expression revealed complete shock. "That wine," she said mildly when she could speak, "must be stronger than you think. I recommend that you let it alone for an hour or so."

Maura laughed. "You'll go with me, of course. Silly, did you think I was sending you by yourself? I'm going to Paris tomorrow, and I want company. You."

Paris! It was only a breath in her mind, but it held beauty, magic, enchantment, an allure beyond words. Paris, City of Light, city of romance, city of dreams—

She could leave for Paris tomorrow!

And the tall Scotsman—he, too, was returning to Paris tomorrow. She had heard the hotel clerk say so.

Maura misread her silence as refusal. She turned persuasive. "My dear, there'll never be a better chance to go. When you marry—and heaven knows what kind of dullard you would have met in that dreadful shop where I found you—you'll learn as I did that all a man thinks about is his own affairs. If he does take you to Paris, he'll watch every move you make. It's hardly worth it, my pet. No, now's the time to go."

"But—but I can't," said Val, listening to an inner voice that balked at the proposal.

Shrewdly Maura said, "No funds, I suppose. Well, you little goose, I'm paying all our expenses. Now I won't hear any more excuses!"

The proposal had charms for Val that her cousin could not suspect. Without Maura, Val alone in London was a lost waif. She had no job, nor were the prospects bright. Mr. Markham was a dangerous enemy.

With all her heart she longed to accept Maura's offer. Paris was her Mecca, her salvation, the object of dreams—anything could happen in Paris! She might even see the Scotsman again. If she did, she would certainly put him in his place!

But a small doubt lingered. Call it instinct, or perhaps Mrs. Grissom's dire warning—she did not know. "Maybe," she said doubtfully, "I could find employment there, and pay you back for my passage."

"Employment? Nonsense. If you insist, you may travel as my maid, at least as far as Paris. Then—we'll see. But we must leave tomorrow."

Val's own need for flight was insistent. "But I haven't anything to wear!"

"Paris," said Maura as though to a small child, "is noted for its fashions."

Later that night, the expedition settled, Val searched in her trunk for the miniature. She took it to the lamp and studied the impetuous, eager eyes of Great-grandmother Finch, as though seeking advice.

"Odd," she said, addressing the miniature, "if Maura had asked me this afternoon, when I was dressed in her clothes, I would have had no doubts. Would you do this, ma'am? Would you trust anyone you had known only three days?"

The bright blue eyes looked back at her without a word. But somehow Val felt comforted when she wrapped the miniature again in soft protecting cloth. That wilful face, those reckless eyes—Great-grandmother would do it, Val was sure. Providence, so far deaf to her pleas, had at last listened. She was putting her enemy and his constables behind her.

In two days she and Maura would be in Paris!

* * *

Maura, mysteriously veiled, boarded the ferry at Southampton, followed by her cousin Valetta in the guise of personal maid. Val was somewhat chagrined to realize that her own meager wardrobe was entirely appropriate for a woman in domestic service.

Val felt the deck move beneath her feet. It was a delicious feeling, evocative of bold undertakings and remarkable daring. Other passengers arrived, hurrying as though by their own activity they could speed the crossing.

Maura gripped Val's wrist painfully. "Don't stand there gaping. Help me to my cabin, before the storm hits us."

Val cast a glance toward the sky, clouded over now by a queer milky haze. She suggested, doubtfully, "If there's bad weather coming, shouldn't we go back?"

"Go back? I can't!"

"I mean, simply to stay overnight in a hotel, and take the ferry tomorrow, or next day." Val's suggestion was futile, for her companion didn't even pause in her headlong progress. She was in a way relieved that Maura had ignored her, for she could well have retorted that Val was too ready to spend money that was not hers. Maura had in truth given evidence of a mean spirit the day before, but had quickly apologized. "I'm just on edge," she had explained, "I want to get away before—" But she had fallen silent then.

Now, Maura flung over her shoulder, "Not possible. Bring that case at once."

Val followed more slowly. There seemed no sense to Maura's insistence upon traveling in haste. Surely they could linger in port for a day or two until the weather cleared, even though Maura could not leave London swiftly enough. But she had said, *before*... Clearly she expected something unpleasant to transpire, something that might prevent her from making her journey. It was not the first time that she had hinted at an unknown obstacle. She had been inquisitive about the man who had spoken to Val in the park—more than inquisitive, Val now decided. She wished Maura would confide in her. How could she know how to help her, unless she understood?

But in the last two days she had begun to learn that Maura was not susceptible to logical analysis. Her cousin was a creature of moods, sometimes gay and insouciant, more often abstracted with what Val believed to be a secret worry.

But hers was not to question, Val thought, hurrying down the iron steps to their cabin. Maura was generous enough to take Val with her to Paris, and the least Val could do was to smile and help where she could.

Their small cabin, to which Maura sped like an arrow, reeked strongly of vinegar and naphtha. It was reassuring to have such unmistakable evidence that the cabin had been recently so well scrubbed, but the lingering smell turned Val's stomach.

Maura, too, was badly affected, but not by the stench. She threw her veil back. Her features were drawn, and her face had turned a pale green. "I know I'm a coward, but I can't help it. I'm a bad sailor."

Val exclaimed, "But we aren't even under way!"

"No matter," said Maura grimly. She removed her hat, then her coat, the high collar of which had partially hidden her features, and handed them to Val. "Just fold the coat, like a good girl, and put the hat somewhere. Hand me my bag."

Obediently, Val did as she was bid. Maura rummaged in the bag until she found a small brown glass vial. She held it aloft. "The only answer," she said. "A bit of this and I'll never know when we leave the pier."

"Laudanum? Isn't that dangerous?"

"Only a few drops. Then, my vexed cousin, I shall turn it over to your custody, until we take to the sea again."

"When we return," murmured Val. "Will that be soon?" She had just started on this adventure. It seemed premature to think already of its conclusion.

"It depends, my pet," said Maura, forcing a laugh. Already the slight motion of the vessel, even tethered as it was at both ends to the dock, was affecting her. She downed the mixture of opiate and water in a few swallows.

"Take this," she demanded, handing the vial to Val, "and put it away. I suppose you don't want any of it, but there's brandy in my bag." She lay down on her bunk. "I wonder if you're such a valorous sailor as you think? My advice is take a good dose of the brandy. It does help, you know. Now leave me alone to my misery."

She turned her face to the wall. Val hesitated, tempted to point out that Maura's tone of voice was a bit patronizing to serve between cousins. She decided not to exaggerate a trifle out of proportion, especially when the trifle was caused by an upheaval in the digestive system.

She sat down on the other bunk. Maura's breathing told her that the laudanum was already taking effect, and she was rapidly dropping into sleep.

From a distance Val could hear the dockhands scurrying about purposefully as well as the shouts and tremors that accompanied the mysterious affair of launching a ferry out to sea. As they moved out of the harbor under steam, she felt the engines throbbing beneath her feet. The floor seemed to come alive. An uneasy sensation awoke somewhere in the region of her stomach and she gripped the edge of the bunk with both hands.

How dreadful if she were to miss the crossing, simply because her stomach rebelled. How dismaying if she could not enjoy every moment of the first real adventure of her life!

She swallowed hard, gulping down the uncertain lump that rose in her throat. She couldn't be sick—she just couldn't!

She remembered the brandy. She found it, but there was no glass. She hesitated, then put the bottle itself to her lips and drank.

The brandy dropped into her empty stomach like a hot coal, igniting whatever it touched like a burning ember in dry grass. She felt the heat of it rising until it flamed in her brain. She thought the walls of the tiny cabin were closing in on her. How very odd! She said loudly to Maura, "Do you see that?"

Maura was not yet fully asleep. She groaned. "Don't talk to me. Just go away and let me die."

Finally, Val believed the brandy had done its work. Her stomach was steady, and she felt fine. Val got to her feet and pulled the thin blanket over Maura. As she bent over to tuck it in around Maura's shoulders the porthole shutter flew open and hit her in the back of her head. She felt as though she had been struck with a sledge.

She stood erect, letting the pain subside to a point where it was bearable. Her cousin was asleep. Suppose the ferry did founder? Val was sure she could not drag an unconscious body up the stairs to the deck, to say nothing of getting her into a lifeboat.

The pain in her head was better, but the close cabin was stifling. She picked up her shawl and went out, closing the cabin door behind her, softly to spare her own head, because Maura was clearly beyond being aroused by anything short of a cannon shot.

She stumbled past other closed doors, wondering whether each cabin held travelers suffering, as Maura did, as much from anticipation as from actual *mal de mer*. The floor of the corridor tilted and she flung her hands out to either side to keep from falling. In a moment the ship returned to an even keel, and she reached the stairs leading to the upper deck. Although she would have liked to explore the ship, at this moment she was aware only of her need for fresh, preferably cool, restoring air on her burning cheeks.

She climbed the stairs, feeling better at every step as she left the musty air of the lower deck behind. She stopped at the top of the iron steps to get her bearings. The open deck was narrow at this point, but to her left, toward the stern, the deck broadened out. There was no one in sight.

She crossed to the rail, grabbing at it for support as the ship plunged suddenly. Leaning against the stanchion, one of many supporting the upper deck, she closed her eyes. She felt the wind blowing away the potent fumes of the brandy, and the motion of the ship now beginning to lull, rhythmically lifting with the waves and settling back again. The jerky movement she had felt below, she now realized, must have marked the moment when the ferry moved from the sheltered waters of the harbor into the choppy waves of the Channel.

At length, feeling somewhat restored, she dared to open her eyes and look out at the sea. The surface of the waters seemed to be in violent motion, choppy waves coming at her from all directions in the turbulent sea, their crests tipped with foam. The sea, gray under a leaden sky of gust-driven clouds, tossed incessantly, sometimes seeming, as the ship heeled, nearly as high as the deck beneath her feet.

Now, watching the ship's motion rise and fall away beneath her, she could not blame her cousin for seeking oblivious sleep. If it had not been for the steadying influence of the brandy, she herself might be moaning on the bunk below. She swallowed hard, and her stomach settled again.

Watching the wild sea hypnotized her beyond any sense of passing time. She did not know how long she stood there, gazing at the waves, letting all the troubles of the past weeks drain away. Fancifully, she could almost believe that the freshness of the gusting breeze was scouring away her griefs.

She felt free from the past. And although the deck seemed to be increasingly unsteady, and a channel growing more menacing by the moment, under ominous storm clouds, she felt happier than she had for months.

The waves, hurried on by the storm winds, towered higher than the ship's rail. She looked into one dark, curving wave, the top of it blowing into spume, and realized she was looking *up*. The sight unnerved her.

Her new self was not in danger now of languishing in Newgate, but was very much in peril from the violence of the seas. The sensible thing would be to escape below, where the motion was less extreme, and the winds could not try to tear her clothes from her as they did at this moment.

She clung to the rail, not daring to trust herself even to cross the narrow deck to the stairway. The wind was exhilarating. Even the sense of danger stirred her pleasantly. In a flash, she realized why. "I'm drunk, on that brandy!" Her stomach lifted and settled. She wished she were even drunker. The liquor had soothed her stomach but now had left only an odd sense of displacement in her head. Danger seemed remote, unable to touch her.

It seemed as though she were standing at a distance, watching this bronze-haired girl laughing back at the wailing wind. It was puzzling—she existed apart from herself in the oddest way, without responsibility, and only a mild curiosity about the phenomenon. She leaned heavily against the rail.

A rough voice sounded in her ear. "Take a deep breath! That's it! Now another! Good girl!" A strong arm lay across her shoulders, holding her steady against the violent motion of the ship.

What on earth—? But she did not speak. She turned, bewildered, to look at the man who had embraced her so rudely. She was surely drunk as a lord, she decided. This could not be the same man! The same rough-hewn features, the same sea-gray eyes, the same Scottish burr—

"You!" she breathed.

Recognition came to him in the same moment. He took his arm away from her shoulders at once. "For God's sake," he demanded harshly, "are you everywhere?"

Nettled, she flung at him, "No more than you, sir! And this time, as you s-see, I am in no need of rescue!"

She expected him to frown in clear disgust and go away at once, but his reaction was surprising. He threw back his head and laughed.

Again, she felt unsettled, so oddly remote. Seeing once more the long face with the stern gray eyes, she realized that he had never left her thoughts. Now that she knew about Maura's existence, she could more readily understand his mistake. He had indeed known Maura in Paris. Val was not quite so ready now to excuse his error. She did not quite know why, but she knew that she did not wish to be taken for Maura, not with this man. She wanted to be herself, and have him desire her for herself, and not because she was a more accessible model of Maura.

And yet, Maura—Val was convinced now—had been accessible. Her cousin could not keep from flirting with any male that was nearby. Maura could not have filled Val's ears with such tales of passion and intrigue had she not had some experience of it.

Maura must have given even this man reason to think she might be willing. If he tried to take advantage of her, Val, she would—

She turned to snub him defiantly, as he had done her in the lobby of the Westminster Palace Hotel. She would wipe that impudent look from his face—

Just then the deck fell away under her feet, and she lost her balance. Unthinkingly she grabbed for support. Her hands caught the narrow lapels of his coat, and she felt his arm wrap protectively around her again. She pulled away and reached frantically for the rail.

"You don't need help, you say?" He was obviously amused.

The tall Scotsman steadied her against the rail. The ship bucked, and she fell against him. His arms were quick to enfold her, and without thinking she laid her head against his chest.

"I really should not..." she murmured, struggling upright.

"Can you stand alone? Somehow I have a feeling we have done this before, haven't you? Or have you forgotten the runaway team as quickly as you pretended to forget last summer in Paris? Oh—I forgot. I promised not to mention Paris again, didn't I?"

"I have never," said Val with excess dignity, "been in Paris in my life. You must be thinking of someone else."

"Lady Thorne, you surely cannot forget the wide swath you cut in Paris last summer? Nor that note of solicitation you slipped into my hand when you stumbled against me—not by accident, I am sure—coming down the grand stairway at the Saint-Cloud Palace? I regret that your departure from France was accelerated—before my duties freed me to accept."

He seemed driven to punish this wench for forgetting that she had once found him attractive. Of course, he would have been simply a diversion for this lady, for rumor insisted that she had greater prey in mind, before her husband had hustled her back to England. Nonetheless, now close to her, he clung to his conviction of the last few days that she must be a greatly accomplished actress to look so young and innocent.

When she did not answer, he pressed on. "I heard that even the emperor himself was smitten by your loveliness. Of course, it would not be *gallant* to wonder aloud whether or not he had had more success than I. Then, again, an emperor might outrank the Laird of Ochill, but only in Paris."

"Laird? Of Ochill? That is a title, I gather?"

"One of great antiquity."

"And yet you are ashamed of it."

His tone altered. "Ashamed? Never."

"But you do not live in Scotland, on your estates?"

His face darkened. In a hard voice he said, "Nor do you stay at Thorne Hall."

"I am not—" Her voice died away. Her mind and body felt confused, out of sync. She seemed to be moving on two levels. On the one hand, her conscious mind insisted: you must go away, you must not stand so close to him, or long to feel his touch again on your arm, or lay your head against his chest, or hear his heart pounding in your ear. But, as if in direct defiance of any known morality, her skin began to move as though possessed, yearning for his strength, crying out to be stroked, to feel his hands ignite the fuse that ran quickly down the length of her body...

And suddenly, she had no control over the unfamiliar

feelings that rose insistently within her. It was that last swig of brandy, she thought, just before she had come up the stairs—one gulp too many. Reeling, she turned to him in piteous appeal. Help me, she cried silently, for I cannot do what I should. Someone else is inside me, someone who knows well enough that my defenses are gone.

Help me—

He reached for her and brought her swiftly to him. Putting a finger under her chin, he tilted her face up to his. He had come to the rescue, she thought dimly, not of herself, but to that other someone inside her skin. Without volition her arms reached up to encircle his neck, and she pressed her body against him.

It was too late to pull away, even had she wanted to. Sighing with pleasure, she could feel his hard body against her softness, his lips searching for hers, nibbling them gently open. Without thinking she let her hands move over the rough black hair at the back of his neck.

He drew away at last, his head bent back, and looked into her eyes, seeking the answer to the question he had not asked. A growl of thunder came from the sky, and not far away lightning flickered as though dancing on the crests of the rioting waves.

Spindrift spattered against them, the salt water running down their faces. "We can't stay here," he whispered. "Come?"

His arm around her, holding her steady against the pitch of the ship, she moved with him to the top of the stairs, and below to the corridor, past a couple of closed doors.

She asked no questions. At the third door they halted. His arm still holding her, he opened the door for them, and bolted it from the inside.

She was safe now from the wind and the rain and the tempest-tossed seas. But oddly it was as though the wildness of the storm had followed them into this cabin, filling it with an atmosphere of tenseness, of crackling electricity, that was more exciting, and dangerous, than the storm above.

He guided her to the bunk and pressed her shoulders, making her sit. He stood before her, searching her features for something, she did not know what. Did he want her permission for—what was to come next? She could not give it to him, for innocence was stilling her tongue. But equally, she knew she could not refuse whatever he wished to do with her.

Later, she could not even remember her last coherent thought. Somehow her clothes were taken from her, and she was thankful that the sodden merino shawl and the drenched petticoats seemed to disappear so easily. He was naked now too—and they were together on the bunk.

She opened her lips to his, deliciously surprised when his tongue lingered on the threshold of her mouth, advancing gently, until he possessed her mouth in a kind of frenzy. She responded, her lips moving incessantly with a feverish greed.

His hands stroked, caressed, seeking out her hidden places and making them his. She gasped once, in surprise, and he hesitated momentarily, before bending anew to teasing her nipples with his delicate tongue.

She did not know what he expected of her, but he taught her, and in truth her body was an apt pupil. She was not clumsy for more than a breath, and more than once her eagerness to answer the questing of his flesh with her own responses led her to match his fever with her own urgency. He growled, a soft leonine purr in his throat, and she knew she had pleased him.

Feeling his hard-muscled leg between hers, aware of his knee bending to press insistently against the entrance to the secret core of her, she caught a long, shuddering breath. He shifted, taking his knee away and settling himself between her spread thighs. She could feel him hard, moist, and pulsing, and felt the muscles in her own belly writhing tumultuously as though demanding to be slaked, until if she could have spoken she would have begged him to—to what?—but she did not even know the words.

She arched against him, obedient to a purely animal instinct, and he slipped a hand beneath the small of her back to bring her to him, ready to receive him. Then—a long, sharp agony burned its way through her from her softness to the top of her head. Somewhere a small, hurt beast whimpered and could not stop, until she recognized that the pitiful cry came from her own throat.

But his mouth stopped her crying, his darting tongue moved frenetically in and out, and suddenly her hurt was forgotten in his suddenly savage driving again and again into her, his swollen, hard, invading manhood pounding in ruthless rhythm. Her softness welcomed him and closed around him, yielding and yet, in some strange way, demanding to release the ecstasy that lay within her.

It was over, too soon. She felt him recede from her, like a tide ebbing, leaving her lonely from his withdrawal, throbbing with remembered pain, and crying.

She turned over on her stomach, muffling her sobs in the blanket. Something was thrown onto her back and she reached for it. It was wet and clammy and she recognized her skirt.

She struggled to sit up, clutching the cold wet dress to her breasts. He was nearly dressed. The room was not so dark now and she recognized the source of the pale light at the window. The storm had passed on.

By the gray light she could see his features, set as though carved in granite. When he spoke, his voice rasped cruelly, so harsh she could almost feel it raking her bare skin.

"A very nice performance," he said coldly. "One might almost think you a virgin."

"Almost?"

"I must admit this is a new experience for me. Virgins have not so far come my way, so I cannot vouch for the authenticity of your performance."

"I don't understand," she moaned.

"Spare me your excesses," he grated. "The act is over and you've had my applause. I congratulate you on a new ploy, my lady. I am convinced you will be an enormous success. None of the *grandes horizontales* have thought of it." He laughed, a brittle sound in the small cabin. "Perhaps I should have provided myself with a sheaf of roses to hand you. But then I had not expected the veteran star to turn ingenue."

He went to the door. Turning to survey her naked body, he grinned wickedly. "Your performance was flawed in one respect. A real ingenue would try to appear a bit reluctant—not turn into a whore at the first touch of her lover's hand!"

Fury at last released her from immobility. She threw her wet garments, her only weapon, at him. They hit the door with a sodden thud as he closed it quickly behind him.

"How could he?" she sobbed. She sat on the bed, forgetting her clothes, forgetting the unlocked door, oblivious of all except his terrible insults, and her grievously bruised body. How dared he intimate such wicked things? She should never have touched the brandy. She had been drunk at the start, but now she was cold sober. *"How could I?"*

The brandy was no excuse, but she could not yet face her own guilt. She had in fact behaved no better than a whore, as he had called her. For now, she would blame her shame on alcohol.

She must move soon, dress, return to Maura, and see to the many duties involved in landing at Calais.

An unmeasurable time later, she stirred. With leaden fingers she dressed, buttoning buttons without thinking, shaking out the wet wool of her shawl, untangling the matted sodden fringe and letting it trail from her hands without trying to drape it around her shoulders. She stepped into the corridor without even a cautious glance to avoid being seen.

There was now only one thing in her mind. She hoped she never saw the man again. If she did, she would, quite simply, kill him.

Chapter Five

Paris in April was like a glass of sparkling champagne, light in color, delicious to the taste, and going quite strongly to the head.

Valetta knew she was not the first to compare this fairylike city to bubbling wine, but in truth she could think of nothing else so *à propos*.

Maura had made arrangements to lease a small third-floor flat in a secluded little courtyard just off the Place Saint-Michel. From the parlor window, if one looked carefully, one could just make out one of the soaring towers of the Cathedral of Notre Dame.

"Too bad that building across the street couldn't have been built a yard or two back!" Val said to their new housekeeper.

Jehane had appeared as if brought by a miracle to the front doorstep the moment that Milady Thorne emerged from the carriage that had brought her and Val from the railroad station. Maura, still veiled, had engaged Jehane on the spot, almost as though she were expecting her.

"We cannot do for ourselves, of course," said Maura. "Surely, Val, you did not expect to do the cooking? You don't even know the difference between a *pâtisserie* and a *jardin potager*. I, for one, do not intend to chance the kind of meals you'd manage!"

"I did not even think of doing the work myself," retorted Valetta. She was beginning to feel that Maura was entirely too prickly to be a satisfactory companion. Even though Lady Thorne had underwritten the cost of this short vacation—for Valetta considered this journey no more than a small lark in the midst of her urgent business of earning a living—Val had not been engaged as a servant, and had no intention of submitting to tyranny. It behooved her to make sure the balance of their relationship was maintained.

"My only concern," she continued sturdily, "was that she came too promptly upon our arrival. How do you know whether she is reliable?"

Maura gave her brittle laugh. "No French servant is reliable. I suppose Jehane is no worse than the others." She dismissed the subject with a wave of her heavily ringed hand and changed the subject. "I shall be gone this afternoon. Monsieur Worth has been kind enough to find time for me this afternoon."

"Monsieur Worth?"

Maura sighed. "How could you possibly not know Worth? Very well, listen. Charles Frederick Worth is an Englishman. He is a designer of clothes. It is said that the empress herself will wear nothing that he has not designed for her. It is he who convinced the empress that crinolines were out of fashion. Of course, they weren't until he said so, and the empress agreed like the sheep she is."

"Gowns? Oh, how delightful! I love clothes." Val hesitated. She was never quite sure how to deal with Maura's quicksilver moods. "Are you going there this afternoon? I have a little money. I should like to go with you."

Maura was sharp. "Out of the question. I cannot bear anyone fussing around me, telling me what they think.

Monsieur Worth is all the consultant I need. And certainly I shall not wish his attention to be diverted to you, with your *little* money."

Lady Thorne watched her young cousin flush. It was so easy to humiliate her. A word would do it, even a tone of voice. Maura was amused. Like shooting fish in a barrel, she thought—hardly any challenge at all. If Val had ever protested, or even fought back, Maura would have respected her more. Baiting this child was not even a challenge, and besides, Maura needed her, even though she had not yet revealed her plan. She must take time to insure Val's goodwill, lest the entire scheme fall through.

"Perhaps another time," she said in a kindly fashion. "But I've got a better idea, Val. Why don't you get to know the city a little? I don't see another trip to Paris in your future, do you? Surely you're not going to meet any eligible prospects in that dingy shop where I found you. Unless you're planning to marry the owner and turn into a woman of business?"

Val hoped she did not reveal the fears that now swept over her. She had all but forgotten the threat of prison, or worse, that lay in wait for her when she returned to London. Her secret thoughts had dwelt entirely on the episode in the cabin of the ferry. Shaken by the terrible realization of what she had allowed to happen, she could not believe that that lovemaking had been more than a maiden's wishful dream. The knowledge that she was no longer inexperienced had driven a wedge into her, so that she felt riven like a tree struck by lightning.

Her life was divided, so to speak, into Before the Man, and afterwards. *Before* now seemed long, pale, and unmarked by meaning. *Afterwards* had driven out fears of Mr. Markham and jail, the probability of starvation from lack of a job, and given her a crowd of rebellious, riotous thoughts and emotions that she could not begin to deal with.

She suspected that Maura could no doubt draw on sufficient experience to help her understand this unforgivable lapse, her unbelievable descent into shame.

She could not confide in her, though. Instead, she swung between blaming the episode on the brandy, and remembering most of the coupling act with disgraceful pleasure.

She had spent hours during the night watches turning over in her mind the scorching denunciations he had flung at her. A fine performance, he had said afterwards—one might almost think you a virgin. How could he think otherwise? But he had assumed Maura would let him run free over her body, and her buzzing head had welcomed the mistake.

The unpalatable truth was too painful to endure. Somehow she had angered him, had failed to measure up to expectations. When she recognized the trend of her muddled thoughts, she knew that more than her body had been invaded. The gray-eyed Scot, whose name she did not even know, continued to arrest her thoughts, waking and dreaming.

Maura had been talking, unheeded. "Enjoy yourself, my pet," she said when Val seemed to hear her again, "while you can."

That afternoon, when Maura, heavily veiled, left for her appointment at Worth's atelier at 7, rue de la Paix, Val dressed to go out. Perhaps if she walked far enough, briskly enough, she might find oblivion in sleep, at least for one night. The only gown that she considered suitable for a stroll on the streets of the fashion capital of the world was the Bismarck-brown dress, mended and mended again, flaunting the cream-colored ruffle as defiantly as though Worth himself had decreed its existence.

But then Val remembered that Maura had never left the apartment at any time without a veil. Perhaps it was the custom in Paris for ladies to go veiled. She did not wish to be taken for a woman of ill repute, as Mrs. Grissom would have said.

"Jehane, tell me," Val said in French, halting but far more fluent than Maura gave her credit for. "Must I wear a veil? Shall I be accosted on the street if I do not?"

"Mademoiselle does not like the veil? Just so. A beautiful woman should not hide her appearance."

"But madame—"

"My lady wears the veil, yes it is so. For a reason, no doubt, but I cannot tell it to you. Perhaps only this piece of a hat on your splendid hair—and *voilà!*—you are ready." She adjusted the hat on Val's bronze hair, giving it a slightly different angle, and with a tiny adjustment making it appear superbly chic.

"I wouldn't have believed—" mused Val. Then, still a London lady even though England seemed to exist in another world, she hesitated about walking out alone. It was odd, she realized, that on her way from lodging to shop, she had never given convention a thought. But now in some subtle way, she had returned to her once-elevated station in life, where a lady never went out without her maid.

"Jehane, will you go with me? To see that I don't get lost," she asked, with the smile that lighted her face. "My cousin believes I cannot even read signs."

Jehane nodded. "I will go with you, mademoiselle, if you wish. With pleasure. But mademoiselle's French is good. An accent of the most charming, of course, but very good."

The French housekeeper who had come to them upon their arrival perhaps too promptly to be coincidence, was broadly built and stocky, with the heavy muscular legs of her ancestors who had once trod mountain paths. Surprisingly agile, she was a fury of energy, and seemed to be in constant battle with dirt. No mote of dust ever lingered in her path. And the meals! *Magnifique!* Val had made an effort, in the days since they had arrived in Paris, to use all the French she knew in conversing with Jehane.

Now, as they went down the stairs to the street, Val told Jehane, "I shall be glad of the exercise. Your *cuisine* will add pounds in a week. Lady Thorne will be fortunate if her new Worth gowns fit when she gets them home."

The housekeeper said carelessly, "Then they will

come to you, mademoiselle, for my lady is already thicker in the waist."

But Val had no illusions about Maura's generosity. Her cousin's expensive gowns would never adorn a figure other than Maura's own.

Jehane returned to the subject. "Do not worry, mademoiselle, for my lady knows well that if she becomes too fat she will no longer attract the—the man she has come to meet."

"What do you mean?" Val demanded as they reached the door to the street. "I know of no man—"

"That is not to say," answered Jehane, carefully choosing her words, "that there is none."

Val suddenly remembered that she was gossiping with a servant, even though she found Jehane far more companionable than her cousin. They emerged from the blue door that opened onto the small square opposite their building, and she put away Maura's affairs for the moment.

The narrow sidewalk beside the building merged into a cobblestone street. In the center of the minuscule square, shallow curbing outlined an oval space, containing a struggling plane tree. There was not a blade of grass anywhere, as there would be in London—only hard-packed dirt. The square was as bleak as the stone apartment buildings that hemmed it in on four sides.

They left the square through an arch at the end of a short street. Valetta could not afterwards have retraced their steps. Jehane indicated points of interest, but Val could not keep them in her mind.

They had not gone far when suddenly Jehane caught her arm. "Wait!"

They had emerged onto a broad street, no doubt one of Haussmann's boulevards, where recently planted chestnuts lined the avenue in both directions. Surely Paris was a city like no other in its elegant open spaces. She had heard of Georges Haussmann and his ruthless destruction of blocks of tenement buildings in order to construct his magnificent city, a plan that would augment the grandeur of the Imperial government. Already other cities were copying Haussmann's designs, she knew—Stockholm, for one, and even Rome.

Now, immobile, she saw the reason for Jehane's strong sudden grip on her arm. Through an arch behind them emerged a small platoon of cavalry, trotting briskly onto the avenue. Val caught her breath. They were a brave sight, their helmets flashing in the sunlight, white plumes bowing in the wind. It seemed as though everything on the horses—save the riders—was a-jingle.

"Imperial guards," Jehane instructed her. "Scarlet, you see, and the headpieces, the casques you call them, all glittery."

"The emperor is approaching then?" She was breathless with excitement. Her first day on the streets of Paris, and already it was possible to see the sovereigns!

"No, of a certainty. These troops are only on an errand, without doubt. When the emperor goes through the streets, one would believe a city of soldiers was on the move. Since the Italian *scélérat* Orsini threw the bomb, there are many, many soldiers when the emperor makes procession."

"The bomb?" echoed Val. "I did not read of that in the newspapers."

"Why not? It was only twelve years ago."

Val suppressed a smile at Jehane's transparent belief that whatever happened in France must be a nine-days' wonder to the rest of the world, to be discussed exhaustively and endlessly recalled.

Val watched the platoon as it turned a corner smartly and left the avenue. "What a marvelous sight!" she breathed when the last white plume was lost from view.

"Always the soldiers," snorted Jehane. "The emperor makes the spectacle every day so the people will forget how hungry they are."

Bread and circuses, the Romans had provided. And Rome had fallen. Could the French Empire be an unsteady structure as well?

It was a sobering thought. Val had not noticed the faces of the people she met on the narrow walkways. She was a tourist, a bird of passage, a guest in this country, and what she looked at were the handsome stone buildings, each attached to the next, lining the streets. Across the way there were similar buildings, apartments for the well-to-do, garnished with flowers wherever one could place a pot. In late April, Paris was adorned with the jewel colors of flowers. Geraniums in ruby hues stood out, even as they mingled with flowers she did not recognize, in shades of topaz, sapphire, amethyst, and, underlying all, the emerald green of the rampant foilage, the velvet lawns, the deep green of the chestnut trees.

This first stroll through the streets close to their apartment only whetted Valetta's appetite for the city. She went out every day after that, and walked for hours, sometimes with Jehane, and sometimes, although she believed Maura would not have approved, daringly alone.

Every day there was a procession of some kind—usually a detachment of cavalry, often a religious procession with choirs singing as they marched down the boulevard. Once, to her great delight, she was fortunate enough to see the young Prince Imperial, of majestic bearing even at fourteen years, on his way from the Tuileries to his own palace, the Bagatelle, escorted by fantastically white-robed Algerian horsemen.

She had caught the wandering eye of the young prince that day. He had bowed gravely to her, as had also a splendidly uniformed soldier at his side. The prince's aide, in fact, turned his head to look at her until the flamboyant procession moved out of sight.

How very flattering it was! And yet, she had been more pleased when the Prince of Wales had bowed to her. The remembrance of that day brought back the Scotsman who rescued her then—and later violated her, even though she had been more than willing.

She returned to the apartment in a lowering mood.

She was alone the day she discovered the Luxembourg Gardens. She had thoroughly explored the narrow side streets near their apartment, the rue de la Huchette, the street surprisingly called Monsieur-le-Prince, and even the Boulevard Saint-Michel, the one Jehane called the Boul' Mich.

This day Maura took an interest in her plans for the day. "I must go again to Worth's, for the last fitting. But you, my pet, what will you do? Go out to walk again?"

"I imagine so, unless you wish me to go with you?"

"Too boring for you. You are such a typical Englishwoman, walking and walking. All you need is country tweeds, and a pair of spaniels to make the picture complete."

"You are laughing at me again, Maura," commented Val without heat.

"Not at all, *chérie*. Have you discovered the Luxembourg yet? I am sure you must not, for you would have overwhelmed me with your praise."

Val bit her lip. Was she really so naïve as to babble in such a boring fashion? Maura could deliver a rebuke in such a fashion that Val did not even recognize the reprimand until later. It was seriously upsetting to think that her more experienced cousin did not approve of her. More than upsetting, Val decided, for she was always aware that she failed in every way to measure up to the companion that Maura expected.

"I shall look forward," she said, her mouth dry, "to visiting it."

"Today is the day," said Maura, with the gay charm that she seldom troubled to use, at least for Val's benefit. "This afternoon, while I am gone, is the best time." Val looked curiously at her. "Surprised that I'm interested? Don't be. Just because I've had some worries of my own, doesn't mean I'm not thinking of your amusement."

Val responded to her cousin's change of heart. "I did think—well, no matter," she said sunnily. "I'll find the Luxembourg this very afternoon."

Maura was satisfied. "About two o'clock is the best time for viewing," she said, "so I am told."

It was approaching two o'clock when she reached the Luxembourg Palace. The gardens were open when she arrived. She was drawn through the wrought-iron gates by the elegant and dazzling vista before her. Everywhere before her were green velvet lawns, adorned with mosaics of bright flowers with elegant statues of beautiful women dreaming forever under magnificent trees. At the center of the gardens was a small fountain, of great antiquity judging by the hoary moss-covered stones circling the pond. In the water the stately lines of the grand palace were reflected, as they had been for more than three and a half centuries.

She wanted to stay in the gardens forever. The spaciousness of the gardens opened up her own thoughts, cramped from the narrowness of their small flat. It was not the physical confinement of the rooms, she decided. It was the jejune, sterile atmosphere of their days. If I had known, she reflected, that Maura would sit at the window for hours, staring down into that scraggly plane tree and that desertlike "garden" in the square, I should not have leaped at the chance to come to Paris, even though the alternative was nothing less than alarming.

But, she remembered, it was not entirely the lure of Paris itself that had attracted her in the first place. It was the fantastic coincidence that had brought her and her only relative together. Even though Val had not known of her cousin's existence, she had been instantly ready to accept her as though they had been childhood companions.

What had she expected? A mirror image of herself? An immediate banishing of loneliness?

Whatever she had expected, she had not found it.

She sat for a long time on a marble bench in the shade. Children played around her, launching tiny boats of bark onto the placid surface of the pond, watching until the agitated waters beneath the fountain seized the bark fleet and sent the little vessels gyrating madly.

The soft plopping rhythm of the fountain lulled her. How wise it was of Maura to suggest coming here!

She thought later she must have dozed for a few

moments. Suddenly, she opened her eyes with an alarming feeling of being watched. A man stood not far away, his gaze turned in her direction. Her memory was playing a trick on her, she thought at first. For a moment she was back on the bank of the Thames, and the Scotsman's frankly admiring eyes were watching her. Her heart lurched in her breast. It could not be—

It was not. This admirer was entirely French, and she was in a French park. Even the approval in his eyes was of a different kind, open, and in a way insulting.

The man was slender of build, with a military bearing that made him appear taller than he was. He wore a thin moustache, and a small tuft of beard that marked him as a member of the emperor's party. He was dressed *à l'Anglais,* in light-colored trousers and a dark sack coat. His hair was hidden under a hard, round hat.

He was, at first sight, attractive. But his gaze on Val was too much, she thought, like that of an effete aristocrat judging inferior horseflesh.

Had she been privy to his thoughts, she would have been astounded. He was, as she saw, frankly enchanted with her appearance. But he was also, as she could not know, struck with her resemblance to the woman with whom he was commencing *l'affaire de coeur.* Not the English lady he had fallen in love with last summer, to be sure, but as she might have been ten years before. He wished he had known Maura then before the sentence of marriage had been passed on them both.

If he could only go back even to last summer, when they had both been frantically eager to explore each other's bodies, to taste the sublime flavors of *l'amour*—before that unlucky day when the threat of scandal erupted and his stupid Clothilde and Maura's husband had intervened. He had promised Maura his undying love. He had not been sincere, but Maura, fool that she was, believed him.

Now he eyed *la petite cousine,* and his loins stirred. Maura would kill him if he touched the nymph. What was a poor man to do?

Nettled by the man's audacity, and irritated because

he had broken the peaceful spell that enfolded her, Valetta left the bench and walked, with a deceptively casual air, toward the gates. She looked behind her once. He was still standing where she had first seen him, watching her.

She hurried home through streets that had become familiar to her. But even as the stranger's boldness had broken her peace in the garden, she was now more than ordinarily aware of the pinched faces she met, the noxious smells that burst upon her from the foul mouths of alleys she passed. Paris, the elegant, glittering city of a million jewels, was revealing the dirty petticoats she wore underneath. The lovely garden contained a bold and alarming worm within it. The quaint streets hid poverty and wretchedness.

By the time Val reached the familiar arch and turned into the narrow cobbled square where she and Maura lived, she had made up her mind. Paris was no longer alluring.

She walked swiftly, around the dusty oval in the middle of the square, and rushed through the blue door. The stranger had not followed her. Why should he have? He was simply a flirtatious Frenchman. She had seen many in the two weeks she had come to know Paris. But for some reason, this man's rude stare gave her an uneasy feeling.

She stopped before climbing the stairs to their apartment. With an effort, she banished him, deliberately, from her mind. Taking a deep breath and gagging on the strong aroma of cooked cabbage, she went up the two flights of stairs to their rooms.

On the landing she stopped short, her hand on the latch. She hoped Maura would be, for once, in a good mood, because Val was going to tell her cousin that she was going back to London.

The decision had not been arrived at logically. It had simply stood there, almost tangible, full grown. She had looked at the idea thoughtfully and liked it. She belonged in London, not idling her days away listening to murmuring fountains and being undressed by a pair of French eyes!

London could be a danger to her, even though she was quite sure that Mr. Markham would not persecute her as long as he was aware she had a titled cousin. But that danger was one she knew. Paris gave her the uneasy feeling that dangers here could take on a shape unknown, and therefore perilous.

She framed her decision in words, then squared her shoulders, and opened the door.

Chapter Six

The sound of the door closing behind Val brought her cousin bursting from the sitting room.

"At last!"

Maura waved a cream-colored envelope excitedly. Seeing that a response was expected from her, Val asked, "At last what?"

"An invitation to Court. This invitation means that the Embassy knows I am here."

"This is a surprise," commented Val, "considering that you have gone to extreme lengths not to appear in public."

"Of course I have. But I've sent you out, you know."

Val stared at her. "Sent me out? Then all the time—"

Maura watched her with narrowed eyes as Val stumbled among her confused thoughts. At length, with a sigh, Maura took pity on her. "You don't really know why I brought you to Paris?"

"Because we're cousins," said Val. "Because we two are the last of the Finches and wanted to get acquainted." Noting her cousin's sardonic amusement, Val faltered. "That was what you told me. Isn't it true?"

Quickly Maura soothed her. "Of course, that's part of it. And I must say we are getting along together better than I had expected."

Val thought darkly, that's because I don't cross you in any way. But she said only, "We're both well brought up, I suppose. And civilized people don't quarrel."

"That's where you're wrong, my pet. I am far more civilized than you, even with your Greek language and your ancient heroes."

"The Greeks were the most highly cultured—"

"But that is, quite literally, ancient history. Refined behavior today is entirely different. It is appearances that count. You will remember that we left London in haste. We have not advertised our presence here."

"But the Embassy is aware of your existence." Val was still smarting from her cousin's casual dismissal of the ancient world in which, thanks to her father's absorbing interest, she had spent much time.

"So here in Paris, all the embassy knows is that the dashing Lady Thorne is strolling in public, decently with her maid—Jehane was good to go with you to give you, as she would say, of respectability the utmost—and behaving with excessive decorum."

"Lady Thorne?" cried Val scornfully. "You haven't set foot out of the apartment for two weeks except to go to Worth's atelier."

"And then, you recall, I wore a heavy veil. But all the time when you were seeing the sights of Paris, I was safely immured here. You see? We have not appeared together at any time."

Valetta realized then that she had moved, until now, upon only the surface of deep waters. Too late she recalled Mrs. Grissom's forebodings. She settled herself in an armchair, crossed her ankles decorously, and said with a sweetness she did not feel, "You may as well tell me everything now."

"I wonder."

Valetta was used to dealing with her father, a temperamental and unconventional man. Now she turned her skill to her cousin, oddly enough, not too different from the classical scholar she had known well. They shared the same devious, secretive ways. "If you don't tell me," suggested Val, "the entire truth about this visit to Paris, then I may make some irretrievable blunder. Only out of ignorance, you understand."

Maura moved to the window and looked down into the street, her back to Valetta. She stood with an arrested air, as though something in the courtyard—or someone—had caught her attention. After a moment, she turned back to Valetta. Her expression was calm, as though she had just received an answer to a vexing question.

"It's hard to explain to someone who has had no *proper* upbringing," she said. "Now don't bristle, my pet. You know that you are hardly aware of the conventions of society. Especially in England, where it matters not what you do, as long as you *seem* to act properly."

"I don't eat with my knife!"

"I knew you'd be angry," said Maura. "That's why I—"

"Come, Maura," said Valetta, giving expression to the disillusion that swept her. "You never gave me a thought, as far as catering to my sensibilities. Best tell me at once, and"—Valetta could not refrain from a telling rapier thrust—"try, if you can, to be honest."

She had gone too far. Maura's neck grew red and the flush flamed upward into her cheeks. She took a step toward Val. Seeing Maura's fingers stiffen into claws, Val tensed, ready to leap out of her way.

But after a moment, the crisis softened. "I suppose you have a right to say that," confessed Maura insincerely. "The truth is—"

The truth was that Maura Finch had fallen out of love with her husband, Sir William Thorne, and into love with a Frenchman. "A general, handsome—so romantic! I'll die if I am not with him."

Valetta guarded her tongue. The problem that Maura

had wrestled with did not seem insurmountable to Val. But after all, as Maura had pointed out, Val's mother had not lived long enough to instruct her daughter in any of the social mores necessary for handling men, including devious feminine wiles. Although Val herself was inclined to act on her own judgment—despite one brandy-induced lapse—she could understand that Maura, a creature of a different and elevated station in society, had to submit to the conventions that ruled.

"And I have come to Paris to be with him. We have to be so careful, and that's where you come in."

"I don't understand," said Valetta flatly. "Why hasn't he come to see you?"

"But he has, my pet. Every day when you, with Jehane, are out getting exercise like a countrywoman."

"Every day?"

Maura had the grace to look guilty. "Not quite, then, since you have such a misguided regard for the truth. But once or twice, when he can get away. But it's not enough."

Val regarded her cousin with distaste. "I dare say."

"You did go to Luxembourg today."

"I did. And I shall not go again."

"Why not?" Maura seemed to wait breathlessly for her answer.

"If you must know," said Val "there was a man—"

Understanding came slowly to her. The man was not there by accident, as indeed neither had she been. "Maura—?"

"I have high hopes for you, my pet."

Maura laughed and seized both of Val's hands in hers. "I shall make a regular *intrigante* out of you yet! The man who stared at you was Raoul. General Raoul Doucet."

Val did not try to hide her dislike. "That man? He was disgusting! I feared I could not leave the park in safety."

Her cousin dropped her hands and retreated. "I warn you, Val, don't play on my good nature. Raoul is mine, and I shall be displeased if I find you are flaunting your innocence to snare him."

"Maura, I merely sat on the bench, according, so I gather, to your scheme. If your general stared at me, it is no fault of mine."

"At my request, Val. So that he could see how much alike we are, you and I. And he is sure you can carry it off."

"But he only saw me a half hour ago."

"Ah, but he came to the square just now, and gave me the signal." She gestured toward the window. "He thinks you will do—as I do."

Val suspected that at last they were coming to the crux of the scheme. She went back to a remark Maura had made a few moments before. "Carry *what* off?"

"The masquerade, of course!"

"Masquerade?"

"The idea is that you will take my place, so that Lady Thorne is seen to be enjoying herself in full view of the Court."

"And where," demanded Val, "will Lady Thorne in fact be?"

"I think," replied Maura judiciously, "that it is best you do not know. But with Raoul, wherever he wishes."

"Then I am to be your accomplice? So that you can romp with that—that fop—in your love nest?" Val's deliberately assumed pose of calm, unshakable acceptance was shattered. "What a hare-brained scheme! You think I would go along with such a snare?"

"Such indignation," Maura pointed out, "does not become one who has taken, and gladly, a good many favors—a trip to Paris, lodging, meals, even clothes. You'll wear the gowns Worth has made for me. I had not thought you ungrateful."

Val glared at her cousin. The shrewd parry had struck her in a vulnerable spot. "Well—"

Maura, knowing she had won, ran to her and hugged her. "I knew you'd do it. There's really no harm in it."

"I would suppose there is, Maura, or else you

wouldn't be making such a great deal of fuss. But tell me, then, what it is I am to do."

She spoke with grudging good humor. Maura's quick changes of mood were almost childlike in their transparency. Val suddenly felt immeasurably the elder of the two, rather than ten years younger.

Having gotten her own way, Maura became confidential. "Sit down here beside me, my pet, and I'll tell you all about it. You see, Raoul is married."

"So are you."

A wave of Maura's hand dismissed poor Sir William as though he had never existed. "And Madame—Raoul's wife, you know—is possessive to the point of lunacy. My poor Raoul is spied upon, harassed—you would not believe how Clothilde keeps him on a string and jerks him back to her at the most inconvenient moments."

"Where did you meet him? In London?"

"No, no. William and I came over to Paris last summer. It was love at first sight—a thunderbolt—a *coup de foudre!*"

"I thought Sir William would never come to Paris—unless, I think you said, there were sheep grazing on the Champs-Elysées?"

"Well, he won't again, I promise you. If I had told you about Raoul, you would never have come with me."

"That, at least, is the truth."

Maura cocked her head to one side and regarded Val with a secret little smile. "I should wish for you a great love affair. Not a marriage, you understand, for a husband is excessively ordinary. Else, why even marry him, you understand? But Raoul—I cannot tell you what he means to me!"

Spare me your ecstasies, thought Valetta. Aloud, she said, "Just tell me what I am to do."

"Well, it is perfectly obvious. While you are pretending to be Lady Thorne in public—very much in the limelight, my pet—then Madame la Générale will know that her Raoul is not with me."

A little secret smile hovered over her cousin's lips. "Best you know nothing. Remember that Madame la Générale is perfectly capable of sending assassins after me—"

"You? Or anyone who enticed her husband away?"

"Me," said Maura with decision. "There is no one else in Raoul's life."

"But if the assassins mistake me for you, I can see that their misunderstanding might be uncomfortable for me."

"That is precisely why you will know nothing of us. You know, I really do care what happens to you. Even that *cochonne* of a wife can't suspect Raoul when she sees you constantly alone in public."

The scheme itself was sordid, but Maura's conscience must deal with it, and of course Raoul's. All Val had to do was to enjoy Paris in the midst of spring, and answer if someone called her Lady Thorne. It was not an impossible challenge, after all.

Paris lay at her feet, as it were. Never in her life would she be presented again with such opportunity, to dance at the Imperial court, to wear the beautiful gowns that emerged from Charles Frederick Worth's studio, to savor this enchanting life to the utmost.

"You'll do it?" said Maura. It was not a question.

"Yes, I'll do it."

In reality, the plan was not quite as simple to execute as had been expected. Lady Thorne did have in hand the coveted invitation to court. She would be escorted by Neal Simmons, an attaché at the British embassy. Raoul would make his appearance at the palace and then, as soon as possible, vanish from the great ballroom, leaving his wife to watch the false Lady Thorne waltz until dawn, if she wished.

But after all was arranged, Maura, to Val's surprise, balked.

"How cruel it is that I cannot go to the ball!"

"But it's all your idea!" Val pointed out. "Go if you wish."

"But Raoul—" Maura bit her lip. She had been oddly

silent that entire day. Val had guessed that she was living out her future, already imagining herself in Raoul's arms. Just as she herself lived, at times, her own hour of the past. "I'm going to the ball," she announced.

Val felt a pang of keen disappointment. Only a week ago she had shrunk from the masquerade, as Maura chose to call it. But now Val felt deceived. She realized she had looked forward to her appearance at court as though she were the most naïve of debutantes.

She managed to hide her feelings. "Fine," she said hardily. "As long as I am not expected to entertain the general in your stead."

Maura shot her a quick glance. "Not at all. Believe me, you are not at all appealing to him. But I have it all planned. I will go, and be presented to the emperor and the empress, and make sure that stupid Doucet woman sees me. And then, my pet, you will take over."

"But that's mad!"

"Mad or not," said Maura, "we're going to do it."

With Jehane's help, Maura chose a gown that would be easily removed when Val arrived at the Tuileries. "A quick change," said Maura, "and you return to the ballroom. A simple exchange, and no one will know the difference."

"But what shall I say?"

"If anyone asks, you went out for a breath of air. You can certainly make that excuse sound convincing, for I have never seen anyone so devoted to outdoor exercise. I am convinced you have traveled over half of Paris on foot."

Maura, caught up in the titillating details of her intrigue, was a whirlwind of activity. She sent instructions to her general. She made Val rehearse a quick change of clothing. "Not that foolish gown, Val. Too many buttons. I do believe your heart is not in this! Here, you'll wear this frock. The color is out of fashion."

Val clung to the Bismarck brown with the creamy ruffle. "That's my only good dress!"

"It belongs in the rubbish. If it were daylight, I would not care to be seen in it. But after dark, no matter."

Maura's excitement heightened the blush in her cheeks and brought a glitter to her green eyes. She whirled around the room in Val's brown dress. Maura's waist was not so slim as Val's, and the seams were under strain. "I wish you wouldn't—" Val exclaimed.

"After all I've given you?" said Maura, dangerously calm. "And you begrudge me this piece of worn-out cloth?"

Val could not promptly think of a retort, at least not one fit to say aloud. Maura had given her companionship at the start, then had taken it away with her selfishness. She had brought her to Paris as a treat, as she had said, then revealed at last that Val was to pay for her vacation with deceit and trickery.

After all Maura had done for her—Val felt no gratitude.

"No one will ever tell the difference between us," Maura purred, holding the brown gown in front of her and examining her reflection in the mirror.

Val caught a strange look on Jehane's face, an expression of Gallic skepticism. Jehane muttered, "In a poor light, *peut-être.*" If Maura heard the maid, she gave no sign.

The carriage from the Embassy arrived, and the genuine Lady Thorne hurried down the steps to the pavement. Neal Simmons, a stolid, square young man with reddish-blond hair and a bristling beard, handed Maura into the carriage.

Jehane watched from the window, Val standing behind the curtain, out of sight from the street. When the carriage clattered over the cobblestones, and under the arch at the end of the short street, Jehane pulled the curtains closed.

"Milady wishes to have her cake," said the maid briefly, "and also to have the eating of it."

Val had learned to like Jehane, and to respect her sage common sense. "You think it won't work?"

"Milady will not admit if it do not work," Jehane pointed out. "She sees what she wish to see."

For a capsule description of Maura, it did very well. "But Jehane, I do not understand. If the general has a—an affection—for Lady Thorne, who is to care? Surely to have mistresses is not an unusual way in Paris, is it?"

"Not at all. Even the emperor—so they say—has a different woman every night. And not the empress, ever! But it is the money, *vous savez.*"

"The money? Surely not my cousin's?"

"That, I do not know about. But Madame Doucet has half the money in France. And she twitches the husband back to her as though he were the small dog."

"One would think—"

"The general has only his pay, and he has the debts high as a mountain."

"How do you know all this?" Val asked.

"We servants know what happens in Paris. I, Jehane, tell you. My cousin is maid to Madame Doucet."

"Did madame send you to Lady Thorne?"

"No, mademoiselle. The general himself. I am no spy." After a moment she went on. "I have many relatives, and—we talk, you know. After all, what is there for us to do but to enjoy hearing about the *haut monde?* It is then as though we ourselves do the gambling, the lovemaking, the—the scheming, you would say."

Jehane was no different from Val herself, she thought—both of us living other people's lives, Jehane and her cousins knowing more about the upper circles than the aristocrats themselves, and Val, living the carefree life of Lady Thorne.

Not precisely carefree, she reminded herself. The masquerade itself was fraught with ugly possibilities. Suppose that she made some ghastly faux pas in court etiquette—bowed to the wrong people, ignored one who must not be ignored. Even, she thought with horror, suppose someone denounced her in public—"What have you done with the real Lady Thorne?"

There was an hour or more to endure before the

general sent his coach to fetch Valetta to the palace. Of course, the carriage from the embassy could not be used for this clandestine trip, and the attaché—Neal Simmons, was that his name?—would never know that Lady Thorne had disappeared.

Could she fool the young man from the embassy? That was not the least of the worries that crowded in on her while she waited. She wore her plain brown frock. Smoothing down the skirt, she remembered the first time she had worn it in London. That lovely Sunday, when she had strolled to the river—the first time she had seen the tall Scotsman.

She put her hands to her face, feeling her cheeks burning. It was not the first time she remembered, of course. It was the second time, the last time—on the ferry. She had managed, somehow, to bury her recollections under layers of vigorous walking around Paris, under the countless demands of her cousin, and even now, as she thought about the disasters that could easily lie in wait for her tonight, she knew she was, at bottom, holding the Scotsman at bay.

She did not even know his name, and yet she knew the feel of his muscled back under her gripping fingers, she knew the wondrous way of his hands, stroking, beguiling. A man she had seen twice in her life and would never see again, and yet she knew the unbearable need in her that he had both unearthed—and filled—

She sank into a chair. She must not, dare not, think of him, for with the ecstasy of remembrance came also the degrading shame of her submission, her immorality that had brought such a blissful reward. Gone now was the bliss, but the shame of it tortured her.

She looked around her, as though she had never seen the room before. With an effort, she returned to the present moment, examining small things as though trying to weave a net of familiarity that would keep her safe. The plain black shawl on the chair, ready to be picked up when she left for the palace, the carefully smoothed coverlet on the bed, the neatly arranged toilette articles on the chest.

At last the coach came, timely in its arrival, for Valetta had dwelt too long on the possibilities of disaster. What if her masquerade failed, what if someone well known to Maura were to emerge from the crowd around the emperor, what if—

"What if, indeed!" cried Jehane at Val's elbow. "Life is full of these what-ifs, *vous savez*. But we go on, nonetheless. I, Jehane, say to you, mademoiselle, you are *tout à fait* in the disguise. There is no need to fear Madame la Générale tonight. She will be completely deceived."

"I still wish—"

"*Tchut!* If wishes were horses, then all may ride horseback. Is it not?"

Jehane saw her into the unmarked carriage sent by the general. She watched the vehicle as it turned into the avenue de l'Imperatrice and disappeared from sight. She turned and slowly climbed the stairs to the apartment.

What a turmoil to make over a simple amorous ruse! These English women had no instinct for intrigue. For Jehane, to weave a web of deceit and intrigue in Paris in the spring was incomparably superior to all other enjoyment, as vital to her as the breath of life itself. The soft air of Paris, scented with chestnut blossoms and the delicate fragrance of spring flowers, beguiled the senses and spoke, at least to the French, of romantic dalliance and, of course, where there was romance there must be intrigue.

The young miss, reflected Jehane, was of a purity not to be believed. She had only to wear Lady Thorne's dress—and such a gown!—for an hour or two this night, long enough for Madame la Générale to see that the attractive Lady Thorne was still in the ballroom after the general left. A mere nothing! Jehane had taken a liking to Val, but she must confess to herself that the English miss was stupid beyond belief to protest such a bagatelle!

* * *

The English miss herself, riding in the general's carriage, was at that moment reflecting that she was as stupid as Mrs. Grissom had hinted. "Why is your cousin taking you to Paris?" she had demanded. "For no good reason, I'll be bound."

At that moment, Val had resented her landlady's skepticism. Her own cousin suspected of wishing her harm! It was not to be considered. But now, as the carriage turned into the Quai du Louvre she began to suspect that she should have listened to Mrs. Grissom's forebodings.

But the scene that unrolled ahead of her now drove all else out of her mind.

The buildings lining the Quai on her right were ablaze with lights. The windows, open to the soft air, allowed strains of lilting music and the shapeless hum of voices and laughter to reach her ears. In spite of her misgivings, she felt her blood move faster from the excitement rising in her.

The carriage, rumbling over cobblestones, turned through a gate and entered the palace grounds. It traveled around the Cour du Carrousel, on her left a vaguely pillared arch, and stopped beside a long building with arched windows.

"Here we are, madame," said the coachman, speaking for the first time since she had climbed into the vehicle.

Where? she thought, but then she discerned a shadowed door in the wall. As she looked, a man in dark clothing emerged from it and exchanged a few words with the coachman. Then he came to open the door for her.

"*Vite, vite,*" he commanded, beckoning her hastily across the yard or two of pavement and through the door, closing it behind them.

She found herself in a dimly lit passageway apparently stretching the length of the building. There seemed to be doors along the walls of the corridor, but the torches were small and far between and gave little light.

How quickly one becomes accustomed to outrageous events! she thought. She gave no murmur of protest as her companion hurried her down the passageway in the semidarkness. They came to another corridor, at right angles, and he guided her into it. She had not even had a glimpse of the man's features. She would not know him again if he stood in front of her—but even though she barely trusted him, she could not wrest herself away from his grip on her wrist, for where would she go?

Finally, they stopped before a door that looked like all the others they had passed. He opened it and motioned her inside.

The room was empty, except for two armchairs seemingly banished from more opulent suites, and a wardrobe standing against the far wall. The windows were curtained, but even in the ill-lit room she could see fragments of threads hanging raggedly from the fabric. Clearly this was a room unused, and all but forgotten.

She turned quickly to her escort. "Where is—" The question died on her lips. She could not ask for Lady Thorne, lest she give the entire scheme away. It was most likely that the man who had brought her here was in the general's pay, but so strongly did the entire deception hold her that she dared not assume anything.

"Wait," ordered the man in a harsh, rusty voice and closed the door behind him. She was alone.

She did not expect to wait long before Maura, eager for the arms of her lover, would hurry in, escaping the disapproving stare of the general's lady. Val dusted the seat of one of the spindly gilt chairs and sat, gingerly. She would not have been surprised if dry rot had eaten away the interior of the legs. But the chair held her.

Her restlessness reflected her tumbled thoughts, fears of disastrous consequences yet unnamed falling down around them. She was not sure she could stand again. What was she doing, sitting so idly on this silly excuse for a chair, when Maura had dinned into her the vital need for a swift exchange of clothing?

"The presence of Lady Thorne in the ballroom,"

Maura had pointed out, "must be continuous, if we are not to be discovered!"

The change of clothing should be easy, for they had rehearsed it several times. First the ball gown was to come off over Maura's head and then over Val's, ready to pull down over Val's slim body after her own brown dress was removed. Then the fastenings of each dress, and finally the jewels transferred. The shimmering dazzle of the Thorne emeralds must be added to Val's throat and ears.

Their heads were already dressed in the same fashion, arranged in a cascade of curls at the back of the head, a far cry from Val's usual neat chignon confined in a severe net. Unbidden, the recollection of her luxuriant hair falling over her bare shoulders—*he* had removed the pins that controlled it—came to her. She sprang up with an impatient word.

Maura was unconscionably long in coming. It was likely she would swirl through the door, irritation honed by her eagerness for Raoul's lips, and with no intention of controlling her sharp temper.

Perhaps Maura's disposition would be better once she and Raoul had found undisturbed time together. Val was not sure how long her own tolerance of her cousin's sharp mood swings would hold out. Her cousin was undoubtedly the most prickly character she had ever met. How appropriate it was that she had married a man named Thorne! Val worked herself back into a good humor.

But she took care to avoid at least some of Maura's castigation—she could at least begin the process of changing garments. She undid the fasteners of her bodice and let the dress fall to the floor. She stepped out of the pool of brown at her feet and stood, suddenly shivering. Even though the night was warm, the thick stone walls of the palace kept a chill in the room.

Except for her petticoat, she had worn only a chemise beneath her dress, easy to take off, for any undergarment she had would show under the *décolleté* of the sea-green chiffon ball gown. At last she heard footsteps outside. Maura, at last! Quickly she pulled her chemise over her head. She would be ready at once to put on Maura's gown.

She had forgotten her new and complicated hair arrangement, and the chemise caught on one of the pins that held her curls in place. The door opened behind her, and she cried out, her voice muffled as she struggled with the chemise, "Maura! Come help me!"

The chemise came free, and she shook it into shape. There had been no answer to her greeting, and, puzzled, she turned.

"Maura?" The word was strangled in her throat.

She stood, arrested. Suddenly she remembered that she wore only the petticoat that circled her slim waist and fell in folds to her instep. Her small, pertly pointed breasts were bare.

The figure that stood within the room, leaning carelessly against the closed door, greedily inspecting her half-bare body, was not Maura.

Very decidedly—not Maura!

Chapter Seven

Neal Simmons, the British attaché assigned to escort Lady Thorne to the Imperial Thursday *soirée,* successfully concealed his irritation at having been kept waiting outside the lady's apartment for the better part of an hour.

His training had even allowed him to hand her, at last, into the carriage with commendable poise, and to sit beside her on the velvet seat, taking care not to disturb the billowing folds of her sea-green skirts.

The ambassador's words still lingered too loudly in Neal's ears for him to be perfectly at ease.

"Lady Thorne's visit to Paris gives us a problem," Lord Lyons had said. "Sir William is highly esteemed by certain persons in the government at home, and his lady therefore must be treated with all courtesy."

Neal waited. Lord Lyons stared into the black, empty grate, lost in his own thoughts. Almost to himself he muttered, "Damn fine woman!"

Then, remembering the presence of his junior staff

member, he added, flushing, "Met her only once, you know. But a beauty!"

Neal, familiar with his lordship's oblique methods of coming to the point, prodded him gently. "Then, my lord, she is likely to be received at court? Then I do not understand what is wrong."

"Well," said Lord Lyons, not looking at his aide, "it's her husband, of course. Where is he? I did hear that he was not at all well, and perhaps is unable to travel. But then, why is she here?" The question did not require an answer, and Neal did not make the mistake of attempting one.

The ambassador continued. "Last year, when she came to Paris for only a fortnight, she turned quite a few heads. Her husband was with her then, and I've no doubt it was thanks to him that she didn't get too far out of line. But there was one incident, in a grotto at Saint-Cloud—thank God we got her out of that. Sir William took her home to England at once. The lady was in a rage!"

Neal guessed, "Was it the emperor?"

"No, sorry to say. His Imperial Majesty knows how to handle his—missteps, let us say. Some general this was, and surprisingly he came out of it well. He swore, of course, that his life was ruined, but I recall seeing him since then, and never with the same woman twice. He recovered."

Neal sighed, relieved. "Then there's nothing to worry about."

"You think not? A woman like that, none too devoted to her marriage vows, alone in Paris? Who knows what mischief she has in that pretty head? But—one must show her the courtesies."

"Of course," murmured Neal, unhappily.

"But no more," said the ambassador on a rising note, "just the courtesies. If she gets into trouble, then it's on her own head. I only hope she doesn't have an eye on a Frenchman, particularly that same one. I don't want to go through all that again."

Lord Lyons let his voice trail away. Neal allowed

himself to speculate on the possible results of Lady Thorne's unreined descent upon Paris. A conventional young man himself, he did not understand all the permutations which might result from an assault upon the bastions of custom. He clearly foresaw, however, that he was once more faced with an assignment that in all likelihood would provide opportunity for disaster around every corner. No trace of his misgivings appeared on his stolid face.

"You'll be at her service," finished his superior. "She may never call on you for anything. But if something—well, let's say, *unusual*—comes up, better talk to me about it."

So it was that Neal Simmons was sitting now in the ambassador's carriage, breathing deeply of Lady Thorne's musky scent, and casting glances at her from the corners of his eyes. Lyons was right—a damn fine woman!

If there were arising in his head dreams of a future private moment when Lady Thorne, miraculously seeing in Neal the very essence of desirable manhood, might take him by the hand and say simply, come with me, he was realistic enough to recognize such a vision for what it was—impossible.

He shifted uneasily in his corner. Lady Thorne was far too alluring, too lovely, too experienced to notice a stocky, reddish-haired underling from the embassy. But he could not rout his dreams so easily.

The carriage turned into the Place du Carrousel. Great bonfires burned for the benefit of the carriages, waiting in line, and every window facing the court blazed with light. The gardens were festooned with colored lanterns, and Neal pointed out the intriguing lamps along the terrace. "The newest invention," he said as proudly as though he had set them up himself, "electric light. A veritable miracle."

At last their turn came to stop before the palace entrance. Neal handed her to the pavement. Through the open doors came a flood of light, the murmur of hundreds of voices like bees in a hive, and the soft strains of stringed instruments, playing in the great Salle des Maréchaux.

Her eyes shining with excitement, she breathed, "How beautiful! I should not have wished to miss this for anything!"

Ushers in brown and gold held them back just inside the entrance. By custom, on Thursday evenings Their Imperial Sovereigns came from the Salon de Louis XIV in procession, to greet their guests in the great ballroom. This night the head of the procession had already passed, and the royal couple were lost to sight in the throng, but there were courtiers in abundance still filing past the door where they were standing.

The sovereigns were now making their way to their thrones on the dais. They had banqueted, so Neal informed her, with only a hundred guests in another room. At the end of the banquet, the Imperial couple had led the way to the ballroom where their other guests were assembled.

The procession itself was something to see. Neal, possessed of a demon of instruction, busily informed Lady Thorne not only of what she was seeing, but also what she had missed.

The elite *Cent-gardes*, in sky-blue and silver, lined the state entrance and the grand stairs. The sovereigns always appeared first, followed by whatever guests they chose to honor, the Bonaparte princes and princesses, foreign ambassadors, the marshals of France—

Lady Thorne turned on Neal. "Why weren't we here to see the beginning?" she demanded fiercely.

He was stung. He had waited an hour for the lady in front of her door, that same hour that would have allowed them to arrive on time. But he bit his tongue. Whether or not he was fully conscious of it, his initial infatuation had just sustained a blow. The lady was lovely, but no man needed to suffer a shrew, particularly without reward.

Straining to move through the crowds at the door of the salon, Maura was able to see the end of the majestic procession. Guided by Neal, she made out chamberlains in scarlet, green-clad equerries, violet-uniformed masters of ceremonies, palace prefects wearing an odd shade of reddish purple.

She tugged at his sleeve. "They are sorted by color, like playing cards!"

Indeed, as Val noticed later when it came her turn to appear in the ballroom, there was an odd resemblance to card suits in the Imperial Court—a two-dimension gaudiness, an air of unreality.

Maura, now, felt more at home here than she ever had at Thorne Manor. She was made for dancing, for flirtation, for being loved and petted. "What are the plumed hats and red baldrics?"

"Beadles," said Neal.

"How medieval."

Neal told her the ritual was unvarying. She was struck by the splendor of the uniforms—where was Raoul? What would he be wearing?—and the glittering pomp of the procession. At last the court had passed, and she and Neal were allowed to move in its wake into the ballroom.

She thought, but did not say, how ridiculous the emperor looked in white silk tights and stockings! But Eugénie impressed Maura against her will. Red-gold hair of a much handsomer shade than Maura's own, the most expressive, limpid eyes—no doubt of it, the empress was a presence! Clad tonight in white tulle spangled with silver stars, Eugénie looked every inch the sovereign.

It was said that the empress had nearly four hundred gowns, mostly designed by the Englishman Worth, and that she often left in the middle of an entertainment to reappear in a different gown. Maura suppressed a giggle. After all, she would do the same this very evening—except that the gown would be the same and only the woman would be changed.

Maura's eyes, seeking only Raoul, scanned the room. At last she caught sight of him against the far wall, his dark eyes fixed in warning on her. She dared not stare at him. At his side stood Madame la Générale herself, dressed in a hideous shade of amaranth, a kind of purplish red that did nothing for her sallow complexion.

Madame Clothilde Doucet—so Raoul had confided—was getting old. If there was one thing Raoul could not abide, it was any sign of age in his women. Well aware of this, Maura took great care to prevent any sign of puffiness or wrinkle around her eyes and throat. Raoul himself was developing a slackness around his thickening waist, but that, of course, was never questioned.

Maura, in Neal's arms, danced closer to the couple. She felt giddy with anticipation. Only an hour or so until she would lie once again in her lover's arms, safe from discovery because her little cousin would absorb the basilisk stare of Clothilde. Close at hand, she noticed those signs of aging that repelled Raoul.

But to be exact, if Clothilde's throat were wrinkling, it was well hidden by the diamond parure she wore, heavy enough to drown her were she to—accidentally—fall into the Seine. God forbid, thought Maura insincerely.

Admiring Raoul, resplendent in his magnificent uniform, and knowing he was hers, Maura could not refrain from sending a mocking, even challenging, glance at Clothilde. Madame Doucet's hand rested lightly on her husband's arm, and at that moment she felt his muscles tightening beneath her fingertips. This, more than Lady Thorne's glance, aroused all of Clothilde's suspicions.

She knew the signs well. Raoul was once again sniffing after some bitch, she told herself, and this time his prey was clearly *l'Anglaise*.

She murmured in his ear, "So? Lady Thorne is here in Paris again?"

With an inept effort at casualness, Raoul said, "I hadn't noticed. Where is she?"

Quite calmly, his wife accused him. "You're lying, Raoul. You see her quite well. I wonder where her poor husband is."

She stole a glance at her husband. How appropriate,

she thought, that since his temptations were entirely physical, so should be the signs of his betrayal. The faint flush creeping up into his cheek told her she was right in her surmise. "I must ask Lord Ronald about the husband. Last year I thought him charming. Raoul, my pet, shall we add Lady Thorne to our invitation list for entertainment when the court moves to Saint-Cloud?"

"Please yourself," replied her spouse, adding with a touch of bitterness, "you will anyway." He moved away and was lost to sight in the crowd.

Clothilde watched carefully, alert for any suspicious circumstance. Lady Thorne, however, continued to move through the crowd, accompanied by the young man from the embassy. Raoul was nowhere in sight. At least they were not together, she thought with relief. As long as she kept Maura in her sight, Clothilde thought, her husband was safe.

The string ensemble put away their instruments in favor of the larger orchestra now ready to provide music for the dancing. The royal pair had reached the canopied dais at the far end, and a hush settled over the crowd. There must be nearly a thousand persons in the Salle des Maréchaux, Maura thought.

The ball was opened in ceremony. The emperor offered his hand to a princess, the empress to a prince, and the dancing opened with a *quadrille d'honneur.* Lord, how these French stood upon their pompous rituals! But the very pretentiousness, their extreme conviction that every gesture mattered in the world, made the intrigue that she and Raoul were to enter upon, this very night, even more delicious!

She smiled radiantly at Neal, who would that moment have died for her. Manfully concealing his devotion, he merely offered his hand to her, and they waltzed away into the throng.

Since the Imperial court was as frivolous as that of ancient Rome, although not so vicious, the advent of a new face to look at immediately gave rise to speculation around the fringes of the dance floor.

Lady Thorne was vividly remembered from her previous visit to Paris, in much the same way as Lord Lyons recalled her whirlwind descent upon the court. A beautiful lady, it was agreed, but odd, and immoral as the French insisted upon believing all English to be. *Les Anglais* were of a different mold altogether, and since one hardly knew what they would do next, it surpassed all logic to try to understand them.

Les Français, on the other hand, considered themselves realists, looking at love squarely as the most delicious of diversions. Not the least of the charms of dalliance—at least to the French—was the spice of intrigue. No one watching Maura Thorne, as she moved like a gossamer bubble now in the arms of Lord Ronald Gower, had the slightest doubt that she was in Paris to accomplish designs that Sir William would have put a stop to immediately. Indeed, it had been a widespread rumor last year that only his stern authority had prevented a scandal of the most dreadful kind.

It remained now only to ascertain the object of Lady Thorne's attentions.

The Vicomte des Loches, who had not met Maura the year before, was now struck for the first time by the bronze-haired beauty with the almond-shaped eyes. He stood near a pillar at the edge of the floor, apparently idly watching the swirling couples before him. In reality, his attention was fixed upon the newcomer.

The vicomte had seen Maura before, he believed. But when? Not the year before, when he had in fact been too ill to leave his villa at Saint-Cloud, but more recently. He searched his memory and found the occasion—this very week, in the Luxembourg Gardens.

Lady Thorne was dressed now in the highest fashion, but in the gardens one would have believed her a naïve young woman without funds, with no style. But he could not be mistaken—surely only one woman in the world had such glorious hair, such a lissome figure. He was aware of a familiar stirring in him and knew that sooner or later—preferably sooner—he must have her, must possess her in his own peculiar fashion. The lady had been alone, and yet there was a man lingering in the shadow of memory—

He had it! That mountebank General Raoul Doucet had been eying her with the intentness of a cat at a mousehole. And yet he had not spoken to her then. But, if the vicomte were not mistaken, and he seldom was, Doucet was stalking the lady, and it would be most interesting to watch the developments, at least until the vicomte himself chose to take a hand.

The vicomte glanced around him. He was, remembering the gardens, not at all surprised to notice Clothilde Doucet glaring at the same lady who had such an unsettling effect on his loins.

The captain of his bodyguard, Alec Drummond, stood nearby, unobtrusively guarding the vicomte's back against a dagger. His work at the moment was not onerous, for it was must unlikely that an enemy would choose to strike in such a throng.

Alec Drummond's attention lapsed. He should have turned this night's detail over to his lieutenant, Jacques Ferelle, but lately, ever since he returned from Scotland, he had been restless and somehow dissatisfied. Better to be on duty than prey to his own black mood, he decided.

But he could not keep his thoughts from straying, as they often did, to the austere scene of his homeland. The pink blossoms of the heather, the sour smell of the sea, the oddly clear light over the water—

But his dreams had altered in the past weeks. Now his thoughts turned more and more toward a woman with whom he could share his home in the Lowlands. Not a woman, he realized—*the* woman. And yet the woman with bronze hair and sapphire eyes was a wanton, and he knew that, if he let himself fall in love with such a one, there would be no peace in the world for him.

With him, awake or asleep, was the sweet bliss of that lovemaking on the ferry, of her gentle moments of hesitation before she submitted willingly to him. If only she was what she had pretended to be!

He had thought her the notorious Lady Thorne, whose reputation, while not precisely tarnished, indicated both experience and willingness to oblige. And yet she had pretended with him to be the complete virgin. He could see through it all, he told himself. A feminine ploy, a female tactic to put the blame of seduction upon the man, and thus keep herself unsullied by the raging demands of desire. Alec Drummond had lost something that might have become very dear to him. If Lady Thorne could only be what she had pretended to be—

Even so, there was a husband—and how could the lady be a virgin when she was married? Proof, if he needed it, that the act she had put on was only that—an act.

But the dream of her had laid firm, unyielding hands on him, and he had not even wished for any other woman since then.

Now, aware at some level of consciousness that the vicomte had moved away, Alec moved dutifully to follow him. It was then that he was struck as though by a fist.

His dream had taken shape before him!

He closed his eyes, the better to evoke the spare slopes of his Scottish homeland, always his spiritual refuge in the bad times. When he opened them, he would—he told himself—see only the bored, self-satisfied faces of the dancers in the great salon. He slowly opened his eyes, dreading to see the lady, and fearing even more to discover that she was only the daft illusion of a crumbling mind.

She was there.

The bronze-haired lady with the laughing eyes was waltzing now with the empress's American dentist, Dr. Evans. She wore a gown seemingly made of green sea-foam, with emeralds around her throat and on her left wrist, and the sight was bitter to him.

She was at home here at court, there was no question about that, and his doubts were gone. Now he wished she had been in truth the inexperienced virgin she had pretended to be, even though he shrank from the role of seducer. But if she had been a maiden, then all things would have now been possible.

He had been gulled. The lady belonged to the world of fashion, wealth, and sophistication. The simple lass—that he had at first scorned, and then longed for—did not exist.

Suddenly he was disgusted with the falseness around him, with the superficial, cruel, pointless existence of the hangers-on of the court. He knew he would very soon have to leave his employment here, or lose all of himself that he valued.

He moved closer to his employer. He could not help but hear the vicomte's conversation with Madame la Générale Doucet.

Des Loches was murmuring, "You know her?"

"The English Lady Thorne," Clothilde informed him.

The vicomte, wily as a ferret, suggested, "The English woman quite puts our empress to shame, does she not?"

Clothilde Doucet's response told him much. "The Englishwoman," she spat, "should fall into a pit!"

"Surely, my dear, there is no need to distress yourself? You need not receive her. Her reputation—"

"She is here with someone from the embassy."

"Ah, then," purred the vicomte, "she has some standing. And friends."

"If you mean my husband," retorted Clothilde, "she will not have his friendship this time, as she did last year."

The vicomte was amused. "I did not meet the lady last summer, for I was confined by the doctors to my bed. This is not to mean, however, that I was isolated from the world. Word came to me that the general, whose bravery we must all commend even though we have not quite the same opinion of his fidelity, was quite *épris* last summer when the lady and her husband came to Paris."

They conversed like the old friends they were. He

had had her once, shortly after the first six months of her marriage to Raoul had ended with her discovery of his unfaithfulness. While she had glimpsed the darker side of the vicomte's nature, she was nevertheless grateful to him for his dalliance with her at a time when she doubted her own worth.

"Gossip is all that was," said Clothilde.

Des Loches watched Maura Thorne with narrowed eyes. She was clearly enjoying the evening. The Duc de Marennes had now slipped his arm around her waist, and even though the waltz was in itself an aphrodisiac, there was no need—decided des Loches—for the duke to draw Lady Thorne quite so close to him.

"Is her husband, the good Sir William, with her this time? He should be."

"I have had inquiries made at the embassy," said Clothilde in a rush. "She is quite alone. She traveled, if you can believe it, with only a maid to keep her company."

"Not quite *comme il faut*. But then, her husband, an amiable cuckold?"

"I do not know, nor care," said Clothilde sharply. "I can tell you, though, my Raoul is not to be the instrument."

"Ah, well, the lady no doubt has her plans."

"Lady! She is no more a lady than Hortense Schneider!"

"La Grande Horizontale!" chuckled des Loches. "An apt description of the Englishwoman, you think?" He did not wait for an answer. "Perhaps I might be of some assistance to you."

"How?"

"If she should be otherwise occupied?"

"I should not wish her harmed," said Clothilde, without sincerity.

"The lady will be willing," said the vicomte. "Trust me."

"I shall make sure of him this time," confided Clothilde. "I will keep her in sight the entire evening."

"Would it not be better to keep an eye on the general?"

"Every man must have his little diversions. As long as that is all they are, I shall not interfere."

"Then you fear milady more than cocottes?"

"Milady is known. He cannot keep a liaison of this nature secret. And I do not wish to appear the fool. Besides, the cocottes are expensive to a man who has only his army pay."

"Whereas milady is an amateur? Do not worry—I shall see to her entertainment tonight, and if I am pleased, perhaps longer than tonight."

Des Loches turned to Alec. "The plain carriage, one hour, at the small door—" Alec followed his greedy glance. "Yes, captain, Lady Thorne. I shall take her, I think, to the Maison Dorée. A champagne supper for this first time, I think—and then we shall see whether she is worth the pursuit."

Alec turned abruptly on his heel. He had no clear idea of what constituted the vicomte's amusements. He had, until now, deliberately stifled his curiosity, leaving his lieutenant, Jacques Ferelle, to follow certain orders. But he hesitated to carry out his instructions this time. He wanted to remember the sweetness, the tender loving, so it had seemed, even though he knew he had been deceived.

He paused on the edge of the floor before sending for the unmarked carriage. He stopped, drawn by a need to take his fill once more of the woman who had, all but unwittingly, stolen his peace of mind. He would not admit that she had also purloined his heart.

In the steps of the dance, Maura turned toward him. He wanted her to see him, perhaps even to reconsider any escapade with the dangerous vicomte. She looked full at him, then, and turned away. She did not know him. Perhaps, he thought darkly, it would be more accurate to say she did not choose to know him.

He turned on his heel. She would deserve everything she got!

But in the end, Alec knew he could not himself contribute to Lady Thorne's downfall. True, she deserved whatever she might receive—cuckolding her husband, willing to succumb to the overtures of a stranger on the ferry. But who had given him the right to judge? Always the realist, he now saw, as though a curtain had been drawn aside, that he was not indignant over Lady Thorne's betrayal of her husband. It was her undeniable dismissal of Alec Drummond that more than rankled.

He was, quite simply, jealous. And, as he had just noted, she did not even recognize him!

A strain from some distant sermon in the kirk he had attended as a boy came back to him—*Vanity, vanity, all is vanity!* Now he understood what the words meant.

He searched for his lieutenant. He would pass on the vicomte's orders, of course. But Jacques Ferelle would carry them out.

After he had found Jacques, he left the room in search of a stiff brandy. He might even make a night of it—brandy and a woman. But not a red-haired woman.

He could never get drunk enough, forgetful enough, to lie again with a woman like that.

Chapter Eight

Val clutched the muslin chemise to her bare breasts and took a step backward, staring at the man who had just entered the little room.

"M-Maura's not here," she stammered.

Raoul Doucet smiled. "I can see that," he said in English, fluent but accented. "I thought once—in the gardens, you remember—that you were much like her. But now I see the difference."

"If you had any sensibility," Val said sharply, "you would go away."

"But I haven't, my dear, and you are much more delectable to look at than my corporal, standing guard outside the door."

She couldn't move. She stared at him, hypnotized, as a small bird watches a serpent gliding toward her on the tree limb. "Go away," she said faintly.

"You think I came to seduce you!" he said, with high good humor. "Not at all. I came only to give you a message."

"What message?"

"That my dear Lady Thorne is momentarily delayed." He paused, but his eyes continued to rove over Val's shoulders, and down over the swelling lines of her breasts, imperfectly concealed by the thin muslin she held. "Yes, she was dancing with—no matter who. She will extricate herself from his embrace soon, no doubt. But in the meantime—"

He stepped toward her. His movement broke the spell of the paralysis that had gripped her. "In the meantime," she said with spirit, "you will do me the greatest favor by joining your corporal, or whoever, in the corridor."

"No talk now, my dear. So little time."

He approached, with clear purpose. She backed up until she felt the cold wall on her bare shoulders. She stared at him, her sapphire eyes dark with fear. "You—"

He reached her and stood close, close enough so that his uniform buttons touched the back of the hand that held her protecting chemise. He cradled her face between his palms and tilted her face to his.

"How much you look like Maura—a young, delicious Maura!"

She would have pushed him away, but he was close enough that her hands were pinioned between their bodies. "Now, my child," he said, covering her mouth with his, his lips moving demandingly on hers. Suddenly she sensed the change in him. While he had at first moved slowly, almost lazily touching her, now he seemed gripped by a growing urgency that frightened her.

With all her strength she freed her hands and shoved at him. "How can you pretend to love Maura, you—you tomcat!"

He laughed softly. "But you *are* Maura, is not that the plan? You will dance the night away so all can see the beautiful Lady Thorne?"

"You know that's only a game!"

"Ah, but *chérie,* so is the grand passion. Only a game, and we are the players of the moment."

He pressed her against the wall. His hands slid from her face, caressing her throat, thrusting inside her pitiful defense of hands and muslin, to cup his hands around her soft breasts. Holding her, squeezing and kneading her, his thumbs flicked her nipples until she could feel them taut beneath his practiced caress.

She felt his manhood hardening against her softness. Her chemise was gone, she did not remember how. His hand slipped inside the waistband of her petticoat, searching fingers playing over her skin.

Muscles in her belly rippled like the sea under a strong breeze. His hard, exploring fingers reached the edge of the delicate triangle of hair, and advanced boldly. She had been shivering before he had entered the room, but now the skin under his incessantly moving fingers grew hot, and waves of flame spread outward from the crisp hair under his hand.

Suddenly she seemed to lie again on the hard bunk of the cabin, willfully submitting to her Scotsman. The brandy had guided her then, but now she was cold sober. The invader this time was not one that her heart welcomed, as it had the bold captain. This invader was a deadly enemy— "Get away!" She writhed against him, seeking escape, but she succeeded only in arousing him further.

He shifted, groaned, and probed her lips until she gasped with disgust. His tongue explored, demanded—and someone far away whimpered. Couldn't they stop? Couldn't someone stop that whimpering? Then she knew the cry was her own.

He let her go, leaving her mouth bruised and wet. He lifted her breast and, stooping, nibbled gently—

"So fresh, so young," he murmured.

The confusion in her body, holding its own memory of that other surrender, was routed. She was angry.

How dare he? How *dare* he!

She forgot any need to protect her nakedness—his advances had long since passed any point of modesty.

She placed the heel of her hand on his chin and shoved. She felt his lips pull at her nipple and let go.

"What—"

She followed up her advantage. Now she became the small fury that a part of her knew existed deep within her. She kicked at him, pushed desperately at whatever part of him she could lay hand on, backing him toward the door.

"You foul—*cochon!*" she cried. Her French was far too removed from the gutter language the situation called for, and she knew no suitable English words either. "*Cochon!*" she cried again and again.

At last, he leaned against the door. No longer greedy, he now gasped for breath. He rubbed his knee in evident pain. She must have kicked him viciously, even though she did not remember.

She feared no more danger from him. Forgetting the protection of the chemise lying on the floor behind her, she stood magnificently, scornfully, erect. "You gave me your message, Monsieur le General, your *entire* message. And now, get out!"

With an attempt at nonchalance that might have in other circumstances been amusing, he brushed his hair back with the flat of his hand. "I see no reason—"

"To tell my cousin?" Val finished for him. "Nor do I, this time. But make sure there will never be a next time."

He appeared to consider the possibility. "I do not promise," he said at last. "There is an English expression that I have heard—a strange choice of words, but I believe I know what it means. I do prefer lamb to mutton, is it not?"

"This lamb," said Val stoutly, "will be on her guard against the wolf, believe me."

His lips twisted wryly. "We shall see."

He was gone. She caught a gasping breath, and then the reaction came. She began to tremble from head to foot. She tottered toward the chair where she had first sat. Absently, she picked up her chemise and spread it across her knees, smoothing out the wrinkles.

As though observing a stranger, she looked at her own breasts, tingling, red tipped. She felt an unfamiliar churning within her, a tumult that in a moment she recognized. She would never again have that first breathless anticipation, the sense of wonder that had come to her on the ferry. Then, she had learned how it was between man and woman, the joy of the coming together that transcended remembered pain.

This was different, of course. Then she had been willing, had followed wherever he led. It was only later that she had been shamed by her own eager responses.

The general, just now, had only disgusted her. How could he dare make love to her when it was Maura whom he loved? How could he betray her faith in him? But she had also learned, just now, that the body lives its own life, and willy-nilly, was capable of taking things into its own hands, totally ignoring any barriers the mind might wish to impose.

It seemed a long time that she waited, startled by the smallest sound lest Maura's lover return, even thinking that Maura might easily have forgotten her cousin sitting half-naked in a strange room in a palace where she knew not a soul. Alone, with her dark thoughts, she waited, brooding.

Raoul's physical presence had gone, but she could still feel his touch as though imprinted on her flesh.

She ought to tell Maura of the general's advances. If he could be so quickly unfaithful, even before Val's masquerade had begun, then the grand passion that Maura claimed united them was distinctly a one-sided affair. But if she told Maura, she was positive that she herself would be put in the wrong. Maura would claim she lied, and Raoul would beg a mild flirtation, adding that the girl simply had read too much into a *politesse.*

Besides, she had already voiced all the protest she could. Val understood, even though she could not entirely approve, Maura's plan to use her as a decoy to deceive the general's wife into believing that he was not at that moment unfaithful with the Englishwoman.

At the start, Maura told her quite unmistakably, "It was a godsend to find you. Now don't make things difficult, my dear. I should not like to turn you out into the street, especially in a foreign city."

"Besides," Maura added when she had resumed her argument hours later, "Raoul is so infatuated with me that he will come to me regardless of what you do. Don't think you can enforce your middle-class prudery on me!"

"Middle class?" roared Val, quite thoroughly angry. "I am a Finch, you know, quite as well born as you."

Maura seized her wrist and dragged her to the mottled mirror in the bedroom. "Look at us," she demanded, suddenly in good humor again. "Such a resemblance was made to be used! No one can tell us apart, you'll have to agree to that!"

Jehane, overhearing them, told herself, "Anybody with the half of one eye can tell the difference. A few years between them, milady says. Bah! It is a lifetime of living between them. Not very nice living, either, if you ask me."

But any differences between the cousins—the drawn, jaded expression of Lady Thorne, the slightly faded tint of the older woman's coif, her barely thicker waistline—were all concealed in the wavy surface of the mirror.

It was, finally, not the accusation of middle-class priggishness that tipped the scales in favor of Maura, for Valetta knew that insincere modesty was not one of her faults. It was simple obligatory gratitude to her cousin for bringing her to Paris, for opening up a world she would never have experienced without Maura's generosity.

"Gratitude?" Maura echoed when Val explained. "I should think you might be grateful. You'd never have seen Paris from that dingy little shop of yours. And never in this world would you have had entrée to court as Valetta Finch. Being Lady Thorne has its advantages, you know."

Then why, wondered Val silently, are you so unhappy?

But that was yesterday, and the week before. Now, she was in this ugly little room, wearing Maura's perfume, spent from fighting off Maura's lover, waiting for Maura.

She came in a rush, her gown of sea-green taffeta swirling about her like the surf, the white ruching trim appearing to Val's overwrought mind like whitecaps on the ocean.

"My dear, it is a mob!" exclaimed Maura in an urgent undertone. Her eyes were shining with excitement, and whether it was the stimulation of the fantastic entertainment she had just left, or the prospect of more intimate delights to come, it was impossible to know.

"What am I to do?" asked Val. It had never been explained fully exactly what would happen when she entered the ballroom in Maura's stead. She knew only that the general's coach would bring her here, and she would exchange gowns. Maura had omitted all other instructions.

"Here is my necklace—my earrings, mind you don't lose them," said Maura, unheeding. "Turn so I can fasten the clasp."

"You didn't answer me."

"Don't get one of your stubborn streaks now, of all times," said Maura impatiently. "You know what to do. The minute you go out that door you're Lady Thorne. You're *me*."

"I know that."

"Make sure that she-devil sees you. Madame la Générale," she mimicked cruelly, "will know then that wherever her husband is, he is not with me."

Val thought that Maura would do well to watch her general as closely as did the general's wife.

"Don't make your bow to the emperor, or to Eugénie," continued Maura. "I've already done that, and it would be extremely odd were you to duplicate that. Plon-Plon is not in attendance tonight. He's the emperor's cousin, you know, a nasty piece of work. Stay away from him always."

"Whom did you dance with?"

"That dull little dentist, Dr. Evans. And Neal Simmons of course. Don't snub him. He brought me, and you'll need to go home with him. And there's some vicomte, and a duke or two—never mind. Just agree with whatever they say, and you won't get into any trouble."

"Am I to—to dance? To converse?"

Maura was now clothed in Val's drab gown. Her thoughts were clearly racing ahead to the tryst with Raoul, and she had all but forgotten her cousin. "Do as you like. But make sure that *dear Clothilde* knows you are in the room."

"How will I know her?"

"She looks like a prefect! She's wearing the most vulgar parure of diamonds, quite outshining the empress, and I should not have thought such a thing possible. Most tactless, of course, but what can you expect? Be sure you stay in her sight until she leaves. Then come home at once."

"Why doesn't Raoul simply tell her to mind her own affairs and do as he pleases?"

"Because, as I already told you, Raoul *is* her affair. She had bought the poor man, and she is guarding him. My darling Raoul!"

Maura gathered up Val's shawl and looked hastily around. "Did I forget anything?" she said, frowning. "Remember, Val. Stay in her sight. The man from the embassy—I told you that—will take you back to the apartment."

She hurried to the door. Pausing with her hand on the latch, she turned. She gave Val her ineffable smile, the smile that lit up her features, taking whatever tribute was given to her beauty as her own right. "Dear Valetta!" she whispered and blew her a kiss.

Maura was suddenly like a naughty child, giggling as she glanced down at Val's gown, a little too tight for Maura, especially at the waist. But Maura seemed not to notice. "I look like a governess, don't I?" she demanded, mischief in her voice, and then she was gone.

Dear Valetta! The insincere words, ringing in Val's ears, mocked her long after Maura left.

She essayed a step or two, feeling the soft silk lightly touching her ankles, getting the feel of the little high-heeled slippers on her feet. Like a governess! Maura had said, laughing, unaware of the hurt she caused Val. Is that what I look like to everyone? Val wondered, her eyes darkening. Would that explain the cruel stinging words the Scotsman had hurled at her in fury?

She had thought—had permitted herself to believe out of pride—that his arms had gone around her, his lips had moved searchingly on hers, his body had taken possession of her, because of the current she had felt flowing between them, a current of irresistible force. Now, told that she looked, in her good brown gown, like a servant, albeit a superior one, she supposed he had just taken her for an innocent moonling, an hour's trifle, to divert him as he waited out the storm—

Governess! Suddenly her irritation deepened. For the first time, she felt cheated. Paris surrounded her, with whispers of love in every chestnut-scented breeze, the mysterious ambience of lamplit darkness, romance and intrigue amidst the pageantry of the Imperial court—and she had as much a right to move in this world as Maura. True, she did not have a title, but titles meant nothing to Valetta. Her breeding was as good as Maura's, and she knew that even in Paris breeding made a difference.

She swept to the door, deliciously conscious of the swish of expensive silk in her cunningly draped skirt, and lifted her head with its magnificently dressed bronze hair. She could easily be here in Paris in her own right, except for a foolish forgotten quarrel two generations past.

Now, she lifted her chin and stepped regally into the corridor, where a servant of the general's awaited her.

The general's servant escorted her through corridors she would not remember, through rooms of varying size, mostly untenanted. At last she could hear far ahead the sibilant sounds of many voices and the intermingled strains of violins and horns in the lilting rhythm of the waltz. Insensibly Val's spirits rose to match her newly acknowledged pride.

"Lady Thorne" was entering the Salle des Maréchaux for the second time this evening, but Valetta Finch, as though she claimed only her own rights and not those of her titled cousin, gazed around her with eager curiosity and not the slighest trace of awe.

The scene was remarkable, one that would forever live in her dreams. Were she ever to have grandchildren, this evening would come to life again when she told them of her first entrance into French society.

The scarlet-clad chamberlain at the door recognized her, murmured "Lady Thorne," and permitted her to enter, believing of course that she had stepped out for only a few brief moments.

Val moved slowly away from the door. She searched the crowd, as she had been bidden, for a glimpse of Madame la Générale. How would she know her? Maura had said she looked like a prefect, a puzzling description. But Val soon learned what her cousin meant.

The French court was infinitely organized. The chamberlains, as she had seen, were uniformed in scarlet, the master of ceremonies, whose duties seemed to be somewhat vague, was clad in violet, and the prefects —minor dignitaries of the palace—in purple amaranth. Fascinated by the complexity of the Imperial hierarchy as expressed in color, she almost forgot to spot madame, who was reported to be wearing an excessively *common* display of diamonds.

She was not difficult to find. Her diamonds, which would have been considered vulgar in England even if worn by royalty, caught the light from thousands of candles and refracted it into miniature rainbows.

Val gave Madame la Générale a long, level stare, as she imagined Maura might do. She was gratified to see that Madame wore a look of relief, as though she had suspected the worst when Maura left the Salle des Maréchaux, and was now comforted to see that, wherever her wayward husband might be, at least he was not reclining in the fair, powdered arms of *l'Anglaise.*

Val allowed herself the slightest of smiles and turned away from Clothilde. It soon became clear that Maura's present legacy to her was not only the most becoming gown she had ever worn, but also a retinue of gallants, smitten by Lady Thorne's charm and beauty, and clamoring for the privilege of the next dance.

She was swept out onto the floor, and the evening dissolved into a blur of faces, some bearded, some with pointed waxed moustaches like the emperor's, and the music played and played, lilting, swaying, hypnotic.

The waltz rhythms went to her head. She felt that her feet no longer touched the floor. She could have danced to the moon, if Monsieur Strauss had but played a little longer.

When her partner guided her near the dais, where the sovereigns sat on the ancient Bourbon thrones, she had her first close look at the emperor, slouched in the enormous royal chair, looking indescribably bored. The empress sat at his side, dressed all in white with glittering spangles sprinkled about her gown like stars. Her amazing red-gold hair shone as though a spotlight were focused on it, and her eyes were fixed on a distant point, as though she disdained to watch the gambolings of inferior creatures.

Val looked up at her partner of the moment and murmured, "I should not like to change places with the empress. How very unhappy she looks."

Her partner agreed. "And she will not allow anyone else to be happy!"

A puzzling statement, she thought, and set it aside to ponder at her leisure.

Some time later, without knowing just how it happened, she found herself dancing, not with one of the young beaux of the court, but with a man of perhaps twice her own years. She broke an uncomfortable silence, saying something polite about the music, but when he did not at once respond with equal civility, she looked squarely at him.

He was not quite handsome, but very nearly so. His expression was marred by deep lines that stretched from his nostrils to bracket his thin, cruel lips, and by the pouches of dissipation under his small eyes.

But it was not the imperfections of his features that arrested her attention and sent a flicker of uneasiness over her. It was something moving in his shallow blue eyes that might be considered only sophisticated amusement in anyone else. She missed a step in the dance. She looked away, oddly breathless as though she had caught a glimpse of something untamed, even dangerous.

"Well," he said, expertly guiding her through the whirling couples, "shall I expect a word of gratitude for my timely rescue?"

"I had not realized my situation was desperate," she countered, relieved to hear her voice was light and frivolous.

"Dancing with mademoiselle?"

"M-Mademoiselle?" she stammered. "I don't understand."

Later she would learn the identity of this partner, who had put his strong arm around her waist and swung her lightly—and that he had another, darker side to his amusements.

Just now her partner's eyes narrowed. Too late, she recalled that she was here in the Tuileries, dancing in borrowed plumage, for a purpose. Clearly this man was suspicious of her—and equally apparent, he had already exchanged with the real Lady Thorne a few words more significant than phrases of *politesse*.

What had Maura said? Val at that moment began to realize that the masquerade might easily result in disaster—and she knew beyond doubt that Maura would escape scot-free, leaving her "country cousin" to bear the brunt of the catastrophe. But she could not turn back now. However, she stored up a few choice remarks to make tomorrow, in the privacy of their own apartment. That is, Maura's apartment—

The waters of deceit that had swirled insignificantly around her ankles at the start were fast deepening.

Val summoned a smile that she hoped sufficiently resembled Maura's to deceive this man with the knowing eyes.

"Aha, so the lady teases!" he exclaimed. "My regrets that I did not meet you last summer."

"Th-thank you."

Suddenly he swung her away from the vicinity of the two Imperial figures, as unreal as pasteboard cutouts. They were moving along the far edge of the floor. In a few moments they would be directly in front of Madame of the vulgar diamonds.

There she was—her basilisk stare resting malevolently on Val and her partner. Into Val's memory crept that odd remark of Maura's: "She is capable of sending assassins after me." At the time, Val had believed Maura indulged herself in dramatics. Now, she was more than halfway ready to believe her cousin spoke only truth.

She tore her gaze away from the general's wife and looked at her partner. Oddly, he, too, was looking at Madame, with a significance that puzzled her. She told herself sharply that she was imagining perils where none existed. Of course her partner, whoever he was, would have gravitated earlier to Maura, and all Val had to do was avoid a misstep—go along with him no matter what he said. She dared not reveal her ignorance of Maura's earlier remarks. And of course her partner would know Raoul's wife, and everyone else in the court.

Maura had done her an evil turn—sending her into this vast assembly without even a hint as to whom she had talked to nor what she had said, particularly to this gentleman now waltzing her expertly, dizzily, around the crowded floor. He was someone of importance, obviously. He was holding her much too tightly, she considered, and she didn't even know his name.

"A bit stuffy in here, don't you think?" he murmured into her curls. Without waiting for an answer, he propelled her dextrously off the floor and through a side door. She had a blurred impression of people in that room, before she was hurried on into another, empty room.

"But I'm—"

"Now, Lady Thorne," said her companion. "I don't advise you to have second thoughts. I do like a bit of resistance, though."

Resistance! The word galvanized all of Valetta's doubts into one healthy protest. If this nobleman believed that Lady Thorne—this Lady Thorne—was an easy mark, he was mistaken.

Her thoughts were jumbled, but she tried to be fair—Maura must have said something that encouraged this cur in his pursuit. She would take that up with Maura, later.

Cold air struck her bare arms. She shivered. They were suddenly outside the building. She felt the cold cobblestones of the courtyard through her thin-soled slippers.

She cried out, "Please take me back. I do not wish—"

She looked wildly about her. It was a scene that recalled nightmare—the black night luridly lit by smoky torches, an unmarked coach nearby, the black horses tossing their heads impatiently, a pair of attendants, springing to open the coach door and let down the steps—

"Monsieur le Vicomte!" said one, saluting.

"Jacques—all is ready?"

They were, although she did not know it, behind the Orangerie, where there was an unobtrusive gate leading on to the Quai des Tuileries, with easy access onto the Pont de Solferino and the far side of the river Seine.

She pulled desperately back, but his arm around her waist was strong and unyielding. She slipped on the cobbles, crying out with pain.

"O-ho! My lady becomes squeamish!" laughed the vicomte. "We'll see to that!"

Maura had brought her to this!

The coach door yawned black before her, and the vicomte's hand was hard between her shoulders.

She had fallen into the oldest trap in the world!

Chapter Nine

Time stood still while her conscious mind took in details as though etched on a pane of glass. The flickering flambeaux, the red velvet coach cushions, the attendants nearby—

The seat was clean, not much worn. The huge wheels were painted black to match the coach body, the spokes picked out with another color, impossible to recognize in the dim light.

The coach seemed to grow larger, and suddenly she realized that the vicomte had propelled her inexorably forward until she stood before the open door, the steps invitingly at her feet.

"No!"

With her protest, she stopped short, her thin-soled slippers skidding on the cobblestones. Her self-proclaimed escort was taken momentarily off-guard.

"I cannot guess what plans you have made for me," said Val mendaciously, "but I really cannot enter into them tonight."

She was babbling, not making much sense, she knew,

but at least she had gained a little time. The vicomte, whose name she did not know, stopped short, and her inevitable progress into the plain coach was momentarily halted.

"But what is amiss, my dear?" Instinctively, she knew that when a man of his address purred in that soothing fashion, danger was most clearly afoot.

"Amiss? I cannot think it at all courteous to steal away from Court in such a dubious fashion."

"Dubious? Not at all. Earlier, Lady Thorne, I believed we understood each other."

Val bit her tongue to hold back her tart protest, "But I am not Lady Thorne!" She dared not give Maura away at the very start, but she had the darkest suspicion that this aristocrat, accustomed to having his own way, would not believe her.

"Please take me back to my escort," she demanded. She sought desperately for the name of the man from the embassy—Maura had mentioned it—and it came. "Mr. Simmons will be most anxious!"

"My dear lady," said her companion, clearly altering his approach, "I do not quite see what distresses you. I had in mind only a simple champagne supper. Not at all a thing, as you say, *peu convenable*. You will be perfectly safe, if that is a concern? But I think not quite dull, madame."

"I do not wish to go," said Val, sensing triumph. "I am sorry if you mistook—mistook my meaning, but I truly do not wish—"

She had planted her small feet uncompromisingly on the pavement, and the vicomte gestured toward the coach door in vain. "I cannot accept this change in tactics, you know," he told her. "I fear you are badly spoiled. But we French do these things differently."

His face was now only inches from Val's. His eyes were shadowed beneath heavy brows so that she could not see their expression, but the cruel twist of his thin lips alarmed her. For the first time, she was truly afraid.

His hand on the small of her back pushed her forward. No spate of words was going to get her out of this trap. She was caught most unfairly. She allowed herself an accusing thought for Maura, whose easy manner must have led this man to expect more than even Maura would give.

Words were left behind. She considered her situation rapidly. There were lackeys on either side of the coach door. From beyond, to her right, appeared another dim figure.

She cried out to him. "Please, monsieur, I beg you—"

The newcomer laughed harshly, and her heart fell. "Ah, good, Jacques!" welcomed the vicomte. "This one may be a handful—"

She vowed she would be.

He pushed her forward. One step, another forced step—the vicomte cried, "Now, Jacques!" and hands reached out for her.

The signal to the men was her signal as well. Swiftly she bent at the waist and took a step backward, under the vicomte's arm. He turned and grabbed her wrist in a vicious grip. She lashed out with one foot. She must have struck his knee, for he released her abruptly and she nearly fell. He held his knee with both hands while a string of full-bodied curses emerged from his lips.

She turned to flee to the shelter of the open doorway. Light was spilling out onto the cobbled pavement. It was faint, but she saw it as a sailor might see beacons at the entrance to a harbor.

"Get her!" snarled the vicomte. "Get her! Before she can talk!"

She was not swift enough. Other hands fell on her, even less gentle than their master's. She kicked viciously. She twisted but the fingers tightened on her. She knew she was being dragged backward, even felt the edge of the carriage steps at the back of her knees—

And then, suddenly, the air was filled with confused sounds. Someone barking rapid French, someone knocking away her captors, a strong arm pulling her to her feet.

"Madame, we regret infinitely this incident. Permit

us to offer apologies for our court. Your honor is safe now, we assure you."

We? Val glanced beyond the slight figure of her rescuer, but he seemed alone. "Oh—," she said softly as she recognized the sad, pain-filled eyes, the impossibly extended and waxed moustache—

She essayed a quick curtsey. "Your Imperial Majesty—my heart-felt thanks—"

"No more, madame. We are greatly disturbed that such a contretemps could possibly take place veritably under our eyes. Monsieur le Vicomte," the emperor added, turning to his guilty courtier, "we believe a month at your country estate might cool your blood."

He gestured behind him. Val saw now that the doorway was filled with people jostling to get a better view of what was transpiring. She wished the cobbles would open up and let her fall into blessed obscurity.

The emperor's lifted hand produced half a dozen attendants. In a moment Louis Napoleon had sorted it out. Guards moved purposefully toward the vicomte. Val glanced furtively at the man who would have ruined her—or Maura. He was not looking at her. Instead, his glittering eyes were fixed on a figure behind the emperor and his men. *"Traître!"* he breathed. Val thought she was the only one who heard him. "I shall remember this."

The subject of des Loches's fury had just joined the crowd. His face was in shadow, but she would have known that tall figure anywhere.

The emperor, whether he noticed the direction the vicomte's hatred took or not, turned to the newcomer. "Captain—" He fumbled for the name. Alec supplied it. "Drummond, Your Majesty."

"Just so. It is our wish that you succor your countrywoman and see her to her carriage. Again, madame," he added, bowing slightly to her, "our regrets."

She curtsied again, and when she rose, the emperor and his attendants had gone. The vicomte leaped into his carriage. She could hear the diminishing sound of wheels as the vehicle lurched out of the courtyard into the street beyond. Only Alec Drummond remained.

She shivered suddenly. The cold from the cobbles had penetrated her thin slippers, and she shook as though she had ague. Alec led her inside and closed the door against the empty courtyard. She blinked in the light. She felt she had been gone a long, long time. She remembered dimly that she was to have stayed in full sight of Madame la Générale. She had failed on her first trial. A cry of dismay escaped her.

"I do not quite understand," said the rangy captain, a mocking note in his voice. "Was that an expression of revulsion? Believe me, I shall not trouble you with my company any longer than it takes to do the emperor's bidding."

"I did not mean that. In truth, I am so distressed I do not know quite what I do mean."

He measured her with a look. She could not read the expression in his stone-gray eyes. Was he too remembering the hard bunk on the ferry, the delicious melting of her body in his embrace?

She felt a flush creeping up her throat and mantling her cheeks. She found it unbearable to stand here, with that shameful, wonderful memory hanging in the air, so vibrant that she could touch it. Her eyes filled unexpectedly when she remembered, too, those hurtful words at the end. She had wanted then to know what he meant, how he could scoff at her inexperience. Now all she wanted was to be free of him.

She had almost erased him from her memory, so she had thought. Now it was all to do over again. It was too much! She stamped her foot in vexation. "I—I truly don't know why the vicomte chose me," she said, almost to herself.

"You don't, Lady Thorne? No need to play the innocent with me, you know. Or do you? I recall now that you did not deign to speak to me earlier in the evening. So perhaps you have forgotten that we crossed the Channel together? Very much together?"

Suddenly the sternness in his features melted, to be

replaced by an emotion very close to hurt. "But of course, the vicomte is a much better prize, even though payment might have been more than you bargained for."

"Prize? You must know I fought him. Indeed, it must have been owing to my cries that His Majesty appeared. I wished no such prize!"

"Not all the vicomte's women are unwilling, at least at first. But what could you expect, my lady? Surely you gave him some encouragement. What changed your mind?"

A wave of fury that was, in part, reaction to her previous fear swept her. "Well, Captain Drummond—as I heard you called—I do not wish to explain to you either my conversation or my actions. I truly cannot see that it is any of your affair. Especially"—she was very near angry tears—"when you have such a mistaken view of me at best."

He had been studying her for the past few minutes, with growing bewilderment. This woman was the one he had held in his arms, and about whom he had even begun to weave little, tentative dreams. He could not be mistaken about this. But he could not believe that woman, whirling in a most abandoned fashion in the ballroom earlier that evening, was the same. There was a puzzle here, and it seemed to him vital that he unravel it.

"My name is Alexander Monteith Drummond. Incidentally, it is my real name."

"What do you mean by that?"

"You call yourself Lady Thorne," he said in a hard-edged tone that he hoped might elicit the truth from her, "a woman who has left her husband, according to Paris gossip. It is perfectly clear that a woman who travels with only one maid does not concern herself overmuch with her reputation. Especially—" He left the thought unfinished, but she understood him.

Especially one who leaps into bed with any handsome stranger!

"Who are you, really?"

"I'm—Maura Thorne," she said stubbornly. She

longed to be able to tell him the truth. Instinctively, she knew that the lie on her lips might alienate him, perhaps forever. But she had promised, and she would keep that promise.

He did not believe her. "Come now, have I not earned your confidence? It is not my intention to demand more than a word of thanks, which you have graciously given me. But I have rescued you twice, you know, and the emperor himself put you in my care now. I don't believe you are the dissolute Lady Thorne."

"Twice?"

"From the horses, and from the storm. You seem to have a faulty memory. Shall I tell you more about your escape from the Channel storm?"

Her cheeks were scalding hot. He had to stoop to hear her. "No, there is no need."

Alec was angry. Ordinarily he kept a tight rein on his emotions. His position as captain of the vicomte's bodyguard grated often on him for he despised his employer, but he was exceedingly well paid, and on his last trip to London had concluded that only six more months in this job would provide him with the funds he needed to repurchase his family home, now in the hands of strangers. He judged the duke's jealous anger by now would be focussed on some other man, since his duchess did not consider fidelity a virtue.

His feelings had played havoc with him this night. The two images—the apparent wanton of the ferry and this blushing victim of the vicomte—could not come together in his mind. He would never have seduced this girl had she in truth been the virgin she pretended. But this shy sweet girl with the unmistakable sapphire eyes did not fit the reputation of Lady Thorne.

He shook his head to clear it.

"Why don't you believe me?" ventured Val. Somewhere she had gone astray this night. She would like to have blamed Maura for making the vicomte's eyes glitter in anticipation of dark delights, for not warning Val about flirtations she had indulged in, but in the end Val was used to shouldering her own guilt.

Nobody had forced her to agree to Maura's scheme. Maura had indeed pleaded, badgered, threatened, and sneered—but in the end Val's lips alone had said yes.

"Where is your bracelet? You came draped with emeralds. Can't you even keep track of them?"

He could not bring himself to explain the deep level of certainty with which he knew that standing before him was his ferry-lady, and not the woman willing to be the vicomte's playmate.

"Your bracelet?" he repeated.

Alarm shot through her as she rubbed her wrist. "How could I be so stupid! She did not—"

She stopped short. She had almost revealed the masquerade. She remembered Maura's clasping the necklace around her throat, the earrings at her lobes. But the bracelet? She must have forgotten to transfer that.

"Answer me!" said Alec. "Did des Loches take it?"

"No, no," said Val. "It's—never mind where it is. It's safe enough."

They were standing together in a small anteroom inside the courtyard door. From far away came the faint strains of the orchestra, still playing as though only moments had passed since she had left the floor with the vicomte. Suddenly she realized that it was in truth only a short time ago that she had been dancing in the ballroom. So much had happened!

She must go back to the assembly, where Raoul's wife could see that Maura Thorne was still enjoying herself apart from the general.

Alec stood between her and the door. "Once more, madame. Who are you?"

"I cannot think you are entitled to quiz me in such a rude fashion."

"Perhaps not," he conceded, taut with anger, "but then you have not always complained of my rudeness."

She burst out, "Oh, why do you insist upon putting me in the wrong? I am groveling with gratitude for your many rescues of me. There, does that satisfy your overweening vanity?"

Suddenly mild in manner, although his gray eyes

still shot sparks like steel on flint, he altered his approach. "You have misunderstood me. It is not your gratitude I seek. It is merely your identity. In case, you know, that valuable bracelet is found, I should like to know to whom to return it."

Reading her hesitation correctly, he pursued his advantage. "To whom shall I return the bracelet?"

She faltered. She was certain that this intransigent man would not let her go until she told him. She was tempted. Why shouldn't she confide in him? She had met him first on the London street, and then, in excessive intimacy, on the ferry. She had known him, in fact, longer than she had been acquainted with her cousin. She had her own life, her own desires—

"I'm not experienced in this," she began, for the first time convincing Alec of her honesty.

He had never been noted for tact. He simply did not see the need of expressing his thoughts in pretty wrappings. He was far from insensitive, but his life had lain among hard ways. Frills were hard to come by, and sometimes even dangerous. Now he said bluntly, "I should hope not."

Val was intent upon her own dilemma. "You've spoiled everything."

Alec, remembering the lascivious glint in his employer's eyes, said, "His Majesty did not think so."

Thinking of Maura's scheme, Val said, surprised, "Why?"

"Do you *know* what that man is?"

"Oh, you mean the vicomte. No." She realized that Maura must have had some prior conversations with him, and she ought to protect her cousin by lying. But she had somehow crossed a line with Alexander Drummond. She had begun by lying to him, but she could not continue. What there was between them now was a bond, however fragile—one rescue from a runaway team and one night on the ferry. She wanted more.

More, if it were to come, could not sustain falsehood. There could be no more deceit between them. She had no guarantee that he felt as she did, nor even that he would not lie to her. But she knew what she must do.

"No," she repeated more sturdily. "He danced with me, just before—he brought me out here. And that is all." No matter what Maura had said to des Loches.

Alec considered her gravely. "I believe you. But he is not someone you ought to advance your acquaintanceship with."

"But he is received here at court."

"Unfortunately, this fact does not of itself provide a cachet of respectability."

Val remembered then the reason they were in Paris at all—Raoul's flagrant deception. "No, of course not. I should have known better. Besides, he is now banished from court." She recalled something she had not had time to consider until now. "How is it that you were so fortunately at hand when His Majesty spoke? Are you—connected to him?"

"For my sins, I am the vicomte's bodyguard."

"Bodyguard! To that blackguard?"

Alec's emotions had suffered greatly this night. He had dreamed, against his will, of this very lady as part of his future, so closely united they could never be divided.

This evening, to his astonished anger, she had looked through him without the slightest sign of recognition. Now, hurt and rage had given way to puzzlement, and suddenly he wanted to shake her name out of her, grab her shoulders and kiss her until she moaned in delight. Instead, he said coldly, "It occurs to me, madame, that you are not possessed of flawless morals yourself."

"You have no right—"

"On the contrary, I have every right. As you noticed, His Majesty himself has charged me for the moment with the preservation of your honor. If, of course, you have any honor remaining!"

He could have bitten his tongue when he heard the hurtful words fouling the air between them.

"You dare to speak so to me!"

"Then explain."

"I—I can't."

Val looked up into Alec's eyes, unwavering and cold. She knew, as she had known moments ago, that, even though she did not understand why, there must be nothing but truth between them. He might not understand, he might be angry, he might turn abruptly and walk out of her life. She lifted her hand in a pitiful little gesture. She could not let him slip away from her, no matter how insulting, how cruel he had been to her.

"At least," she said in a wee voice, so that he had to stoop to hear her, "not here, not now."

He was not satisfied, but he realized that he would get no more out of her this night. He suspected strongly that she was not Lady Thorne, no matter how stoutly she had maintained that fiction, but he did not know how he knew this. But who, then, was she?

If this one were indeed Lady Thorne, then who was the other one who danced so wildly through the evening, flirting dangerously with the vicomte?

"All right," he said quickly. "Meet me—do you know the Pont des Arts?" She nodded. "All right. Just after noon tomorrow. But I'll get you home tonight."

"Oh, no, you mustn't. At least, Mr. Simmons from the embassy will expect to escort me home."

So, he thought, she has the protection of the embassy, as Lady Thorne would have. But still he was not satisfied. "Do you wish to return to the dancing?"

"Oh, no, I could not. But I should—"

"You are in no way fit to meet people now."

He stepped to the door and spoke briefly to someone outside. "Well, then," he said to her, "we must not keep the good attaché waiting."

He took her arm and guided her through a warren of corridors, so that she did not have to enter the ballroom again. She dreaded every moment she might meet someone who knew Maura, or who would ask questions she did not wish to answer. But at last they reached a door that led onto the rue de Rivoli, where the embassy carriage waited, Neal Simmons standing beside it.

Alec handed her up without a word, and when she

would have thanked him again, she saw that he had turned his back and was walking rapidly away.

She did not know what she said to poor Mr. Simmons. She spared a thought to his evening, devoted to duty that he must find distasteful, judging from his expression. If Maura had offended him, as she well might have, let Maura make it up to him at some future time. Val herself had been surfeited with the debris Maura left in her wake.

She lapsed into dreamy speculation. Would she meet Alec the next day or not? If she did, she would have to explain the entire deception, and betray Maura. But if she did not meet him, then something very precious might be lost forever.

She would decide in the morning. Now, she realized again that she had not followed Maura's instructions to wait until Madame Doucet had left the ballroom. She had been told she must stay in Madame's sight constantly. But it was surely not Val's fault that Maura had promised the vicomte favors that she expected Val to provide.

The rhythm of the carriage, the monotonous grind of the wheels on the cobbled streets, insensibly lulled her. She was grateful for the small respite, the opportunity to arrange her thoughts in order. When she left the palace, she had been ready to throw her hand in and say farewell to the only journey she had ever taken. She had tucked away a small amount of money before she left London. She had planned to spend it on a falderal to serve as souvenir of Paris, but now she thought better of wasting it on a trifle. She now was pleased that she had kept some money by her, for she was learning—and quickly—that she dare not place unquestioned reliance on the promise of her cousin.

The carriage turned to cross the river toward their apartment. The lights in the magnificent houses along the broad boulevards, the elegantly dressed couples descending from carriages along the way and walking up the steps to attend parties, the snatches of Offenbach tunes from string orchestras, were indescribably alluring.

She would be sad to leave Paris.

For one who had worked hard for her father, lived on his scholar's sketchy income with never enough left over for even the simplest pleasures, she reflected that she could with unsettling ease accustom herself to the pursuit of leisured life.

It was past midnight when she climbed the stairs to their apartment. At one in the morning, she felt wide awake. There were a couple of subjects for discussion with Maura before they went to bed. She needed to know, first, precisely where the emerald bracelet was. She thought Maura had still been wearing it when she went off to Raoul, but Val wanted to be reassured.

Two, she would point out to her cousin that she could not carry out her part of the schemes unless Maura were more forthcoming in her plans. Surely, Maura must have dallied just enough for the vicomte to believe her willing, even eager, to accept his hospitality or whatever one might call it. Val wished to make certain that Maura watched her step—or, as it happened, Val's step—in the future. She wanted no more hair-raising escapes. Besides, the emperor might not come upon the scene so providentially the next time.

Maura was not at home. Val made ready for bed, knowing that sleep would not come for hours. She hung the sea-foam gown in the wardrobe and placed the necklace and earrings in Maura's blue leather jewel case. The bracelet was not there. Maura must be wearing it.

At last, when the little clock on the mantel stood at three, she heard faintly the sound of wheels on cobbles from below. Maura's quick steps came at once on the stairs.

Even at first glimpse, Val's heart sank. There would be no talking to Maura tonight. She swept in, leaving the door open, and danced a circle around Val.

"You're drunk," pronounced Val.

"If music be the food of love," sang Maura, out of tune, and glided around the room to her own rhythm.

"Maura, I must talk with you—"

She might as well have been shouting down a well, she thought, for all the attention her cousin paid to her. She reached out to catch Maura's wrist, to stop her on one of her dizzy rounds.

She felt metal beneath her fingers. "Oh, the bracelet! Thank goodness you've got it."

Maura was oblivious to everything around her. "Tomorrow," she crooned when Val stood directly in front of her, "I'll talk to you tomorrow, maybe if *mon cher* Raoul permits me the time."

Val eyed her in some disgust. Her cousin's display of wanton passion seemed almost unnatural. "Too much brandy!" she diagnosed.

"No, my sweet," laughed Maura huskily. "The most intoxicating—the most intox—"

She dropped into an armchair and collapsed like a rag doll. Laying her head back, she closed her eyes, losing herself in her own private dreams. Val watched her, uneasily, glad in a way she could not follow Maura's uncontrolled thoughts. Maura's smile made Val uncomfortable. There seemed to be something almost evil in the upturn of the lips, puffy from recent passion. Val shook herself. Maura could not be evil—it was only that Val herself was exhausted and her judgment therefore unbalanced.

But for the first time Val noticed the coarseness of Maura's complexion, the heavy bags under her closed eyes. What was it Raoul had said in that small anteroom? Lamb rather than mutton, that was it. If he could see Maura now, he would be more than ever convinced that his darling Maura had crossed the line to mutton.

Funny, Val thought suddenly—the vicomte and Alex Drummond had all but erased the recollection of Raoul's untimely arrival in the changing room. Good, she thought, she would not have to think about him again.

It was best that she could not share Maura's thoughts. Sometime in the future, Maura suspected, when the fever of living had ebbed, and desire was only a delight feebly remembered, she would forget this night just past. Perhaps then—but perhaps never.

Maura had travelled far in the years from the naïve miss she had been on her wedding night. William, aware of the more than two decades separating their ages, had initiated her gently, even tenderly. Too gently, she would have told him had it been possible to discuss such matters between husband and wife.

Her mother had instructed her in the dark side of married life, foretelling with lugubrious relish the pain, shame, and disgust—but never revealing to her the delirious ecstasy that was possible.

Maura's wedding night remained no mere revelation to her but soon flamed into an obsession. William had never suspected that raging fires blazed so close to him. A regular once-a-week encounter was sufficient for him, or so it seemed.

Maura, unsatisfied, was soon looking farther afield. Hunter Dyson, William's nephew and heir, supposing that Maura produced no son, kept his bachelor household a short way across the fields, a distance that Maura found it easy to cross when William was otherwise occupied.

Even Hunter could not satiate her greedy appetite. Last summer William had brought her to Paris. It had been a fateful trip. Her first meeting with General Raoul Doucet had been a *coup de foudre*. It made no difference to either that both were married, and they had met often, blind to scandal erupting around them.

This night just past, in Raoul's tiny pied-à-terre, no more than a garret in a house near the Pont Neuf, far surpassed any sensual experience she had ever known. She was far from inexperienced, no matter if William, and Hunter, each believed himself the only lover she had.

This night—delirium—wave after wave of savage pain and throbbing rapture had so intermingled that she could not even now separate them, swept away as she was on a tide of sensations. Raoul's hands had taken possession of her, explored crevices in a way that no man had before dared, rousing her to that terrible sweet clamoring that made her arch to his demand, welcome him into her softness, cling to him with fury and digging fingers until she felt adrift, without life support on the ocean's heaving breast.

Afterward, spent and gasping, she tried to tell him what she felt. "Hush, my love," Raoul had said, enforcing his demand by covering her mouth with his, and then to her surprise she felt his urgent, unwearied manhood again swelling against her belly, moving wetly up to stroke one breast, and then the other, hardening, arousing her until she cried out.

His knees held her hair fast to the pillow. She could not move her head as he towered over her. Her world diminished to the exquisite sensation of rubbing on her open lips, teasing, bruising.

She cried out once in surprise, and then, once again, gladly.

"Maura?"

Val's irritated voice came to her as though from across the far hills. She shuddered with the shock of return to the present.

The image of Raoul faded. She could let it go more easily now, for she would be with him this coming night, and the next, and the next.

Chapter Ten

Val spent a sleepless night. Whether it was from the enormous excitement of the ball the night before, or the near-tragic episode with the vicomte, from which the emperor himself had rescued her, or more likely—she decided just before dawn—the reappearance in her life of the tall Scotsman that kept her from sleep, it would be hard to say.

Alexander Drummond—at least she knew his name now—seemed to have become a part of her life, of the very odd way her life had changed. Ordinarily, she mused, a gentleman was introduced to a lady, the couple then explored and tested their compatibility, all within social proprieties, the lady's father or brother took care that the man was of sufficiently good character to be considered a suitor. Then, as months dragged on, at last the gentleman would declare his intentions and all would move on, merry as a wedding bell.

Alec Drummond fell into no such recognized routine. In him she sensed a fierce independence that would not be tamed. Not so much a flouting of convention, she decided, but simply a ruthless dismissal of any reason to conform to standards and customs he did not care for.

With Alec, the consummation came first, the acquaintance later. She no longer felt the acute, humbling shame that had consumed her when he had left her in the ferry cabin.

Paris had altered her in intangible ways. She hardly knew herself any more. She was of course Valetta Finch, when she was not Maura Thorne. But in a strange way she stood aside from the Valetta Finch she had known for twenty years, putting that well-bred young lady aside as one packs away an out-of-season dress in the wardrobe.

In mothballs, she thought wryly.

She felt unsettled, in a strange land with odd customs, and everything she had been taught seemed not to fit anymore. She would, no doubt, return to the staid young person, without prospects, when she set foot again on English soil.

In the meantime, it was easy to drift along in Maura's wake, like a chip tumbling behind a fast-moving boat, and let the day take care of itself.

She resolved just before she finally fell asleep that this day would contain a firm discussion with her cousin about the need for a full briefing before she appeared again in disguise. But this day would not see her meeting Alec Drummond at the Pont des Arts. She dared not see him again, for reasons that had little to do with protecting Maura's scheme.

That decision made, she fell asleep.

When she arose, Maura was still abed, even though it was shockingly late. The quiet gave Val the chance to shape her arguments, to fashion her complaint that Maura's carelessness flirting with the vicomte had put Val into real danger. She had the strongest foreboding that she would never be able to penetrate Maura's mood of ecstasy. Certainly her cousin was more than a little intoxicated last night, or rather early this morning, when she returned, and whether it was the aftermath of illegitimate passion or more simply too much brandy, the result was the same.

Suddenly Val felt overwhelmed. The view from the window, into the heart of that spindly plane tree that struggled to live in the midst of concrete and stones, only pointed out all over again that she was alone in an exotic and possibly alien land. Only one landmark stood in the distance, like a lighthouse in the foggy dark, waiting now at the Pont des Arts.

Blithely ignoring her decision not to meet him, she now remembered she had promised she would be at the Pont des Arts. She therefore would be there. When a Finch gave her word—but apparently this point of honor did not apply to Maura's branch of the family.

She dressed with great care. She deliberately passed by the gowns hanging in the wardrobe, most of them not yet worn. The dresses were fresh from the hands of the *couseuses* in Worth's atelier, their tiny stitches so small as to be nearly invisible.

Val had an undiscovered flair for fashion, and Worth had taught her much as she examined his work. But, as becoming to her as these costumes were, she chose, instead, one of her own. She would pretend to be her cousin when she had to, but this afternoon she must be herself entirely—at least, the French version of herself.

She put on an unassuming frock of poplin, one she had made to wear in Mr. Markham's shop. How long ago that seemed now! The amber fabric perfectly complemented her hair. Ready to bind up her curls in a no-nonsense net at the nape of her neck, she hesitated. Alec had told her, in that cabin on the ferry, that she should throw away her snood, and let her glorious hair ripple as it would. She stood without moving, dreaming, as she felt again his strong hands removing her hairpins, smoothing the luxurious curls away from her shoulders, her bare shoulders—

She shook herself. She was not ready to let him tell her how to dress. Swiftly she tucked her curls into the concealing net and smiled at her demure reflection in the glass. One thing he would have to admit—she did not look in the least like the notorious Lady Thorne today.

She picked up her parasol, said a word to Jehane, and hurried down the stairs. She had no idea how much time it would take to walk to the Pont des Arts. If she were late, he might not be there. Perhaps he would have decided she was not coming. She told herself in that case her problem would be solved. She would not have to explain to him even the barest outline of the masquerade, would not feel his cold gray eyes disapprove of her.

In the distance now she caught sight of the towers of Notre Dame and knew she was nearing the bridge. She slowed her pace. She must think clearly—decide exactly what she would say to Alec if he were still waiting for her, how much of Maura's secret she could reveal.

Within sight of the bridge, she stopped short. There was still time to go back, to take refuge in Maura's apartment, and hope to avoid Alec Drummond forever.

The Pont des Arts crossed the Seine at a point just upstream from the Imperial palaces of the Tuileries and the Louvre. She approached the bridge, suddenly shy. She could make out Alec Drummond's rangy figure watching for her along the approach. She was not prepared for the sudden breathless feeling that claimed her when she saw him. He was taller than average, angular, clearly of another breed than the smaller, slightly-built Frenchmen who were passing nearby. This contrast, surprisingly, stirred her.

He caught sight of her then and hurried across the avenue. His glance at her was fleeting, but something moved behind his casualness and for a moment she thought he was going to kiss her. He didn't.

"This place is too open," he said, as though answering her unacknowledged fear. "I've got a carriage waiting."

He put her into it, climbed in beside her, and they moved off. They rode in silence for some minutes. She was quiveringly aware of his closeness. At length, the coach stopped and Alec helped her down. They were at the edge of a great mass of trees and grass. A paved walk led into the park, and at a distance she could see the bright colors of flowerbeds, like jewels tossed haphazardly on green velvet.

"I don't know where we are," she ventured. "Not the Luxembourg Gardens?"

"The Bois de Boulogne. Too far for you to walk, but the park has some private places." He looked hard at her. "Are you afraid of me?" The tone of his voice was mocking, even harsh.

Bitterness edged her retort. "What more could you do to me than you have already done?" She was gratified to see that a flush appeared on his high cheekbones. "If you don't approve of me, as I must conclude from your close examination, will you please give me directions to find my way home?"

"Nonsense," he said curtly. "Don't be so quick to see an insult. I simply wanted to make sure that you could not be recognized as Lady Thorne." His mouth turned down at the corners, in self-deprecation. "It would do my lady no good with her general to be seen with a gentleman in a closed carriage."

Unable to choose among the words of comfort and denial that trembled on her lips, she said nothing.

He touched her arm and they moved into the peaceful shade of the Bois. The walkways were broad and winding, and, at this time of the day, deserted. Feeling great daring, she tucked her hand into the crook of his elbow and smiled to herself. A passerby might think they were lovers out for a stroll, instead of man and woman at odds, probably on the knife-edge of a quarrel.

The silence between them, surprisingly more companionable than angry, was broken. He said, in an approving voice, "You look like yourself today."

"I was myself last night."

"At the end, yes. But I will wager my employ that there are two Lady Thornes. As though one weren't enough."

"How could you know? You are a stranger to me."

He stopped short, and, her hand still in his arm, she swung to face him. He put a finger under her chin and tilted her face up. "A stranger?"

The poignant recollection of that hour on the ferry gripped her so sharply that she felt as though buffeted by a high wind. "But still," she breathed, "you could not know which of us—"

"I was a fool then," he said with an appearance of calm. "But—we can talk about that some other time."

Clutching desperately for any scrap of remaining dignity, she cried out, "There won't be another time!"

"No?" He smiled coldly. "And what if the vicomte attempts your virtue again? Louis Napoleon cannot be everywhere!"

"It is not generous to remind me," she cried, "of how much I owe you."

"Scotsmen are not known to be generous."

"Besides, the vicomte is banished."

A crunch of carriage wheels could be heard in the distance, muted by the buffers of thick shrubbery along the winding path. Far from reminding her that she was in the very heart of Paris, the remote sounds increased the sense of intimacy surrounding them.

"How did you know?" she said at last.

"That you were not—the other, whoever she is?"

"Yes. Was it the bracelet? It is at home, safe, as I told you."

"Not the bracelet."

"What, then?"

"You struggled. I heard your cries at the same time as His Majesty did. I was right behind him. The emperor was fooled, but I wasn't. You were different from the woman who was dancing at the first. You are not much like her, you know."

"Maura would not have struggled?" She noticed the gleam in his eye. Before he could pounce on her cousin's name, she continued hastily. "Don't think you have caught me in a slip of the tongue. I had already decided to tell you everything." Almost everything, she said to herself.

Ungraciously, he told her, "It's about time."

"Can I trust you?"

She felt the muscles in his forearm tense beneath her fingertips. She had wounded him, again. What a prickly man! She set herself to mollify him.

"It's simply, Captain Drummond, that the secret is not mine alone."

He removed her hand from his arm. "Now let us understand each other," he suggested, his frosty gray eyes holding hers. "Either you trust me, or you don't. I make no mention of what has already passed between us. If an apology is required, I shall oblige, later. But I have a strong feeling—"

Belatedly, he recognized the strong feeling. It was an entirely personal desire to hold her and protect her against all peril, for now and forevermore. Strangely in his ears, the extent of his desire sounded much like marriage vows. If so, then so be it. But now was not the time for frankness, at least on his part.

"A strong feeling?" she prompted him.

"A strong feeling," he repeated, "that you are in deeper trouble than you know."

She did not meet his eyes. He had echoed the unspoken uneasiness that dwelt just beneath the surface of her conscious thought. Slowly, she said, "You may be right." More briskly, she said, "I told you I would explain it all. My name is Valetta Finch. Did you know that?"

"Finch. Isn't Lady Thorne—"

"Maura Finch. And I haven't known her long at all. My father died in January, the last of the family. I was told that the other branches of the Finch family had died out. And since I was entirely alone, I came to London. I had to earn my living, you see."

She told him briefly about her employment in Mr. Markham's shop. She had not intended to relate anything of that last dreadful day there, but, once started, she could not halt the spate of words. She had not before realized how much she had needed to talk about it. Instinctively she had not confided in Maura, and now she knew she had been right to hold her tongue. Maura was not above using any weapon to gain her own way.

Alec listened in silence. She glanced at him once, but his face was a mask, and she looked away. She came to the afternoon of that last day, when Miss Wilson was talking about summoning bailiffs, and Maura had entered the shop.

"The very image of me," explained Val. "Of course we knew at once that we were related. A mirror image!"

Not quite, thought Alec dryly. He had not seen Maura Thorne at close range the night before, but Val was clearly more shining, more alive, more fresh and clean than her cousin. He smiled inwardly at his description of Val. He dared not speak, though, lest he interrupt the narrative that he must hear.

"You cannot know," continued Val, "how really *miraculous* it was to find that I had a cousin. And such a cousin! So charming, so knowledgeable, so kind."

"And so," he said when she paused, "you came to Paris. Lady Thorne doubtless had her reasons. Did you know what they were?"

"Not then," she confessed. "At first I thought it was for my company. Because we were cousins, you see. I did not want to let her go away when we had just met, because I didn't want to be alone again."

"And you supposed she felt the same way?" He caught a glimpse of the deep loneliness of her, one caused not only by her father's death. He suspected that she had rarely received what she needed—comfort, companionship, love. And the shame of it was that she did not expect anything more. "Come," he said, emotion roughening his voice. "Let us walk on a bit."

They resumed their stroll, but this time she did not take his arm. "When did you find out," he resumed, "that she had brought you to Paris for what we may call her own reasons?"

She was struck by his harsh tone. But she had started on this tale and, oddly, she wanted someone to know the whole of it, lest something happened to her. She gasped inwardly—what could happen? She had no clear premonition, but there had been times in this venture that she had felt swept along inexorably to some end. Unconsciously she now reached out for a figurative handhold.

"Just what do you do for her?" demanded Alec.

"Well, you have seen it."

"There's more."

"How do you know that?"

"I know the type. Full of her own importance. The world must dance to her tune. Selfish, thoughtless—"

Maura exactly, reflected Val. But with an oddly pathetic gesture, she protested. "Don't."

More gently, he urged her. "You take her place, of course. Like last night. Your cousin came to the ball, though, and then—you exchanged places with her?"

"Yes. That is what happened about the bracelet. She forgot to give it to me."

Now that he had guessed so much from the little she had revealed, she told him the whole of it. He knew the deliberate bringing of Val to Paris, and the masquerade. Now she told him the reason—Maura's infatuation with Raoul Doucet, and their scheme to deceive Madame Doucet.

When he finally spoke, after a long silence, he did not say what she had expected to hear. "What of your reputation?"

"What of it? Don't you see? Nobody even knows I'm in Paris. Everybody thinks I am Maura."

He did not tell her that this anonymity was her most potent peril. If nobody knew she, Valetta Finch, were here, then nobody would know if she disappeared. He felt a cold *frisson* at the back of his neck. It was his Scottish second sight, no doubt. He gripped Val's hand.

"What happens if the general, jealous of Lady Thorne, wreaks his vengeance upon *you?*"

Val said wryly, "Raoul can tell us apart."

Startled by her tone, he exclaimed, "He made advances?"

Her flush betrayed her. Alec, studying her intently, was learning her little ways, the signs of thoughts and emotions. This flush told him Raoul was not indifferent to her. If he found Lady Thorne attractive, how much more desirable must he see Val! Her refusal to meet his eyes indicated that more had transpired between her and the general than she would tell.

"Well, then," said Alec, not deceived, "if the general is already unfaithful, you can see as well as I that this so-called idyll is destined to see an early termination."

"Well, then," echoed Val, regaining her spirit, "you can see, too, that if it is soon done with, then there's nothing to worry about."

"What happens," Alec demanded, "when Lady Thorne comes to realize that the general is straying?"

"I don't know," said Val slowly, "I really don't know."

They moved now in a shadowed walkway, the air tinted a shimmery green by the interlacing leaves overhead. Even the cries of children and the calls of anxious nursemaids were left behind. The quiet was almost tangible as they moved together in an intimate world.

This, she thought, must be the real Paris, the heart of the city's romance. The parades, the hard clip-clop of horses, of troops passing in review, the rumble of carriage wheels, and the constant metallic jingling of harnesses—all was stripped away like steel armorplate to reveal a soft, yielding body beneath.

Alec took her hand and placed it again within the crook of his elbow as they moved farther away from the sunlit gardens. The walk was deserted. They were alone.

"Valetta." She looked up at him, her heart beating a little more loudly in her ears. "Val?" he said again, but this time it was a question, a question of which she knew the answer but dared not give it.

He smiled, a wry one-sided smile that in another man, or at another time, might be called bitter. "My dear," he said, amused, "you have never been spoiled by that hypocritical upbringing that so many of your contemporaries have endured."

"What do you mean?"

"Every well-bred lady, you know, has been carefully taught to conceal every emotion that comes to her."

She forced a laugh. "How do they ever—get along?"

"Get along? You mean, get married? Because they fancy it is their mission to deny their husbands any glimpse into their own feelings. They shut him permanently out of their lives."

His eyes darkened momentarily, as though he was looking at an unwelcome memory. He took her hand and pulled her to him. "But not you. I can tell every thought that runs through your pretty head!"

With spirit, she retorted, "Don't be too sure of that!"

His arm around her waist, he held her close without moving for a long time. It seemed to her the most natural thing in the world to lay her head on his shoulder. He stroked her hair, soothing, lulling her. At length, without guile she lifted her face to his. He kissed her, not as he had on the ferry, but gently, almost chastely.

Not until she opened her lips willingly did he move his own back and forth against them, teasing them, darting his tongue in and out until she thought she would scream with sweet agony. He pressed her against him, so close that she could feel his body hot through her thin gown. His hands on her back molded her to him. Nothing loath, she pressed against his hard length thinking vaguely, how well we fit together—

Abruptly, she thrust him away. The remembered response to him sang in her very blood, but she also remembered the hurt. "I wonder at you, sir."

"Now what?" He was exasperated. "What maggot's in your head now?"

"I should not consider it a maggot, Captain Drummond. But I see your memory is faulty."

He stood apart from her, his legs spread, his hands belligerently on his hips. "I remember that you put up no such maidenly protests before!"

"So I am no maiden," she flung at him furiously. "And whose fault is that? You flung your contempt in my face—and now you seem to have forgotten—what you have done to me!"

She put her hands up to hide her face.

"I remember," he said his voice taut. "I was wrong.

I thought you were Lady Thorne, and knew what you were doing, willing enough to enjoy the man at hand."

"You knew then?" She spoke in such a low tone that he could not hear the rest of her sentence. He put a finger under her chin and forced her to look at him.

"Knew what? That it was your first time? Yes, I knew at the end, too late to do any good. It was disgust at myself that made me accuse you."

He bent to kiss her, but she turned her head so that he felt her bronze curls beneath his lips. "Val—"

A harsh note in his voice—could it really be pain?—moved her. Something about this man—and no other man in her life so far—demanded honesty. She could, she knew, send him away as punishment. He deserved it, for his arrogant assumption that she would come to him any time he beckoned, that she was captive to his lust—

The punishment, no matter whether he suffered or not, would be devastating for her.

"I'm so ashamed," she whispered.

"Ashamed!" He let his hands lie loosely on her shoulders. "There is nothing shameful about love, my dear. Exciting, tempestuous, full of upheaval and sweetness, and many other things. But never shameful. Remember that."

"But you never said love."

Nor will I, yet, he thought. I am not ready, not ready. But he could not lie to her, he realized with some surprise. He lifted her hand and kissed her palm. He felt the quivering within her and knew she did not hate him, at least not yet. He watched her, an odd light in his eyes, a strange expression on his features. "Love? It is sweet, my dear, for the most part. Sweet beyond the telling of it."

She heard him as from a distance. The tumult in her mind was so riotous she could not believe he did not hear it, too. She removed her hand from his and stepped away. She straightened her clothes nervously. She was aware of Alec, his body, his nearness, the tantalizing aroma of his shaving soap. Her body recognized its master, but she dared not give way to the throbbing ache in her. At last, she was in shaky control of her voice. He was still watching her, his glance never wavering.

With a coquettishness she hadn't known she was capable of, she said, "What are you thinking?"

He laughed. "Not what you might imagine. I was remembering a Scottish hillside—the slopes pink with heather, a fine breeze coming up from the burn below, and overhead the kestrels flying."

Chagrin made her flush. She had not expected such a response. She had braced herself, hopefully, for a passionate declaration of his love!

"And, my darling Valetta, you, climbing the hill with me."

The tender look in his eyes moved her beyond belief. "Ah!" It was only a breath. At that moment, if he had said, "Come with me this moment to Scotland—or the world beyond—," she would have put her hand in his, gladly, with all her heart and never look back.

He said, "But I can't go home again, not yet."

She would always remember this moment, she thought. The green leaves overhead, the oddly moving splotches of filtered sunlight in the path, the exotic scent of flowers—the dead taste of ashes on the tongue.

She turned and walked briskly back the way they had come. It would be a long way home, but—she had nothing else to do with her time, not now. She hurried blindly, not caring but achingly aware that he followed, his stride lengthening to catch up.

He finally caught her arm and held her, at the edge of a paved boulevard that wound around a smooth expanse of water.

They were not alone. To her amazement, a seemingly endless procession of vehicles was promenading around the lake, like a living carrousel.

Alec pulled her back quickly, and she looked at him in surprise. "The demimonde. Actresses and—others."

Obediently she turned her back on the glittering parade and walked away. She said nothing, but she did wonder—why had that blonde woman in the open, velvet-lined carriage, smiled at them? And, if Val had not been mistaken, she had actually *winked* at them. Or, more probably, at Alec. Val was suddenly aware of an irrational pang of dislike for her.

Unsettled by this encounter with a world so aggressively alien, she was less than pleased with Alec when, as they finally neared the carriage that waited for their return, he took up again the subject of Val's masquerade.

"It's dangerous," said Alec, breaking the long silence that had painfully settled between them.

"What is?"

"This masquerade."

So much had transpired between them since she had revealed the extent of Maura's scheme that it was hard to imagine she had given him her confidence only an hour before. "Nothing will happen."

"You can't be sure! That cousin of yours thinks nothing of setting the world on its ear."

"Who knows of this masquerade, as you call it?" she pointed out. "Only Maura, and Jehane, of course, and the general, and me. And now you."

"And the coachmen, the servants, even Worth the designer."

"No, no. I did not go to Worth myself. Only Maura did, and veiled."

Alec then proved himself surprisingly conversant with feminine affairs. "What if someone from Worth sees you in his gowns?"

"What if, then?"

"The gowns—at least that green one you wore last night, does not fit you. You are slimmer than your cousin."

"Worth will not notice."

"Believe me, he will. I have heard that he sends his own people to court functions to inspect his work—as well as that of his competitors."

"I had not thought of that. But"—she regained her poise—"what of it?"

"Lady Thorne is a woman of loose behavior. Now

don't fly into the air. You have already suffered from—mistaken identity, may I remind you? To my own infinite regret." He smiled wryly. "I do not regret the occasion—only that I was the cause of injury to you. But surely you are aware that it is not the thing to run away from your husband and meet a married lover—"

"She has reason."

"You mean, overwhelming passion, I suppose."

She lifted her chin. "Why not?"

"Why not indeed? I wonder whether you know the difference between love and passion? Never mind. I shall instruct you."

"I shall not need to trouble you on that score."

Sheer bravado, she realized, wishing for all the instruction he could give her.

He resumed. "She—your cousin—is a woman of much practiced charm and coquettishness. She may promise more than you, in her place, are willing to proffer. The vicomte's attempt bears witness."

"Nonsense. Maura is wrapped up in her general."

"You think the vicomte simply chose you at random?"

She considered certain things the vicomte had said, certain hints reflecting shared intentions. Reluctantly, she admitted that Alec's contention was well within reason.

She grew uneasy, knowing that at least a portion of Alec's warning was *à propos*. "But I can't leave her, not yet."

"Why not?"

"Isn't it obvious? Where would I go, except back to London?" And jail, she added silently, if Mr. Markham were to catch sight of her. "She is the only family I have. This fever of hers will burn itself out, and then we'll return to England."

"And then?"

"Then she'll go back to Sir William."

She refused to examine, even to herself, her own undesirable prospects in that event. Alec, doggedly

Scottish, persisted. "If you won't listen to common sense," he began angrily, but she, torn by her own doubts, turned on him in fury.

"You have control of all of the common sense in the world, I suppose? How much sense does it make to turn my back on my only cousin, who is all kindness to me, to choose to go back and work in a dark shop and live in a tiny attic room, instead of staying a little longer in Paris?"

Incited by his fear for her, he flung an accusation which he knew to be baseless. "Then your views are entirely based on material benefits to you?"

"If you were to choose a dreary life rather than a sunny one, then I wonder at *your* common sense!"

She turned on her heel and started, blinded by tears of rage, across the street.

He caught up with her and put her into the carriage. They rode in utter silence until he said farewell at the far end of the little courtyard with the plane tree. He watched her until she reached the blue door, and waited, hoping for a wave of her hand. He was disappointed.

She climbed the stairs, tears welling unchecked. She was angry, she told herself. Not sorry, nor desolate, nor ashamed. Simply very, very angry.

Chapter Eleven

Alec was angry.

May passed and slipped unobtrusively into June. The emperor and his empress moved, as was their habit for the summer, to the palace at Saint-Cloud. Many of the *haute noblesse* joined the exodus, heedless of storm clouds gathering over France.

Prussia was flexing its new muscles. Bismarck made savage and unrealistic demands that France would not meet. Everywhere there was talk of war. Half of Paris thought that France should capitulate, thereby preserving for them at least the lovely indulgent life they knew, while the other half found Prussian antics merely amusing.

Alec, purely and proudly Scottish, found nothing to admire in either. His regret was that the vicomte, surprisingly, had much to do with the government at this moment, and, with his exile over, had returned to the capital. His captain of the guard, therefore, had to also stay close at hand.

Alec found Paris a desert, in spite of the lush greenery of the parks, the throngs making their rounds of the Bois, and his employer's demands. From time to time he caught a glimpse of "Lady Thorne" from a distance. Valetta, playing her part well, looked at him and passed on without a sign of recognition.

Had Alec been physically closer to her, he might have caught the momentary appeal, the vulnerable hope, in the sapphire eyes. Instead, he contented himself with setting his own features in granitelike sternness, lest by some mischance he disclosed Maura's scheme of which he disapproved so greatly.

It was for Val's sake, he told himself. But in truth he was loath to reveal his own naked longing for her.

The first days of September came all too soon. Alec, alone in a job he disliked, working for an employer he despised, decided it was time to talk to his greatest friend in Paris. He set out toward the Champs Elyseés.

Hortense Schneider (she who had winked outrageously at Alec in the Bois) was one of whom the French called, with devastating accuracy, *les grandes horizontales*.

Originally, she had been an opera singer, the star of Offenbach's *La Grande Duchesse de Gerolstein,* bringing audiences roaring to their feet night after night. But an audience of hundreds standing in ovation was less to her liking—so it was said—than one or two in other positions, throwing substantial sums of money her way in the semiprivacy of her opulent house in the Champs-Elysées.

There were other courtesans competing in this Second Empire Paris, many of whom earned fabulous sums of money. One Cora Pearl was reported to have earned and spent more than sixteen million pounds in her short career.

But it was Hortense whom the Prince of Wales, visiting incognito, asked for—and, of course, always got.

She appealed not only to the lonely English prince, but to a varied clientele. This very morning, when Alec Drummond was making his way toward her house, she was reported to be considering a stunningly magnificent offer from the smitten Khedive of Egypt.

But besides her magnificent body and her equally generous distribution of her expensive favors, she possessed a fund of common sense. Offenbach's brightest star, an actress of the most winsome charm and inimitable allure, Hortense was at heart a Bavarian *hausfrau.* Her sojourn in Paris at the pinnacle of the demimonde was an exercise, often in the most literal sense of the word, in building security for her later years.

She had been heard to say to her faithful Anna, "*Grüss Gott,* I get so tired of their hands and their eyes and their loose mouths, and their—their complete arrogance to think I can be bought for ten thousand francs."

"Why not?" countered Anna. "You can."

"But only my outside," argued Hortense. "My real inside is—well, you know where."

"In a castle," came the ritualistic response, "in the forest above Regensburg."

"Another year of this, Anna. Then we'll just fade away."

Her companion's eyes darkened. "From what I heard the other night, from General Comte Reille and the Prime Minister, Ollivier, I don't know that we can last the year out."

"What do you mean?"

"You remember, they once said that the French army was invincible. Three hundred and eighty-five thousand men, ready to rise up at a word. And the emperor gave the word, of all the *bêtises.*" Anna stopped, clucked her tongue, and went on. "Imagine coming out with a French word, as though good German wasn't all a person needs. We've been here too long, that is certain. I wager the emperor wishes now he had been struck dumb before he declared war."

"The Prussians overran the French at Sedan—I know that. But surely the French will rally?"

"When the French boast, it is a good idea to believe the opposite, which you will recall, I did. What, Madame Hortense, shall we do, now that France is defeated?"

The stocky, stolid Anna, more a companion and memento of home than a maid, did not wait for an answer. She set up a big copper tub before the empty hearth in Hortense's own bedroom.

Hortense loved these moments of privacy. Her clients were never admitted to the third floor of her splendid house, which she kept apart, inviolate from her profession. The leisurely bath with which she started every day was a sybaritic luxury in which she reveled.

She dropped handfuls of scented powders into the warm water and watched the bubbles rise and cover the surface. Then she took off her red satin robe, tossed it carelessly toward the narrow bed, and slid into the foamy water.

The warm silky water coddled her in its embrace, and she closed her eyes in sheer bliss. But the world could not be kept at bay for long.

The odd conversation Anna had overheard, and, as always had relayed to her mistress, was puzzling. Hortense let the warm water relax her tense muscles and sank down into the tub, resting her head on the cushioned rim. She gave herself up to the sensual caress of the water lapping about her body at her slightest movement.

But her mind could not let go so easily. If the time to leave Paris came sooner than expected, she must be ready—she would have to be. She dared not take a chance on losing everything. She had no illusions left. While she had many friends in Paris, the crowds wildly applauding her performances, and those admitted to her private circle who enjoyed influential positions in government and society, she knew that at the first cold breath of adversity she would stand alone.

"You did not answer me," said Anna, bringing another pitcher of hot water. "What are you thinking?"

"I am thinking," said Hortense in their native tongue, "that it is time to move our arrangements ahead."

Over the years the two had developed a kind of cryptic verbal shorthand. Now stolid Anna expressed satisfaction. "How soon?"

"If the armies fall back on Paris, we shall not be here. There is time, yet, Anna. We have our plans made. If there are fortunes yet to be made, we must have our share of them."

Anna turned thoughtful. "And yet, to use your words, there is also the danger of losing it all." She sat holding a pair of thick towels. "It is no secret that we are German."

"Bavarian, not Prussian, don't forget."

"To the stupid Frenchman, is there a difference? I think not."

A note in Anna's voice caused Hortense to look sharply at her. "If you want to leave now, Anna, I shall not object. Where will you go? Back to your uncle's hovel? I had thought you loathed swine, and the chickens—"

"You don't need to remind me what I owe you, Hortense. And you know very well that I shall stay with you no matter if it costs me my life."

Hortense gave a sniff of contempt. "Not likely."

Anna almost smiled. She had planted the seed as she knew well how to do. Now she must summon the patience to let it grow.

"Captain Drummond is waiting below."

"Why didn't you say so?" cried Hortense. "Bring him up at once!"

The captain of the bodyguard of the Vicomte des Loches, though not a client, was counted a friend. He was welcomed in Hortense's house at any time, although he was careful not to intrude when she was "working."

Captain Drummond was a lonely man in a foreign country. In her he had found the only friend he could trust, and she had never betrayed him. Therefore, he often stayed away when he longed for her company, noting without criticism the impressive and recognizable carriage of the Khedive of Egypt, or that of a visiting English prince incognito, standing before her door.

He had been raised in an austerely religious home, and occasionally he wondered what his mother might have said about her son's friendship with the most famous courtesan in Paris. He hoped she would have understood that the lady was honest, free of the double-standard morality which bore heavily on most women, while leaving men free to follow their inclinations.

Like Alec—and this was perhaps the most durable bond between them, that made them friends instead of lovers—she had a goal of a certain sum of money that would buy her a certain castle on a slope of the Bohmerwald, the range of mountains between Bavaria and Bohemia, studded with lakes, and far from the glittering pretense that pervaded her life in Paris.

Anna, of course, would share that new life, and they would keep house in good peasant comfort. And no men in sight! At least for a while.

Alec's dream was no different in substance, even though his goal was not a castle, but a solidly built stone house, somewhere near Tillicoultry with a fine view across the sheep-dotted plain to the Ochill Hills. And, just as she sold her body for her dreams, he sold his sword arm.

Val had unaccountably begun to appear in his vision of the Scotland haven he longed for. He had a grave suspicion that the house would have no appeal unless she moved with her light grace through the rooms. But the chasm between them was unbridgeable. She would never see her masquerade for the dishonest and dangerous ploy it was, nor could he convey to her his real fear that she was risking more than her reputation.

He could not talk to her without becoming angry. For the first time in his life, his passion overpowered his good sense.

Maybe, he thought, if he had not been so quick to take her to bed—even though he had believed her to be the tarnished Lady Thorne—he would stand a better chance now with his Valetta.

Val! Would she ever be his? He knew now that, unless she came to him, willingly, her sapphire eyes alight with love and desire for him, only for him, the dream stone house might as well be a ruin, and the Ochills naught but a raised hummock in a fallow field. She held all the joy in his life in her small hands.

In his lonely hurt, he remembered Hortense. He had not seen her for some time, not since she had winked at him so outrageously in the park. He smiled to himself, recalling her boisterous good humor and her immense kindness to him. It was noon before he was free to make his way to her splendid mansion.

He found her in her bath. It was significant that he felt no more embarrassment than had she been his brother.

"Ah, my friend!" she greeted him. "Just the one I wished to see. You can tell us, I am sure."

"Anything I can."

"Anna says it is time for us to leave Paris. But I see you do not expect trouble."

"How do you see that?" he countered. "Perhaps I came to say farewell."

She wore an arrested look for a moment. Automatically, she cupped the billowing suds in her hand and let them slither over her magnificent shoulders. "Did you, Alec?"

He thought for a moment before answering her. "My dear," he said at last, "you know the French are abominable fighters."

Anna snorted but said nothing.

"Yes, Anna, you told me so. But, Alec, three hundred eighty-five thousands? Could they all be dead?"

"Krupp's cannon," said Alec in terse explanation, "outranges the French. And all the supplies for the army, I'm told, instead of being in the north to face the Germans, have to be brought from somewhere near Rouen. It's a crime. They're toy soldiers with fancy uniforms. They think the whole thing is nothing but a parade down the Champs-Elysées!"

"Ah, my friend," laughed Hortense, "if you had the running of the world, things would be different, *hein?*"

Yes, he thought, Val would be with him, leaving that selfish pig of a cousin behind, and—

While his thoughts scattered he had glanced around

Hortense's bedroom. It contained only a narrow bed, austerely covered with a plain quilt, a small chest of drawers, two chairs, and a fireplace. There was hardly room for the copper tub in which Hortense still lay, covered by foamy bubbles. Her blonde hair was pinned casually at the top of her head, while Anna stood nearby, waiting for the moment to hand her mistress one of the enormous bath towels. On a signal from Hortense, Anna silently left the room.

A shrewd look at Alec's drawn face had told Hortense much. She knew men, and this one was particularly dear to her, mostly because he did not consider her as an object of his lust.

"Alec—?"

With an obvious effort he roused himself from his lonely thoughts. In an attempt to tease her, he said, "Not gone to the Egyptian harem yet?"

She matched his mood. "I'm waiting for you to escort me. With any luck, we'd never arrive!"

Alec quirked a black eyebrow. "You know we shouldn't suit."

"We're much alike, *mon ami.* We both sell ourselves."

"Ah, why so bitter this morning? The city has not fallen yet."

"It can't still be morning, can it?"

"Of course. Ordinarily I would never appear at your door before noon. I have a regard for my head."

No one else was permitted to see this facet of Alec. His humor was droll, not swift and rapierlike. He felt completely free with Hortense, since there was no pull of tension between them, only an easy friendship. If there had once been passion, it had not endured.

He frowned now, wondering whether he would ever feel as free with Val. Would there be friendship at the last, after the fever of desire was gone? Or would they grow apart, and come to be strangers at the end?

Hortense set herself to beguile him out of his mood. She had a new *bonne bouche* about the Duc de Morny, whose diversions usually involved dressing in his wife's clothes and, wearing a wig, sometimes regaling the emperor's household troops with a ribald cancan, leaving no doubt of his sex before the dance was finished.

Since Paris in recent weeks had lost much of its effervescence, she reached back in memory to amuse him. "Do you recall, Alec dear, that dreadful stunt that Rigolboche performed?" Rigolboche, the professional cancan dancer, the toast of certain elements of Paris, had once crossed a broad Paris avenue stark naked, while the Duc de Gramont-Caderousse applauded from the curb. Frightened the horses, it did, Hortense laughed, to say nothing of the honest Parisian tradesmen passing by at the time.

Alec reluctantly allowed himself to smile.

"Were you at the Maison Dorée, Alec, the night that that slut Cora Pearl had herself served up on a silver salver—wearing no more than a sprig of parsley? Limp parsley, at that. The gentlemen applauded like the fools they are. It would have been more *à propos*, I think, had she clutched an apple in her teeth, as the English do with their great pigs!"

Alec was amused. "You know you're not nearly as malicious as you try to make me think."

"Ah, you have me there! But it is the gossip which attracts, you know. One must be *au courant* with the latest."

"Or even fabricate a little, if necessary?"

Hortense shrugged. The movement started little rivers of bubbles sliding down her shoulders, to be lost in the larger sea around her. "Blanche d'Antigny's new diamonds, you must have seen them?" she resumed. "They are gaudier even than Madame Doucet's newest parure. And that, they tell me, is of the utmost bad taste, for you must know that the empress was greatly displeased when she set eyes on them. She feels the diamonds of the world should be reserved only for her own serene majesty! Ah, Alec my friend, the world is full of fools! And I am not the least."

"Nor I, I am afraid," he agreed, thinking of his unrequited longing for Valetta.

"*Mon ami,*" said Hortense, anxiously peering into his face, "what is it? Is it the Lady Thorne? Do not, I beg you, do not tell me that *she* has you in her—I was about to say clutches."

"Clutches would be right," sighed Alec. "The woman's a harpy. But no, I am not in her clutches."

"But," objected Hortense, puzzled, "it was she you were with in the Bois that day, *n'est-çe-pas?* And the rumor ran that you did her a service one night at the palace, as well."

She eyed him narrowly. Her own magnificent house was a central gathering place in Paris, and many rumors and truths passed there that would have astounded even those who considered themselves *bien informés* concerning the world's events.

Alec could not betray the secret Val had trusted him with. "Not Lady Thorne," he repeated.

"Then," said Hortense matter-of-factly, "it is the other one."

Alec's jaw dropped. "Wh-what?"

"Did you think, *mon vieux,* that this foolish Thorne woman practices her deception undetected? Pah!"

"Then," said Alec slowly, "there *is* danger to the girl."

"Hand me the towel. This water is cold."

He brought the towel and waited while she pulled herself erect in the tub. The bubbles slid lingeringly down her marble skin into the water around the ankles.

Obediently he brought a pitcher of scented water and poured it over her shoulders. In spite of himself, he was aware of her ample pink-tipped breasts, her narrow waist, her broad hips. There was no hair on her body. With a shock he realized that she had shaved her pubic hair.

His surprise was evident. She watched him, amused. "One of the ladies from the court of some Maharajah or other, here for the Exposition, was most helpful in some of the tricks of the trade. I am told that novelty is the price of continued success."

She stood in the tub, the towel held loosely in her hands. She looked the very embodiment of desirable womanhood. It was no wonder, he thought, that princes fell at her feet.

She smiled, tantalizing, teasing. She was as aware as he of that desire now stirring in him. At length he broke the silence with a huge sigh. Roughly, he demanded, "Where's your robe? I'm not a eunuch, like your Khedive's men. Are you going to turn him down?"

"I should exile myself to a wasteland of camels and sand?" she cried with little regard for geographical truth. "And palm trees? When I retire from the world, *mon cher,* it will not be to sit with a gaggle of women in a harem. Remember that."

"And yet you are disgusted with men?"

She looked sheepish, caught in her own trap. "Well enough. But women and their silly chitchat disgust me even more." She fell silent, pulling the red satin robe closely around her superb body. "Men are fools, dear Alec, but sometimes they make sense. In spite of themselves."

Alec sat down again in the chair. He sensed that Hortense was unusually troubled. She needed time, though, before confiding in him. He crossed his legs leisurely. Even as Hortense was his dearest friend in all of Paris, so he knew that she too considered him, a fellow alien, as one of the few she could trust. He was willing to wait for her to speak.

Besides the special feeling that bound them together, she was fascinating entertainment. She had a bright and lively mind, but she was at her most amusing when she was unbending with intimates. Purposely challenging her, he said, "I should like to hear of a time when men—that is, *your* men here—made sense. You wine them so well."

"There was an episode," she said quietly, "that sticks in my mind like the cocklebur. It was at the first, when the war had just begun." She thought for a moment, then resumed obliquely. "You agree that these Frenchmen thought the world would fall on its face as soon as it saw their so handsome men in their so handsome uniforms. *Ja?*"

Alec nodded.

"But then, while they preened themselves like so many roosters someone said a word that closed them all up, like a trap." She gestured with her hands. "Shut! Like so. What did it mean, my friend?"

"Since I do not know the word, Hortense, I shall refrain from speculating."

She snapped her fingers. "I knew I would forget all the facts when I told you. I cannot think— Oh, yes." She lowered her voice to a conspiratorial whisper, giving the word an ominous importance. "Sadowa."

"Sadowa," repeated Alec. He thought for a long time. The bubbles dying in the bathwater filled the air with tiny little pops. She glanced at him several times, watching his frown come, seeing his face settle into hard, uncompromising lines.

"What is it, *liebling?*"

"My first war," he told her, his voice harsh. "I was a fool of a kid, wanting all the excitement of being a soldier, wearing a brave uniform—women ripe for the taking—all of it."

"For the women," she told him softly, "you never needed a uniform."

He seemed not to hear her. He moved abruptly, as though giving way to emotions long stifled, now boiling up irrepressibly.

"All right, I'll tell you what I know. You know Sadowa? The Austrians call it Koniggratz, in Bohemia. The Germans fought the Austrians there, for reasons that I doubt even they understand. Our esteemed emperor thought the Germans and the Austrians would fight each other until they were exhausted, and then he would come in and pick up the leftovers. A typical ploy of his—scheming to gain the lot without fighting."

"And you were there?" Hortense knew her men. This one before her was now reliving some of the most painful days of his life—so transparent were the reflective eyes, the strained voice, the white knuckles.

"I was there. On the German side as a mercenary. I

was not the only Scot there. Many a younger son found it more profitable to leave home—even some elder sons."

"And the Germans won."

"Indeed they did. They had a new gun—a weapon called a Needle Gun." He answered the query in her eyes. "Because the cartridge was exploded in a new way, by a needle piercing the case."

"But what does it mean? Why did they speak the word in my salon and then all look so grave?" Her mobile features suddenly mimicked a pompous and forbidding expression.

He gave her a one-sided smile that held no amusement. "Because the Germans have the Needle Gun, and no army in Europe today can stand up to them. Not even the much-admired French battalions in their gaudy uniforms—the uniform which includes, my dear girl, as part of it a sword. Now you can see what Sadowa means? Not quite literally—but near enough to make no difference—a sword, for God's sake, against the most significant killing weapon known to man."

She shivered. Shaking her head, as though coming out of a dream, she said, "The fools." Then, deliberately lightening the mood that had fallen between them, she leaned toward him, letting the red satin robe fall open as it would. "Alec?"

He shook his head. "I can't afford you."

She touched his shoulder. He became aware of the heady scent of the jasmine crystals she had dissolved in the bathwater—perhaps another trick courtesy of the Indian lady—and knew that once he would have succumbed to the clear invitation. But the bright limpid image of Valetta came to him, and he held back.

"For you, *mon ami*, this is without cost." She gestured, her fingers touching her breasts lightly, and, moving downward, stroked her rounded hips invitingly. "All of it."

"Charity?" he asked wryly.

"Honesty," she amended, "for the tie that is between us."

He smiled. He lifted her hand to his lips. "An honor, my dear, believe me. But—not now."

"Ah, well, you cannot blame me for hoping," she said philosophically. She wrapped the red satin robe around her again with a curiously innocent gesture and sat in the other chair.

At last, he left her, dismissed because some duke was expected in an hour. He slipped through the garden gate into the quiet street behind her house.

If Hortense had not managed to arouse his physical desire sufficiently, she had succeeded in releasing the fey mood that plagued him. A Highland Scot, Alec Drummond shared his ancestors' susceptibility to dark moods and gloomy forebodings. The worst of it was that, almost without exception, the ominous oppressiveness heralded trouble of some kind. If Alec felt an unwonted chill, as he did now, he could be sure that menacing clouds would soon appear on his horizon.

In a restless mood, he searched the conversation of the last hour for some clue, some suggestive remark that might have caused his present anxiety. There was nothing he could recognize.

He tried to force his thoughts to more pleasant things. He wished he had been present at the Maison Dorée, when the flamboyant Cora Pearl had herself served up, adorned with a mere sprig of parsley, on a huge silver tray. His wayward thoughts slipped back to Hortense—this morning she had not bothered with any concealment.

Suddenly his longing for Valetta, to hold her in his arms again, was so overwhelming that he stood still, willing his desire to recede, demanding control of himself. At last, he felt calm again. But next time, he doubted he could quell the mighty urge that swept him like the surge of the ocean.

Ocean?

He cocked his head, listening intently, acutely aware of the far-off rumbling sound that he knew now was not in his mind. He felt cold, as he recognized the meaning of the distant roar.

Paris was on the move—a mob, a full-throated protesting mob, no longer human, no longer reasonable.

Paris had heard the news of the defeat, and rejected it.

He was not armed, being off duty. He planned swiftly. First he must return to the vicomte's town house on the rue de Courcelles, to get his pistols, and then he must find Val.

He hoped she had sense enough to stay inside the apartment, until he could get there and see what could be done about getting her out of danger. Paris on the march was sinister, powerful, and invincible.

Chapter Twelve

That Sunday morning, Val was on her way to the rue de Courcelles, Maura's note tucked into her small reticule. Her errand, if she were to believe her cousin, was simple enough. She was to hand the note to the Vicomte des Loches, receive from him a small wash-leather bag heavy with gold, and return.

Val sought a diversion while she considered her cousin's instructions. "Why should this vicomte hand me money?"

"Because I am asking him to," Maura said. "Kindly do not pry into my business."

Val had to be content with that meager explanation, for it was all she was to have. The atmosphere of uneasiness, even of impending disaster, that had permeated the apartment the last few days had deepened until this morning, when it weighed on her with the force of imminent doom. She knew that the war was not going well for the French. Also, she was painfully aware—

judging from Maura's vicious temper—that Raoul Doucet had followed his regiments to the battlefront.

Now, as she moved quickly along the pavements this morning, she had the odd feeling that she had been set down in an alien city, one she had not seen before.

Sunday mornings in Paris always had a gala air to them. Shops were closed, children and parents dressed in their best going to church, and later to outings in one of the lovely Parisian parks. But this morning, although the shutters in the shopping district were closed as usual, few people were on the streets. She walked almost alone, without seeing another person for blocks at a time.

It was eerie.

From far in the distance came a muted roar, a hum like that of bees around a disturbed hive. She remembered once, when her father had taken her to view the sights at Brighton on a rare holiday, she had heard a rumbling sound much like this. Papa had told her it was the sound of the sea. But surely she could not hear the sea all the way from Paris!

She could not understand the sound. The battlefront was miles away—at least so the latest news had informed Paris. It could not be the enemy at the gates, could it? Her step faltered, and she stopped. She looked around her. There was no place to hide, no one to ask for help, no one—

She took a deep breath and then another to settle herself. It was quite impossible for the Germans to be at the gates of the city, for the entire French army lay between the enemy and the capital. She was, she told herself, on a simple errand to the vicomte—to get money for Maura. After a bit, she felt her confidence returning and walked on. Her confidence was flawed, though, for she realized that she did not in the least trust her cousin.

As she walked along toward the rue de Courcelles and the vicomte she looked back over the summer, searching for a clue to Maura's intentions, striving to convince herself that she had no need to fear for herself. Maura must have at least the basic decency to see that the two of them returned in due course and safety to London, together—

Lost in reverie, Val recalled she had found it harder and harder as the summer wore on, to distinguish one day from the next.

Maura's general had been much in evidence, although Val thought that was not quite the word. She hardly ever saw him, but, judging from Maura's frequent absences, he was still pulling the strings of Val's life from a distance.

She no longer thought that Paris was the romantic, feminine city she had believed it at first. Maura had hired a carriage, and after the *cocher* had driven Lady Thorne to her rendezvous with Raoul, he returned to drive Val as "Lady Thorne" around the Bois de Boulogne, where she could be seen publicly for two hours, very much alone.

"Wouldn't it be simpler," Val suggested once, "for me to go with you to your destination, and then go on alone to the park? The coachman would not then have to come back for me."

Maura glared at her suspiciously. "And how did you learn just where Raoul's little flat is? How do you know it is on the way to the park? No, little cousin, I think not. I've watched you, you know. You are filled with jealousy. It shows in everything you do."

"Jealousy?"

"Don't think I haven't noticed. You're always asking when I am going to him—"

"Only so I know what to plan for myself," protested Val.

"You want Raoul for yourself!"

"Ridiculous!" scoffed Val. "Why would I want him?" When, she added silently, there is Alec.

"Envy, of course. All English spinsters are alike. They would give their souls to be loved as I am." She swept Val from head to foot with a contemptuous glance. "You probably will not die a virgin. After all, you do resemble me somewhat. Sometime you may find a man of sorts. But be well advised to keep your clutching hands off my Raoul."

"Maura, you're mad!"

"By the way," Maura continued, ignoring her protests, "the coachman is not to be bribed, so do not attempt him."

"I wouldn't touch your so-called gentleman," cried Val, indignation swallowing up her caution, "for any sum you could mention. But you're living in a fool's paradise if you think he's going to be faithful to you forever."

The expression in Maura's eyes, then, turned inward. It had been mid-July when Maura so baldly accused her, and France had just declared war on Prussia. The armies were mobilizing, and it was only a matter of time before Raoul Doucet would be with his men, leaving both Clothilde and his adoring Maura to mourn his going.

"Don't worry, Maura," Val said coolly, "your Raoul is safe from me."

"Believe me," Maura said, throwing consistency to the winds, "you don't give me any qualms. Raoul loves me to distraction. He has no time for anyone else."

Without guile, Val wondered aloud, "How can he get away as often as he does? Surely he must need to be with his soldiers?"

"The army is totally ready," Maura boasted. "Mark my words, there will be no war. The Prussians are simply swaggering like little boys. Raoul is busier than before, though. Once in a while he is late. But when he comes he is more *ardent* than ever." Maura preened herself.

Val wondered now, as she drew nearer to her destination on this September morning, if it would have made any difference if she had told Maura then about the small incident she had witnessed shortly before their quarrel.

It had meant little then, but now, looking back, she could see that it held a certain significance. Maura's coachman was driving her toward her daily appearance in the Bois. Suddenly he swerved around an obstacle in the way ahead. Val glanced idly out of the window, to see what impeded them.

A carriage had stopped along the sidewalk directly in front of them, and as she looked a gentleman descended from it. She gasped in recognition. The look on Raoul's face, turned toward the passenger still inside the vehicle, held rapture mingled with masculine self-approval. Val had surmised at once that the lady within was Maura. Quickly Val turned her face away, lest Raoul catch sight of her, and accuse her of spying on Maura.

But as she was carried on her way to the daily promenade, her mind worried around the edges of the incident. Surely Raoul would not be taking his leave of Maura at that hour—she had just been taken, supposedly by her coachman, to meet him at his *pied-à-terre.* But here was Raoul, in another carriage, taking an amorous leave of *someone.*

Suppose it were Madame la Générale?

Val was amused. How very *French,* to be certain that if a man were involved romantically with some woman, that woman was positively not his wife!

She even felt a pang of sympathy for the poor general—what a tangled life he must lead, with his peremptory wife, his equally demanding English mistress, and his unknown *amour!* How many other women did he think he could satisfy?

Maura had boasted that Raoul was more passionate than ever. Val realized she was skeptical in the extreme. She noticed that Maura spent more and more time, those July days, before her mirror, with reason. The hectic pace Maura had kept, her nights with Raoul, and afternoons as well, several times a week, was taking its toll. Her skin was no longer fresh and clear, and pouches began to appear underneath her tired eyes.

If Val had been told then that, in addition to being late at times for his rendezvous with Maura, the general oftentimes did not appear at all, she would have better understood the hunted—no, *haunted* was the better word—look that flickered occasionally across her cousin's features.

Val was now, on her way to the vicomte, near enough to the Seine to see the towers of the Cathedral of Notre Dame rising to her right. The sunlight of this luminous September morning slanted at a lower angle than in midsummer, sending elongated shadows across the cobbled streets. She was hardly aware of the increasing volume of the once-distant roar she had heard. She was caught up in her mood of reminiscence. She and Maura had begun this adventure with light hearts and an eagerness to embrace whatever happy things might come to them. Little by little that comfortable companionship had eroded. Maura's intention was to use Val for her own purposes. And Val had her own secret to cherish.

In her daily ride through the park, Val had searched the fashionable crowds for a glimpse of a tall Scotsman with cold gray eyes. She would not die a virgin, as Maura, unaware of Val's secret, had said. But she might as well consider herself so, for without Alec Drummond her life would be a wasteland and unbearably lonely.

She had tasted such an emptiness during this long summer. The fashionable court had gone, early in July, to St. Cloud, following the Imperial couple, who usually spent the summers in their palace removed from the hot city. There had been no sign of Alec.

Maura had not left Paris. She might airily dismiss the threat of war with a wave of the hand, but her general was needed here in the capital, he said. The talk in the Paris salons, at least the ones Val attended in her cousin's stead, was brave enough—the armies were ready, the Prussians would find they had blundered into a hornet's nest, there would be no question of defeat since the French were invincible—

But underneath the bravado ran an ugly current of fear. Germans were spat at in the streets, and toward the middle of July, several innocent members of the German community in Paris were beaten and left for dead in the street.

Val had not tried to follow the stages of the quarrel between the two nations. She knew little about politics, and believed, rightly, that the real Lady Thorne would not be interested. There had been "the telegram," to which the French took exception. Val had been astonished then to see her history books come to life. The Gallic temperament in action meant crowds milling along the boulevards, great throngs of people roaring out the revolutionary "Marseillaise," marching along Haussmann's broad avenues like a ragged army, shouting, *"À Berlin!"*

For one fanciful moment, she could believe she stood on the Paris streets of a century before, watching the wretched, ill-fed mobs fight their way toward the Bastille. Suddenly, that day, she had been struck by a strong foreboding. She longed with all her heart for sedate London, where crowds were good-humored for the most part, at least decently behaved. Not that Londoners shied away from making their wishes known, but these crowds gave off an almost animal stench, made up of a fury and brutality far from the surface.

Paris the romantic and alluring city was showing her dirty petticoats.

On July 19, Val recalled, had come the fatal word from Saint-Cloud—the emperor had declared war on the Prussians.

Everyone said, only a couple of weeks and the French armies would be on the Rhine—a false and cruelly deceptive hope. The news from the front was bad. Maura was immovable in her determination to stay in Paris.

But yesterday, the third of September, Maura's resistance crumbled as surely as had the French at Sedan. That was the first Val had heard of Maura's acquaintance with the notorious Vicomte des Loches.

"Maura, I won't have anything to do with the vicomte. Have you forgotten? He tried to kidnap me!"

"Not you, my pet," said Maura, preening herself. "Me."

"It would have made no difference in the long run. You or me. He would have done—horrible things."

"You don't know that. In truth, Val, I wonder at your prudery. From what you told me he merely invited you to a champagne supper. What's so wrong with that?"

"If nothing was wrong with it," Val maintained stubbornly, "why would he have had to force you?"

"My dear, he would not have had to force *me*. Now then, forget it. That's all past, and whether you know it or not, we are in most uncomfortable circumstances."

"How can *he* help us?"

"You won't even have to see him. Just take a note to him, and bring back—what he gives you. Surely you can do that much, after living on my bounty all this time?"

"I've earned every penny of my keep!" flared Val. "Playing the role of the notorious Lady Thorne has not been easy!"

"But easier, I am persuaded, than clerking in a draper's shop," purred Maura, "or Newgate Gaol."

A cold shiver ran down Val's spine. Her words choked in her throat. "N-Newgate? How did you find that out?"

"You told me."

"You're lying. I told you nothing."

Maura's smile did not reach her eyes. "You told me, my pet. Just now. Did you think I would not remember when I first saw you? In the clutches of the constable, you recall, and those scraggy peasants furious at me for taking you away?"

"You don't know how it happened."

"I made inquiries, my pet. A wanton, said your Mr. Whatever—seducing him quite out of his senses. And taking money from the till!"

Val, stung, cried out, "He lied!"

"But at least he wished you in gaol. Now, my child, I shall put it frankly before us. We have no money—"

"You could sell one of those fantastic emeralds."

Maura laughed. "They are gone—sold."

"Sold—?"

"What do you think we've been living on for these months, you ungrateful wretch?"

Val sank into a chair, her knees unable to hold her. "But the general?"

"What about him?"

"He didn't pay for anything?"

"Of course not. That bitch of a wife won't let him have any money of his own."

Val tottered on the verge of hysterical laughter. Maura seemed to have no understanding of the outrageous things she was saying—imagine blaming a wife for not giving her husband funds to support a paramour, or—remembering that moment when she had seen Raoul taking amorous leave of yet another lady in a carriage—even two.

But logic had never been a part of this mad expedition. Even Val's common sense had been put away on a high shelf for the occasion, allowing Maura's headstrong will and her own romantic leanings to carry them through. Alec had shouted to her about common sense, and she should have listened to him.

"What are you going to do, Val, sit there like a duck on a pond? We've got to get out of here before the Germans come in. Do you know what they do to women?"

Drily, Val answered, "Hardly worse than what the vicomte has in mind, I imagine." She stood up. "Suppose the man gives you money, as I suppose you are asking for. What will you do then?"

Maura sensed that Val was weakening. She hastened to pursue her advantage. "Us, my dear. You do not think I shall abandon you? After all, we are cousins."

"Somehow," said Val crisply, "that does not carry much weight with me. I'll get the money. But not if I have to see the vicomte. I'll deal with an underling—"

Perhaps the captain of the vicomte's own guard—if she could just see Alec again—

"No matter, my pet. The vicomte has said he'll lend me the money."

Something in Maura's tone jarred. "What did you

promise him in return? Don't lie to me, Maura. It's going to take both of us to get out of the city and back to London. Jehane said that the trains have been jammed for days with people leaving Paris. It's no time for us to fall out. What did you promise?"

"Nothing, believe me. Except that when he gets to London, he won't find my door closed against him."

"He's coming to London?"

"Don't be skeptical. London will be overrun with *émigrés*. You have nothing to do with this, Val. It's a private agreement between the vicomte and me."

"I wish I could believe that."

"Don't argue with me now!" cried Maura. "We're on our own. We've got to get out of Paris. You don't have any money." Her expression altered. "Do you?"

"Only a little that my father left me."

"Well, then." Maura went to the window and looked out into the parched little park in the *place*. "No time to lose, Val."

It was clear enough. Maura depended on Val to rescue them, to get the funds that would provide transportation to the Channel, and passage to England. Besides, her cousin gave every sign of collapsing in sheer panic. She would do well to get Maura away as quickly as possible.

Besides all the arguments she presented to herself, she was aware of one underlying hope. If she went to the vicomte's house on the rue de Courcelles, she might have a chance to talk to Alec, one more time, to tell him she was leaving Paris.

She would get the money and come back, gather her own baggage and her hidden hoard of gold. Perhaps by nightfall, they would be in a train, or at least a carriage, on the road to the Channel.

Now, on her way to the rue de Courcelles, she walked briskly. There seemed no longer to be any need to cover her hair with an anonymous shawl to deceive the general's wife. That entire masquerade had held little in the way of romance. It was simply an exercise in indulgence of two willful persons, each used to scheming to get his own way.

She did not think she herself could have deceived a husband and helped to deceive a wife, all for a summer's love. But she had certain shame-filled memories of her own. How could she cast a stone at her cousin?

The river and the rue de Courcelles lay just ahead. The roar, now that she paid attention to it, had grown in volume. The day, which had begun in a luminous mist, had turned cloudless, a perfect day for a Sunday stroll. Usually, much of Paris would be abroad on a day like this, strolling through the parks, promenading along the sidewalks, exchanging bright greetings. She had learned one thing about the Parisians—they were inordinately proud of their city and never seemed to be done with admiring it from all angles.

But today appeared, somehow, different. Empty streets, abandoned parks— She caught sight of the first placard. *Vive la République!* But France was an empire, wasn't it? Another poster carried the answer—*À bas l'Empereur!*

She turned the corner into the rue de Courcelles and stopped short. The street was jammed with people, from sidewalk to sidewalk. It was impossible to make any headway. She believed the house she sought was halfway down the block, but she had no hopes of ever reaching it. And without the purse that Maura had persuaded her was waiting for her there, she and Maura would be virtually prisoners, unable to get out of Paris, to say nothing of returning to their homeland.

Paris was living up to its volatile reputation! One defeat, the deathly sick emperor surrendering, unable to bear the sight of further bloodshed, and all of Paris was in the streets.

The crowd, pushing and shoving impatiently before her, was on its way to some destination beyond, a goal she could not even guess at—perhaps the Hotel de Ville where the government offices were, or the Palais Bourbon where the Chambers met, the French equivalent of the Houses of Parliament?

She followed along at the rear of the moving throng, her eye on the white entrance door midway along the street, the door she guessed was her destination.

Suddenly the character of the loud throng-humming altered strangely. The rumbling of many voices was coming from behind her as well!

She wheeled to look in the direction from which she had come. And the street was full.

She had time only to notice that the men in front, all poorly dressed, looking as though they had not had time to don their Sunday suits, were advancing toward her on a front that stretched from one side of the street to the other.

It was, she thought just before she was engulfed, like a giant wave, born of some massive storm somewhere beyond sight, rearing its entire ponderous body to its full height before falling of its own weight.

The men in the front reached her, lifting her from her feet. She began to fall backward and knew that if she went down, she would never rise again—the tramping feet, the heavy boots that made the pavement tremble, would stamp out her life's breath in an instant.

She reached out blindly to save herself.

She felt rough cloth beneath her fingers, and grabbed for the fragile handhold. Hands went beneath her elbows, and although she moved her feet as though walking, she felt nothing but air beneath the thin soles of her slippers.

She was swept along on a wave of humanity that smelled strangely of garlic and unwashed garments. Also—the oddest thing!—she could *feel* the vibration of many voices, grumbling, low, unmusical, surrounding her, behind her, and ahead as they caught up with the mob preceding them.

A tune—that was it—they were singing!

The man beside her, reeking of the smell of fish, jerked her arm painfully. "Sing!" he commanded. "You a Royalist? Sing, then!"

But sing what? she wondered, and then, with her wits sharpened by desperation, she made the connection. Her voice quavered with the first words—"*Allons enfants de la patrie*"—but as she continued she grew more confident, and toward the end she was singing as loudly as the rest.

"*Qu'un sang impur—*"

One part of her mind pointed out how inappropriate it was for a modest English maiden to be joining in this frenzied exhortation to "fertilize the fields with the impure blood of the enemy!" But then, she thought, it was only French blood they were after. If her own English blood were not to flow, she must join the throng for the present. But at the first chance to escape, she must be ready to seize her opportunity. Perhaps when they reached a wider avenue—she tried to think ahead. If they reached the Concorde, that would be the best place to escape from her unwelcome companions. The broad stretches of pavement there should invite a spreading out of the crowd, and they would never miss her if she made her way to the edges of the mob, then suddenly vanished.

The great mass of people, jammed together in the narrow rue de Courcelles, flowed out of the mouth of the street and eventually reached the Place de la Concorde. She saw at once that she had badly misread the events of the day.

Far from being a small throng that could readily be encompassed in a narrow street, it looked like all of Paris was already gathered in the Concorde. She would not be surprised if the mob stretched from the chestnut trees of the Tuileries all the way to Mont-Valerian beyond the Bois de Boulogne behind her. With a sinking heart, she realized that escape was farther away than ever.

There must be tens of thousands on the march. She grabbed the man next to her for support, stood on tiptoe, and peered over the heads of those around her. There was nothing but people as far as she could see.

She tried to move, but bodies pressed against her on all sides. Far from escaping, she now found it difficult to breathe. A sense of panic arose in her. She thought she screamed, but surely she would not have shrieked, "*Aux Tuileries!* To the Tuileries!" The words became a full-throated roar, like a pride of angry lions in the Zoological Gardens.

The shouts settled into a rhythmic chant. Suddenly, the dreadful purpose of the crowd became apparent—clear and somehow contagious. Thousands advancing like one long serpentine monster, they moved ahead full of purpose.

The bright gilt eagles on the gates of the Tuileries gardens were torn away. The empress's flag on its high staff fluttered in the slight breeze, and then descended, for the last time. The gates to the Tuileries gardens were as a rule locked, Val knew. The mob would be defeated at last—

Val was aware of the events of the next hour as though a nightmare unfolded itself for her particular attention—and horror. She was jostled and shoved, barely able to keep her footing. Elbows struck her head, and once a beldam hit her on the shoulder, for no reason, with a stout stick. She no longer saw the people around her as factory workers, shopkeepers, women and children. They had turned into howling imps, dancing around some amusing enterprise of destruction.

The senseless devastation had its own horrendous fascination.

The gates of the ornamental railings dividing the Tuileries Gardens from the Place de la Concorde, securely locked, were no match for the pressure of thousands of bodies. They gave way, and the first-comers scrambled desperately to stay on their feet, against the thrust of the mob behind them. They almost fell on the second line of railings, protecting the private gardens. The railings fell like straw before the reaper.

It must be midafternoon by now, thought Val disjointedly. What was Maura doing now? She would be furious when Val did not appear with the purse of gold she had been sent for. But Maura's anger could be dealt with later. Just now, Val's struggles were bent with single-minded intensity toward getting toward the edge of the mob that engulfed her.

The rioting Parisians, intoxicated by their success, now took up a chant that must have struck a cold chill in the empress if she were still within the palace.

"*Dé-ché-ance! À bas l'Espagnole!* Down, down with the Spanish woman!"

The shouts thrummed rhythmically, like the pulse of a great monster bent on destroying the empire that had betrayed their hopes. Val thought if only she could use this rocking beat— She swayed with her neighbors like a clock pendulum, gaining a little headway on each return to her right, an inch or so, and sometimes as much as half a yard, sidling between bodies intent on reaching the great doors of the palace.

She was making progress, but slowly, too slowly! She glanced back once, to measure how far she had come. Someone gripped her arm with iron fingers! She turned, gasping with pain and fright.

"What are you doing here?" demanded Alec Drummond.

Instantly nettled, she retorted, "What does it look like? I'm going to burn down the palace, of course!"

"Hush!" he said fiercely. "All they need is to hear the word, and they'll be doing it within the hour."

"Don't think I can tell them anything they don't know," she said. "They're the experts."

Without her noticing, Alec had pulled her the rest of the way to the edge of the crowd. Suddenly she realized she was free of the nightmare. She began to shake and could not stop.

"Oh, Alec! Alec!"

"Come on," he said urgently. He put his arm around her and pulled her with him. "We've got to get out of here."

She had a confused notion that they moved along the sections of railing that had not yet fallen. Then, it seemed that another man came along to take her other arm, and they were running, running—

They were inside the palace. "Hold up a moment,"

said the newcomer. She recognized him without surprise—Lord Ronald Gower, an Englishman visiting Paris, whom she had met several times.

"Lady Thorne," he said, "my compliments. I cannot conceive how you came to be caught up in that—that unbelievable *thing* out there, for one cannot call them human beings. But, old man," he added, turning to Alec, "I cannot think you wish to linger here? I should not like to take my chances on that pair of doors holding. Must get Lady Thorne out, right?"

"I agree. I wonder if the empress is still here. I would not give a groat for her life, if they find her."

"Not our immediate problem, Captain," Lord Ronald pointed out. "This lady—a bird in the hand, you know. Reminds me of what that Carlyle fellow wrote about the French Revolution." He stopped to consider, and added judiciously, "The first one that is, for if this isn't another revolution, I'll be—" He glanced at Val. "That is, I'll be much surprised."

"That bunch out there's getting closer," said Alec.

"Right you are," said Lord Ronald. "Time to move on."

They hurried through rooms Val hardly recognized. The emptiness and the signs of a hurried departure made them sadly altered.

She glimpsed a toy sword halfway out of its scabbard, dropped on a sofa. There were empty jewel cases tossed on a table in a small withdrawing room, side by side with a Sevres plate holding some small crusts of bread and a half-eaten egg.

Once they entered a room where a pair of servants were scuttling out a door in the opposite wall. Lord Ronald spoke swiftly to them and nodded in satisfaction at their answer. "The empress has just left, only moments ago, according to these fellows."

Alec glanced behind him. "That crash—"

"They've broken down the doors," said Lord Ronald calmly. "Look, you take Lady Thorne and I'll stay here—"

"You won't have a chance," Alec said urgently.

"Nor will you if you don't move on, my dear chap. I'll just slip through to the Palais Royale. No problem if I go now."

He vanished in the wake of the two servants before she could even thank him. Alec grabbed her wrist. "Come on, Val, for God's sake!"

He took her hand and they ran through the dusty, littered halls of the palace. Alec had, in his employment, learned the little corridors, the secret staircases, the obscure side doors of the palaces.

She ran with him, losing track of the many turns they made into side corridors, through small rooms and large, the draperies adorned with the Imperial *N* and eagles. How long would they last under the furious hands of the invading Parisians?

They came at last to a plain door that stood ajar at the end of a stark passageway.

"Thank God," muttered Alec. "I was afraid this door would be locked. But the key's still in it."

"Suppose the empress came this way?"

Alec nodded absently. "Quickly, Val." She heard the sound of running feet behind them. "Alec!" she breathed. He hustled her through the door, taking the key out of the lock, and locking it behind them. "That will give us a minute or two."

She knew where they were now. They had left the Tuileries and were now standing in the deserted Louvre. They hurried through the empty Great Gallery and the Pavilion of Apollos. When they reached the Hall of the Seven Chimneys, they stopped. She had a stitch in her side, but she stifled her groan. They were nowhere near out of danger yet.

Alec let her rest while he prowled the room, looking cautiously out of the lancet windows onto the street. She watched him, wondering how he had ever found her in the confusion outside. His hard lean body held the strength of a coiled spring, and she recalled just how those iron muscles of his back had felt under her stroking fingers, how warm his demanding lips could be, seeking her response—

She shook her head to clear her mind of memories best left forgotten. Alec was only concerned with her because she was a helpless Englishwoman lost in the midst of a foreign revolution. He had told her she had no common sense, that he had nothing but contempt for her idiocy. He had pointed out the essential dishonesty of her role in her cousin's masquerade, hitting too near the mark for her to forgive him. The quarrel that had erupted so swiftly between them had deepened, by neglect, into an abyss.

The thought came to her that, if she were never to see him after today, if she could not spend her days with him, then she did not care whether she lived or died.

"Let's go!" said Alec, unaware of her depression, but rousing her back to the immediacy of the present dilemma they now shared.

They hurried down wide steps into the Egyptian Museum. He guided her to their right, toward a side door. "This is the only way the empress could have come. I hope it is still safe."

The door was, fortunately, unlocked. They emerged on an empty cobbled square. Across the way was the small church of St. Germain l'Auxerrois. The crowd's chant had not ceased, but the vast bulk of the palace succeeded in muting the sound so that it did not seem dangerous. But the comparative peace was illusory.

She sobbed for breath, and he stopped at last. "I think we're safe enough for the moment," he said. "That bunch will sing and tear things up for a few hours yet before they spread out over the city."

"But what will I do? How will we get out of Paris?" She spoke more to herself than to her companion.

"What did you intend to do?" he demanded with interest. "You surely weren't trying to get out of Paris when I saw you. What on earth possessed you to join that mob?"

"I didn't join the mob. They joined me," she protested. "I was simply doing an errand for Maura—" At the sight of his suddenly grim expression, her voice died away. She should never have mentioned her cousin, she knew. Clearly the quarrel that had erupted all those weeks ago still lay like an open wound between her and Alec.

"An errand for her, to des Loches? I see."

"You don't see at all," wailed Val. She was conscious now of an unbelievable fatigue. She did not think she could take another step. But she felt shriveled beneath Alec's scorching gaze. No matter what it cost her, she would not take any more help from him. She started to walk away from him.

"You little fool!" he snarled as he caught up with her. "Where do you think you're going?"

"Back to the apartment," she informed him coolly. "Maura will be wondering where I am."

"I should like to see that scene. I'll come along with you. You think she intends to leave Paris?"

"Of course. That's why I went—where I went," she said. "She was to get the railroad tickets while I—" She broke off. "Why should I tell you anything? You loathe me. I know you rescued me. As I remember, you set great store by being thanked. Thank you, Captain Drummond. And now you can leave me alone, having done your duty."

"Why do you always rip me up? I suppose it's delayed reaction from your revolutionary activities of today. I confess I was surprised to see you shouting slogans with the best of them."

She had had enough of small talk, of petty fighting with him. How close was love to hate? Sometimes it was hard to tell them apart. She was sure she hated him now, for his contemptuous superiority, for his moralistic judgments regarding her lack of intelligence and Maura's lack of integrity. It did not help her to realize that he was right.

As her thoughts jumbled together she knew that she owed him this day her very life. Without thinking, she reached her hand out toward him. He took it at once, enveloping it in his own warm, comforting fingers.

They crossed the Boulevard Saint-Germain and hurried southwest away from the river behind them along the rue de Rennes, and then more westerly along the rue de Vaugirard. Then they plunged into the mass of small streets lying between Vaugirard and the railroad lines that terminated in the Gare Mont-Parnasse. "Maura was to get our tickets at the other station," Val told him, "the Gare Saint-Lazare? To go to the coast."

"You still trust her then? After all she's done to you?"

"Who else should I trust?" she demanded hotly, and an uncomfortable silence fell between them.

It seemed only moments before they were approaching the archway over the street leading into the small *place*. He held her back as a pair of horses emerged pulling a heavy carriage and then turned in the opposite direction from them.

As the carriage moved past them, slowing for the turn, she caught sight of the occupants. The veiled passenger on her side turned directly toward Val. Val's cry of recognition held shock, then anger, and finally disappointed rage.

"Maura! And she's not going to stop!"

Alec's hand under Val's elbow steadied her. "That woman was veiled. Are you sure?"

She turned on him, her sapphire eyes blazing. "If you dare to say I told you so," she hissed, "I will quite simply strike you!"

"I will tell you nothing you don't already know," he said gravely. He looked down the street after the vanishing carriage. "What will you do now?"

She hesitated, torn by indecision and a woeful longing to throw herself into his arms and surrender to her despair. She would have cursed the day that Maura found her had she had been able to put her mind to it. But there were other things to do first.

"Maybe Jehane is upstairs. Maybe Maura left a note for me."

She knew her voice wavered, echoing her doubts. But she crossed the *place*, aware of Alec following her, and climbed the stairs to the top floor.

The door was not locked. She entered hesitantly, not

quite knowing what to expect. There were signs of hasty departure, much like the disorder she had seen in the Tuileries, not an hour since. Unwashed dishes on the counter in the kitchen, beds unmade.

"But where is Jehane?"

"The second woman in the carriage, I believe."

"I didn't see— There's no note."

"Naturally," he said with perfect calm. He appeared to have made up his mind not to quarrel with her, she thought, and she suddenly felt strangely alone. It was as though he no longer cared anymore, if he ever had.

"Perhaps the bedroom—"

She disappeared down the short hall. There was no note. Even worse, there was no sign of Val's two guineas. Of course not, for how had Maura hired the carriage if she were as penniless as she had pretended? Val's two guineas had trotted off down the street moments ago, she was sure.

She should have felt desolate. In a strange, riot-torn city, alone, without funds save for the few coins at the bottom of her purse—fortunately, she had saved that. She fumbled at her belt. The purse was still there, miraculously, after all the shoving and hurly-burly jostling by the mob.

"Find anything?" It was Alec's voice from the living room. "We'd better hurry."

We—what a wonderful word. Suddenly her spirits lifted illogically. "Coming!"

When she reappeared, she carried a cloak and a shawl over her arm. She had tucked as many of her toiletries as possible into her pockets. "I'm ready, Alec. Where are we going?"

He looked at her without speaking. She could not read the expression on his thin face. Had he been ill this past month? Suddenly shy beneath his concentrated gaze, she mumbled, "Perhaps my portmanteau—"

"No!" he said sharply. "I don't fancy walking down the road with a straw carry-all."

"W-walking?"

"Who knows?" he countered. "I take it she didn't leave any money?"

She detected a critical note in his voice and immediately turned defensive. "I have a little of my own. Here in my pocket. I trust it will be sufficient to serve as a retainer for your services as guide. If not, I shall remit the balance when I arrive in London."

A rash promise, if ever there was one, she thought, but she could no more control her temper with him than take wing from the apartment window and fly to Deauville. He was not deceived by her pretentious air. His lips twitched, but all he said was, "Let's go."

He flagged down a passing carriage when they again reached the rue de Vaugirard. Val was surprised when the coachman stopped, but if she had seen, as the *cocher* did, the heavy pistol in Alec's belt, she would have understood.

The streets then passed by as though in a dream. This western part of the city was new to her. They turned right on the Boulevard Victor and crossed the river again. By devious turnings they emerged on the Boulevard Murat, then turned left after a bit through the Porte d'Auteuil, a gate in the feudal wall that still surrounded the city.

Traffic was light, and most of the travel was headed toward the city. Their way lay along the southern edge of the Bois de Boulogne, where Val had driven in Lady Thorne's place every day for weeks. Surely that had all been a dream—or perhaps her present journey was not real. Of the two, she would rather be here with Alec, knowing nothing of what lay ahead, just content to ride beside him in the closed carriage forever.

Forever was impossible. Suddenly her dreamy idyll was cut short when the coachman pulled his horse to a halt. "No more, monsieur. No matter you shoot me here, I go no more."

Alec jumped to the ground and strode forward to argue with the coachman. At length he came back. "Sorry, my dear. This is as far as we ride, for a while at least."

He helped her to the ground. She looked around her, concealing her dismay. The night light, that blue luminosity of a Parisian twilight, was deepening. In an hour, it would be too dark even to walk along a well-defined road. "Where are we?" she said just above a whisper.

"That's the river ahead of us—"

"We crossed it once."

"Ah, but it curves back again. Don't give up, Val. I know where we are."

Chapter Thirteen

They crossed the Seine twice more, hurrying, as Alec said, to make the most of the remaining light. They had walked through the small town of Saint-Cloud, seeing the jutting towers of the emperor's summer palace rising above the trees to their right.

They walked fast for nearly an hour. Somewhere beyond the town, fatigue came down around Val like a smothering gray blanket. It seemed to her that they had been traveling for hours. Riots and tumult still beat upon her thoughts. It seemed she had not slept for at least a month, and she could not remember when she had last eaten.

That very morning, though it seemed an eternity ago, she had been living in another world, one of peace and order, a world she knew.

Her feet dragged because she could not summon the will or the strength to pick them up. Alec had held her hand, urging her forward when she lagged behind him. Now, she could go no farther. At least she had to catch her breath.

Pulling her hand from his, she let him go on ahead. She moved, hands outstretched before her, toward a dark pillar-shaped object, hoping it was a tree. It was, and she leaned against the trunk, closing her eyes because she lacked effort to hold her lids open.

She pulled air into her lungs in great, shuddering breaths. She would be surprised if the stitch in her side did not return before long. Her legs felt like lead, and she doubted she could ever set them in motion again. If she could just stay here, leaning heavily against the tree, for a week, she might be ready—

She knew when Alec came back to find her. The clean fragrance of his soap was strong, and she opened her eyes. She could see him faintly against the dark greenery along the road behind him. He was not looking at her but instead was peering intently down the road ahead of them.

The road itself was hardly more than a carriage track, the ruts thick and soft with summer dust. She realized suddenly that night had not fallen, as she had thought. The darkness was simply because the lane was bordered in tall grass, protected as well by heavily leafed trees coming together overhead to form an ever-shifting ceiling.

How far they had come from Paris! And how infinitely farther had she traveled from the company of her cousin. She summoned up that last glimpse of Maura, at the arched mouth of the street leading from the square where they had lived in comparative friendship, even at times with affection, for the past four months—Maura, heavily veiled in the carriage, looking directly at Val, deliberately turning away and traveling on, abandoning the cousin she believed was without funds or friends.

It was small wonder, though, that Maura, never the most courageous of women, had fled in panic before the crowds. The mobs of Paris had been transformed before Val's eyes into a savage animal with many ravening heads. She remembered now that she had recognized Maura's coachman, that cousin of Jehane's who had often driven Val through the streets of the capital. Val tried to recall—the shadowy figure beside Maura, the one Alec had seen—was it Jehane? It was more than likely.

Val gave it up. She had been so stunned to see her cousin hurtling past, not stopping to pick her up, that she hadn't noticed much else. She had not believed that Maura would abandon her. Even now, she sought excuses for her cousin's selfishness.

No matter that she now knew that Maura thought only of herself, that she had used Val shamelessly for her own ends—nonetheless, her one-time joy at finding one relative, when she had believed herself alone in the world, was hard to erase.

That one relative, she realized sadly, had plunged her into a world of deceit and lust, of gambling, vice, of manipulating other people without conscience. Surely one relative was enough. What state might she be in now supposing she had found more than one like Maura?

But the loss of her dream, wispy as it had been, cut her like a knife turning slowly in her breast. She felt the tears sliding down her cheeks. As though he sensed her distress, Alec turned to her. "We can't stay here. Can you go on now?"

She did not know how she could. But she forced a smile and told him, "Yes, Alec."

He peered at her in the dusky light. She knew he didn't believe her, but they had to keep going until they found a safe place. It was out of the question to take a train—

She thought she heard the words only in her mind, but then she realized that Alec had spoken aloud. "If your cousin does manage to get aboard a train, crowded as it will be with refugees fleeing Paris," he continued, "she may be recognized."

"As Lady Thorne?"

"That doesn't matter. She is clearly English, and arrogant, and her title will do nothing for her. You haven't forgotten those mobs so soon?"

He spoke in a terse manner, as though he were directing his energy toward one goal of vital importance. She remembered the mobs crying *"À bas!"* to everyone. *À bas* the empress! Val hoped she had escaped from the palace. She realized that Alec and Lord Ronald had guessed they were only moments behind Eugénie and her party. If only the mobs hadn't remembered the rear doors to the palace, and been in time to block them! But perhaps the empress had preceded them to that quiet square, and thus escaped.

À bas the English—for not coming to France's rescue in her war with Prussia. Down with all foreigners, for some might be Germans! *À bas* the monarchy, the Bonapartes, the rich, the priests, the Americans—

She began to recognize the miraculous good fortune that had brought Alec to her rescue, with his quick wits and his strength, and his knowledge of the city and its people.

He had started down the road without her. She hurried, running a few steps to catch up with him. She could not feel her feet, but at least they did not pain her. He reached back to take her hand and added his strength to hers. They walked down the road. Alec looked over his shoulder from time to time, but there was no one in sight. The grass verges gave way to high hedges and then to a wall of trees. If someone did pursue them, there would be no way to escape at least as far as the curve ahead.

They had almost reached the bend in the road when Alec stopped. He studied the wall of greenery along the left side of the road.

"Do you know where we are?" she asked. "Are you looking for something?" She spoke automatically in a whisper. She did not know why, for there was no one to overhear.

He nodded. "Right in here there should be—ah, here it is!"

He pushed branches away, careful not to break any to give sign that someone had passed this way. At length he grunted with satisfaction. Hidden in the hedge was a small wooden gate, no more than a yard high. Long disused, the shrubbery had overgrown it and hidden the once-used path that led away into the woods beyond.

"The hinges will be too rusty to work by this time, Val. Here, I'll put you over."

He slid one arm around her shoulders, bent to slip the other beneath her knees and lifted her easily over the gate. He followed her by only a step. She moved and felt her skirt tear, caught on some shrub.

While he was restoring displaced tree limbs to their former position, giving no hint of their intrusion, she looked around her. Judging by the gate, they were clearly in someone's private park. They stood amidst a growth of medium-sized trees. There must have been a path through these woods, but it was not visible now, at least in the dusk. But Alec was clearly familiar with these grounds.

"Where are we?" she asked when he again stood beside her.

He did not answer her at once. He placed his hands on her forearms and turned her to face him. His deep-set eyes searched her face, seeking some reassurance in her features, perhaps even some sign that she had sufficient courage for the task ahead. She did not know what he needed from her, but whatever it was, he seemed satisfied.

Slowly he bent to her, pulling her closer to him, and gently placed his lips, moving slightly, on hers. With an effort she could sense in his body, he pulled away, but he did not release her. "My darling Val," he said, amusement in his voice, "I am surprised that you have trusted me this far."

I could do nothing else, she thought, but knew at once that if she had been given a choice, she would still be standing here in the darkness with him, wishing the moment just past had not ended.

"Where are we?" she wondered.

"I'll tell you later. Just now, you must do as I say." She nodded agreement. "We will go in that direction, away from the road. I will lead. Make no sound whatever, if you can help it."

"Is it far?"

"Not far. It is possible that there may be people somewhere ahead of us. Would you like me to scout ahead to find out?"

"And leave me? Never."

They were speaking in whispers, so low that their words were inaudible a few feet away. Nonetheless, his next words were even more hushed. "Never, I promise." He turned and moved in the direction he had indicated.

Val, clothing torn, almost penniless, no place in the world to go and with a very precarious future, followed Alec with the highest spirits she had felt since she had come to Paris.

She could not see where they were going. Indeed, she did not much care. Her horizon had diminished to the broad tweed back moving ahead of her, along with the terrible need to make no sound at all.

Leave her never! The words sang in her head, and once she looked quickly around in alarm, fearing that her thoughts were loud enough to ring out through the woods.

When Alec stopped abruptly ahead of her, she could not stop quickly enough, and she bumped into him. Her eyes stung from the sudden sharp pain in her nose, and she must have made a sound, for he put his hand out behind him in an urgent gesture of silence.

She closed her eyes against the smarting tears and listened. There was nothing—not even a bird-song, but she remembered that this was September, when most birds hushed. There was not even a dog barking in the distance. At length, satisfied, Alec moved ahead, more cautiously than before.

A building loomed on their right. Before she had time to wonder at it, Alec veered toward it, found a narrow door in the side wall, and vanished within.

She felt desperately alone. She swallowed hard, to rout the scream that quivered in her throat. And Alec, blessedly, reappeared and beckoned her to him. He closed the door behind them, silently, and shut out the night.

She recognized the smell that came to her, a mixture

of hay and axle grease, of ancient bran mashes and the unmistakable odor of horses. They must be in a building that in England would likely be called a carriage house—and apparently abandoned.

If she could see now what she would see in the morning, she might have shuddered. But although the familiar aroma spoke of long disuse, she could not see the great cobwebs, heavy with accumulated dust, hanging from the corners of the building.

"What is this place?" she asked. Her voice sounded hollow in the empty building.

"It's a barn on the grounds of the vicomte's summer estate. Nobody's used it for years. They used to store carriages here, but they built other stables, more convenient. We'll be safe here."

For how long? she wondered. Wisely, she did not put her doubts into words. He had rescued her from real peril and had charged himself with her safety. She would do nothing to burden him further.

But she did wish to know their plans—his plans, she should have said. She certainly had no intention of trotting along beside him like a faithful retriever, stopping on command, brought to heel—

She marveled at the little flame of rebellion that flared up in her from time to time. She preferred to call it mature independence. She thought darkly that she knew what Alec would term it—female stubbornness.

She was exhausted from the day, the flight, the long walk, the terrors that flickered around her and clouded her thoughts. But Alec had said he wouldn't leave her, and she would soon return to herself again—when she had sat down a while, and especially if she had something to eat.

He touched her shoulder and pointed. In the darkness, she made out, nailed to one of the hewn wooden pillars that held up the roof, a series of ladder-rungs ascending into the mow. "Up with you."

It was certainly not the first haymow she had ever seen, but it was without doubt one of the highest. Who knew what might be concealed in the hay, what variety of vermin had crawled in to nest for the winter?

"Up," repeated Alec. Blindly setting aside for the moment her resolve not to do his bidding, she handed him her cloak and shawl. She picked up her skirt with one hand and, reaching up to higher rungs to pull herself up, began to climb into the mow.

The haymow was far from full. He followed her and made a hollow in the center of the sweet-smelling hay. "Put your cloak down first," he ordered, "it will be more comfortable." When she was settled, he added, "it may be cold later, but—I'll take care of that."

His meaning escaped her. The silence of the barn, the faint starlight filtering in through a slatted window far over her head, gave her the comfortable knowledge that she was safe, able to rest at last in a cave that her rescuer—her one-time lover—had provided.

"I'm hungry." The words surprised her as much as they did him. She had not meant to complain.

He grinned. "So am I." He touched her shoulder. "Lean back and rest," he said. "I'll be back." He crawled on hands and knees as far as the edge of the mow, and then, descending the ladder, he was gone from her sight.

Replete with the crusty French bread and the cheese that Alec had brought back with him—the best food she had ever eaten, she informed him—she leaned back against the soft hay. "Sleep if you can," he told her. "Tomorrow—could be as hard as today was."

She knew he was right. Worn out with the day's fatigue, she slept heavily for half an hour. She woke then with a start. It took a moment or two before she knew where she was. When she fully came to herself and realized she was lying in an abandoned haymow somewhere in France, without a home, with only the garments, now slightly torn and soiled, that she now wore, and with nowhere to go, she gasped involuntarily. Too late, she remembered she was not alone in the barn.

Cautiously she turned her head toward him, fearing

she had awakened him. Even in the darkness, she could see the shine of his opened eyes.

"You're awake," he said softly.

"Yes. Can't you sleep, either?"

"Not very sleepy, I guess." He reached out and found her hand. "What are you thinking, my dear?"

"What will happen tomorrow. What I'll do when we get to England. I'm so confused—"

He raised himself on his elbow and looked down at her. The moon must have risen, she thought, because it's lighter, I can see his face, how gentle he looks—

"Don't be," he told her. "Don't worry about what's past."

It came to her in a flash that he was not talking about the riots in the broad avenues of Paris yesterday. Nor was he referring to her bad judgment in trusting the cousin she resembled so much and had longed to love.

He set her hand gently away and laid his palm softly on her cheek. Then she knew he was remembering, as she was with the sweetness belonging to things past that will never come again, that afternoon on the ferry.

No one could ever take her virginity again, with gentleness or with anger. No one, not even Alec, could bring her to that first surprising recognition of her own vulnerability, of her first, trembling steps into the blissful mystery that bound, even while it separated, a man and a woman. A certain woman and a very special man—

The sigh that escaped her lips, that he felt warmly on his cheek, was ragged, full of anguish, of pain that ripped through his own heart as well as hers. He had done the unforgivable to her, and yet he would always cherish the sweet memory of her submission, of her loving generosity to him. She had woven herself into his dreams, and into his life. He dared not, for his salvation, let her go again.

He remembered the cold hand that had clutched his heart that very day when, after retrieving his weapons, and the small amount of money he had in his room at the vicomte's house in the rue de Courcelles, he had stepped out of the front door, amazed at the mobs in the street. To his horror, he had seen the crowd pick up the slight figure with the magnificent, unmistakable bronze hair and sweep her away, as tiny and helpless as a dried leaf on the current.

The dreadful fear that had driven him to find her then was only now beginning to recede. He had found her, true, but they were still in an alien land, a country where the English were presently being blamed for the French army's defeat—"If the English had come to the rescue, we would have won the battle, and Paris, the center of the civilized world, would have been saved!" They were a long way from the Channel and safety.

The days ahead could be as dangerous as the day just past. Without money and without friends, the road to Deauville fairly bristled with perils.

But they were safe for now. It might be, he thought, that these few hours were all that Providence was to allow them. An infinite sadness stirred within him.

"Val?"

In the gathering moonlight, she turned to him.

His fingers tucked her hair behind her ear, smoothing it, caressing her forehead with delicate strokes. Then, bending, he found her lips. Nervously she made as though to move away, but, though her mind commanded, her lips clung to his, tasting the lingering sweetness of bread on his tongue, before he drew away.

Her arms went shyly around his neck, and he let her pull him down across her breasts. He murmured something into her throat—a sound like a great cat purring, she thought—while his lips nibbled wetly along her jaw. The touch of his teeth gently on her earlobe seemed to stir a coiled spring deep inside her and she cried out softly.

Never again would come that first time, she had thought. But she had never dreamed the second time might be sweeter.

She felt cool air on her breasts and knew that he had drawn her frock down to bare them. His hands moved constantly on her breasts, with butterfly touches teasing the nipples into hardness.

She could not remember whether she had helped his awkward hands remove the rest of her clothing, her pale yellow muslin dress, her starched petticoats. But somehow she was naked before him, glad of it and obscurely proud.

With a couple of movements, he thrust his own garments out of his way. When he turned back to her, there was no barrier between their flesh. She felt his body slide warmly along hers, fitting himself to the curve of her hips, the length of his thigh paired, matching, to hers.

Even though she was aware that his nakedness was joined with hers, limb for limb along their entire length, yet she knew nothing but the movement, incessant, soft, yet masterfully demanding, of his hands. His fingers moved delicately, constantly, over her, bringing the flesh of her breasts to a tingling heat of desire before his hands slid downward, lingering over the tiny cup of her navel.

His eyes followed his hands gliding over her smooth flesh, opalescent in the mysterious golden light from the high window. He heard her soft sigh, and turned greedily to her, taking possession of her mouth. He nibbled at her lower lip, endlessly moving back and forth until she gasped for breath. His tongue thrust into her mouth then, a forerunner of another invasion yet to come.

His lips moved purposely into the hollow at the base of her throat. He threw one leg across her thighs and cupped her breasts in both hands, before he bent to kiss the hardening nipples, to suck them and then tantalize with his ceaselessly moving tongue.

She was burning. Every nerve was taut with expectation. Even her skin seemed to clamor for him. It was as though she stood somewhat aside, watching her body, greedy for love, respond to his, hearing her breathing become shallower, surprised to feel her body arching to meet his, her palms holding his face tenderly between them, stroking, holding his dear head close to her.

If her conscience stirred, she was not aware of it. She only knew the craving desire of her body to take him into her, to hold his maleness safe within her until they were truly one flesh.

She could not bear the excruciating tension. She moved from side to side seeking ease, but it did not come. "Alec, please!" She heard herself pleading with him. "Help me!"

He moved over her then, placing down his long body carefully to fit her, settling down on her with a sigh of comfort and desire for her.

She felt his manhood harden against her, and suddenly she felt she possessed the secrets of the universe, the stars sang around her, and she felt enlarged to the limits of the earth—

She—and she alone at this moment—could ease her lover's anguish. She, and she only, could fold him within her, feel his mad, irresistible thrusting, and know that he belonged to her, and she to him. She held him fast in her heart. And she did not know how she knew this. All the wisdom of all the women in the world was hers, this night.

She pressed herself upward against his hard chest, feeling the exquisite pain of the pressure against her sensitive nipples. She put her arms around his neck, lifting her face to claim his lips. Her hands slid down over his broad, powerful shoulders, pressing her fingers hard into his flesh. Deliberately she lifted her hips and moved them slightly, rhythmically, from side to side.

He grew suddenly very still. He pulled his mouth away from hers and looked down into the dark pools of her eyes.

"I was a fool," he said at last, his voice a mere breath in the dark. "Before—when I thought you were—someone else."

A shiver ran up her back, although the night was warm. "Now I'm the fool?"

"I want you to want me." When she did not answer

at once, he tasted again the sweetness of her lips, but, mingled with his overwhelming desire for her, came a haunting and bitter conviction that all his days had gone wrong.

He moved to slide away from her, in his grievous disappointment, but her arms held him all the tighter. Bursting with glad surmise, he whispered, "Shall I stay, then?"

Suddenly her new-found wisdom allowed her the luxury of mischief. "No, darling Alec. Don't stay. Come even closer." She opened her thighs, willingly, inviting to him.

With a glad cry that was muffled in her thick hair, he entered her, but far more gently than that first time—her very first time. He slid into her slowly, inexorably, thickly. She felt poised on the brink of a precipice—one more moment, one more movement of her would send her crashing over the edge. She felt the waves beginning to build in her, the ripples widening around his pounding deep within her like the surface of a lake disturbed by a tossed stone—but more, much more violent than that.

She lingered, poised on a knife edge of anticipation, her whole being centered on his deliberate movements—his rhythm insistent, demanding, engulfing her. Her body answered him, matching him beat for beat, until they moved together as one flesh.

She clutched him tightly, desperately, as he swung her with him somewhere out beyond the stars until they fell together, one body fused together, in an ecstasy beyond believing.

Chapter Fourteen

They had been walking since daybreak.

Val moved in a kind of dream. It was quite beyond belief that only yesterday she had been safely inside the flat that she shared with Maura, facing an obscure square containing a dying plane tree in its garden island.

She wondered now how she could have been so naïve as to believe that, simply because she was an Englishwoman, she was invulnerable to hurt. She rubbed the hurting place on her shoulder. This morning, as she had dressed, she had become aware of the darkening flesh, throbbing with pain.

She thought back and vaguely recalled the incident that must have caused the bruise—a sharp blow, like a thrown rock, hitting her. But she had been at that moment in real danger of losing her life, and the occurrence had passed without notice. But Alec had come, and then Lord Ronald, to rescue her from the irrepressible tide of angry Parisians behind her.

Alec noticed her discomfort. "You're in pain? Did I—"

The night just passed was on his mind as well as hers, she thought, gratified. "No, Alec," she said quickly. "I think I got hurt by that terrible mob. It's only a bruise."

The road ahead of them stretched out straight and narrow. They had left the barn, veiled by the mists of another golden dawn, and crept through the coppice the way they had come, over the small gate and into the road. She had brushed the hay from her gown as well as she could, and then put her cloak on, grateful for its warmth against the early morning chill. The night's dew on the small weeds in the woods had dampened her skirts. She could feel the hem of her cloak heavy against her ankles as she walked.

She was acutely aware of the man who walked beside her. Even with her eyes open she could still see in her mind his narrow face bending over her, searching her eyes to discover her thoughts. The first time, on the ferry, he had believed her to be Maura Thorne, practiced, far from innocent—in fact, very near to an unpaid prostitute.

Now he knew who she was. But, although he might wish that first violation of her undone, she shrewdly understood that, had he not already breached her virginity, the bliss of the night just past would not have come to her.

Instead, he would have, with strong self-discipline, moved far enough away from her in the haymow so that she would feel private and safe from him, but not so distant that she might feel alone and abandoned.

He had been watching her covertly from the corners of his eyes. Now he asked, "What are you smiling about?"

"I don't really know," she told him, although she knew well enough.

Belatedly, she recognized that, while he surely recalled their night of love with as much pleasure as she did, he had turned his thoughts to the needs of the moment. Judging from his frown, he was worried.

"We're still in danger, aren't we?"

He nodded. "You can't walk all the way to Deauville," he told her, "and there's no assurance we can find a boat to take us across to England."

"Why aren't we going to Calais, then, and taking the ferry?"

"Because the ferries will be watched. It's not safe."

She did not understand. He had unconsciously lengthened his stride, so that she was forced to run a few steps to catch up with him. "Watched? Why? For English? I'd think they'd want us all out of the country if they dislike us so much."

He looked at her sharply. "That hair of yours—can't you cover it up?"

Abruptly the joyous love for him that sang in her veins turned into active loathing. She stopped in the center of the road. "Captain Drummond," she began firmly.

"Spare me your displays of temperament," he told her. "Are you coming, or not?"

"I should like to know where we are going, sir," she said icily. "I should like to know, as well, why I must cover my hair—that same hair that you told me once was too glorious to be hidden—and I should also like to know why you—" Her voice broke and she bit her lower lip hard to keep it from trembling. Why had he turned against her this morning, when he had been so—so wonderful last night? What had she done? How had she offended him?

Something of her distress reached him. He came back and put one arm around her, pulling her to him. His other hand pressed her head to his shoulder. "Don't you really know?" he murmured.

"Know wh-what?"

He suppressed a sigh. He could not expect his sheltered darling to understand what worried him. He had developed the habit of reticence in his employment here in France. He dared not exhibit his loathing for his vice-ridden employer, nor his growing contempt for most things French. It would be hard to find words now, to explain to Val his fears for her, but on a deep level of understanding he realized that she deserved from him nothing but honesty. Suppose, he worried, that something happened to him so that he could not go all the way with her, to keep her safe, to watch out for her well-being? She needed to know certain things—

"Come here," he said gently. "Do you mind sitting on the grass? Spread your shawl."

He led her the few short steps to the grassy bank bordering the dirt track they had been traveling. When she was comfortable, he dropped to sit beside her.

"Now, my dear, listen. You know that the mobs were howling for the empress's blood yesterday. You heard them, and you know how close they were behind us." She nodded impatiently. "You know then how much the French hate the empress, because she is Spanish, and—for many other reasons, I suppose."

"But she got away from the palace, you thought?"

"But she'll not be safe until she is no longer on French soil."

She held her hands tightly in her lap, to keep from reaching for him, from seeking reassurance in his touch that she was safe, that she was loved. Today's Alec bore no resemblance to her lover of last night.

"What has the empress to do with me— Oh!"

He nodded. "You see it, then. That hair of yours is nowhere near the reddish color of Eugenie's, but it is close enough to deceive a nation of dark-haired, dark-eyed Frenchmen."

"You think they would mistake me for *her?*"

He agreed. "They destroy first and ask questions later."

She was silent for a long time, turning his idea over in her mind. "But then, if Maura left Paris, she's in danger too."

"Let's not worry about Maura. Surely you don't have any idea we should hurry to warn her?" His voice was harsh.

"I know you don't like her," she began, "but she's been good to me."

She reached into her pocket to find the scarf she had snatched up in that brief moment in the apartment, after Maura had treacherously gone off in her own carriage.

He nodded approval. "You do believe me then."

She was troubled. The danger was more urgent than she had guessed, thinking only that as an Englishwoman she was unwelcome in France. Now that Alec had pointed out her superficial resemblance to the fleeing empress, she felt a cold hand clutching at her. There was no way she could warn Maura, nor, to be honest, did she think her cousin would be glad to see her. She had made her feelings entirely clear, even through the disguising veil.

He did not understand her reluctance to admit that he was right. She had sufficient common sense to recognize logic, he knew, for she was covering her glorious hair as he had instructed. Perhaps she had no confidence in him?

Drily he assured her, "I'll get you to England, don't worry."

Something in the tone of his voice alarmed her. "But you, Alec? You speak as though I were merely a bundle that you have engaged yourself to deliver, like a basket of washing. Aren't you going to England yourself?"

He would not meet her eyes. He was silent for so long that she prodded him. "What is there left for you in France?" She cast her mind wildly about for the reasons that must be uppermost in his mind. "You said you've probably lost your job with that evil vicomte—because you are here with me and not with him."

"I would have quit him before long anyway," he said. "There's no place for a foreigner here, now that the Germans are winning the war. No Frenchman, no matter how noble, would be allowed to maintain what, after all, is a private army."

"What will you do then?"

He had no answer for her. Left to her own imaginings, then, she was carried beyond the limits of logic. If he had no place in France, then he must stay in

England. But he spoke as though he were simply going to drop her on the first safe and convenient shelf, and then go his own way.

How could he so casually forget the night just past? He loved her, he had whispered so in her ear over and over, beguiling her mind while his body took possession of her flesh. It came to her then—the difference between Alec's kind of love for her and her own blind and willing submission, how she shamefully accepted his professions of love at face value. Inwardly she writhed, remembering how eagerly she had welcomed him into her most private self. They moved down the road again. She trudged along beside him, in wounded silence.

From time to time she glanced at him. He seemed now to not even notice that she was there beside him, matching her strides to his, with her Englishwoman's country step.

Only last night, she had thought that she could love him forever. She had erected a structure of dreams on the flimsy structure of a passionate *incident*—a weak word, perhaps, but just the term he probably would have used—and now, in a handful of words, he had destroyed her future like a housewife's broom sweeping away cobwebs on the ceiling.

He would get her to England!

He refused to answer even her most urgent questions: What would he do, once he had gotten her safely out of France? He had spoken once, nostalgically, about his Scotland home in view of the Ochills. Would he go there? She did not know.

But the answer to the question she dared not even form in her mind—would he take her with him?—was already apparent. Whatever he was planning for his future, he clearly did not expect her to be a part of it.

Well, then, she would quietly—desperately—cut him out of her dreams. He was simply a man who spoke her native tongue, a man bound by his sense of duty to bring a fellow English citizen out of a land ravaged by war. And she would be suitably grateful for his efforts—

but not at all in her previous manner. A simple thank-you in words would have to suffice.

Grimly satisfied with her decision, she tightened her lips and concentrated on keeping up with his faster pace. She would not allow herself to lag behind, lest he lash out at her again. She would never, never beg him to let her rest a moment!

They walked on endlessly. The poplars bordering the narrow road on either side seemed to pass by her sight as slowly as in a dream. The exertion deadened her thoughts until the world's horizons drew in and she could see only the brown dirt track ahead, the monotonous unrolling of the gray-green columns of trees at her right, and on her left the silent, stern figure of the man she must think of as merely a guide.

As a guide, she thought, he was a failure. He had barely found her anything substantial to eat, and she was increasingly aware of a ferocious gnawing pang in the region of her stomach. Indeed, he did not even seem to have food on his mind.

But she was determined that she would ask for nothing from this man. She was pleased to note how far she had removed herself from him—he had started out, this morning, as "darling Alec" in her thoughts, and now he had become only "this man."

Suddenly she saw that the character of the road ahead had altered. They must be coming into some kind of village. She glanced at him for enlightenment. He said only, "We've reached the railroad."

"Then we can ride to the coast?"

"Do you have money enough?"

"I—I did have, but—"

He nodded curtly. "I suppose you gave it to that woman. No need to answer. I can see it in your face. I suspect that your money paid for that coach she rode off in."

"She was going to buy train tickets for us both! Why didn't she?" cried Val. "I didn't know she disliked me so much!" She turned to Alec, forgetting that she loathed him. "Where do you think she is? Maybe the general sent for her, and she's hidden away in a rendezvous, waiting for him."

"You think so?" Alec said, sarcastically. "Not that woman! Saving her own skin, you can be sure of that. Headed for the coast, without any question."

"On the train?"

He shook his head absently. His gaze focused intently upon the cluster of houses ahead. "Quite likely the train was already packed full of refugees leaving the city. Besides," he added cynically, "there wouldn't be room on the train for all her luggage."

"But she said she would get tickets for us both," Val repeated. Her heart could not accept the truth her perceptions had fully witnessed—that Maura had fled the city without her. She herself would not have abandoned her cousin, to say nothing of stealing all the money she had.

She had, while she puzzled, stopped walking. Alec came back to her. "Still mooning over that b– that cousin of yours? If she did board the train from Paris to the Channel, she's even more witless than I thought she was. The French lose their heads, you know. Didn't you hear them shouting for the empress in the palace garden? If they had caught her, they'd have torn her to pieces."

"But Maura—"

"You remember what I said before. Picture a woman with fair hair, a tinge of red in it, well dressed and arrogant, facing that incensed mob."

He had claimed that Val could be taken for the runaway empress. His argument, she knew, could apply equally to Maura.

"If she managed to board the train, she has by now likely been pulled off of it and thrust into a jail somewhere—if she were lucky."

"She had the carriage, I thought, just to take her to the station. But could she travel all the way to the coast in it?"

"The only chance she'll have," he said grimly. "Now

let's forget her. She's brought nothing but trouble to you. We've got a few things to worry about ourselves."

The railroad and the village were not far ahead now. She could make out the whitewashed cottages lining the main street, and flowers spilling over window boxes in festoons of red and yellow.

She was suddenly frightened. Alec had pointed out the possibility that she might be mistaken for the hated empress. Suppose people poured out of the little houses and came at her—she closed her eyes, seeing vividly again the passion-distorted faces of the mob that had carried her along inexorably to the palace.

She pulled her scarf tighter, flattening her hair. She fixed her eyes on the village ahead, trying to summon sufficient courage for whatever lay before them.

There was no sign of life, not even a dog. Suddenly, Alec guided her into a smaller lane at right angles to the road. A few yards down the lane stood an unpainted wooden outbuilding. He pointed to it. "Stay there till I come back."

She had a myriad of questions at the tip of her tongue, but he was gone before she could ask the first one. He did not come back. She had time to consider all the unresolved questions she dared not ask him—

Today, with the harsh sunlight beating down against her, she thought Alec was no better than Maura. He had used her, too, perhaps in a different way but no less cruelly. No wonder he fumed about what he called her obsession with Maura—he wanted her only for himself. If anyone were to take advantage of her, he probably thought, it would be Alec Drummond.

Did they make a fool of her, or was she already half-way to folly?

Then, of course, there was Alec. Had she not been on that ferry, or had such a close resemblance to Maura, Alec would not have given her a second thought, would he? How much she would have missed! But how much better off she would have been, deprived of all that Alec had brought her—the soaring bliss of love, the disillusion that wrapped her now, the unfriendly sun beating hotly on her, the real likelihood that she would not live to see England again.

She had read it somewhere—"Love is the wisdom of the fool—" What was the rest of it? Something unpleasant, no doubt.

The squeak of dry wagon wheels startled her. She opened her eyes, alarmed.

It was only Alec. But a transformed Alec!

He had acquired a broad-brimmed hat that threw his sharp features into shadowy disguise. He sat on the wooden seat of a two-wheeled farm cart, holding the reins of a chestnut mare. He pulled the cart to a stop opposite her, no difficult feat, for the mare of questionable age had obtained no great speed.

"Here you are, madam!" said Alec, in high spirits. "Better than a carriage any day." He reached down to take her hand and pull her up to the seat beside him. "Lots of fresh air, and time to enjoy it."

"How did you manage this?"

He clucked the mare into forward movement again. "We shall not reach the coast in a hurry, even providing this rig lasts the distance. I have to tell you I am not impressed with the stability of the cart."

She looked behind her. It was a small wagon, the bottom covered with a deep layer of straw, fresh from reaping. It was September, and harvest time in the rich fields of Normandy.

But the wheels wobbled and creaked as though they could not remember the last time they had felt axle grease.

"At least it's better than walking," she smiled.

"That it is," he said. They rode on in silence. She was not entirely reconciled to her own folly. And her instinct told her that her misery might well deepen as time wore on. But for now, she was sitting beside her only lover, the aroma of new straw rising about them, and some very pleasant memories.

Besides, his gloomy forebodings could not be ignored. He was not at all sure they would reach the coast in safety. She finally realized that characteristic optimism had glossed over the true depth of the peril they were in.

She spared a moment to wonder where Maura was, how she had managed. Probably she was already in England, having had a head start in her own carriage. Perhaps she had already returned to Thorne Hall, to give Sir William whatever explanation she might find that would put her escapade in its best light, and to forget about Val completely.

She tried to stifle a sigh without success. Alec turned to her and reached out to cover her hand with his.

Despite what had happened to her, forgetting how her nearest—Maura, and her dearest—Alec, had used her, she was still alive, this day was good, and if they rode on in this fashion for a month, she would not complain.

It was nearly dusk before they came upon the evidence.

They had ambled through the lush late-summer meadows, dotted in the distance by grazing, peaceful cattle, and had crossed little streams by way of broad stones imbedded to provide a ford.

There were apple orchards, and woodlands, and comfortable homesteads of brick hidden behind hedgerows, and church spires seemingly floating on rounded green treetops.

Alec said little, but the silence that fell eventually between them was kindly with companionship, and Val, contentedly seizing the moment, set her doubts at a distance.

The sun, moving westward, bathed the bright wide skies with gold, and struck long shadows behind the cart and its passengers. The light of Paris had been almost tangible at dusk, an indigo chiffon veil kindly softening the harsher aspects of the city. But the light of the countryside faded gently, imperceptibly. There was no need to shade any ugliness, for there was none. The landscape was bright and clear even after the sun slipped behind the tallest trees, as though the entire scene were done carefully in imaginative cloisonné.

She was the first, though, to see the dark objects on the road ahead. "What in the world, Alec? Is it an animal, a cow?"

He smothered his own exclamation and slowed the mare. Suddenly, the placid animal shied to one side and shook her head fitfully against the reins, fighting the bit.

Animals know things, Val thought, vaguely alarmed.

They drew closer. The thing in the road took on recognizable outlines as they approached. It was a carriage—the remains of a large carriage, a four-wheeled, four-seated vehicle. One of the four wheels stood at a crazy angle against the body of the coach, another, its yellow spokes shattered, lay a little distance apart.

"Hold the reins while I look," said Alec, jumping to the ground.

Automatically she took the leather reins, peering all the while at the unexplained debris in the road. The carriage, of course, had met with an accident. The shafts were shattered and the horses gone, either liberated when the harness broke or led away by the survivors, if there had been any. Filled with vague alarm, she speculated on what must have happened. The passengers in the carriage could well have been injured, perhaps severely enough that their rescue would be of primary importance. Baggage was tossed about haphazardly, one of the portmanteaus broken open and gowns spilling out over the dirt—gowns that she knew well, had herself worn—

Her throat tightened. "Alec!"

Startled, he looked back at her. She wrapped the reins around the cornerpost of the cart and scrambled to the ground. She ran to him and grabbed his arm. "Maura! That dress, look. This is Maura's carriage! What could have happened?"

He wore a cold, arrested look. He was holding a cushion from the carriage, and now he looked at it as though he did not remember picking it up.

His voice came as though from a vast distance. "Are you sure?"

"Of course I'm sure," she said impatiently. "I've worn that dress myself. And that deep blue one with the ivory lace, and that—Alec, what could have happened to her?"

In response he held out the cushion to her. "Don't touch it!" he warned sharply. "See that? Where the light catches the smear?"

"What is it? Not—"

"Blood. It's not quite dry yet."

The carriage seemed to rise up and tip, swirling around her in the most fantastic, dreamlike fashion. Alec gave a muttered exclamation and grabbed her arm. "Don't faint, for God's sake!" he said sharply. "I haven't time for that!"

She could clearly hear a sarcastic retort in her head, but she knew she could not speak aloud. Instead, she clung to him as though he were a lifeboat in a stormy sea. His coat smelled of straw. Feeling his strength flow into her, she laid her head briefly on his shoulder.

He scanned the area around them warily. "Come on, Val." He still held the blood-stained cushion in his right hand. He looked at it suddenly in disgust and dropped it. He rubbed the palms of his hands on his trousers before he grabbed her wrist. "We've got to get out of here before they come back."

"Th-they?"

There was no time for discussion, no matter how pertinent it might be. He did not appear to hurry, but she had barely gathered her skirts and climbed onto the seat before the cart was again moving ahead, carefully skirting the wreckage.

"Alec, we can't just go on!"

"Why not?" he said tightly. "She left you behind without a backward look. You do remember that?"

"Of course I do. But she's in trouble. That blood means something."

"Certainly it does. It means that someone thought she was the missing empress. Possibly they frightened the horses—"

"And dragged Maura from the wreck? Alec, we've got to help her."

"And how do you propose doing that?" he demanded fiercely. "I've got my hands full getting you out of here. She got what she deserves."

He persuaded the little mare to a fair burst of speed, doubtless faster than she had trotted since she was a colt. But still they seemed to make little progress. When she turned to look back, she could still see the dark smudge across the road that was the crippled carriage, the only tragic clue to her cousin's fate.

The road rose before them and they struggled up a long hill that Alec said would lead them to Bonnières. "I expected that perhaps we could find an inn either here at Rolleboise or at Bonnières. But we dare not stop now."

"Because of me, I know. I'm sorry to cause you so much trouble."

He reached for her hand and patted it. "Not so much trouble."

She knew all he had said about Maura was true—she had callously left Val behind, she had selfishly taken Val's guineas, she had courted disaster from the very moment she had left the shelter of Thorne Hall. And Maura had had no qualms about dragging Val down with her.

At the top of the long rise she turned to take one final glance at the last traces of her cousin, the pathetic remains of Maura's most cherished possessions, the lovely gowns, now gritty with dirt, the dainty satin slippers, all the fripperies of a frivolous woman. She had known her such a short time, and not even a happy time, yet she felt as though, because of their shared Finch blood, she had known her forever.

When they started down the other side of the hill, Alec pointed out the village lying in the valley below them. "There was not much blood," he said at last. "Perhaps they merely put her in jail."

"She could prove she is English, then," Val concluded, somewhat comforted. "And of course Jehane was with her. She could explain."

His features wore for a moment an odd expression.

She understood him—supposing Jehane were injured or even dead? The possibilities seemed endless.

While they had paused at the wreckage, night had crept closer. The afterglow of the sunset had stolen all the colors from the land, but it was still possible to discern woods and meadows, strawsticks and hayricks.

His hand was suddenly warm on her trembling thigh. "Trust me?"

Without waiting for an answer, he pulled the mare to a stop and turned to Val. "Come here," he said and held his arms out to her. She hesitated only a moment before leaning into his embrace. Gone were the doubts that had been so tormenting, when he had left her in that village hours ago. Now, she settled against him like a beautiful yacht coming into safe harbor.

He tilted her face to his and quietly kissed her before letting her go. "Come," he whispered again, "there's not much time."

They left the road and crossed a small field where hay had recently been cut. The sharp stems of the grasses crackled sharply beneath the wooden wheels of the cart. On a small rise a short distance ahead lay an ebony belt of trees. She caught her breath sharply at an obscure shape that loomed directly ahead.

"Strawstack," he said briefly. "Around to the back of it, away from passersby on the road."

An odd note in his voice caused her to look quickly at him. It was strange, she thought, that up here, even in the shadow of the woods, the light was not yet gone. Twilight had come to the valley below, and she could not even make out the track they had just left. Dusk in Paris was soft, caressing, sensuous. But here this time of day held nothing romantic in it—evening simply an hour marked by waning daylight before, and absence of light afterwards.

Val could see him clearly now. The little mare pulled the cart to the edge of the woods, before Alec unhitched her and led her to a grassy place. Val sat obediently in the cart, waiting for him.

It was a lovely, peaceful scene. But she hardly saw

it. Instead, before her eyes rose the vision of the carriage toppled on its side, the bloody cushions, the pitiful debris of Maura's existence. Val wondered what Maura's last thoughts would have been. She imagined the crashing violence of the wreck, the crowds dragging Maura, and Jehane, from the carriage, and shouting crazy slogans—she had heard them herself in Paris, only yesterday.

"*À bas l'Impératrice!* Down with the empress!"

Had Maura thought, wondered Val, in those last moments, that Raoul and his passion for her was worth it all? Did Maura regret her headstrong, willful departure from her husband's protection?

It came to her with a start that she was thinking about her cousin as though she were already dead, as though she had in fact seen the torn bodies of Maura and Jehane. In fact, she realized, she had seen nothing of the sort. A few satin rags, a slipper from which the heel had been torn away, a bloody cushion, and that was all.

Alec came back to the cart. "We're safe here," he said in a low voice and put his hand on her shoulder.

Somehow his gentle, warm touch released her fears and her regrets. They poured out over the rigid wall she had erected to hold them decently inside herself.

But she could not help herself.

There was no room for him to sit down beside her, so he stood, pulling her close, stroking her hair, her shoulders, soothing her as though she were a child. But his solid strength calmed her, by degrees, and at last except for an occasional strangled sob she weathered her storm.

"Do you th-think she's dead?" she ventured at last.

"I can't say. It is impossible to say whose blood was spilled." She moved, and he sat beside her. "Darling, I know you hate me for not trying to find her." When she did not answer, he went on. "I could have gone after her. I could have followed whatever trail the bandits had left, and probably found her. Suppose I had found her—and she was fortunate enough to be alive. I would then have drawn my gun, threatened at least twenty villagers, and dragged her away."

"But you didn't!"

He ignored her interruption. He seemed anxious that she understand his reasons. "I would then have had to leave the maid in the hands of the village men, who would in all likelihood be incensed at my interference. That would not have done the girl any good, would it?" He pulled her closer.

"N-no." Her voice was small and muffled against his chest.

"And then I would have had to bring your cousin back to where I left you in the cart."

Suddenly all was clear to her. She pulled away and sat up. "You think I wouldn't have been there? You think I would have run away?"

"Not by choice, no. But if Lady Thorne resembles the empress, whom the French people blame for the German victories, then—"

He waited, letting her work it out for herself. "Then," she said at last, "so do I."

"Exactly." He put his arm again around her shoulders. He put a finger under her chin, and lifted her face to him. "I've got to get you safely to England. I dare not take a chance on anything happening to you. You are far too precious to me—"

He bent to touch her lips with his, gently at first, and then demanding, masterful. How could he make love to her now, knowing that the wreckage site had set her adrift on a current of grief for Maura—not for what she was, but for what she might have been, and the strong bonds of family that might have come to bind them?

She had danced to Maura's tune—so willingly at first—until she wearied, until she could dance no more. Now even the silken threads of her gratitude to her cousin were ruptured. Instead, she would belong to Alec Drummond, last night and forever.

Even the taking of her maidenhood in that empty cabin on the ferry had set her in bondage to him. Always, he would be in her heart the one who set her apart from innocent childhood, the one who brought her to the realization of her womanly capacity for bliss, her ability not only to take, but to give him pleasure in the fullest measure.

She felt his arms gently urging her into the bottom of the farm cart. The smell of fresh straw rose around her, and she giggled. He made a questioning sound in his throat, but she did not answer him. From this time on, the smell of a barn, the pungent odor of the little mare, would stir her memories.

Romance, she had once believed, was nurtured on the fragrances of jasmine, of meadowsweet, exotic spices—not the earthy smells of straw, of barn dust!

But romance was not to be bound by trappings. Romance was here now, untying her cloak and pulling it away from her, opening her bodice, laying her breasts bare, stroking her chilled flesh until it warmed under his hands.

She would never ask for more than the soft straw beneath her, and Alec, dropping nibbling little kisses along her earlobes, letting his tongue flick in and out of the little hollow at the base of her throat.

Maura might be dead, her body torn and trampled, and Jehane gone, too. But this night, she could not, would not, grieve.

This night she must affirm that she was alive, that the flame of life within her still urged upward. With a little moan, she raised her arms to encircle his neck, to bring him down to her, and arched her body to meet him more than halfway.

After a time that could not be measured, Alec removed himself from her. She sighed, reluctant to return from the blissful country to which he had taken her. Abruptly, without intending to speak at all, she heard herself saying, "I'm hungry!"

His deep chuckle came. "A good thing I know my Val," he said whimsically. "Any man who takes a trip with you had best stock up a week's provender!"

Faintly, and seriously, she echoed, "*Any* man?"

He seemed not to hear her. He pulled himself to the back of the cart and rummaged for a few minutes. Any man? She would not be taking a trip with just any man. She felt a tear slip from her wet eyes and slide toward her ear before she brushed it away.

He returned, on his knees, with a French loaf and a quarter round of cheese. "Sorry," he said. "No fancy Maison Dorée within walking distance. This will have to do."

They ate in silence. She realized she was ravenous, and the bread and cheese tasted like a feast. She had pulled her cloak over her, in an unconscious defense against his "any man," but Alec did not notice. Naked, he sat next to her in the narrow cart, his knees drawn up to make more room for her. She could see his pale body against the deep obscurity of the night that surrounded them.

From deep in the woods she heard the scream of a big hunting owl. The meadow they had crossed was alive with the sounds of night insects, raising their high-pitched hum to the faint stars. A peaceful night scene—

Alec tensed. "What—," she began, but his free hand came swiftly over her mouth, silencing her. He did not move, but she could feel all his senses focused on listening.

She listened, too. There was nothing to hear. She glanced at him, and he made a sharp gesture indicating quiet. Then she, too, heard what his sharp ears already had caught. The pattern, far away, of horse hooves, coming closer.

The moments stretched out interminably. The horse was only walking, and although she thought she could detect the presence of more than one animal, she could not be sure. She reached out to Alec. Her fingers closed on nothing.

She sat up sharply. She could barely see Alec, his opalescent body truncated and receding in the dark. She was shocked at first, but then she realized that he had pulled his trousers on and was on his way to reconnoiter. She dared not call to him.

She sat alone in the dark, the pile of straw still flat where Alec had lain beside her. She was prey to the most frightful misgivings—who had traveled on the road below them, and why had Alec been so suspicious? Was it possible that he had learned more from the wreckage of the carriage than he had told her?

It was the loneliest, most desolate time she had ever spent. She thought it must be near daybreak before a dark shadow emerged beside the cart. She almost screamed.

"Hush!" he said and threw his leg over the side of the cart and dropped beside her. "It's all right now. They've gone."

"Who? Who's gone?"

He hesitated before he answered. "A handful of men."

"Who were they?"

His answer was evasive. "No one we want to meet."

"Alec—I thought you were never coming back!"

The night had grown chilly, or else her fears had made her shiver. She was sure, though, that she would get no more satisfactory answers from him than he had already given her. And in truth, there was no need for her to know more. She trusted him. And while she was happy to be with him, to put her own life in his hands, yet, she realized, there was nothing else to do. She had no choice.

In a movement that she thought strangely domestic, and oddly endearing, he pulled his trousers off and folded them neatly over the seat at the front of the cart. Without thinking, she pulled her cloak tighter around her. Her gesture, designed only to comfort herself, did not go unnoticed. He lay down, slowly and deliberately, beside her. Supporting himself on his elbow, he broodingly looked down on her. With his free hand, then, he took hold of the neck of her cloak. "Val? Are you trying to shut me out?"

The trembling in his voice was irresistible. "Never," she breathed and opened the garment to him. For a long time he made no move. Then, slowly, almost casually, he began to stroke her body, long sweeping strokes that calmed her fears at the same time as they grew more demanding.

"Do you mind?" he asked, the slow rhythm of his caresses continuing. "I can't keep my hands from wandering all over you. You're so beautiful!"

He was silent for a time. Only his hands spoke for him, telling her he found her desirable, without words declaring that she belonged to him.

She was suspended in the small world he was building for her, a world where only the two of them existed, each for the other's delight—

He shattered the enclave they shared. "Val. Listen to me."

With a sigh she returned to the present. "All right."

"We've got a long way to go to the coast. I don't know whether this nag we've got can make it. I'm not even sure the wheels won't fall off the cart."

"I'm not questioning you, Alec, but is there another way? Do we have to get to England?"

He did not answer, but she could feel his fingers tightening as they moved on the flesh of her thigh. "Of course, Alec," she conceded. "We can't stay here."

He didn't go on. Abruptly, she knew what he was thinking. "It's something about those people on the road. Alec, you *did* recognize them! Were they after—us?"

"I don't know. But it wouldn't be hard to guess the road we are taking. It's the most direct way. But we have the advantage, for they don't know where we are. Nor do they know we saw them."

She moved as though to sit up, but his hand went gently to her shoulder, to push her back again onto the soft straw bedding. "But we've got to be sensible," he told her. "Suppose something happens to me. You've got to promise me that you won't try to help me. Or look for me if I disappear."

"But Alec!"

"No buts, my darling. Do you know how to shoot a gun?"

Reluctantly, she nodded, and then realized he could not see her in the night, so she spoke aloud. "I have, but not often. But Alec, I can't go on without you!"

"You must. I'd hate to think," he added, deliberately making himself sound selfish, "that all my trouble in getting you out of Paris had gone for naught." He let her think for a moment before he pressed her further. "Promise me, that if something happens to me—and remember, it well could, because that was my man Futrelle out there on the road—Jacques—and a patrol of the vicomte's men."

"What do they want?"

"Let's hope it is not me. The vicomte has a score or two to settle with me." Not least of which, he remembered, was his witnessing of des Loches's humiliation at the hands of the emperor, that night at the Tuileries Palace. He did not speak of this to Val.

"What we'll do tomorrow—" he planned aloud.

Such a curiously domestic scene, she thought, pleased. Just like two married people, lying in bed, talking over the small events of the day, considering—together—the incidents likely for the morrow.

What would the morrow bring this time, the most uncertain future she had ever known? Even in her wildest trouble in the past, Miss Wilson and Mr. Markham stiff with accusations, she knew the worst that could happen was to be thrown in jail. While that had seemed then to be the end of the world, what waited for her now was infinitely, damnably the worse.

"What will we do tomorrow?" she prompted him.

"I shall teach you how to fire my pistol—in case, sometime, I do not come back to you. And you'll promise me that you'll take it—and use it if you need to."

She shivered involuntarily. His fingers tightened, in sympathy, on her thigh. But still he was not satisfied. "My darling Val, you must listen. If something happens to me, you are to take my gun and run for the coast. Get there any way you can. Deauville is your best chance. Find a fishing vessel, if possible. and get back to England. You won't be safe anywhere in France."

"Or England," she said, too low for him to hear.

"Promise me."

She could not promise him that she would leave him behind for any reason. It was tantamount to asking her to leave her blood behind and run away without it, or her breath, or her wits.

"I—I can't."

"Tell me why not," he asked in a coaxing tone. His fingers that had stroked softly over her thighs, and hips, moved faster. They slid now to caress the inner part of her leg. She could feel her skin shiver under his touch. Her breath caught. He sensed his approaching victory. "Come," he teased, "tell me."

Abruptly, she sat up and pushed his hand away. "Alec, I don't want to leave you."

"Don't try to save me," he said again, as though by sheer repetition he would gain his end. His voice came out of the darkness, from somewhere near her knees, disembodied, separate from the lips that touched, fleetingly, here and there along her trembling leg. "Go on to England."

She listened to him, listened, too, to the warring thoughts in her brain. The words came out without her willing them, softly, plaintively. "Will you come—later?"

He did not answer. She was not sure he had heard her. She was not even sure she wanted an answer from him. If he did extinguish all hope in her, then she might—barely perhaps—endure whatever lay ahead of her. For she was now convinced—as if her destiny were written clearly in the night sky—that parting was inevitable. Perhaps the separation would be temporary. But—

The conviction came to her that he did not love her as she did him. She was there to satisfy a need, and he was taking her to the Channel out of an obscure sense of duty. She stiffened inwardly, but he sensed it. His hands ceased their exploring.

"Val? What's wrong?" When she did not answer, he lifted his head to kiss her breast, making a loving sound as his free arm reached around to bring her closer to him.

She had meant to put him in his place. But her body knew better than she did where his place was. She felt, someplace deep inside, the first melting of her resistance. Her own body turned traitor to her. Finally, she cried out, "I cannot think properly when you do this!"

His voice, soft as a purling stream, a current of triumph strong in it, said, "When I do what, my love? This? Or perhaps *this?* Which?"

Her words sounded strangled by the exquisite sensations that sent tremors through her. "Don't! Don't—"

"No need to think, darling," he said. "Just promise me that you'll do as I said. Take the gun, go to England."

What use was it to argue? Her body had betrayed her again, seeking beyond her will the ecstasy that only he could bring. Her flesh was as much in thrall to him as though she wore gyves on her wrists.

Days without Alec? He was thinking in terms of weeks, months—she would not, even in her mind, say the word "forever." If he wished to see her safe, as he said, then she must submit. And at least she would have this night.

"I promise."

He answered vaguely, but she could not distinguish the words. She leaned over him to hear better. Her thick hair, of a color infamous enough to place her in political danger, had long since come loose from its pins. Now it fell freely as she bent to him, making a curtain enclosing them from the night. The only sound in the vast stillness was the crunching of grass as the mare grazed, and the rising and falling hum of the night's insects.

Instead of repeating what he had said, he nuzzled along her throat, his teeth finding and biting gently the lobe of her ear. The cart—her entire world—rocked gently, and she knew he had shifted his body. She felt, suddenly, with a shock of recognition, the wetness of his eager mouth on her nipples. Her stomach muscles contracted in a spasm of desire. He felt the movement and caressed her stomach in a movingly reassuring gesture.

She could no longer measure time nor space. The only sensation in the world was the urgency of his lips, his mouth moving ceaselessly, thrusting at her breasts. His hands slid along the inner part of her thighs, pushing them apart. He probed delicately until he reached the delicate triangle of hair, where he paused, toying with the sensitive skin.

The intensity of her emotion, sparked by his commanding mastery of her secret entrance, sent quivers through her. Her skin felt as though she were bathing in champagne. The bubbles rose up in her, and she knew she was as drunk as though she had swallowed a magnum of the wine, even though she had had only cold spring water for supper.

His probing, teasing, caressing fingers grew bolder, more intimate, stroking her private self until she could feel the moisture on his fingers, and knew that the wild clamoring somewhere inside her must be satisfied—and soon.

A sound purred in her throat. He did not understand, and to her sorrow he moved away from her. He reached up to take her shoulder and pull her down to him. His voice was warm in her ear. "Shall I stop?"

"No!" The word came on a sob.

He moved, then, with swift purpose. He shoved her legs apart, pulling her left leg across his thighs, and pulled her down on top of him. She felt his hardening manhood moving along the tender inner part of her leg and gasped. His hands were on her hips, settling her down astride him. She felt the stiff straw against her knees. She did not at once know what he wanted of her.

He found her hand and wrapped her fingers around his male hardness. She trembled, feeling him moving in her hand, tickling her fingers. The night turned stormy—except that the thunder was only in her head. His hand covered hers, guiding her in the way he would have her go.

Her skin was aflame, like a fire on the surging sea.

The most exquisite sensations swallowed her, like a wave on the ocean, a wave that was rising up, and up, the crest of it still not visible.

His hand still over hers, he guided her to rub him against the downy triangle guarding the core of her, and then, at last, to the private part of herself that was opening to him. Imperceptibly, his movements began to take on a rhythmic stroking, his manhood sliding tantalizingly against her, and she moved with him.

"Take me into yourself when you're ready, my love."

When I'm ready! She would do it now! But not yet. She was excruciatingly aware of him, of his needs. She could hear his shallow breathing, the inarticulate sounds coming from his wet, open lips. His hands were everywhere on her, wildly fluttering, in an agony of rising tension.

Suddenly, the inner core of her dissolved in a molten, unbridled joy. She let the tension, deliberately, build in her, knowing that, his manhood in her hand, she could bring them both to bliss at any moment. But, her instinct instructed her, joy the longer delayed is the greater.

She took a new delight in holding back, in letting the rhythm of their bodies move together, in feeling the sinews of his strong, powerful thighs supporting her. How vigorous was this swelling part of him in her hand, thrusting against her fingers—

Suddenly, as though a great gong had struck, vibrating in the night, she knew that it was time. She slid him into her. The delayed invasion overwhelmed her in a crashing crescendo of driving pulsations. She collapsed on his chest, fainting with the immensity of the desire still exploding within her.

He was all around her. His arms held her safe against his furred chest, his legs guarded her back. His maleness was deep, deep inside her, pounding, making them one flesh—now and forever. Together they soared, ecstatic, beyond the stars, free of the earth, free of all but the wondrous abandon of union.

Whatever the morrow might bring—peril, or parting, strife or desolation—all was forgotten. There was only this night.

Late the next day, Alec calculated they were almost in sight of the Channel.

"How do you know?" she asked. "That rise ahead looks just like the last one to me."

"Don't you smell it, darling?"

She breathed deeply. "The air is different."

"Salt. The smell of the sea. We don't have far to go now."

She fell silent. Even though she knew they were still in danger until they left the soil of France behind, she was reluctant to come to the end of their journey. Alec had evaded her questions about the future—*their* future. If she believed only what he had said, she would not think they had any future together at all.

If anything happened—he had said. But what could happen so close to the Channel and safety? Separation was the worst, and the fear of it filled her thoughts. She reached out to touch his arm, a small plea for reassurance. He put his hand over hers and smiled down at her. Sensing her need, he bent to kiss her.

The sound of horses coming fast toward them interrupted their sweet moment. Springing away from her, Alec reached for the gun, on the floor of the cart, but it was too late.

Across the track before them, barring their way, was a patrol of eight armed riders, the sun striking sparkling glints from their weapons. Their uniforms were vaguely familiar. Soldiers of the emperor? It was all a mistake, she thought, managing an expression of calm. When the men discovered they were English, they would leave them alone.

One of the men shouted, dispelling her illusion. "Ho, there, Drummond! You almost got away!"

Alec leaped to the ground, facing the soldiers. "*Captain* Drummond, Pierre."

"Not any more." The leader of the group gestured to

his men, and they moved back. "His Excellency, the vicomte, has no more need of your services."

"I thought you had given up the search for me."

"You saw us?"

Alec nodded. "Last night, on the road." He laughed. "I hardly recognized you in your new finery, Jacques. I suppose you finally wormed your way into my job."

The leader's face darkened. Oh, Alec, Val cried silently, don't insult him—just let's be on our way.

Nevertheless she moved the gun with her foot so it would be easier to pick up, if there was need.

"I have that honor," said Futrelle stiffly, "and my first assignment is to bring you back to Paris. His Excellency, by the way, did not specify in what condition."

"For what reason?" demanded Alec. "I owe him nothing."

"He has the odd idea," explained Futrelle with a laugh, "that no man leaves his service except by his own wish."

"Nonsense!"

"Eccentric, I give you. But my own position is not so secure that I can afford protest." He dismounted. His men followed his lead.

Although the man's voice seemed to reflect high good humor, Val knew that Alec was strung tight with wariness. She must follow his lead. The cart horse, somnolent till now, stamped restlessly. She picked up the reins and steadied the beast.

The small movement caught Futrelle's eye, and for the first time he looked full at her.

"Aha, the elusive Lady Thorne!" he cried in triumph. "You know, Drummond, His Excellency has never forgiven you for interfering that evening at the palace."

"It was the emperor!" Alec spat out.

"Ah, but the emperor is out of reach. You are the more vulnerable. If we take you both back—you and the lady—there should be a tidy bonus for us, eh, men?"

Alec, his pent-up rage bursting out, moved forward. "Take me if you must—but not her!"

Everything happened at once—one of the men casually lifted his rifle and struck Alec's temple. She watched in horror as he staggered backward. Struggling to his knees, he still moved forward toward his assailant, his fingers clutching air. He had almost gotten to his feet when Futrelle gave the word.

"Get him!"

The blows rained down on Alec's defenseless head and shoulders. Val was unable to move. She could do nothing—

Alec grabbed a rifle, parrying its blow, and yelled, "Val—run. *Run!*"

The warning sapped his remaining strength. He dropped to the ground, exhausted. The enemy soldiers surrounded the prone figure, and she could see no more.

"He's dead."

Futrelle answered, "No matter. Des Loches would have killed him anyway."

They had forgotten Val for the moment. She slapped the reins sharply on the mare's rump. Surprised, the animal leaped forward, and the cart rattled off toward the Channel port.

Fearing pursuit, she glanced over her shoulder, but the little knot of men still stood in the road, staring down at their fallen victim.

Alec was dead! The words pounded in her brain. Alec was dead, dead, dead.

She no longer acted consciously. She remembered, later, entering a small town, looking for the waterfront, searching for a fishing boat to take her to England. She found one, noting vaguely that the crew seemed anxious to follow her orders.

Only much later did she recall that she had held Alec's enormous gun in her hand the entire time. She held it tightly—all she had left of him—and at last the English coast rose before her staring eyes.

Chapter Fifteen

The nightmare no longer came every night. These days Val could perhaps sleep every other night through till morning. Now, though, she writhed in her sleep, feeling the evil coming, knowing the dream must run its course, certain there was no escape—

She was in a cart, surrounded by a happiness that was almost palpable. A city in the distance, at the end of the road, a city they were destined never to reach.

The soldiers were coming from the city. At first a dark splotch on the horizon, a smudge that looked oddly like an overturned carriage, but it wasn't. It was only a handful of men, in uniforms, unexpectedly carrying enormous cannons in their hands.

Then the dream—more real than truth and just as menacing—broke down into great jagged menacing splinters like the smashing of a large window.

The soldiers spoke in little fragmented French words. "The vicomte wants you back . . . nobody leaves the vicomte . . . without permission . . . maybe the lady . . . a sop to his excellency...give us the girl and we'll let you go...."

Alec struggling, restrained by powerful arms. The man called Jacques, beating Alec with his gun stock. Alec throwing his gun toward her, shouting. Run, Val. No, Alec! Run, Val, RUN!

She couldn't leave Alec, his blood streaming out onto the ground, his leg bent oddly beneath him. She ran a little way to him, and somehow she had a gun—Alec's gun—in her hand.

"Idiot Pierre! You've killed him. He's dead, dead, dead!"

RUN, VAL!

She ran. She could hear her feet pounding, louder and louder. She tiptoed, but the pounding continued, and someone called out.

"Lady Thorne! Lady Thorne! It's me, Colby!"

The door opened, then, and Val knew she had been dreaming. She felt drugged with pain, and yet she knew she was not hurt. Only Alec had been hurt, was lying dead when, obedient to Alec's orders and her own fear, she had taken flight, toward the Channel.

Val groaned. She took deep shuddering breaths, trying to come back to the present. She dared not think of the past, of Alec's head sagging, his feet jerking in response to the blows of the rifle butts on him.

Colby came to the bed. "Another nightmare, my lady? They're worse now than when you came."

"Oh, no, Colby. Last night, wasn't it last night? I slept all the way through."

"But just now you were shouting fit to raise the roof. I'd best see that tomorrow night you get something to make you sleep. I've got a potion that my mother set store by."

Val threw back the comforter and swung her feet to the carpeted floor. The housekeeper bent to the grate and stirred the fire. "Thank you," said Val, pulling her robe on, "for not mentioning a guilty conscience."

"Your conscience is your own," retorted Colby. "Though I don't mind saying I'm glad it's not mine."

"There wasn't anything more I could do," said Val. "He was dead—they said so." How strange it was that logic seemed to have nothing to do with conscience! It would have been better if she had stayed and died with Alec. At least it would be over by now.

The fire was blazing now. Colby turned to look at Val. The housekeeper had a squarish figure, with no yielding curves in sight. Her robe, snatched up when she heard Val's shouting, was gray flannel, uncompromisingly shapeless. "I'll get some tea. I wager you'll not be going back to bed?"

Val shook her head. She sat in an armchair and stared into the flames. "Bring a cup for yourself," she said absently.

She must banish the sights and sounds that lingered before her mind's eye, brought to life again and again by the relentless nightmares.

Deliberately, she brought herself to the present, slowly burying that terrible day on the road outside Deauville. Perhaps one day she would bury it deeply enough that it would never surface again. Perhaps even that fearful memory of her broken lover would fade. But if she dared not remember the terror, then she could not remember the glowing remembrance of happiness, for the one faded inexorably into the other. Union and parting, splendor and ruin—each existed inseparable from the other.

And here she was, safe enough, in Thorne Hall, still caught up in the deceitful web of Maura's weaving. She hardly remembered how she had come to this place. While she waited for Colby's return, she let her memories take over and felt herself drifting into a past that held no promise...

Colby came in with a tray.

Colby poured tea and added a generous dollop of brandy to Val's. "Drink it. Even if you sleep in a chair, it's better than not sleeping at all."

After a bit, Val said, "Do you think Sir William was awakened? I would dread disturbing him."

"No," said Colby promptly. "Besides, Fenton would

tell him something, even if he did hear. A dog on the heath, perhaps."

Val's sense of humor was returning. "Did I really sound like that?"

Colby shook her head. When she spoke, it was on a different subject. "When you came that day, I didn't believe you'd still be here a month later. Did you?"

"No. I wish—I wish I hadn't come at all."

"But you've made all the difference to Sir William, miss. Oh, dear, I had best keep calling you my lady. I'll make a mistake, sure as I'm born."

Val had never intended to keep up the masquerade that Maura had begun in London. She had finally resigned herself to taking Maura's place in the glittering salons of the Imperial court, now destroyed, but she had never considered taking Maura's place at Thorne Hall.

She could still recall in precise detail the expression on Colby's face when she had presented herself at the front door of Thorne Hall. Her hired carriage—paid for by the coins Alec had entrusted to her that last day as though he had had a premonition of what was to come—waited behind her on the drive. Colby's eyes had darkened, and her hand had flown to cover her mouth against a scream.

Val's first words had been ambiguous. "May I come in?"

Colby automatically dropped a curtsey and stepped back, and Val had walked through the door into Thorne Hall. Her first impression had been of solidity and spaciousness, not a gracious house but one built for comfort. "My lady," said Colby and stopped helplessly, not knowing how to go on.

"I am sorry to arrive without warning you of my coming," Val began. "But I have bad news for Sir William."

Colby hesitated, her eyes scanning Val's face as though searching to read her thoughts. "Lady Thorne?"

"Please let me come in. I shall only take a moment. I have asked my carriage to wait. May I see Sir William?"

Colby opened the door wide. "Yes, my lady. I am sorry, but you took me so by surprise. I—we did not expect—"

"You are making a mistake, you know," said Val quietly. Colby held out her hand for the cloak, and Val removed it. Val was moving like a doll, without life—without Alec.

"A mistake, my lady?" said Colby, adding stoutly, "perhaps it is your mistake. You'll find nothing for you here, ma'am."

Val turned her beautiful sapphire eyes on the housekeeper, puzzled. She did not understand Colby's quick intake of breath. "I must see Sir William, for a moment. Then I will go."

Go where? She did not know. Nor did she care greatly. She must tell Maura's husband what she believed had happened to Maura. She owed Maura that much, but no more.

"But you are not Lady Thorne," said Colby. "I wonder at your nerve, miss."

Val interrupted. "I did not call myself Lady Thorne, did I? Let me see Sir William at once, if you please."

Colby, for once in her life, did not know what was best to do. This imposter might do terrible damage to Sir William. And yet, Colby knew quality when she saw it. The poor lady was pale and obviously exhausted, almost as though she had just suffered through a great ordeal. And yet she was gentle—and determined. Colby was convinced that the lady would simply keep insisting upon seeing Sir William until the housekeeper gave in.

"I'll take you to Sir William, miss." She hesitated. "What name shall I give, if you please?"

"I shall tell him myself."

Val did not expect what she found. She was escorted down a corridor, into a room removed a short way from the entrance hall. A manservant rose, startled, to his feet when he caught sight of Val in the doorway, behind Colby. The book he had been reading from dropped to the floor, unheeded.

"What—" he began, but fell silent at a fierce gesture from the housekeeper.

This was clearly the room of an invalid. The fire in the grate blazed, and the room was hot and airless. Even so, the invalid in the chair seemed unaffected. A woolen blanket was wrapped around his legs. He turned toward the door, curious.

"What is it, Fenton? A visitor? Who—" The voice was thin, as though coming from a great distance. "Fenton—I can't see."

Neither Colby nor Fenton spoke. Val took a tentative step into the room, and then another. The silence stretched. Val's rehearsed words fled into the void, leaving her lips unable to move. At length, she stammered, "I—I came—"

The invalid moved in his chair. "My dear," he faltered, "no need to explain. You have come back, Maura. My dearest wish—"

Tears of joy and weakness choked him. He reached a shaking hand toward her, and—fatefully—she took it in both of hers. She mumbled something, she did not know what.

Sir William's man, Fenton, stood beside the invalid's chair, alert as a whippet. Val was aware, too, of the vigilant presence of Colby standing behind her. It seemed hard for Sir William to reach her, so she knelt, still warming his cold hand between hers, and looked up into his old eyes.

Maura had called him old, but she had not hinted that he was ill. Now he was only a shell, confined to his chair, his pale eyes kind but without sharp focus, his speech impaired. She knelt without moving for a long time. His hand quavered toward her head, and, understanding him, she took off her bonnet. He stroked the bright bronze hair, believing he caressed his wife once again.

She did not move until he laid his head back, wearied. Only then did she get to her feet, stiffly after the long moments of kneeling. Colby had not moved. Now her features had discarded the expression of disbelief that they had worn at first sight of Val. Instead, her bright blue eyes glittered with suspicion and distrust. Val glanced at Fenton, but he seemed already to have forgotten her. He wore an anxious frown, as he eyed Sir William.

Maura's husband had gone beyond his strength. His eyes closed, his breath coming in shallow gasps. His pale, aristocratic face, though, wore a trace of a smile.

Val looked long at him. He seemed on the verge of dying. She stretched out a hand as though to pull him back but let her hand drop futilely to her side. Holding her bonnet by the strings, she left the room.

Uncertainly, she stood in the hallway. Colby went past without remark. When the housekeeper returned, she said impassively, "I have sent the carriage away, my lady. I hope I did right."

"Carriage?" echoed Val, as though the word were foreign.

"The hired carriage," repeated Colby, "the one you came in." Without sincerity, she added, "My lady."

Val roused herself. She had not been the prey of bleak thoughts, for she was past thinking. The old man had thought she was Maura. She was not able to tell him otherwise. She felt adrift, waiting for someone to tell her what to do next.

Colby was not a hard woman. She was nearing sixty, and more than two-thirds of her life had been spent at Thorne Hall, first in the service of Sir William's mother, and then, running Sir William's household. She had nearly left Thorne Hall when Maura Finch came as Sir William's lady. As it happened, her well-loved master had more need of her then than ever.

She led Val into a small sitting-room just off the main hall, stirred up the fire, and took her bonnet. A cheap, flimsy thing! Colby thought. Not at all Lady Thorne's taste! But then, Colby was well aware that the lady seated before her was not Lady Thorne, not in the least!

"Well, madam?" said Colby sturdily.

"Well?" responded Val. "I had not thought—I did not know—"

"That he was ill?"

Val looked up into the servant's face, seeking answers, even looking for questions. "He is very ill, isn't he? Is he—dying?"

Colby did not flinch. "The doctor says he cannot recover. Oh, he speaks, and his mind is coming back. But he can't move his right side, you know. And he's lost half his vision. But you knew that before you came, didn't you, madam?"

Slowly it came to her. "You think, you really think I am pretending to be Lady Thorne?"

"Aren't you, madam? I did not hear you deny it."

Val shook her head. "I only came to tell him—" The incongruity of her explaining herself to a servant, almost as though she were begging for understanding, did not occur to her. The image of Sir William's desperate hunger for his wife's return was imprinted on her mind. She doubted she would ever forget it.

Colby stood, implacable, the symbol of all the hurt that Maura had inflicted on her husband, her one-time household. Val, not for the first time, was ashamed of her blood. To be a Finch, she once thought, was to be a member of a proud, though extinct, family. Now, she must once more take on herself a portion of Maura's shameful behavior.

She took a deep breath and began again. "I am Valetta Finch. Lady Thorne is—was—my cousin. I only became acquainted with her this summer, by chance." She thought about what she had said and corrected it. "By mischance."

Colby broke in. "I beg your pardon, madam. You said, *was?*"

"I believe so." She told Colby about Maura's flight from Paris, escaping the tumult in the streets. She finished with finding the overturned, bloody carriage on the road. "It's beyond probability that she is still alive."

"I can't say I'm sorry," said Colby.

Val scarcely heard her. "I must go. You sent away my carriage? Oh, dear—"

"You can't go, madam. Not now and leave him—again."

"I never left him at the start!"

"But he thinks so. Madam—it's a hard thing for me to say. But the master—he can't last long. If you leave again, I put it bluntly, I know, but—" She shook her head. "If you go again, you'll kill him."

"I am not responsible for him," said Val. "It's really too much to put on me. I could tell him—"

Colby shook her head with decision. "No, madam. He's been deceived enough. I've seen it all. She was a wicked woman, no matter if she was your cousin. He gave her everything he had, and she threw it away with no more thought than a spoiled child. But still he loved her. The Lord knows why, for I don't. He didn't want to live anymore when she left."

"And that's why—?" She gestured in the direction of the sickroom.

"A stroke. The doctor says from the shock. But you've come back, don't you see? At least, he thinks so."

Val was pursuing a trail of her own. "But didn't he know where she went?"

"Not one of us did. I'd have let her know when he had the apoplexy, if I'd known where. Not that she'd have cared."

"They did travel, though—"

"Aye, they did. That trip to France last year. And when she came back, anybody with half an eye could tell something had come about. Happen you know what it was?"

Val nodded. "Yes. The beginning of it all."

The housekeeper nodded, not surprised. She had disliked Maura from the start and had made no secret of it. Her resentment had deepened, had turned into loathing. She had little feeling now for anyone but Sir William. It seemed logical that Lady Thorne's cousin should make amends for her wrongdoing.

"You'll stay, then?" she insisted. "Not—spoil it for him?"

For a long time, Val could not answer. At length, she sighed, resigned. Once again she was caught in Maura's toils. Even though Maura was surely dead, a victim of her own folly, she was still stretching out a hand to trap Val as surely as though she stood once again—at the beginning of that bright summer—and said, "You'll do what I say, my pet, or else."

"I have no place else to go," said Val, truthfully. "And I can see you are right. If I left him now, he might well have another stroke. Yes, I'll stay."

That had been a month ago. A month filled with growing appreciation for the very kindly, gentle man who had failed to satisfy her selfish cousin—a month, too, filled with the soothing influence of regular, uneventful days. If it had been only the days, Val could, perhaps, eventually have come to terms with her altered life. But the nightmares, terror filled, devastating, full of great loss and inconsolable grief, would not let her forget.

To the amazement of the doctor and the entire household, Sir William began to improve. His right side was no stronger, nor did his full sight return to him. But his mind became clear. His eyes followed Val around the room, and Fenton reported that he was hard put to calm his master when Lady Thorne was out of the room.

None of the other servants penetrated Val's identity. Even Val's eyes, sapphires instead of emeralds, did not give her away, as they had in the first few minutes with Colby. Colby explained that some of the servants were new since Maura's time, and others, including Pollifex the estate factor, had had little enough to do with Lady Thorne, since she had taken no interest in the farms.

Val settled, if not happily, at least with some contentment into the routine imposed upon Thorne Hall by its master's illness. She spent an hour or so in the morning with him, in the suite of rooms adapted for his care. Previously, the rooms had been a study and an office for the running of the estate, but they were on the ground floor, a fact that made it easier for his staff to care for him.

In the afternoons she sat quietly with him. It was a safe haven for her, a quiet place to recover. She felt nothing but compassion for William. She had no more than that tepid emotion to give him or anyone else. All passion had been spent, she believed. She would never again want a love like Alec's, even if such a thing were possible. Passion made one raw and vulnerable, unsettled, miserable. She had come through alive, barely, and was satisfied to stay in the backwater forever. She could not survive more days like that last one with Alec. The only way to exist was the way she existed now, buoyed against collapse with the small tasks of getting through one day after another.

Sir William had been saving issues of *The Cornhill Magazine,* expecting to read the current serial when it was complete. But his stroke had intervened. With charming diffidence he asked her if she would read to him. "I know you never liked to, Maura, my dear, but you have changed so greatly that I venture to make a request—"

"Of course, William," said Val. "I'll be glad to."

She ignored Fenton's brief expression of surprise. Clearly she was not living up to Maura's reputation.

In truth, reading to William was one of the more enjoyable tasks of her day. Before long she was greatly caught up in the affairs of Bullhampton, a village of Wiltshire, where Anthony Trollope dealt capably with the obnoxious Marquis of Trowbridge as well as the vicar and independent Miss Lowther, who could not make up her mind as to which man she loved.

The woman doesn't know what love is, thought Val, or she'd know well enough *which man!* But the mild passions displayed in the long book were soothing, and William's gratitude to her went a long way toward healing.

She had been in residence at Thorne Hall for six weeks when Colby came to her with an odd request.

"Will you rent the Pavilion, madam?"

Val stared at her. She had come to find comfort in the woman's sturdy honesty, her support in the difficult path she had to tread. They were allies, with Sir William's ease, both of mind and body, as their sole goal. "The Pavilion? What is that? And why should I rent it?"

The Pavilion was a small building set well beyond the rose garden, out of sight of the house, except for its exotic roof. Sir William's mother had come from a wealthy brewing family, and it was her money which had built Thorne Hall. Finding it ugly beyond endurance, that Lady Thorne had built a small and private refuge, well away from the house. She had fancied a teahouse in the Japanese fashion, where she could spend hours with her books or her needlework—and, as she had told Colby, refresh her soul among beautiful *objets d'art.*

William, for love of his mother, still kept it in order. And now, someone wished to rent it.

"I don't think—" said Val doubtfully.

"We dare not bother Sir William with it," said Colby firmly. "Pollifex says it's going to ruin without someone in it. This poor man, a poor crippled thing he is, so Pollifex says, won't hurt it."

Val still hesitated, undecided. Pollifex was the estate agent, and Val trusted him. If he said the Pavilion needed human occupancy to preserve it, then she should agree. But she herself would have asked more questions: Must she go down and set the Pavilion in order for the new tenant? Would the poor crippled man need a maid to take care of him—?

But Fenton came with a summons from Sir William, and Val said quickly, "Go ahead. It makes no difference to me." Later, she would have cause to remember those words.

She hurried to William. Always fretful when she was not in his sight, he calmed down when she came in. He had found a miracle in his last days, he believed. He had always thought Maura the loveliest woman he had ever known and had hardly dared to ask her to marry him. He was too old for her, he knew, and yet at the first they had been happy.

At least, he had been happy. Recalling what had happened later, he wondered now just how much he had deceived himself. Had Maura been dissatisfied from the start?

He put aside such thoughts. Maura had come back to him, much gentler, much sweeter, and a joy to his declining years. He had no illusions about his future. It would be short, and he would be fortunate indeed if it held no more pain than he had endured already. He smiled up at her as she dropped a kiss on his cheek. How much she had changed! Even her scent was lighter, more feminine.

"What will you like today? Shall we go on with Captain Hastings? Trollope can certainly draw a weak character, can't he?"

He nodded, and she picked up the issue of *The Cornhill Magazine* that she had been reading the day before. Her voice read the words, but her mind moved on its own road. She was more than fond of William. He was so patient with his handicaps, so grateful for the help that he required. How could Maura have left him? How could she have chosen that grand passion for Raoul? Didn't she see his meretricious glitter, his shallowness? Wasn't she aware of his pawing at every woman who came near? Val knew from bitter experience that Raoul had had no intention of ever being faithful to her cousin. That entire summer had been one enormous deception.

But Raoul and Maura had no monopoly on deceit, thought Val, sitting in Lady Thorne's chair.

She turned another page. William looked stronger to her. Even the doctor had turned cautiously optimistic. "You've done him a world of good, Lady Thorne. While his condition must always be considered serious, I do not see any immediate danger to his life."

While her prison was comfortable, even luxurious,

she knew it to be as much a jail as the Old Bailey, which, if Miss Wilson had had her way, she might even now be inhabiting. She had no wish to escape from this confinement, though, for her life was over. It had ended that hot day in France, the white dust of the road rising to cover the trail of blood from Alec's head—

"What's the matter, my dear?" came William's anxious voice. "I've tired you. Best stop reading. After all, there's always tomorrow, isn't there?" She nodded. There was always tomorrow, and tomorrow, and tomorrow—one empty day after another stretching into infinity.

Chapter Sixteen

Some time in the next day or two, she remembered that William had mentioned one or two of his mother's favorite books, a leather-bound copy of *The Corsair,* for one. She smiled. How little his mother's romantic taste had rubbed off on William! His choice ran to the prosaic doings of true-to-life villagers.

She thought she should go down to the Pavilion and retrieve a few books from his mother's library. She had no fear that the tenant might damage them. The walk to the Pavilion was more in the nature of needed exercise. She had been brought up a countrywoman, and long walks in the country were a part of her. Indeed, her custom of walking had served her well in France—

She shook her head to rid herself of that image. She found a dark green cloak of Maura's, of fine broadcloth and lined with squirrel. Maura must have intended to return to Thorne Hall when her passion for Raoul waned, for she had left all her elegant winter clothing in the cedar-lined closet.

Maura was not one to leave behind her possessions

unless absolutely necessary. She had needed the carriage to take all her Worth gowns with her away from Paris.

The late October air was crisp and welcome. She had forgotten how good fresh air could feel, after the stuffiness of open fires and airless rooms. She moved quickly across the broad lawn and through the rose garden. At the far end of the rose garden, beyond the pergola, covered now with dead vining canes of the summer's climbers, she found the entrance to a path that she judged must lead to the famous Pavilion.

She had grown enamored of the idea of slipping away from the Hall into a private, romantic little building. She could feel kin to William's mother. She paused a moment and looked back at the unattractive building she had just left. The yellow stone of the house was quarried less than a mile away, in a quarry on Thorne land. The architect, William Butterfield, was well known for his solidly built, churchlike houses.

He built for eternity, apparently. It was hard to think of anything short of a natural catastrophe that would move one stone, one red brick of the trim, one slate on the high hunched roofs out of their original setting.

Even in 1854, when the house was built, certain amenities were lacking—like bathrooms, running water even for the kitchen sink. There were great tanks of water in the cellars, she had been told, from which water had to be pumped up by hand.

William Thorne's father had not believed in frills.

She turned her back on the Hall with a sigh of relief. Whatever the Pavilion was, it would be a welcomed change.

The path wound along the edge of a neglected knot garden before it plunged into the deep woods beyond. She could hear the water of the little river murmuring to her left. An opening now and then indicated small footpaths that no doubt led to the river. The paths had been unused for a long time, judging from the undergrowth that threatened to obliterate them.

On her right hand, she passed a path that was as

wide as the one she walked on. She paused a moment to peer down it. In a short distance, the path curved sharply. Was this the path to the Pavilion? She should have asked Colby before she left. She decided that the path striking off at an angle had not been trodden for a little while. She saw a footprint ahead of her on what she considered the main path and set out to follow it.

But one day soon she would take the other path and see where it led. It was then, at that moment, that she realized she had already made the decision to stay here with William.

Why? Because she had no place else to go? Reason enough. But underlying the prosaic common sense of staying for William's sake was the knowledge that one place was the same as another—all desert without Alec Drummond.

She was sure he was dead, both from the terrible wounds he had already sustained while she watched helplessly, and from whatever injury was yet to come to him. Only Alec's gun in her hand had kept the men from attacking her as well. She could have died there, with Alec. She considered the possibility with regret.

She did not know how long she had been walking, at a slower pace now that the woods were around her, when the path opened abruptly into a clearing. And what a sight!

There was the Pavilion. A miniature pagoda, painted red and black, now peeling in spots. Red tile roof, eaves sweeping upward as though to leap from the building into the heavens. A grand staircase—more French than Oriental—marching up to a front door which was covered, if one could believe one's eyes, in Delft tile.

She stood, her breath arrested in sheer awe. An ornamental pond lay before the building, so that the romantic hideaway of the late Lady Thorne was reflected in it. One such building, she thought with a shudder, would have been enough.

She did not know how long she stood at the end of the path. She felt at last the dampness of the earth stealing through the thin soles of her slippers and knew it was time to move.

She skirted the pond, noticing that the reeds and a few water-lily pads spoke of neglect. She went up the stairs, thinking what she would say to the tenant in explanation of her visit.

She did not have to knock. As she climbed to the top step the door opened, and the tenant stood in the doorway, blocking it.

She gasped as though she had just received a blow in her stomach. The poor, crippled man who had rented the Pavilion, the man who stood now, favoring his left leg, in the doorway—

"ALEC!"

Alec's lips twisted wryly. "As you see."

"But where—you're alive! You're hurt! Alec, what happened?" Her flow of quick questions slowed at last, and she noticed he had not moved. "Are—aren't you glad to see me?"

"I did not believe it," he said. Even his voice had changed, she realized. Gone was the tender softness she loved. In its place was a harsh rasping, hard as Scottish granite, cold as his sea-gray eyes.

"Believe?" He had hurled his words at her as though they were stones, meant to hurt. She could only echo him in bewilderment.

"What are you doing here?" he demanded.

With the sight of Alec, she felt suddenly more alive than she had for weeks. Alive, yes—and angry. "I am freezing on the doorstep," she told him, with some spirit, "and, if you are as badly wounded as I have heard, you will take your death of pneumonia."

Grudgingly, he backed away from the door. While he was not welcoming, at least he made it possible for her to enter. She did, looking around her at William's mother's interpretation of romance. A pavilion where she could be herself, it was said—and Val could only be thankful that the red velvet hangings, the vast ottomans and divans, the vermilion-enameled furnishings were not a reflection of her own self.

"I see you're still at it," said Alec, not retreating from whatever battle he wished to fight.

"I wonder what you can mean?"

"Still pretending. Still masquerading as the infamous Lady Thorne. But now of course, there's more at stake, isn't there?"

"Alec! You've got it all wrong!"

"Yes? Your factor Pollifex described my landlady to me. Bronze hair, bright eyes. Oh, yes, all of it. Lady Thorne, indeed."

Sparks flew from her sapphire eyes. Oh, yes, she was alive again! "What did you expect me to do? You said I should return to England. And I did. Obedient to the end, Captain Drummond!"

"England, yes," he granted. "But not to return to the bed of a husband not yours."

His voice had lost a little of its cutting edge. He was wavering now, and she knew it. She realized with astonishment that she knew him—on the basis of a few days of unremitting companionship—very well indeed.

She said, gently smiling, "If you only knew— Dearest Alec, let me in out of the cold."

He stepped aside and she crossed the Pavilion's threshold for the first time.

She had been shaken to the core by the unexpected sight of her dear love whom she had believed dead. Her first instinct was to comfort him, to croon over his injuries, and in solacing him, gain ease for herself. Rage rose in her for the dreadful cruelties inflicted on him, for the ruin of a man vastly superior to those who had hurt him. But he had held her off—at sword's length, so to speak—and flung insults at her, and all she could do was to repay him in kind.

They stood, incongruous in that pavilion room of wild, exotic furnishings, so out of place in this quiet corner of England, and glared bitterly at each other.

Suddenly she saw in his eyes a vulnerability that was foreign to him. Always, he had known what was best to do. He wore an air of competence, authority, even mastery. He had not hesitated to dominate her, telling her baldly where her duty lay, pointing out the essential dishonesty of her cousin's plan. As though she couldn't see it for herself!

He had made no allowance for the obvious fact that she was caught in Maura's web, in Paris. But he had made sacrifices to set Val on the way to safety, to take her as far as he could toward England. She had thought he was committed to her. But now—

She was so bitter of heart that it seemed as though her thin body could not hold it, must break with it, and she turned away. But in the act of turning, she caught his eye, and saw the hurt appeal, the ruined look of a man who gazed without hope upon the ashes of his life. She believed she recognized the dismay of a man who, handed his life's dream, doubts that such happiness could be his, and spurns it.

She hesitated. Her hand reached out in her own vulnerable appeal to him. "Alec?"

The barrier between them was swept away as though it had never been. He pulled her to him, holding her tight with his good arm. He rained kisses on her upturned, laughing face. The nightmare, she believed, was over.

The weather turned a week later. She pulled her squirrel-lined cloak tightly to her throat as she hurried along the darkened path back to the Hall. It was later than she thought. Evening was closing in, earlier now than when she had first come.

It had been a memorable week. She could hardly contain the happiness that simmered in her. If she had thought that her love for Alec lay only in the ecstatic abandon of their united bodies, she was wrong. Alec, apologetic, had informed her that he was but half a man—"at least, for the moment. The doctors couldn't be sure that—it—would come back to me."

No, there was more between them than the exquisite torture of the senses. There was passion between them in the quiet probing of each other's thoughts, memories, of the fitting together of their complementing selves.

The passion of learning to know each other—this was more exciting than she had ever dreamed!

The Pavilion had come to be theirs alone. William's mother's ghost no longer lingered, even in the exotic room they had discovered upstairs. Heavily draped with red velvet, the room seemed transported here, intact from a harem somewhere in Arabia. A broad coach, covered in satin the color of Devonshire cream, dominated the room from its imposing position on a dais raised a step above the floor, in the Oriental fashion.

They had climbed to the seraglio room only that afternoon, reveling in its privacy. "I'm recovering," Alec had said, looking with surprise at his swelling crotch.

"Oh, darling, and I must go back to the house!"

"Next time, for sure."

The path through the woods was hard to make out. She had no fear of taking one of the overgrown paths to the river by mistake, but the broader one that led off into Thorne farmland, as she thought, was hard to distinguish in the twilight. She did not wish to waste time by taking the wrong track.

But her way ran true, and she hurried across the lawns to the door of the kitchen wing. She met Colby just inside the door.

"Oh, dear. Am I late?"

"Sir William," said Colby sternly, "will soon be asking for you."

Val flushed. "He was asleep when I left. I thought he would nap for an hour." She was vexed with herself. There was no need to explain herself to Colby. The housekeeper had no right to put her in the wrong. But then, Colby was her only ally in this house.

"He did," said Colby. "You've been gone for three."

"Three? I can't believe it!"

"It's true, madam. I'll send one of the maids to tell him you'll be down at once."

"Oh, yes, Colby. Please do. But I must smooth my hair—"

Val needed a few moments to arrange her expression, to cover the happiness she knew was obvious. Even Sir William, seeing only half of what there was to see, might well discover the joy that sang in her, and wonder. It was simply a necessary chore, like changing her frock from the gray flannel, bordered with traces of mud and damp from the path, to a green muslin, more suitable for the sickroom, always kept at a temperature just under greenhouse levels. William was always cold.

Colby followed her up the stairs. When she closed Val's bedroom door behind her, she spoke her mind. "I expected," she began, "better from you, madam. I did not expect to see the lady of Thorne Hall sneaking out to what amounts to a lovers' meeting—no better than a kitchen wench romping in the haymow."

"Haymow!" Val exclaimed, remembering. Her laugh bubbled like a newly opened bottle of champagne.

Colby was not amused. "Or worse. You pretend to have Sir William's good at heart. I don't see that spending half the day with another man is going to help him any. If he finds out—"

Val twisted feathery curls along her forehead and eyed the result in the mirror. "He won't find out, Colby, unless you tell him. And I don't think you will."

She had the right of it, thought Colby. But she had spent anxious times, unhappy with the advent of the tenant in the Pavilion, and the false Lady Thorne's foolish running down there every chance she got. Besides, if Colby wasn't mistaken—

Val turned to face her. "I do not expect to hurt William, and I do not intend to account to you for my actions. I am not Maura Thorne, and I do not break any vows to Sir William, for I made none. If I choose to visit the Pavilion, it is entirely my affair."

"Not while Sir William frets, madam. You are pretending to be Lady Thorne—with good excuse, I know that—but you can't be both—an unattached female and a married lady."

"Isn't that up to me?"

Colby knew Val was wrong but she had not the words to express herself. She could only try again. "Who is he, anyway?"

Val could not be angry for long. Besides, Colby had come to be her friend, and they both sought only to protect William.

"He—he's the man I told you about. The man who helped me escape from Paris."

"But you're not *wed* to him?"

"No. There was no time."

Time enough for leaping into bed, thought Colby grimly.

"I wonder, Colby, if you have any idea of what France is like?"

"Full of heathens," said the housekeeper promptly.

"It's so beautiful, like the loveliest city you can imagine, even in your dreams. The flowers in the park, the air that can make you forget your name, that long blue twilight— No, Colby, I did not lose my head over them. But—you do know that my cousin went to Paris to—to be with someone?"

"I heard there was someone last year," said Colby slowly. "And the master brought her home in a hurry. Believe me, she wasn't pleased with that! There was no living with her for months." Curiosity nudged her. "Was it him—that same one—she went to?"

"I am not sure what her initial plans were. But when she saw me, she must have thought me a godsend. She invited me to Paris, you know, I thought as simply a new-found relative. But then I found out what she meant to do." Val was speaking slowly, trying to explain the mad scheme so that it sounded at least reasonable. "She meant to spend time with—her lover—all the while I was out in public, at court, walking in the gardens." She gave Colby a level look. "You don't see it? Valetta Finch in Lady Thorne's clothing—pretending to be Lady Thorne so that her lover's wife would be deceived. While I went to balls and so on, I—or rather Maura—was not suspected of being with him."

"A decoy, would you call it?"

"A piece of bait in a trap," said Val wryly.

Colby thought for a bit. "But the gentleman at the Pavilion now—was he the lover?"

"Oh, no! He thought I was Maura at the first, but then he found out the truth. I didn't see him much until that day when the French surrendered to the Germans." She could not tell even Colby about that final scene in the apartment. Maura had sent her to the vicomte to get her out of the way while she ransacked the apartment for Val's money and fled, leaving her to her own devices.

She told Colby about the rioting in the streets, the mobs ready to tear the empress to pieces, and Alec helping her to escape through the labyrinth of the palace.

"And we walked and walked, out of Paris. Finally we hired a cart, and it was easier then. Captain Drummond was afraid, you see, that I would be mistaken for the empress. Her hair is bright, you know, like mine."

"And like Lady Thorne's. But she was killed, you said."

"She must be dead. There was blood in the carriage, you know. She could not have made it to England by herself."

The silence that fell between them was more friendly now. "So you see," Val finished, "there wasn't time to be married. It would have been dangerous even to go into a town. They shouted such dreadful things in Paris, you know."

"That explains it, then."

"You see, Colby? I am not a wanton. I knew Captain Drummond before I ever came to Thorne Hall."

"I suppose that changes things. Does he know?"

"Know? What?"

"I thought it was too soon. He came only a fortnight ago."

"Colby, don't try my patience. What are you talking about?"

The housekeeper gave the impression of settling herself solidly on her feet, then launched her bombshell. "Does he know you're carrying?"

"Carrying—" Val's voice died away. "So—"

She sat down abruptly. She had not given any thought to the possibility that she might be carrying Alec's child. But she knew now that Colby spoke the truth. Odd little signs that she had dismissed as the result of the strain of pretending to be William's wife, the ordeal of that week on the road, fleeing Paris, told her without doubt that Colby was right.

"That's it, then." Those wonderful nights when Alec had explored her as he would, had taught her to give, to respond with all the ardor she could summon—never a joy without a hardship. She covered her face with her hands, feeling tears spilling from her eyes and sliding through her fingers. "Colby, what can I do?"

The housekeeper found she could not maintain her rigidly moral stance. The question was indeed doubtful, for whatever Val had done, whatever passions had driven her, all had happened before she had come to Thorne Hall. Colby, always honest, had to admit that even Sir William's pathetic needs could not prevail over the demands of a new life coming.

"It's hard to see the ways of Providence," said Colby in an altered voice. "To think that you came here just in time to bring Sir William back to himself—I can see a clear hand in this. But this other—I just don't know."

Troubled, she fell back on doing the things she knew well. She stirred up the fire in the bedroom grate and put another block of wood on it. "I suppose—" she said, uncertainly, "will you leave with *him?*"

"I can't. How can I do it? How could I begin to apologize..."

"It would kill him," Colby said flatly.

"He's never harmed anyone. I can't leave him. If he had a stroke when Maura left, then he could—have another one—"

"Or the loneliness afterwards," the housekeeper pointed out. "That's what was doing him in before you came."

They remained silent for a bit. Everything had been said that could be said. There was no conclusion, no escape from this dilemma. How cruel life was—and each of them doing their utmost to be kind—Alec saving her from the Parisian mobs, sacrificing his employment and his health for her, and she finding no other way to get to England. And William, the most innocent, mourning his wayward wife and rejoicing at her return—only to be more vulnerable than ever.

Maura was to blame for it all—but Maura had doubtlessly been avenged by her captors on the road. But then again, Val had been in no way reluctant to surrender herself to Alec. They were all to blame—and blameless.

Finally, Val pulled herself to her feet. "Well, Colby, at least I can go to Sir William now. There's not much time, I suppose, before I must decide what to do. But that's tomorrow, and today—is today."

William's face lit up when she entered the room. She felt a pang of guilt but quickly smothered it. She crossed to him and dropped a kiss on his wrinkled cheek. "Sorry I am late, William."

"No matter, my dear. I am much too selfish, wanting you with me. I know I'm a boring old invalid—"

"Hush! You're no such thing! I just—went out for some fresh air, and the time got away from me." She hoped his failed eyesight could not detect the flush on her cheeks.

"Of course, my dear." He fell silent then. She noticed a couple of sheets of paper on his lap—a letter. For no logical reason, she felt that the papers were important to her. A letter from someone telling him that Val was an imposter? Or from an unseen observer who felt compelled to expose Val's sojurns to the Pavilion? Or even, her fancy flying out of control, a letter from Maura in France?

Better to know the worst at once. Steadying her voice, she asked, "The post has come?"

She was right. The letter was troubling. William

frowned down at it. He picked the sheets up with a trembling hand and said, "My dear, can I trouble you to read this? Fenton has read it to me, but I should like to hear it again."

Gingerly, as though the letter might explode in her hand, she took it and began to read aloud. She worked her way through the neat professional handwriting, at first not comprehending the legal language. At last, when she finished, she looked up in dismay. "An inventory? Your lawyer is making an inventory? Why? Is something wrong?"

"Now, Maura, my dear. Nothing to make a fuss about. An annual chore. Put off because of my ridiculous helplessness."

"He should not trouble you with this," she fretted.

"But I need to know. The estate is entailed, you know, and since I will have no sons, I must hand it over to my nephew as I received it." His fingers moved restlessly on the blanket covering his knees. Heat poured from the crackling blaze in the grate behind him, and yet he shivered from time to time. "I do not like to ask, Maura. But I must. Where are the jewels?"

The room was so hot. She passed a hand over her forehead. Were the walls receding into the distance? She closed her eyes. She dared not faint. What would Maura do, faced with such a question? She would defy William—tell him lies! Val, with sudden humility, realized she herself had strayed far away from the habit of truth. She dared not cast any stones, even in her mind, at her cousin.

"The jewels?"

"The Thorne emeralds, my dear. And I believe you'll find on the list a ruby brooch—one my mother wore when she was presented to the queen—I forget the others, but they're on the list."

Val forced herself to examine the list. They were there all right. The emerald necklace and earrings that she had worn on the occasion of the first masquerade—when she had changed clothes in that little anteroom, and when, later, Alec had rescued her from his unsavory employer. The rubies, which she had not worn because they clashed with that glorious bronze Finch hair. A few diamonds, a sapphire or two—

And all the time, ringing in her ears, were Maura's words at the last, standing in the apartment, making plans to spend Val's last coins on their escape from war-surrounded Paris: "I've sold the lot, idiot! What do you think we've been living on these months?"

Sold the Thorne jewels, she had, to pay for her mad worthless passion for that faithless general. Robbed the estate—and there was no way to retrieve the loss.

"My dear!" came William's gentle voice, laden with concern. "Are you ill? I should not have troubled you with business. I know you have never had any interest in our affairs."

"No, William. It's all right."

"I am sure that you have them someplace. I do not care much for them myself. It is only that my nephew is not a lenient man. But let us not think of that for the moment."

The plan struck Val with such force that she thought she must have cringed. William's mild gaze was upon her, and she forced a smile. "Shall you like me to read to you?" she offered.

Trollope's mundane prose fitted her mood. With one part of her, she could beguile William for an hour, and yet her own thoughts could flow unimpeded to the things that loomed large as disaster before her.

The child—I could have the child and we could call it William's. He would have an heir then—and the accounting for Maura's jewels could be postponed to another day. But, she told herself, why should I cover up again for Maura? She took the jewels and she sold them. I didn't even know they were gone until that last day. Likely the last day but one of Maura's life. Val was prone to take too much blame to herself, Alec had told her—

Alec—what will I tell Alec? That his child is to be a sacrifice to Maura's sins? I cannot tell him the child is William's because he wouldn't believe me for a moment. Nor would William—who of all men would know better. I cannot tell him, "The child is Alec's, but we'll just pretend it is ours," and bribe the doctor to say William could be the father, and threaten the servants, and suborn Colby—

And know all the time I'm getting more and more mired in the quicksand of deceit! I won't do it!

As she read on, her thoughts spat out the unpalatable truth—she could not continue in this way of deception, for the child growing within her would make that impossible, nor could she tell the truth to William, lest he have another stroke, and this time most likely, a fatal one.

There was, quite simply, no way out.

Chapter Seventeen

The rising moon, nearly full, shone brightly enough to make the path through the rose garden clearly visible in the autumn twilight.

When she reached the edge of the woods, though, she bent to turn up the wick in the lantern she carried. She had never come this way by night before. The shadows leaping across the path as the lantern swung back and forth from her hand startled her, but she was not afraid.

In fact, she had no room in her mind for fear. She had only an immense need to be with Alcc, to feel his arms around her, to hear him tell her that she need not fear that Maura's sins would catch up with her, to tell her that he knew precisely what was best to be done for them all.

William had had his light supper and his sleeping medicine. Fenton would, as always, sleep on a cot nearby, and Val was free until morning.

She slowed her pace when she moved under the trees. The path no longer seemed familiar in the distorted light. Usually she checked her progress by noting the little openings where the paths branched off, some on the left toward the river, the larger one on the right. She had promised herself one day to follow the wider path to see where it led, but she had not yet had time.

Alec would know what to do. She had so much to tell him. Would he be pleased to know about the child? He must be! If he grew angry, she would be destroyed.

He could not be angry. They had spent hours learning to know each other better, exploring their hopes and dreams. His injuries, severe enough at the first, were healing rapidly. In fact, this afternoon she knew that he once again desired her, and only the lateness of the hour had kept him unsatisfied.

She emerged from the woods and skirted the ornamental water. She stumbled once on the broad steps and nearly dropped the lantern. The door—to her surprise—yielded to her touch.

In the dim light of the lantern, the garish Oriental red of the main room of the Pavilion was softened to a warm glow. The room was empty. She walked across the floor, taking care to make no noise. She knew he slept in a room to the left. If he had already gone to sleep, she would not wish to awaken him. The room was empty.

She stood in the hall, perplexed. Where had he gone? Surely he had not come to the Hall to see her, or she would have met him on the path. She had counted more than she realized on seeing him. It was, perhaps, the recognition that he had fully recovered that had drawn her this far, the knowledge that her desire had grown as strong as his from long abstinence.

She did not want to leave the Pavilion. The silence surrounded her like a cocoon. Oddly, William's mother came to her mind. Lady Thorne—disdaining the yeasty smell of the brewery whose prosperity built the mausoleumlike Hall—escaped into this *bijou* of exotic fancy. Val thought she could even smell the remains of incense or perhaps musky perfume. It was well known that musk was the strongest of aphrodisiac aromas, and even the faint memory of it stirred pleasingly along her nerves.

Then she heard the noise. The soft thud of a footfall—the faint brushing sound of a bare foot on thick carpet, she thought—over her head. Alec must be upstairs, in the room so out of place in a Japanese teahouse. Without conscious volition, she moved to the stairway, seeing the seraglio room in her mind, and began to climb.

He lay on the low white divan. He had heard her footsteps approaching and watched the door. She stood in the doorway, her eyes locked with his across the firelit room.

"You came?" he said in soft wonder. "Or are you only my dream again?"

"I'm here, dearest."

He reached out for her. "Then come."

She shook her head. Smiling slightly, she began to unfasten her bodice, to lift her petticoats over her head.

Even these homely gestures moved him with an allure that tightened his loins, stirred that desire for her that lay always close and ready, like something vital and powerful moving just beneath the surface of a pond.

He watched, loving the lissome grace of her body, the enchanting web of seduction she wove with every smallest movement. She was aware of the powerful urge she was stirring in him. He moved to sit on the edge of the divan, as though his impatience would bring her more swiftly to him.

The divan, wide and long and soft, was once at home in a harem, set in an Arabian garden. He had no wish for a seraglio, for the one woman in the world for him stood just across the room.

He moved ahead into her thoughts, always so close to his own that they seemed as intertwined as their bodies would be. She was as ready for him as he was for her—she would glory in his nakedness, and a glow of passion would light her lovely face. He could not disentangle his dreams from reality. But she was here, her magnificent bronze hair shining in the firelight, and the words she spoke now in her low, sweet voice were tender and loving.

With difficulty he held his impatience in check. Yet a shuddering sigh slipped from his lips. But he waited, curbing his hunger to hold her so close that they would be but one body entwined, her mouth to be his, his tongue soon to savor the sweetness of her like the rarest of fine wine.

The fire leaped in the grate, bringing the scarlet velvet hangings into a maze of muted colors. Now she stood naked before him, rosy in the flickering light, one long tress slipping waywardly to caress her left breast. She let him look at her for a moment, almost feeling his gaze touch the shadows at her throat, glide lovingly over the satin skin of her full breasts, his eyes traveling like a tender finger to touch her here and there.

He made a sound in his throat. He smelled the clean innocent fragrance of her and saw the message in her eyes, so full of unashamed desire for him.

His heart stopped in his chest, stifling his breathing. When it started again to beat, his pulse pounded so loudly in his ears he thought she might flinch from the thunder of it. She seemed aware only of him, sitting at the edge of the divan, his eyes filled with hunger for her. She put her hands on his shoulders, kneading his flesh briefly with her strong fingers, pulling him to her.

His arms went around her, and he buried his face in the soft scented hollow between her breasts. He had known women, many women, but it was now as though they had never existed. This woman alone, this golden girl with the sapphire eyes, this perfectly formed mate, was his alone. He alone had the right to nibble along the precious curve of her breast, to tease the rosy tip of it with his tongue, moving lightly as a butterfly's bite, until it proudly hardened.

He alone knew the secret places, knew the caresses that pleased her most. She was his, endlessly desirable, endlessly enticing, forever tempting. She was his—but in the same fashion, he was entirely hers. He was her slave, bound by his newly recovered desire to give her pleasure, glorying in the ability of his body to slake her thirsts.

She placed the palms of her hands on either side of his face, and, with infinite gentleness, pulled his head away from her. She could feel the wetness left by his mouth on her, feel the tingling of her skin as though it had come into a life of its own, responsive in itself to his maleness. She tilted his head so she could look down into his eyes, dark in their hollows. She moved one finger along his left eyebrow, smoothing the hairs in a tender caress.

She gazed into his dear face, the features that she knew so well by sight, knew even better by the touch of her exploring fingers, knew almost mystically by the taste of him under her hungry mouth. She felt his head turn beneath her palms, and his tight embrace relaxed as he set her a few inches away from him. She shivered, feeling cold where his arms had been. His hands, warm and promising, lingered on her waist. He kissed her, lightly on one breast and then the other, and followed with his lips the glorious valley between. His tongue dipped lightly into the tiny cup of her navel and then slid farther down.

Her muscles quivered, writhing under his lips, stirring a similar convulsion within her. She caught her breath. The slight sound of her gasp reached him, and he laughed, a throaty sound full of triumph at the leaping desire he had awakened in her.

He leaned back on the divan and pulled her down on him. She felt beneath her the hard evidence of his restored manhood, swelling and moist. Her body sang, knowing that she had aroused him, knowing, too, that she knew well how to satisfy him, how to bring him to a forgetfulness of all barriers between man and woman.

But not yet. She eased away from him, inviting him to follow. He understood her, though no words passed between them. The bond that linked them was for the moment one of hands and lips and tongues and eyes. Eyes to enjoy the splendid tapering proud length of her, the provocative thrust of her generous breasts, the sleek and silken thighs that parted, welcoming him to the very private core of her.

Her jewel-bright eyes sent him all her love and tenderness, darkening to the color of the deep wild ocean as she felt his hands caressing and gliding over her, stroking until her skin kindled beneath his touch, bringing a clamant insistence of its own, a fiery hunger for union, a greedy demand to be fulfilled in oneness.

He pulled her to him, feeling her softness, her generous and yielding curves the perfect complement to his hardness. Although she lay beside him, with not the slightest space between them, he felt she was still apart from him. But the growing bonds between them, woven by probing tongues and uniting mouths, by eager restless hands and by sensually welcoming limbs and teasing, stirring passions, were still strengthening. He was aware of the altering scent of her, knew she was joyously matching his need, his hunger, coming swiftly to meet his passion and in the same moment yielding to his male mastery.

She could feel stirring against her breasts the hard, furred muscles of his chest. She moved against him, hearing a moan of pleasure deep in his throat, knowing that by her own delights she was bringing to him an ecstasy that he would return to her tenfold.

He moved then, spreading her quivering thighs and taking sovereign possession of the core of her, the chalice of her femininity that she offered to him for his comfort and easing.

Their bliss enwrapped them for an unmeasurable time. Their bodies were one, and he held her, feeling her the dearest part of him, cherishing her sweetly, soothing her, reassuring her by the imperceptible touches of his lips, by his lingering within her so she could feel his nearness, that she was his other self, the one woman in the world who could fill his emptiness. His dearest dear, his eternal desire, his glorious love—

Later, much later, they lay sated on the divan, Alec's long body touching hers along its entire length. She knew that she could no longer hold off the moment of revelation. Their coming together this night had filled the empty places in her being, convincing her she was not alone. Even now, he pulled her to him, feeling her softness against him, his impassioned need of her rising again.

Even though he had only moments ago withdrawn from her, yet the nearness of her stirred him again. He moved against her, feeling her tender nipples hardening once more against his chest. She moaned in her throat, knowing that her pleasure was kindling a flame that would flicker ever brighter between them.

She smiled into his eyes, those hard gray eyes that sometimes held the chill of the North Sea, and sometimes—this very moment—held a lurking devilish laughter. No more time for teasing—

He moved then, spreading her welcoming thighs and taking, again, sovereign possession of her. Once again he stayed within her, letting her know without words that she was his other self.

Later, she heard her voice saying, fearfully, the words that she had not intended—not yet, at least—to say. "Alec, I'm going to have a child." He was at once still, unmoving, for a long time. The log in the grate burned through and fell with a soft sound into the ashes.

"Alec? *Darling?* You're not angry?"

"No." After a moment, he demanded, "How soon?"

"In the spring—May."

"No, no. I mean how soon can you pack up?"

"Pack up? What do you mean?"

Alec's thoughts had leaped ahead. "We had probably best get married in England. Easier than waiting. We don't want any questions asked when we get home. I want my son to be born a Scot."

He was not angry. But she wished, in a way, that he were. This immediate taking control of both their lives—her's and the child's—jarred. "You could at least say you're pleased."

"I am pleased. You can't doubt that? Why else am I taking you home to Scotland with me?" He slid away from her, leaving her strangely bereft. "What's wrong now? I'll not say I'm overly surprised."

"Nor should I have been."

"You haven't told me how soon we're leaving."

Lover he might be, father of her child he certainly was, but master of her life he was not. "You haven't," she said deliberately, "asked me to marry you."

He sat on the edge of the bed. She saw that he favored his left leg and knew the pain throbbed in him. She would not make allowances. "Nor," she added, "did you ask me whether I would go to Scotland with you."

He slewed around to look at her. "Ask you? Good God, what else? Of course I expect to marry you. And where else would we live but Scotland?"

"I do not plan to leave William."

She felt the gathering storm in him, even though they were not touching. "Not leave William? That invalid? I think you have forgotten it is my son you're carrying."

"My child, too, Alec." She hated the pleading note in her voice, but she could not change it. "I can't leave William at least until I explain. It will kill him if I desert him."

"What is he to you? Don't tell me you're settling down as Lady Thorne in earnest! As I suspected all the time. The Laird of Ochill can't compete with Sir William's fortune. Is that it?"

"Alec, no! Just give me time to work it out with him!"

"There is no time. May, you say? We'll have to be settled before the snows come, for Scotland's a cruel land in winter. It may not be as luxurious a life as you seem to enjoy here—"

"I can't be heartless to a man who has been all kindness to me."

"But," he said, feeding on his anger and jealousy, "you can reject a man who has risked his life for you!"

She sat up now, the change in position lending her confidence. "You always did wish," she pointed out coldly, "to be thanked profusely for whatever services you performed. Very well. Thank you for risking your life for me. Thank you for using my body to slake your lust on. Thank you for giving me a child that will, without doubt, lead to my ruin. Is that sufficient?"

He stood naked in the middle of the overfurnished room. Hands on hips, he glared at her. She thought he might well strike her. She steeled herself against flinching.

Why did she, ordinarily a compliant and giving person, rise up so angrily—and so often—at him? The answer lay deep within her, and instinctively she recognized it. He was part of her and always would be. He had invaded her body and her mind. But she would not let him engulf her soul. She had to fight him, lest she be swallowed up by his domination.

"I demand that you forget this business of staying here. I'll expect you to be ready to travel by the end of the week."

"You are not allowed to demand anything from me!"

"You are carrying my son. That is my warrant."

"You do not own me. It's my body, not yours, that is bearing a child. Your part in this is done."

He was so angry, so frustrated with jealousy and the inability to reach her, that he could no longer speak sense. He dared not stay in this hot decadent room with her because his hands itched to seize her and shake some kind of reason into her. He was afraid that his wrath would not stop there.

He picked up the clothes she had—so tantalizingly!—taken off only an hour ago and threw them at her. For a moment she was back on the ferry. She clutched a petticoat, heedless of all but the sound of her dear love—her fulminating enemy—clumping stiffly down the stairs.

Alec had rejected her—the coming baby would turn William against her. She had nothing left to her but ruin. She began to cry. She pulled on her clothes—Maura's clothes—and went downstairs. The door to Alec's room was closed, and all was silent within.

Still sobbing, she went out into the night.

* * *

The fog, as it did in autumn, had come up. The only light was the feeble glow from her lantern, about as much use, she thought, as half a dozen fireflies. She moved carefully down the broad steps, feeling her way with her foot. Before she realized it she had stepped onto the wet grass. She could not see the ornamental water, but she knew how to get around it safely.

She directed her footsteps to the left, seeking the path that would lead her home through the woods. She found it without difficulty. It was only a few minutes' walk, but it would probably take half an hour in this thick darkness. She was wrong. She would not get home to Thorne Hall that night.

At first, the fog did not seem heavy. The brave little light from the lantern showed the way a yard ahead, and the path was clear. She went slowly into the woods. Little gray wisps floated harmlessly across her path. Soon, however, the misty threads thickened and joined others, until the lantern beam turned back on itself, unable to penetrate the obscurity.

She stumbled, took a few rapid steps, and fell. Her breath was knocked out of her, and she lay unmoving for a minute. It would be easier simply to lie there, weary with the passionate lovemaking just past, and unable to take thought for the days ahead. She could lie there in the fog and sleep.

Her eyelids grew heavy. But the fog touched her cheek with a cold, damp finger. Moved then by the knowledge, still new to her, that she carried within her a living creature to whom she had a duty, she struggled to her knees. The lantern still threw out its light, a yard away from where she had dropped it.

She picked it up and threw its ray back the way she had come. What had she fallen over? There it was, a root stretched across the path, loose enough to catch the toe of her slipper in it. She must be more careful. She went on.

She traveled some distance. She thought that soon she would break out of the woods and find herself in the gardens of the Hall. She stopped, looking around her. Nothing seemed familiar. Even the root, she now remembered, was strange. She remembered none along the regular path. Was it possible that she had taken the wrong turning?

Thinking back, she could not be sure. The root didn't belong on the path—but then she had always come in daylight and perhaps had not noticed it. She was still in the woods, but she could only see a couple of feet ahead of her at a time, and distances could be deceiving.

She started ahead, again, but even the trees, the bushes, were unknown. She started back, but if she were really lost, she might go in a circle all night—

She felt panic rising into a lump like a fist in her throat. The path must come out somewhere, she told herself.

A low keening came to her, and she stopped to listen, the hair rising on the back of her neck. The wind—that was it, the wind in the trees. She sighed in relief. If the wind rose, then the fog would dissipate.

But she had been too long in the cold and the damp, had struggled too much against Alec's arrogant assumption that her life and her child were his to dispose of without so much as a discussion. Her knees had begun to shake, and she knew she must rest soon. Something was not right. She should long since have been crossing the knot garden, hurrying through the rose garden with the lights of the kitchen guiding her.

Uncertain, she stopped and swung her lantern around her. The trees had thinned out and she felt thick grass yielding beneath her thin-soled slippers. The light beam fell upon grass, little scrubby shrubs and yearling trees. She recognized nothing.

She must keep going. She took a step, sliding a little on the wet grass. To catch her balance, she swung her arms, and the lantern, describing a great arc, showed her what lay ahead—nothing.

Nothing!

Blackness, where the grass fell away before her. Beyond was emptiness, the void of what appeared to be a great hole in the ground—

Bewildered, unbelieving, she stood staring at the edge of the grass, a couple of feet in front of her. Another step, and she would have walked into air.

The quarry!

The excavation from which had come the stones that built Thorne Hall. William had told her of it. And now she had found it. Almost found her death in it.

She felt her knees turning to jelly. She must back away. It was not safe so close to the edge. If she could simply make her legs move, backward.... Odd, she had been ready to lie down and sleep her life away, letting the impossible decisions drift away on a tide of blackness. Now, she was desperately anxious to survive, to back away from this bottomless pit.

The keening of the wind in the trees had changed its tone. Now there seemed to be a long call riding on the deep cello tone of the rising gale. A long sound—calling her name. She believed her mind must be fevered. She was exhausted, of course—that must be why she thought she heard Alec's voice. It could not be, of course, because he had shut himself off with his senseless fury inside the Pavilion. It was impossible that he could be riding the rushing winds and calling her name.

Her skirt was heavy with wetness. Even her shawl had soaked up the mist, and she felt sodden clear through. When the call came again, she could not keep from answering. It must be the wind, but it sounded almost human.

She turned, quickly, to lift her lantern like a beacon, to send her call in the direction of the cry. The wet grass slipped beneath her sodden shoes. Feeling her footing go, she tried to recover, grabbing at support that was not there. As she fell, feeling her back strike the heavy, wet grass, she lost hold of the lantern.

She clutched at the wet grass under her fingers, feeling the blades slide out of her grasp. Turning with an involuntary cry, she saw the faint beam of the lantern describing a lighted arc far into the blackness below.

At that moment she began to slide, her hands clutching at air, as the blackness of the pit came up to meet her.

Chapter Eighteen

She drifted, weightless, in a twilight filled with misty faces, distorted as in a nightmare. The faces came, showing themselves to her and receding, and bringing the odd smell of medicaments, even the unlikely smell of ether. None of it made sense, and she followed the faces, hands out, pleading for something undefined.

Now and then the fog lightened to trailing misty wisps, and she was cold, shivering as though she would never again be warm. Disembodied hands wrapped her in more blankets, and she slept.

When she emerged at last from the fog, her lips dry and her throat parched, her surroundings came slowly to her. A crackling fire in the grate, somebody sitting in a chair nearby—her mother? No, it couldn't be. She groaned. The woman in the chair brought her a drink of some kind, nasty tasting, but she slept again, and when she awoke this time, she was herself.

Colby came to look down at her, worried. "I see you're back with us, madam. We almost lost you."

"I don't think I remember what happened." Nor did

she want to. At the edges of her memory she could feel lurking great dark shapes of fear and wretchedness. She did not want to know.

Colby told her. "You hared off to the Pavilion in the night. Dark as Dick's hatband with the fog, and nobody but a moonling would think of doing such a witless thing." The housekeeper could not keep the crossness out of her voice. Caring for Val with the doctor, she had come to recognize her own strong affection for her. Not knowing how to tell her, she took refuge in scolding.

"In the dark?" Val protested, memory surging back. "I had a lantern."

Colby relented. "Did you? They didn't find any."

"It went—down."

"I always told them they ought to put up a fence around that quarry. But you may be right. There's a lantern missing."

"Who found me?" Val wondered after a bit. "I was at the bottom of the pit."

"Not quite. A ledge a few feet below the rim. You lodged there. If you had looked, you would have seen you couldn't have thrown yourself away, because of the ledge."

Val struggled to sit up. "Throw myself away?" She regarded Colby with horror. "You think I—did it on purpose?"

The housekeeper's silence was answer enough. Val tried to throw back the covers, struggling to get out of bed. Colby was instantly beside her, pressing her shoulders back against the pillows, covering her again.

"I've sent for tea," she told her. "You'd best wait for it."

Val was not sorry to stay in bed. The warmth of the eiderdown was making inroads against the memory of that cold night, and the foglike limbo in which she had wandered for so long. To think she was in her bed all the time!

But there were gaps. She must remember—she had gone to the Pavilion at night, carrying a lantern. Why at night? But Alec had been overjoyed to see her and to hear her news—

Her news!

"You've lost it," said Colby tartly. "Wasn't that what you wanted?"

"How could you believe I'd try to kill myself?"

"Many another in the same fix has done it."

There was nothing more to be said. The hot tea came, heavily sugared and marvelously restorative, and she slept at once.

The next day she got out of bed and dressed. Her reflection in the mirror showed traces of the accident. Deep purple smudges under her eyes, a new hollowness in her cheeks—but outside of a certain weakness in her legs and a tendency of her hands to tremble, she was well again.

"I must see William," she told Colby. "How much did you tell him?"

"I said you had a cold. Didn't want to give it to him."

Val nodded. She reached out to grasp Colby's shoulder. "You don't really think I threw myself over into that—that pit?"

Slowly the housekeeper shook her head. "At first, madam. For you know the quarry is far off the path. We didn't see how you could have got there, lest it was on purpose, don't you see? But the fog does change things around so that you see what isn't there."

"That it did." She thought a moment, catching hold of something Colby had said. "You said *we*. Who found me? Alec?"

Colby did not answer her directly. "Best we go down to Sir William, madam."

Val hurried downstairs. William's lively welcome pained her. She gave him the excuse that Colby had made up for her. Would she ever be done with lying?

She spent the afternoon with him. He looked frailer today, as though his skin had become translucent. She had been right to tell Alec she could not leave this man. She now remembered, vividly, the quarrel that had sent her out, distraught, into the misty night. It was Alec's fault—but her own as well. She would see him as soon as she could, and this time she would listen to whatever solution he might have devised.

But not tonight. Fog, rising from the river, drifted past the window. She shuddered. She had no wish to go to the Pavilion after dark again.

She had dinner with William, giving Fenton a few hours to himself. When she finally left William to be put to bed by his devoted Fenton, she found Colby waiting for her.

"I think it right, madam," said Colby without preliminaries, "to inform you of what happened that night. Your man from the Pavilion came raging up to the door. I don't know what went on between you two—and I'm sure I don't want to know—but he was right outside himself. When we couldn't find you, he went wild. I called Pollifex, and he and Carter went with him, more to keep an eye on him than expecting to find you."

So Alec was wild! He must have regretted greatly his outrageous behavior, his arrogant demands on her. He must have come swiftly to apologize.

"It's not like him," said Val, secretly pleased, "to lose control like that."

Colby said shortly, "Every man has his folly."

"Folly? You think that? I must ask him."

"You'll find that hard to do, madam."

They had been climbing the stairs during this exchange, and they went together into the master bedroom—Maura's bedroom. Colby helped her off with her dress and into a robe. Automatically Val sat down at the dressing table and began to brush her hair.

She echoed, "Hard to do? What do you mean?"

Something in Colby's stance alarmed her. When she spoke, Val knew why Colby had waited for her tonight. "He's not there anymore."

"Not where? He's at the Pavilion, isn't he?"

"He left."

"He couldn't have!" Val wailed. "Not without saying good-bye. Not without telling me where he was going!"

"Left the next day. Not a word to anybody. A pretty suspicious thing to do. He sure doesn't want any part of that baby, does he?"

Val bristled. But Colby was her only friend, and she needed to talk, needed reassurance that she had done the right thing. "I told him I couldn't leave William."

"What did you plan to do then?" demanded the other. "Have the babe? Break Sir William's heart?"

"No," said Val in a low voice. "My own."

After a moment Colby said in an altered tone, "You think it's none of my business, I suppose. Well, Sir William and I grew up, you might say, together. I've known him since he was a baby and I was Tweeny here for his mother. A sweeter child was never birthed, and I grieve my heart out for how he is now."

The simple words were eloquent with tragedy and grief. Val forgot her own troubles. She set the brush down and crossed the distance beween them, not only the few feet of carpet but also the greater distance between mistress and servant. She put her arms around Colby and hugged her close. "We both love him, in our different ways," murmured Val, "and the more so because what has happened to him was not of our doing. I have suffered a little, myself, from my cousin's selfishness." The tears that streamed down her cheeks mingled with Colby's. In the end, Colby was first to pull away. She straightened her skirts roughly, as though they had offended her, but her eyes brimmed with the affection that the real Lady Thorne could never have earned.

After Val had told her all that Alec had said and wept for a little, Colby said, "And Sir William, ailing as he is and not to get well, will never have an heir."

Val sat up straight. She wiped her eyes with a lace-trimmed handkerchief—an *M* embroidered in satin stitch in one corner—and glared at the housekeeper.

"You think—Colby, you *cannot* think—that if he recovered sufficiently—that I would—that he would—Colby, you shock me!"

"You make a better Lady Thorne than your cousin. Too late, of course, now. More's the pity."

Val stood, smoothing her hair. "You forget that had he not been an invalid I should not have stayed."

Colby refused to meet her eyes. "Just the same, madam," she said, abandoning all logic, "it's too bad it couldn't be."

Later, in bed, Val lay awake. Alec invaded her thoughts tonight. He was gone, so Colby said, and without a word to her. He probably did not learn before he left that the baby was lost. If he had known, would he have stayed with her? She could not trust herself alone with him again, for she dared not risk another pregnancy.

When she needed him most, he had fled from his responsibility. While she had flung in his face the truth that his part in making the child was done, she had spoken in anger. He had not tried to hide his concern, not for her, but for his son.

How did he know it would have been a boy? His pride demanded a son—and she was only the means to an end!

She sat up and pounded the pillows into a new shape. But the argument continued. He had rescued her, coming after her, searching till he found her.

But he had made impossible demands on her—cancelling for her a bride's cherished decisions—whether to marry at all, when to wed, and where to live. Out of legitimate rage, she had flung the words back in his face, wounding him, but destroying herself as well.

She did not sleep that night.

The days slid by noiselessly and without friction. There was no word from Alec. Pollifex told her that the tenant had paid rent on the Pavilion until the end of the year. She dared not follow her recurring wish, born in fits of stormy anger at him, to throw out into the snow every single shirt, jacket, hat, book, that he had left behind. Only then could she be certain to erase every trace of the passion they had once shared.

Gone, he might be, but never forgotten. Basically a giving person, she was now haunted by doubts. Had she given enough to him, in her great love? Had she flung his faults at him too hard and too often, wounding him beyond repair?

She could not forget the unforgivable taunt she had last shouted at him—his part in producing the child had been simply a source of pleasure to him, and now it was over!

Her stomach muscles writhed with the remembered turbulence of shared passion. A source of pleasure to her, too, and even denying it brought the warm glow of splendor past.

Even during her hours with William, reading the long novel about the sad affairs of Captain Hastings, who had (so Trollope had said), been cheated of what he thought were his rights, Alec's face swam insistently between her and the printed pages. Dear Alec, that hungry light shining in his eyes especially for her—

This way lay misery. She would never forget him if she carried on in this fashion. The only way to erase his features from her mind was to picture them cruel, angry, domineering. The model was clear, from the last time she had seen him. He had been white with apparent fury. It did not occur to her that he might have been railing at his frustrated helplessness to care for her.

The weather closed in. The northeasterly winter storms swept in from the North Sea on raw and raging winds. William's health worsened. Fenton told Val that even before the disastrous stroke Sir William had always been prey to aching muscles and stiff joints whenever bad weather came.

Even Val, seeking relief from the stifling heat of William's sickroom, could not stand against the blustery gale. The doctor came and shook his head. He had nothing but contempt for Val, since he had treated her when she fell and knew well that the child she lost was not, could not be, William's. He gave his report grudgingly to her. Sir William could linger on for years. He would not improve beyond his present state. He could slip away tonight, or ten years from tonight—it was beyond his skill to predict. He turned stony eyes to her, and she knew what he was thinking as clearly as though he shouted it at her. "Ten years waiting hand and foot on an invalid, Lady Thorne, is fit punishment for any adulteress."

William grew frailer as the winter deepened, but the glow in his half-blind eyes when he turned toward her still burned. The weeks wore on toward Christmas. She spoke to Colby about dressing the house for the holiday.

"Wreaths of evergreen, we always had," recalled the housekeeper nostalgically, "and ivy. Chains made out of greens tied on stout twine, to make the ropes you know. In and out of the balustrades, chaplets, Lady Thorne used to call them, around the mirrors. A basket of mistletoe here and there—" Her voice died away in remembrance. Abruptly she shook herself. "That's dead and gone, madam. But if you wish it—"

Val's enthusiasm had been a frail thing, at best. "I don't think so, Colby. William couldn't see much of it. I really don't know that he even knows Christmas is at hand."

In this she was wrong, though. In a day or two, when she sat alone with him, he beckoned her to him. "Look," he said, with the weak hoarseness of the very ill, "in that drawer."

She pulled out the drawer of his night stand and, as he gestured with long bony fingers, took up a small bag of blue suede.

"Your Christmas, my dear."

The bag was heavy, chinking, in her hand. Opening it, she caught a glimpse of gold, mint-gold, the gold of sovereigns.

"William! Oh, but it's too much!"

She sank to her knees beside the bed, setting the

bag down on the table. She took both his gnarled hands in hers, as she had that first day at Thorne Hall, and held them. "So much, William. You mustn't be so generous—"

"Why not?" She could not tell him. "I've got all I want right here, my dear." He squeezed her fingers. "I must tell you again, my dear Maura, for I may not have much time, you know, how grateful I am for your care of me. To think you came back to me—it's almost a miracle, you know. I did not expect ever to see you again."

She stayed with him, kneeling, warming his cold hands in hers, until, with the suddenness of an invalid, he fell asleep.

If William gave her gold for Christmas, Alec sent only anguish. His note arrived, informing her that he was at Harwich, at the White Hart, and wished to see her at once.

Val, while Colby watched, tossed the note into the fire in the morning room. "I thought he had gone to Scotland," she said as casually as she could, "but now he's in Harwich."

"What does he want?"

"I don't know. I don't care. I owe him my life, I suppose, since he came after me that night. But of course I wouldn't have been out that night were it not for him."

Colby eyed her warily. "I mistrust this."

"No more than I do. But it matters not. I shall not go to Harwich. William is better today, Fenton says, and I shall not leave him."

Colby fished out the note from where it had fallen on the hearth and smoothed it out. "It's only a couple of hours' ride, you know."

"You're on Alec's side!"

"He did act worrited. Like he had a feeling for you." Colby had grown to love this girl, for her sweetness, but also for her loyal devotion to Colby's ewe lamb, Sir William. And, Colby knew, to be fair about it, she'd had a hard time getting back to England, the French acting like the heathens they were.

Val was through with Alec. She could not allow him to come back to her only to break her heart again and again. During that long summer in Paris, when he avoided her, when, as he supposedly lay dying, he had sent her away to a future of loneliness and again when he had left the Pavilion without a word.

Three times were enough.

"A couple of hours, madam," suggested Colby with guile, "and back soon as kiss your hand."

Val told her, "I'm not going," but her voice lacked conviction.

With satisfaction Colby said, "I'll order the carriage."

Her mistress could not endure this seesaw business, she thought. The man was daft over her, no matter how it looked, and in a way he had the right of it. No man should have to see his son brought up in another man's house. And if the madam had only waited—instead of running off and getting herself into the quarry—he'd have come around.

Sometimes, decided Colby, Providence knows what it's doing. If Captain Drummond was at Harwich, there was likely a reason.

Standing before the door of the White Hart, Val steeled herself for the encounter with Alec. She had decided to put Alec out of her life, and she must tell him so. Yet, the conviction was strong in her that at the sight of his lithe, sinewy body—the body that was even now a part of hers—she could well melt into his arms. She tightened her lips and went through the door.

"The captain is not here at the moment, madam," said the innkeeper, hardly concealing his curiosity. "But the captain's lady is. Will you see her?"

His lady? *His lady?*

How could he send for Val only to introduce her to the woman he had chosen to take to Scotland, since Val had refused to go? Could he be so dastardly, so—so cowardly, so—she could not think of words sufficiently scorching. Besides, he was not there to hear them.

Well, she had no intention of staying long enough to tell him to his face what a poltroon he was. She turned on her heel. "Is there a message?" urged the innkeeper, but she did not answer.

She had reached the door when she heard her name called, in a voice she had never expected to hear again.

"Val, my pet!"

She wheeled, shaken. It was indeed Maura, leaning arrogantly against the door leading to a private sitting room.

"I thought you were dead!"

"As you can see, I am not."

There was nothing for Val to do but to join Maura in her room. "What happened to you?" demanded Val, irritated. "There was blood on the cushions, and your clothes all over the road. We thought they had killed you. Didn't you even bother to let anybody know you were alive? What did you do with Jehane?"

"She saved her own skin. She turned on me, you know."

"Too bad you didn't save the ruby brooch for emergencies. You could have paid your way home."

"How do you know about the brooch?"

"It's in the estate inventory. William has been asking me about the jewels."

Maura grabbed her arm. "What did you tell him?"

"What could I tell him? You said you'd sold them all." Struck by an odd expression in the green eyes, Val was convinced of the truth. "You didn't sell them! You lied to me, Maura!"

"What if I did? At least I brought them back. I had a terrible time, Val."

"I can believe it." Maura had aged ten years since Val had first met her, only last April. Val could almost feel sorry for her. Almost, but not quite. But it could not hurt to pretend.

"I am sorry for you."

"You don't sound sorry, my pet. But you should be.

I come home after an ordeal I wish to forget, to find that you have stolen my husband."

"Stolen! Don't tell me you value him."

"I value my position. I value the security that I married and nice clothes, and someone to cook for me and bring me tea, and scrub the floors—"

Involuntarily Val glanced at the ringless hands Maura held out to her. The skin was reddened and cracked, signs of hard physical labor that must have been more of a trial to her than any threat to her life.

"And now, Alec tells me, you've taken my husband."

Val's thoughts darted desperately, searching for some way to stave off Maura's return. William simply could not face the misery that she was sure to bring. He had told Val more than once that he loved the sweetness, the kind devotion that she had brought to him. So different from what she had been, he had said.

"Why are you here at the White Hart, anyway?" Maura was asking. "I suppose dear Alec sent word that he was here, and you come running every time he crooks his finger at you." Maura's smile turned vulpine, wanting to see Val squirm under her poisoned words. "No answer? I hit too near the mark, I imagine. Tell me, my pet, couldn't my dear husband tell the difference between us? Didn't he feel puzzled to find a near-virgin in his bed?"

"He didn't—he can't—Maura, listen to me."

The older woman waved a hand, as though brushing away a fly. "Alec, now—Alec can tell the difference between us. And he prefers, I may tell you, a woman with experience, sophistication— You're blushing! How charming!"

If Alec had chosen Maura—the innkeeper had called her the captain's lady—then she wished him well for his bargain. She thought she had exorcised him from her mind, but the sharp bitterness Maura's words stirred up in her told her otherwise.

She could still salvage something. She could save William.

"Maura, you can't go home."

"I can't? Why not? Don't tell me that monstrosity of a building has burned to the ground?" She attempted a light touch, but Val thought her sarcasm almost macabre, contrasting with the glassy windows of her haunted eyes. Maura had truly suffered, but—so had William.

"His right side is paralyzed. He cannot help himself, but must rely on Fenton—you remember Fenton?—for nearly everything. He can get out of his chair and take a few steps, on his good days. There aren't very many of them. His sight is dim."

"Then he will not know when I come and you leave. Because, dear cousin, the minute I come in that front door, you will be out of the kitchen door. The servants' wing. Most appropriate. I warn you, I mean it. If you're not gone in half an hour, the constable will drag you out. Not a new experience for you, of course. But not pleasant."

"You're not paying attention to me, Maura. William's wits are alert. Are you ready to read to him every afternoon? Will you enjoy hours in his sickroom while he tries to talk to you? I doubt it."

"So. He is an invalid, if I am to believe you. And I don't. But I must suppose that you have not had to suffer his deadly lovemaking. Nor will I, I promise you."

"Maura, you're not listening. If you come back, and act like you did before—you'll kill him."

Maura's eyes narrowed. "You've settled in, I see. Dear Alec told me so, but I could not believe you had it in you to accomplish such a cowardly fraud!"

"Fraud! Who are you to accuse me of deception? You taught me all I know of trickery!"

"You've found a nice snug place, I see. I did listen, you know, especially when you said *if* I come back. Well, my pet, I'm coming back."

"The shock of seeing you after he's used to me will bring on another stroke. This one could be fatal."

"You think the return of his dear wife would upset the poor little man? But he thinks I've already come—doesn't he?"

"Y-yes. But we are different people, Maura. He's used to me now. He's been getting better."

"He will have to get used to me again, then." Maura was quieter. "Never fear, my pet. He'll get accustomed all over again to Fenton, for you may well imagine my tastes do not run to sickroom duties. No, Fenton will have to do it all."

Slowly Val said, "I can't stop you."

"Very true."

"At least give me time to prepare William, to make some excuse to him so that he won't feel abandoned."

"My, how touching! I shall very soon feel just the teeniest bit jealous of you."

Val stood ramrod-stiff. She knew her hands were clenched into fists, and she hid them in the folds of her cloak—Maura's cloak. "No need. He'll be no trouble to you *that* way."

"You mean, making love? No matter. The tenant in the Pavilion—*my* Pavilion, remember—will be more than sufficiently amusing to me."

"You wouldn't."

"That hurts?" smiled Maura. "Why do you think Alec came to find me in France? He'd had enough of substitutes." Her eyes stayed on Val, judging the effect of her sneers. "In some ways, he is more adept than Raoul. But you wouldn't know."

Val felt her blood recede and suspected she was white as flour. She knew she had received a wound intended to be mortal. She could die at her leisure. But just now she must make a valiant attempt to save William.

"Why don't you and Alec"—how much it cost to say his name without a tremor!—"stay here at the inn for a week? Give me time to prepare William for your coming. It would save trouble in the long run. And surely it makes no difference to you."

Maura turned reflective. Val watched her face eagerly, trying to follow her thoughts. "Very well," she said at last. "One week. One week only, my pet. Don't try to fob me off a moment longer, for I won't have it.

You're a cuckoo in the nest, and your next stop may well be gaol for impersonating me. Poor William!"

"You wouldn't dare! After all, you did plot the masquerade from the beginning!"

Maura had tired of toying with her young cousin. She smiled now, and said calmly, "You were a fool!"

Val rode back to Thorne Hall in a daze. She had expected to meet Alec, and likely enough quarrel again with him. Her firm resolution had been to keep from hurling herself into his arms. She had been totally unprepared to meet Maura. She especially had no defenses against Maura's insinuations about Alec.

Did Alec really go to France to find Maura because he found me useless? Or because he found her bewitching? Was I too naïve for him? Was he angry because I was carrying his child? Should I have been more yielding, more submissive?

There was nothing to gain by going over and over the past. It was the future she must worry about. She could not, of course, stay with William. At best, she could prepare him for the truth—that his wife had not suffered a sea-change, but was still the cruel, heartless, selfish woman who had deserted him nearly a year ago.

But maybe she would not have to tell William the truth. Maybe she could simply let Maura slip into her place, and trust that he would be deceived. Again. Colby would know what was best. By the time the carriage turned into the drive at Thorne Hall, her body was stiff and cold and her mind numb with confusion.

She had not even noticed that the wind had changed and drifts of snowflakes were beginning to descend from the darkening sky.

Chapter Nineteen

"The captain," pronounced Colby, having heard all that Val could tell her, "should have minded his own business. No reason why he should go bucketing after Lady Thorne. We did well enough without her."

Val sighed, agreeing. "But sooner or later she would have come back, Colby. She had no place else to go. Her general was through with her. She was so thin, so worn. If you had seen her, you would have felt sorry for her."

"She made her bed," said Colby.

Val and Colby both were agreed that Maura's advent would prove to be disastrous for William. But while Val staggered under the burden of knowing that she was, in truth, an imposter, Colby clung single-mindedly to the conviction that Maura's return would be the death of Sir William. Poison she had been to Sir William, and poison she would always be. And while there was any life left in her stout body, she would do anything to preserve her master.

She was, though, only a servant after all, helpless

in the face of upper-class injustice. She had a week to make her plans. She trod carefully though, daring not take Val into her confidence. But one thing she promised herself—Maura must not return.

The week's grace, depended on by the two women at Thorne Hall, dwindled in Maura's mind to two days. She did not break her promise since she had never intended in the first place to keep it. Alec had come to France to find her, starting at the place in the road where the carriage had been wrecked, and discovering her in veritable slavery in the kitchen of an inn farther down the road.

She offered herself as payment for his timely arrival, but he had declined. She was more than a little afraid of him, if she were to be honest. She knew men, and she recognized that Alec Drummond was not vulnerable to beguilement. She gathered, from the answers he refused to give to her questions, that he and her foolish little cousin were in love.

Maura was used to blaming someone else for her predicaments, however small. It was easy, therefore, to place the guilt for her own folly on Valetta. Val's tortured face, as Maura recalled it, had been balm to her. If Val wished Maura to stay away for a week, then that was reason enough to wait only until Alec was away from the inn for at least a couple of hours, and call a carriage to take her to Thorne Hall.

It was hard going for the horse because the snow that began when Val had returned to the Hall, two days before, had continued to fall, piling up in the corners of the fields, and lying thick on the roads.

It would be worth the trouble, she smiled, to see their surprise when she entered. Surprise? More like being struck by a thunderbolt! Maura hugged herself in anticipation.

At last the carriage turned in between the stone gates and went up the drive to Thorne Hall. Nobody had heard the carriage on the snow-packed ground, for nobody came to help her down. Doubtless Val had run a lax household, spoiling the servants. There would be a few changes in the coming days.

Maura lifted the knocker and let it fall loudly twice before the door opened. The expression on Colby's face was all that Maura could have wished. The housekeeper could not have been more shocked had Satan himself stood there, swishing his tail. In truth, Colby's emotion on seeing Lady Thorne would not have been much different if she had been the devil.

"You!"

"I do not quite like your manner," said Maura, smiling without amusement. "Keeping me out in the cold? Stand aside, Colby."

"You said a week."

"Did I? No matter. I'm here now."

"You'll kill him."

The lovely green eyes glittered beneath slitted lids. "She's converted you, I see. Well, I shall take care of that."

"It's the simple truth, my lady. He can't stand the shock."

"You have never made a secret of your dislike for me. I imagine you will not have to endure your situation here for long. I will not abide insubordination."

Maura had stepped inside, but, never one to attend to details, she left the door swinging wide behind her. Desperately Colby stood her ground in the foyer. "His condition is due to you in the first place. You don't care for that. Another shock will kill him, though." Colby cast discretion to the winds. "You'll be no better than a murderer."

"I shall remember that, Colby," cried Maura, her voice rising, "when I write my letter of recommendation upon your departure. Which will be quite soon, I assure you. In the interim, I am confident that the return of the true prodigal wife will raise my husband's spirits. Out of my way!"

Val was sitting with William. He seemed better today and had made his way unaided from the bed to his armchair by the fire. There was no sound in the room except for the soft puff of a burnt log as it dropped into the thick bed of ashes, and the hiss of the snow, now turning to rain, on the windows.

The argument in the entry hall came clearly through the sickroom door, left ajar. Val saw that William's fingers clenched into a fist on his knee. "William, what is it?" He did not answer.

His face stiffened, as though struck by a dreadful memory. His eyes held a leaping flame of anger, as though someone had blown on an ember to bring it to life. She watched him, horrified, as he put aside the blankets with trembling hands, and struggled to his feet.

She sprang to his side, but, very gently in a gesture at odds with the fire in his eyes, he set her aside and tottered out the door. "William—!"

She stumbled over the blanket on the floor and nearly fell. She lost a few seconds. William had, with astonishing speed, reached the foyer by the time she caught up with him.

He put out his hands on both sides, flattening the palms against the walls to hold himself up, while he stared at the two women. They were as though turned to stone. Colby whispered once, but Maura made no sound, no movement.

Val stood on tiptoe to see over William's shoulder. She touched him, but the horror of the confrontation kept her from moving. She did not know what to do to help him. She caught a glimpse of Maura's hag-ridden, worn face, staring unbelievingly at William. *I told her,* Val thought briefly, *but she wouldn't listen to me.*

Maura's face felt stiff with shock. To see William so gray, so terribly thin, with the sure touch of mortality on him, had shaken her foundations. She had built her plan on William as he had been. She had thought Val had lied to her, saying he was ill, just so she could continue living in the comfort that Maura craved.

When she could speak, her voice came harsh as a raven's croak. "Aren't you glad to see me, William? The prodigal, returned."

Her words seemed to release some spring inside him. He knew his wits were unreliable, and he thought he must have gone mad. But when Maura spoke, he understood at last. The dear wife who had been such a comforting nurse, such a sweet companion these last weeks, did not exist. He did not quite know who she was, but he did know, from the depths of his crippled being, she was the one he loved with a strength that was, even now, causing his heart to burst.

He turned, faltering, to look at Val behind him. He had been massively bewildered, but no longer. He put out his hand to her in a gesture that spoke where he could not—a gesture of regret, of apology, and of love. His voice croaked, but no words came. Val cried out. She crossed the small space between them and put her arms around him. "Dear William—" she said brokenly. "Come away—"

The look he gave her she would remember always. A sorrowful, listening look—listening to the approach of his mortal end. With an inarticulate cry, a choked gurgling sound, he slipped from her embrace, and toppled, slowly, with great dignity, to the floor.

Val, with an anguished sob, dropped to her knees beside him. She took his hand in hers, and with her free hand smoothed a lock of hair from his forehead. The awful struggle to speak, reflected in his eyes, tormented him. She bent low to him and said, with soft tenderness, "I'll always remember—"

He understood her. His gratification shimmered for a moment in his eyes, and he died.

Colby watched her master die. She was not even aware of Maura standing a little apart, her foot tapping impatiently. Maura hid her feelings behind an inscrutable mask, but there was no mistaking the enmity in her green eyes when she glanced at Val.

Colby's own days at Thorne Hall were past. She had made up her mind to that, almost at the instant she had recognized the unwelcome presence of Lady Thorne. She had no more reason to stay here, now that the master was gone. She looked up, then, after Sir William's body relaxed, as the spirit that held the flesh together departed, leaving only a bundle of old clothes behind. She caught Maura's eye, and a message passed between them. *You killed him—you're a murderer!*

Behind Maura, through the open doorway, Colby recognized Alec Drummond, breathless from hard riding, his coat wet, limping more distinctly than ever. His bright look went searchingly from one to another, taking in what had just happened.

"I got back to the inn too late," he said, "to stop her."

Maura's lip curled. He could not have stopped her anyway. She had come, headlong, to claim her rights, and now the damage was done. Her husband lay dead on the floor, and the usurper was kneeling beside him, still holding the dead hand, and sobbing quietly.

Enough, said Maura to herself, is enough.

She spoke to Alec but he did not hear her. His eyes were all for his darling, grieving on the oak parquet floor, and he could not help her. Her hair had slipped from its pins and fell in a cascade hiding her face. He was instantly taken back to that night in France, lying together in the soft sweet-smelling straw, her hair loosely brushing over his face—

He took a step toward her. Suddenly she became aware of him and looked up. Her sapphire eyes glowed with a scalding fire as she recognized him. She turned away from him, deliberately, hurtfully.

He had lost her.

Val had gone. Colby, with one last defiant glance at Maura, had followed her. "Val," Alec called, but she did not heed him.

"Give it up," said Maura. "She's stubborn."

"You really don't see what you've done, do you?" he marveled.

"What *I've* done? All I did was return to my home, to my husband. What that cousin of mine has done was try to weasel into my place here. A nice plushy life—

until I came. No wonder she was so anxious to keep me away."

Alec stared at her. "Lady Thorne, I have known you only a couple of weeks, since I found you in that hell-hole in Normandy. In that time you have exhibited all the redeeming qualities of a viper. You have been the cause of your husband's death, done untold damage to Valetta, and I am exceedingly thankful I am not your housekeeper. I believe Colby is a virtuous woman, but I would be very careful about the food I ate, if I were you."

"Alec!" It was a wail. "You cannot abandon me now."

"Watch me."

He looked down at his hat as though he did not remember why he was holding it. He turned to leave. "I suppose you have left your carriage horses stand. I'll send them away."

"Alec, you must help me. What shall I do? Who shall I call?"

"The doctor, I suppose. And I suggest a clergyman, for yourself."

He was gone. Maura ran to the door to call him back. The rain pelted into her face, and she pulled back inside. She closed the heavy door.

She went into the small sitting room. It had not changed since she had left. At least Val hadn't redecorated the house. Maura called Colby.

"I suppose you haven't had sense enough to call the doctor. Do it at once."

"He's on the way, my lady."

"I want that woman out of here before he gets here. No need to confuse the issue."

"He won't be confused, my lady."

"Don't answer me with that insolent expression on your face. Get Valetta out of here."

"It's not fit weather outside, my lady."

"She will be packed and out—and I do not expect to see any of my clothes walking out on her back, either—in thirty minutes. You will not leave for a week, Colby. I need you here."

Colby hid her thoughts. It would not help to get into a slanging match with Lady Thorne. She had her own plans in mind, but with a week to work them out, there was no hurry.

She went back to the kitchen. Val was there.

"Where did you get those clothes, madam?" Colby cried, "I thought I had put them in the attic out of sight."

"I got them down after I saw Maura in Harwich. Colby, I never thought it would end like this. William gone, so bewildered in the end—"

Colby ventured to put her arm around Val's shoulders. "Madam, don't fret yourself now. Sir William's safe as ever was now. He wouldn't have liked the change, now that Lady Thorne is back."

Val nodded. "I know it. But somehow I can't quite feel that it has all happened. Colby, how will you do with her?"

"Don't worry about me. You're dressed to go? Your cloak?"

"On the chair. Yes, I must go at once. She told me, you know—thirty minutes after she came, or she would call the constable. I can't be the cause of such scandal, not with William lying dead in his own house. He doesn't deserve that."

"I can hide you, there in the pantry behind the kitchen. She'll never know. She's not one to come into my kitchen. Do stay, madam. I'll worry myself sick if you go now. Where will you go?"

Val had taken up her cloak. Now she set it down again. "Truly I don't know. Where did you say I should hide?"

Colby set her in a dark corner behind the big stove. It was warm there and dark. Colby knew best, Val thought. Maura would never catch sight of her here, and she could sleep, and leave in the morning. She was so tired, so very tired.

She must have slept. When she woke, she was alone in the kitchen. She did not remember for a moment why she was there, but suddenly it all came back in a bitter flood. Maura, William dying, Alec a traitor to her, leaving her without a word of explanation, and bringing back such trouble on her.

Maura was a fiend—Maura could not be merciful—Val dared not risk Maura's wrath for Colby, who had hidden her. She stood and put on her cloak. She felt numb. It would not matter if she went out into the storm, for she had no feeling. Nothing could hurt her now. She moved quietly to the door and stepped out into the windy dark.

The rain had turned to snow again, lightening the way. She did not think she was foolish to start out, haphazardly, in the winter night. She did not think at all.

She walked blindly in the storm. There was shelter someplace. The Pavilion would be safe enough now. Alec was no doubt sitting comfortably in the house with Maura. She must not think of Alec.

She slipped now and then as her foot struck a frozen rut on the path. Then she heard the sound of hooves. It did not seem strange when the horse came up beside her and the rider reached down. It was Alec. Of course, she thought, in dreams all things are logical. He lifted her to the saddle, and somehow they were at the Pavilion.

He stoked up the fire and set her before it. He took off her cloak and her dress and wrapped her in a blanket. He talked gently to her—not to persuade her, but only to provide comforting sounds that perhaps, somehow, might penetrate to wherever she had gone in her mind.

Had she loved Sir William so much?

He made her swallow brandy. She sputtered at first, but he was patient with her. The warmth of the spirits spread out strongly from her stomach, breaking up the frozen shell that enveloped her. His words began to make sense.

"She promised me, too, that she would stay the week.... Colby told me where you had gone to.... She told me about the baby. I'm sorry.... She may have a hard time of it.... Maura will send her packing soon, you know.... Do you think she'd like Scotland?"

When at last Val found words, they were not the ones she expected. Without volition, the question that obsessed her came out. "Did you go after Maura because you loved her?"

"Did she tell you that? You know better than to believe her. She's twisty as a snake."

"Then why?"

"To set you free."

"What do you mean?"

"You were bound to Thorne, and it wasn't your duty. It was Maura's job, not yours."

"You were wrong. You see how wrong it was for her to come back."

"Trying to live without truth is wrong."

"The truth," she said with returning spirit, "is cruel."

"Cruel? Perhaps. But suppose Thorne had lived another twenty years. He would not have wished you to sacrifice your life to him. Not if he knew the truth." He fell silent for a bit. "If Maura had returned to him at the beginning—or never gone away—he would not have had these happy weeks with you. You have given him much more than you know."

She said nothing. He was not sure she heard him. Finally, he stood up. "Well, Val, you're not listening, so I might as well leave you alone. Your room is over there, the room I used to sleep in." He stood looking down at her, an odd expression on his face. "I'll be upstairs, in the Turkish room."

He had caught her attention at last. She looked up quickly, almost apprehensively. He shook his head. "It's up to you, Val. This time, though, if you come to me, you'll never leave me again."

She stood up and wrapped the blanket tightly around her slender figure. She didn't meet his eyes. She walked stiffly across the room to the door he had indicated and entered the empty room. He stood watching her but she did not look back. Instead, he heard the door close with a sharp, final click.

He sat in the chair, still warm from the heat of her body. He stared into the fire for a long time. The flames fashioned pictures for him, as though his life—the only life that had meaning for him—unfolded before him.

Val on the ferry, sweet and innocent—God, how innocent!

Val never complaining, the perfect lover whether in cart or in barn, or even on a harem divan.

Sapphire eyes sparkling like jewels, brimming with love for him—so he had thought, gallantly following wherever he led her, trusting him to get her out of danger.

And last, the picture he could not get out of his dreams, her limp body lying apparently lifeless on the grassy ledge, so close to disaster.

But it was all over. She had finished with him. She had told him so. He had been wrong to interfere, she said, but he could not love her and not be responsible for her welfare.

The only thing to do was to leave her. Maybe she could make a life of her own, one that was more to her liking.

He went slowly, limping as though he were already an old man, across the room. He had given up the ground floor bedroom to her, and now he pulled himself painfully up the stairs to that foolishly exotic room, where they had come together that last time.

Was this how it was to be his life long, he wondered, not knowing that he echoed Val's own earlier thoughts—gray, dreary, and solitary?

The fire died down behind the screen that Alec had set in place before he went upstairs. The door to the bedroom opened soundlessly. A slight figure, clad in a bathrobe too big for her, shook her head to let her thick hair fall over her shoulders. She crossed the foyer to the stairs and began to climb.

Moments later, the silence was broken—by a sharp, glad cry, loving murmur in response, and the closing of a door upstairs.

Epilogue

He lay on the wide bed, looking out the window into the night. From here he could see the familiar outline of the Ochills against the sky and rejoiced once again that he had come home.

The door was ajar, and he could see her shadow, painted in wavering candlelight, across the heavy curtains as she reached to unfasten her bodice, to lift her petticoats over her head...

She would come through the door, as ready for him as he was for her. She would revel in his nakedness, and her words, like the touch of her hands on him, would be tender and loving.

Her feminine figure was a little fuller now than it had been, her responses to him warmer, and zestful, and never tiring. He held his impatience in check. A shuddering sigh escaped his lips, but he forced himself to wait.

The shadow on the curtains seemed to listen, and then he heard the cry himself. A small, demanding cry from another room, instantly hushed. Colby, he knew, would be bending over his son's cradle, quieting him with loving hands. His son—their son.

How many times in the last year had he waited thus? More than he could count. She blew out the candle and moved toward him. The flickering firelight bathed her pearly skin in its warm glow. She stood for a moment, letting him look at her. She reached out her hands and touched him, kneading his shoulders briefly with her strong fingers, pulling him to her.

This woman alone, this golden girl with the sapphire eyes, this perfect mate, was his alone. He alone knew the secret places of her.

He was proud of her. He loved her with all his being. And there was no place nearer to Heaven than they had already come, and would come tonight, and again, and again.